SHOPPING CART ANNIE

Cordy Fitzgerald

www.cordyfitzgerald.com

ISBN: 0692932070
ISBN 13: 9780692932070 (Shopping Cart Annie) ©

Library of Congress Control Number: 2017912171
Shopping Cart Annie, Denver, CO

ACKNOWLEDGEMENTS

I live in a wonderful city that has marvelous resources for people who read and write profusely. I've used all of these resources and I want to thank them: all of the Denver Public Libraries, Rocky Mountain Fiction Writers, and The Lighthouse.

Then there are the individuals whose skills slowly and with effort increased mine. There is no room to list critique members, but I owe you so much. Most of all, the skills of Judy Stirling and Anita Mumm are legendary in my mind.

I especially want to thank my former neighbor, Ethel Hayden, for memories of her kindness that continue to strengthen my resolve.

EPIGRAPH

"I only regret that I have but one life to lose for my country."

Attributed to Nathan Hale

TABLE OF CONTENTS

1	Fall, 1982 Denver, Colorado	1
2	Spring, 2009 Park Hill, Denver	6
3	June 1996 North of Bagdad	16
4	Beginning of Summer, 2009 Denver, Colorado	19
5	Beginning of Summer, 2009 Denver, Colorado	28
6	Beginning of Summer, 2009 Denver, Colorado	31
7	A week later, 2009 Park Hill, Denver	43
8	That same afternoon, 2009 Denver, Colorado	51
9	June 1996 North of Bagdad, Iraq	52
10	End of Summer, 2009 LoDo, Denver	63
11	Four hours later, 2009 Park Hill, Denver	71
12	Two hours later, 2009 Park Hill, Denver	75
13	June 1996 Outside Amman, Jordan	78
14	End of Summer, 2009 Park Hill, Denver	86
15	Later that night, 2009 Park Hill, Denver	94
16	Next morning, 2009 Park Hill, Denver	96
17	June 1996 Aqaba, Jordan	105
18	End of Summer, 2009 Denver, Colorado	112
19	End of Summer, 2009 Denver, Colorado	121
20	June 1996 Aswan, Egypt	126
21	End of Summer, 2009 The Highlands, Denver	137
22	End of Summer, 2009 Downtown, Denver	148

23	Early Summer, 1998 Outside Kandahar, Afghanistan	151
24	End of Summer, 2009 The Highlands, Denver	162
25	Fall, 2009 Downtown, Denver	168
26	Early Fall, 1998 Road to Kabul	173
27	Fall, 2009 Downtown, Denver	176
28	Fall, 2009 Denver Tech Center	185
29	August 2008 Islamabad, Pakistan	195
30	Fall, 2009 Denver Tech Center	202
31	September 2008 Kabul, Afghanistan	205
32	Fall, 2009 Denver Tech Center	215
33	September 2008 Kabul, Afghanistan	220
34	September 2009 Denver Tech Center	228
35	January 2009 Wakhan Corridor, Afghanistan	238
36	Fall, 2009 Denver Tech Center	251
37	February 2009 Wakhan Corridor, Afganistan	262
38	September 2009 Denver, Colorado	269
39	February 2009 Hindu Kush Mountains	275
40	February 2009 Hindu Kush Mountains	283
41	September 2009 Park Hill, Denver	291
42	September 2009 Close to Asadabad	297
43	September 2009 Park Hill, Denver	309
44	September 2009 Close to Asadabad	313
45	September 2009 Park Hill, Denver	317
Epilogue Spring, 2010 Park Hill, Denver		321

1

FALL, 1982 DENVER, COLORADO

At three years old, Kadija Campbell sounded out words on a page. By four, she read her mother's child psychology books behind their sofa. When her mom told her she was too precocious to ever stay home alone, Kadija was four and felt forever doomed. Would she always have to wear her one-piece long johns on their midnight ride to the grocery store?

The store was ten minutes away, yet they usually made it in five, mashing Sammy Subaru's guts to the floor. It didn't help that by age six, Kadija spoke fluent mama drama and would let her mother know just how ultimatums sounded. *Raising a daughter alone isn't easy,* she'd say in that same theatrical voice her mom used, *while going to school at night to learn skills for a better tomorrow, yet making every dime count today.*

By seven, Kadija fancied her mom to be an Elizabethan at heart, a pale beauty, who valued education above men. Her mom could talk weeds into self-immolation, fortify a two-person family against all attackers, and create magical incantations. For example, whenever she interviewed for jobs or haggled over a bill, she'd render Kadija invisible. Her daughter's features blended into mall fixtures, library shelves, and wall art better than most pouty lipped, light-skinned, brown eyed, kinky haired kids her age.

On this night, Kadija had already begun to make herself invisible, by climbing onto the mechanical horse.

"Don't hog that horse," her mom exclaimed. "It's for little kids. Get off if somebody wants a ride."

" 'kay."

Turquoise tights kept her skinny legs warm, while they dangled past the horse's motor. Preoccupied with a search for sustenance through her coat pockets, she hoped to find a penny for the machine or a broken cookie from recess. Eureka! Her fingers found a whole piece of chewed gum, restorable with spit.

Cold wind exploded through the store's wide entrance, forcing her to button her coat and sit in the saddle on both hands. She chewed gum ferociously and stared at honey-colored lights bouncing off newer cars in the lot. Funny how crime lights created shadows large enough for people to hide in.

The white haired security guard leaned against the customer service counter, chatting with a tired store clerk. "There goes Shopping Cart Annie. Thought I'd missed her today."

Kadija leaned over the horse's head to follow the guard's line of sight. In the dark distance moved a mountain of a woman pushing a cart. Annie was somebody everybody knew. Wrapped in one shawl atop another, she'd mumble out loud along side a cart that reeked with every manner of plastic bag and corrugated box.

Kadija remembered their first encounter. "Look mama! I'm Snow White with African hair and she's Snow Black with hair like mine. See?" She poked fingers through the woman's shawls, trying to climb up to her head.

Kadija's willowy mom had turned pink, before scooping her daughter into her soft white arms, as if Annie might harm a small child. But Annie ignored her mother and from that time on, smiled at Kadija, as if she knew something no one else did. They became soundless buddies, waving at each other from long distances away. The mountain was waving now, as Kadija enthusiastically returned the warm feelings between them.

"Never seen her this slow," said an employee leaning against the floor polisher display. "Wonder where she intends to sleep tonight."

His words, like a blow to the throat, made Kadija swallow her gum whole. Annie was homeless? No apartment, no hospital, no church to belong to? No family? Why? What made her poorer than she and her mom?

Maybe mom would let her stay the night. Kadija stood on the base of the horse, stretching to see down the nearest aisles. Where was her mother anyway? Not seeing her, she looked out the entrance and watched Annie turn away from the front opening. Maybe she had a place to stay after all.

Kadija felt protective of Annie because she was the only person who had figured out what Annie was really doing. She recited license plate numbers as she walked past each one. Although Kadija never saw anyone around her, it was as if Annie spoke into a hidden microphone as she said each number on the license plate clearly before going to the next one. She hadn't told anyone about it because no one seemed to care.

From the corner of her eye, she spied a bearded young man marching towards the store's entrance. His black cape furled in the breeze. No more eccentric than anyone else in Park Hill, he likely came from services at the AME church a few blocks away. He stopped beside Annie's cart. Store lights bounced against a metal shaft, as he swiftly raised both hands. He swung the metal object above Annie's head several times, sometimes pulling the shaft like a saw. Kadija peered into darkness, seeking the occasional glint of light.

Something heavy plopped into Annie's cart. Her body slumped to the ground. Stunned, Kadija stopped breathing. The man reached into the cart and pulled out a wet coil of wire. Then bending over the lump on the ground, yanked more wire from under Annie's body. He dropped the shaft before stashing the wire into his cape, then walked toward the entrance, straight toward Kadija.

She inhaled, never breaking her gaze from his eyes, so deep they were like shiny black holes that blinked with occasional light. Kadija felt certain he was about to speak. But didn't he know she was invisible? Suddenly he looked away. He walked further into the store. She was invisible after all.

Kadija exhaled forcefully as she plopped onto the horse's saddle. Was the store moving? A woman screamed then dropped her purse. Two carts rammed each other and an argument ensued before the sirens could be heard everywhere. Everything blurred.

A security guard swept past her. "Don't step in it!" he shouted. "Keep back! Everybody!"

Kadija shut her eyes.

"Let's go!" Her mom shoved a grocery bag into her hands. "Take this and stay close. Something's happened. Can't tell what. We've got to get out of here before they block us in. Follow me."

Her mom's conspiratorial voice gave Kadija something to focus on. She thought of nothing else but her mother's instructions, while she kept part of her body touching her mom's. They darted between gawkers, avoiding what everyone else saw.

Words, unspoken, skipped across memories. While speeding home, Kadija put the window down, letting the wind dry her tears before they were noticed. If only she was like her dad. Nothing ever scared him, no Viet Cong, nobody.

She set her grocery bag down before reaching the front door and rushed to the bathroom. Her knees dropped to the floor as she hurled the contents of her stomach into the toilet. It was over in an instant. Yet she was cold and shaking.

"Kadija! Why'd you leave that bag outside?"

Instinctively, her hand slammed the bathroom door shut. "Couldn't hold it any longer."

Though breathing hard, she felt better than she had a minute before. She trembled; afraid to talk about it, scared that if she ever attached words to what she saw, those horrible images would live inside her as forever nightmares.

"Feel okay?" her mother called through a closed door.

"Uh huh."

She flushed everything away.

Without taking off her coat, she climbed into bed and pulled the sheets over her face. Noises her mother made, while putting groceries away, comforted her. As long as she never spoke of this night to anyone, she'd be fine. She was sure of it.

2

SPRING, 2009 PARK HILL, DENVER

"Praise be to God!" Dr. Inez Buchanan's words slid past her lips, as she stared admiringly at food she'd spent hours preparing. Sunday's breakfast was always gourmet cuisine. Today her cup held pecan coffee, while her plate boasted two eggs-over-easy, firm fresh lox, topped with paper-thin slivers of crisp red onion and enough cayenne pepper to clear her sinuses for the entire day. Capers rested in hollandaise sauce along the outer edge of the plate and cheesy grits filled the only vacant space left.

Colorful cookbooks looked down from shelves mounted close to the ceiling. They sat like exotic passports to dishes she could barely pronounce. Deliberately, she kept those books inaccessible to the casual neighbor and exploring child. And in a secret space behind the refrigerator was a five-foot grabber for her use only. As if God heard her praise, the sound of two pieces of barley bread popped up from the toaster to acknowledge her thankfulness.

After all, she was entitled. Her entire breakfast, she believed, was the fruit of her retirement. After forty years of the kind of work that could drive most people insane, God blessed her with good food, decent shelter, nobody's ass to kiss, and cloth napkins to keep civilization headed in the right direction.

Just then her doorbell rang. She jumped. Visitors were rare. Inez stood quite still. Any movement could be seen through the sheers at her windows. Meanwhile the smell of pecan coffee became harder to resist. Slowly she savored one long swallow.

Again, the doorbell rang. Determined to put an end to it, she marched through the dining room, stopping at one of several ornate mirrors hung there for a purpose. The decorating had been a former neighbor's stroke of genius. Inez adjusted her bra strap, because being lopsided was never an option, not alone on a Sunday morning or even after a seventeen-year old mastectomy. Perhaps enough time had passed and plastic surgery could be an option for a survivor with a tumor so close to her breastplate. If she remembered, she'd look into it sometime during the week.

Abruptly, she opened the front door wide. There stood a white haired woman in a navy Chanel suit, navy pumps, an oversized matching purse, white gloves, and a navy pillbox hat. Inez coveted the woman's white hair; her own had turned a drab gray. But the woman wore clothes Goodwill craved, straight from 1950s haute couture magazines. Deep leathery wrinkles on her face and neck also gave testament to long hot days beside a swimming pool or two, probably without wearing a stitch of sunscreen.

"I'm Dolly David from over on Albion Street." Her voice was masculine and her thumb curved towards Pikes Peak.

Not knowing anyone with that name, Inez responded with a half smile and closed the door ever so slightly.

"Maybe you've heard of my husband. I'm Colonel Tucker David's wife, till he died this past January."

Why would Inez have heard of her husband? Inez's eyes strayed across the street, pondering the enigma and inching the door further in, as the woman's mistress-of-the-realm voice regaled the virtues of her late husband's military career. Inez refused to tell her she was sorry for her loss. That would only encourage her.

"Actually," the woman continued, "I'm Teddy Wabely's godmother."

"Oh!" Inez shouted. "Why didn't you say so? Come on in."

The woman's perfume was stronger than it should have been, though reminiscent of the verbena and lemon her mother had worn. Instinctively, Inez decided to leave the door open awhile longer.

"That's so kind of you. I was hoping we could talk. I'd been meaning to call you ever since ... I just left church services up the street, thought maybe I'd tell you ... I guess I should start from the beginning, but ..."

"Listen," Inez interrupted. "I was about to eat ..."

"Oh, certainly not! I've had breakfast, thank you. But I wonder if I might sit with you while you eat and tell you a few things about my granddaughter. You see Teddy's told me so much about you and those Chinese officials you kept from ..."

"I'm no detective, Mrs. David. I don't do private investigations. If that's what you need, you're better off calling the police."

Inez had recited those words often. News services still recounted the way she exposed China's attempt to outsource its espionage against the United States, even though it had happened nearly six months ago.

The woman placed her gloved hand on Inez's arm. "Teddy told me in strictest confidence," she whispered, "that you're very intelligent for a black woman. And I ..."

There it was from nowhere, a deep deliberate stab to the helium balloon holding up Inez's self-confidence and individual determination. She heard the balloon's skin twist and turn. Inez grabbed the doorknob and said, "Teddy would never have said anything like that. Are you even his godmother?"

"Oh, my dear," Dolly said breathlessly. She backed away towards the dining room.

Inez continued to talk into the screen door, "Can't remember when I last heard that sorry piece of racism." One demeaning incident after another swiftly passed in front of her eyes. "Used to hear it everywhere. Anyway, don't let me take up any more of your time."

Dolly took another two steps backwards and staggered under the weight of her large purse that both her arms now cradled. Her eyes widened. "I *am* Teddy's godmother. I haven't seen him in years, but our families have lived in Denver for several generations. And no one has ever called us racists. Never!" She straightened her back. "I'm proud my godson helped you. But see here, I'll beg, if I need to. I'll do anything, fly you anywhere, pay you anything, if you'll just find my granddaughter and bring her home."

Inez leaned closer to carefully watch the woman open that large purse of hers. What was that child's name, the one who carried those over-sized bags at Shoshone Middle School? Inez tried to remember, but was distracted. One of Dolly's hands fished inside the purse, apparently finding what she searched for. She pulled out a silver flask.

The rude gesture made Inez groan audibly. The woman unscrewed the top, flung her head straight back, her hat falling to the floor, and guzzled down the liquid. Inez slammed the door shut and with nostrils flared, marched past the odor of alcohol and into her kitchen, where she sat down to finally eat breakfast.

"Door's not locked," she shouted back. "See yourself out."

For a moment, the only sounds came from Inez's fork against her plate and her groans of satisfaction after each bite. A short time later the woman shouted, "My esteemed doctor prescribed this …this …"

"Then FIRE his ass!" Inez shouted back.

"Ah! You have a horrible disposition. I don't know why I thought I …"

Silence again. Was Dolly David pilfering? Inez wasn't worried. Retired schoolteachers have nothing worth stealing. Besides, she knew Dolly's type, the kind of woman who could persuade a doctor to dull the pain of reality, should it ever force itself upon her life.

Eventually, Dolly stepped inside the kitchen, dabbing dry eyes with a crumpled tissue.

Inez's anger had dissipated with the taste of good food. "There's coffee on the counter," she said. "Cups are in the cabinet above it." She was also slightly curious.

Instead of getting coffee, Dolly dropped her purse to the floor and sat at the table across from Inez.

"I'm so sorry," Dolly said. "I didn't mean to offend you. It was the last thing I intended. I'm just frustrated. I can't get anyone to help me."

And why would anyone help her? She could probably afford prescriptive relief at any level. Inez couldn't relate and got up to pour herself another cup of coffee.

"I've talked to police," Dolly continued, "my elected representatives in Congress, the FBI, CIA, Departments of State, Defense, the U.S. Embassy in Afghanistan."

"I'm impressed," Inez said. "Is she military?" she asked, as she sat down.

Dolly shook her head, no.

"How old is she?"

"Mid thirties."

"So it's possible your granddaughter is where she wants to be. And that begs the question, doesn't it?"

Ted Wabely, her former neighbor, once told Inez that he felt blessed in having absentee parents, while growing up. Perhaps those feelings included his godmother. "Isn't that like trying to save her from herself?" Inez asked.

The woman grabbed a wad of paper napkins from its holder and sobbed real tears into them.

Inez ate quietly then asked, "You have friends you can talk to?"

Without answering, Dolly got up and poured the coffee Inez had offered earlier. She took her time, silently adding the right amount of sugar and cream, sticking her finger in it to determine the temperature, tasting it before adding anything else.

While her back was turned, Inez observed Dolly's hands tremble. Was pouring coffee the maid's job or was she a functioning alcoholic, or both?

"The Colonel, bless his soul," Dolly replied, "was one of my best friends." She kept her back toward Inez. "But we didn't talk much.

He forced everything in his life to fit two camps: good or evil, black or white. You followed him or got left behind. There was no gray. He disowned our daughter years ago so he never knew his granddaughter existed."

Dolly twirled around to face Inez with the kind of smile political candidates used on television. Then she walked back to the table, sat down, and crossed her legs to one side, without spilling a drop of coffee. Well, thought Inez, she's practiced that routine more than once.

"You know," said Inez, genuinely fascinated, "if you just want someone to listen to you, I can do that. After all, you are Teddy's godmother."

Dolly stirred her coffee, leaned forward, and began hurling words at her the way machine guns hurl bullets. "People think I belong in an insane asylum, when I tell them my granddaughter is in Afghanistan with a Taliban husband. But I know they've been living there for the past few years."

Without thinking, Inez tossed her head back and chuckled. "Who told you that story, Mrs. David?"

Dolly squinted hard, yanked her purse from the floor, and pulled out a pink nylon wallet with a rabbit's foot dangling from it. Lacey, Lacey Cunningham was her name, the girl who always brought her large purses to class. Greek letters in blue ink covered both sides of the nylon. It couldn't possibly have belonged to Dolly. With wrinkled yet nimble fingers, she pulled out a photo and smacked it on the table, as if playing a spade on a trick of cards. Inez was not about to pick it up or give Dolly the satisfaction of showing overt interest.

The young woman in the photo was uncommonly beautiful. Her movie star features could have been a mixture of several different races, Caucasian and African among them. She could have been a pin-up girl for a global society, replacing the half-century-old photos of Lana Turner and Marilyn Monroe.

The photograph spoke volumes, providing a likely reason why Dolly's husband disowned a daughter. She'd had a baby by an African American or Aborigine, for all Inez knew, or very possibly by a soldier within the jurisdiction of the Colonel's far-reaching command. It could even explain why Dolly was asking for help from an African-American woman she didn't even know.

"Call me, Doll," the woman said smugly.

Fat chance of that, Inez thought. "Well, she is beautiful."

"And she was raised right here in Park Hill."

"Her husband," Inez questioned, "the man you say is Taliban. You have his picture?"

"Would you believe me, if I told you someone broke into my home and stole my only picture of him, but took nothing else, and I have no way of proving any of that?"

"Why would you lie?" Inez asked.

"Thank you," Dolly said, placing her bare hand on top of Inez's. Dolly's eyes watered up again, while Inez slowly moved her hand away.

"Let's start again," Inez suggested. "Your granddaughter told you she was married to a Taliban soldier? How do you know she's in Afghanistan? Who told you that part of the story?"

"Why do you keep calling it a story?"

"Guess it's my own bias," Inez admitted. "I didn't know Taliban ever married, much less married American women. To be honest, I've never thought about them until now. But I've taught many girls from Park Hill over the years. This isn't a community in which extremist Islamic beliefs about women flourish or go undetected. The average schoolgirl here believes she could be President of the United States one day. Whatever way the Taliban defines intellectual activity, they don't want females involved in it. Maybe I'm giving more credit to the girls in this neighborhood than I should, but that difference alone would impede such a marriage, don't you think?"

Glancing again at the photo, Inez continued, "And your granddaughter doesn't appear developmentally ..."

Dolly stood up abruptly. "You're not smart for a black woman! You're an arrogant bitch! You started by insulting my psychiatrist, a learned Syrian, who knows my needs better than some Ph.D. retired schoolteacher. And now you talk as if my granddaughter has to be retarded to marry a Taliban. Her IQ you might as well know, is much higher than Teddy's ever was." She picked up her purse from under the table again. "Just who do you think you are? You're not listening to me." Opening it, she again searched its contents just the way Lacey Cunningham would have.

Inez mashed her lips together, sliding them from side to side. She regretted the speed with which she'd opened her door to an alcoholic and remembered the morning Lacey brought two bags to class.

I need you to open that bag Lacey, so I can see what's in it.
Why's that, Dr. Buchanan? It's just my lunch.

"I'm so sorry, Dolly," Inez began. "You're right. I should have been listening and learning with my mouth shut. I got caught up in your granddaughter's history. There's so much I don't know. Like what about your granddaughter's father for example?"

Instantly, Dolly plopped into the nearest chair, purse and all, as if exhausted. "You say you got caught up in her story?" she repeated. "There are some who think her father was an honorable man, more honorable than the Colonel. Are you interested enough to help?"

"Listen," Inez announced, "I've told you before, I'm not a detective. I …"

"No, you listen!" Dolly was on her feet again, squeezing her purse against her chest. "My granddaughter called me a few weeks before her grandfather died. She's all I've got. Her mom, my daughter, was killed in a car accident years ago, speeding. That's when I finally stepped up. I wasn't going to ignore my granddaughter, the way I'd ignored my daughter.

"She said she needed money, Afghan women needed it. She knew I had money. I paid her college tuition, got her started in her first apartment. She gave me detailed instructions to get the money to her. Didn't say how much she needed. It was up to me. Said she'd be just outside Jalalabad until the end of the year. After that they were moving into the mountains, and I'd never see her again, particularly if the money didn't come. Her words shocked me. Whether she gets this money or not, I believe she may be killed." Her voice disappeared into her throat.

"And you could tell it was her, from her voice, even though you hadn't heard it since when?"

"She knew things about her mother only a daughter could know."

"But you said you and your husband disowned your daughter. How much could *you* have really known about her?"

Dolly shook her head. "None of that's important. I did what she asked. But no one showed up. I've got to try again."

"Well," Inez responded, "if you're anxious to throw money away, Western Union will deliver every dime you give them. Grandparents are always taken in."

Dolly set her purse on the counter and paced the floor, walking up and down the narrow space between the counter and the kitchen table. She stopped suddenly.

"Okay. I can believe that the Taliban may want my money for whatever they do with money."

"Read the papers, why don't you," Inez shouted. "That'll give you some idea what they do with money."

Dolly balled her hands into fists. "What if it's not for Afghan women? What if it really is a ransom?" Her voice broke. "I need to know she's safe! I need to bring her home! And I need help."

Still seated, Inez blinked quickly to stop water from collecting in her eyes. She understood this woman's pain perfectly. So what, if Inez had no family of her own, or perhaps because of that, she could vividly imagine the anguish of a grandmother unable to rescue her granddaughter. Unobtrusively, she wiped her cheeks with the back of her hand, but felt Dolly leaning closer.

"Help me," Dolly pleaded. "I need to know where she is, dead or alive, raped or not. If she's being held against her will, I need someone to go get her."

She pulled out the pink wallet again. "This was found in a trashcan near her last apartment in Fort Collins. Police thought a student murdered her. I want you to have it. It's got her driver's license, social security card, proof of insurance …"

"Dolly, I can't take that. I'm not sure what I can do." Inez took a deep breath. "But I promise I'll make a phone call to someone I know at the FBI."

"I want you to have this, too." Dolly turned her purse upside down. A heavy gray gun, the word Glock printed in bold sunken letters on one side, dropped onto the table.

Hysterical, Inez scrambled to her feet, the smooth bottoms of her bedroom slippers sliding out from under her. "What the hell!" she screamed.

Dolly ran yelling. "I was going to shoot somebody, maybe myself," she added. "Don't need to now. Don't worry about money. I'll send you some."

Inez picked up the gun with a potholder and scurried after her. "Stop," she yelled. "Take this thing."

But she was gone. Inez stood on her porch, marveling at that eighty-something's speed. Lacey Cunningham had kept a seven-inch knife in *her* purse.

3

JUNE 1996 NORTH OF BAGDAD

"**M**ad Man'll torture them, won't he?" she screamed.

Uday barely heard her. Mad Man's Imperial army, some three hundred strong, slashed, pillaged, looted, and butchered people in their slow path down each echoing corridor; creating enough noise to drown out her words as the two ran for their lives.

Uday's ears, however, remained sensitive to the sound of her flat leather thongs against a marble floor. She kept up with him, but he was the better runner and a full leg in front. Storm boots thundered ahead of them. For an instant, he regretted having given his gun away to a fellow agent. Reaching behind him, he grabbed her arm, yanking her behind a wide Romanesque column, only two steps from the top of the staircase.

"Won't he?" she yelled.

"Shut up!" He smothered her mouth with his sweaty palm, while ear-splitting shrieks and cries for help rose above the first floor. Heavy-footed soldiers ran downstairs again. The odor of gasoline and burned flesh told them what was happening below.

Again they ran, this time stumbling down the back service stairs to doors at the bottom of the building. His neck bulging, his veins popping, Uday pushed his right shoulder against pneumatic doors, the last ones scheduled to be chained shut. In scorching sunlight, they galloped across burning sand toward a mud caked 1950s Citroen. He hoped the motor was running, but couldn't hear anything above continuous agonizing screams and mortar shells ripping away the east wing of the building.

Uday flung open the door of the aging sedan to shove Sabeen inside, all the while watching a bewildered soldier standing behind them at the back door they'd just exited. Chains hung from the arm of that soldier as he held the door open and stood motionless. The soldier's other hand held a rifle. Uday slid into the back seat next to Sabeen and hollered at the man behind the wheel to do something, anything.

The car's original two-cylinder motor had been switched out for a Maserati engine that idled loudly. The driver came to life, waving one arm out the window, bidding the befuddled soldier to come closer. As soon as the soldier released his hand from the door, the driver pointed his customized revolver and fired one soundless bullet. The soldier fell on that same stretch of burning sand behind the headquarters of the Iraqi National Congress, a building destined to become rubble.

The sedan driver, wearing a military cap and a khaki colored shirt resembling the uniform of Mad Man's army, pressed his foot against the floor, making dust rise from the road behind them.

Sabeen had already torn away her full body hijab, all the while staring at Uday. "You know what he'll do to them, don't you?"

"Damn right I know," he said. "You volunteered us for this gig, remember?"

"Well, I don't know what he'll do. So don't tell me!" Tears actually flowed down her cheeks, but her voice remained steady and strong. "If you tell me, if you use the words, then I'll remember those words and I'll picture it and have never-ending nightmares about it. But if you don't tell me, well ... then I'll be okay."

"How many times, Sabeen, will you tell me this?"

Uday, rapidly pulled on new clothes from a plastic bag on the floor of the back seat. Mentally, he was attempting to change his persona from a professorial interpreter to a pilot with swagger. Making others suspend their judgment of him was all he had to do. But to do that, he needed mental space, space to conjure up a new version of himself. There was no time to focus on Sabeen's psychological needs.

She changed into another hijab, all black and less elegant than the one she'd worn. But this time she added a burqa as well, revealing only her red swollen eyes. She constantly chattered about their decision to work apart, to take missions in different countries, and their feelings that it would help their separate careers.

"Almost there," hollered the driver. "Soldiers watch everyone. Get down on the floor."

The driver pulled off the main street behind a large bakery truck with its side door opened. He took off his military jacket and cap, dropping them over the back seat into yet another bag. Then he slid a white tunic over his head and began driving again, while he covered his holster and gun that lay between his legs.

Twenty minutes later, the driver asked, "Ready back there?"

With one hand, Uday grabbed the back of Sabeen's head and pressed her mouth hard against his. With his other hand he made sure he'd never forget the hardness of her nipples or the softness between her legs. His hands were rough and he kept at it until the palms of her hands pushed harder against his chest. He tried to smother himself in her scent, happy to drown in it, even if she did talk too much. Over the past year, their love, marinated in adrenaline, had been his potion of choice. And yet he was excited about his next mission, his first without her.

Finally, he released her. "Ready," he announced.

The driver kept the car at a crawl beside a long indiscernible opening at the bottom of a wire fence about a quarter of a mile from a 747. It was the largest of four planes on the tarmac.

As Uday hopped out, Sabeen, holding both hands together and head bowed, whispered, "Namaste, my Uday, my love." Still on the floor, she stretched to slam the door shut behind him.

4

BEGINNING OF SUMMER, 2009
DENVER, COLORADO

From her front porch, Dr. Inez Buchanan watched a Black Mercedes stop at the curb. She folded her arms tightly across her chest. Darkened windows kept the car's occupants a secret, but Inez knew who they were.

In the far corner of her eye, she recognized movement farther up the street. A lanky teenaged boy ran down the sidewalk and up the path to her front door, carrying a medium sized box of chocolates, which he protected like a football in play. She turned in his direction and gave him an unyielding look. The boy threw himself against the wall beside her open door and continued to breath hard. Briefly, she watched him bend over to catch his breath, then turned her attention back to the sedan at the curb.

With what Inez thought was a Nigerian accent, the boy said, "I'm raising money for East High School. But I'll be back later. I see you've got company coming, don't you."

Her only response to his observation was a smile over one shoulder. She appreciated the red blur of his sneakers, once he regained his speed. Off he ran across the street and up to the next block. She was known as an 'easy touch' by most fundraisers. School solicitations were as common as butterflies in Park Hill.

Two men had emerged from the shiny black car to trample over her Kentucky blue grass, as if they owned it. Each carried a file box in one arm and a brief case that dangled from the other hand.

Using her livid schoolteacher voice, Inez's lips barely moved. "Grass does not grow on trees, which is why I have a cement walkway. And," she said, staring at their boxes, "when I consented to have you in my home, it was for introductions only."

Inez stepped aside to let the suit-wearing, baggage-laden men through her doorway.

Again she was surprised when they continued through the entryway and into her dining room without asking permission. The short one even displayed a phone in his ear. And for what, Inez wondered? To show that someone thought him important enough to call. The audacity.

Swiftly following them, Inez continued her admonishments. "As I explained over the phone, I have no intention of asking Dolly David to pay for anything. I only phoned one friend, who is able to find out anything there is to know about crime in this state and I'm still waiting for him to return my call."

"Who could that be?" asked the taller of the two, the one who looked old enough to have played basketball at the turn of the twentieth century.

"That's *my* business, isn't it?" Inez quipped.

The short younger man sighed with drama reminiscent of a burlesque show, and said, "We saturated the entire Fort Collins area with private investigators, when she disappeared. We even searched abroad. You really should have come to us first."

One hand rested on his hip, his pinkie in the air, while the other held his briefcase, which in one jerky move, he slammed atop her mahogany table. Although it made a soft supple sound of leather against wood, Inez hastily picked it up and propped it against the leg of the chair closest to him. Soundlessly, they glared at each other, she daring him to put it back.

"Don't get us wrong," said the tall man, who'd placed both his box and briefcase on the floor where they belonged. "We appreciate the fact that you consented to see us, however reluctantly, but understand that I advised Dolly against coming to you in the first place. She considered you her last resort and I considered you useless. By the way, what did you do with the gun she gave you?"

Inez turned from the short man to glare now at the tall one. The man's sense of privilege was well oiled. But before she could open her mouth, the short man shoved two business cards under her chin.

Inez read directly from the cards the short man held, making no attempt to touch them herself. "Why are you asking, Mr. Allen Bradley, Esquire? Or are you the legal secretary, Mr. Joseph Alonzo Stronsky, Junior?"

"Just curious and I'm Bradley," answered the tall man. "Please excuse my manners. I meant to introduced myself as soon as I came in."

"And I'm the secretary you talked to on the phone," said Stronsky. "Trust us. We wouldn't be here, if it wasn't necessary."

He tossed both cards on the dining room table, as if playing craps. She remembered telling him about Dolly's gun and made a mental note never to volunteer information to them again.

"You think Dolly hired me, don't you?" Inez asked. "Well, she didn't. I'm simply researching something for her, as I would for any friend or acquaintance. And when I'm finished, that'll be the end of it."

"Sit down, Doctor Buchanan. Please." Bradley directed. "Circumstances have changed, since you last talked to Dolly."

He pulled a dining room chair closer to her, but didn't sit. Stronsky was already seated, placing his box on the table and pulling papers neatly from it. She continued to stand, as did Bradley.

A peek in one of her mirrors, made her straighten her back more.

"We kept this out of the papers," Bradley said, "for reasons we'll explain later. Mrs. David committed suicide three days ago and she …"

"No. No!" Inez heard her voice rising as she shook her head. "That can't be."

"… and she's named you the primary executor of her estate."

Breathless, Inez tried but failed to pull the chair back further from the table. She gave up and sat on it awkwardly. Bradley sat, too, across from Stronsky.

Acid began to pool at the top of her stomach. After several minutes, in which she silently affirmed life's precarious nature, she realized, looking into the faces of both men that they hadn't said a word and probably wouldn't speak again until she did.

But all she wanted was time alone to think, because the Dolly David she briefly met would never have committed suicide. Inez was very certain that, even though Dolly brought a gun in her purse, it wasn't for suicide, but to kill the next person who refused to help.

She quietly summoned her memories of Dolly, her silver flask, her emotional swings from pride to fear, her determination to seek help for her granddaughter, her racial ignorance, her curiosity, until finally she blurted, "But why?"

Bradley spoke up first. "We have papers for you to sign because…"

The loud teacher-in-control voice she used to interrupt him could probably be heard outside. "Will I need to hire my own attorney to get my questions answered?"

"I'm so sorry," Bradley said. "We're here to help *you*. I didn't realize you'd be affected by news of her death. You only met her once. I'm sorry for being so callous. What was your question again?"

She knew this man wasn't sorry for *being* callous. He was sorry his callousness had been noted. She took a deep breath before starting. "*Why* did she commit suicide? Did she leave a note? And *why* didn't she just leave her estate to her granddaughter? Dolly said she had something to live for now."

The first time she realized Bradley wore glasses was when he pulled them off. His bald head, gray eyes and skin, his lack of eyebrows gave him the face of a naked newt. Embarrassed for him, she looked away, while he wiped his lenses.

"As to the first two questions," Bradley began, "There was no note. And although I've known Dolly for decades, I was her husband's attorney first. Later I became her attorney, when her daughter died in a car accident. After that, Dolly tried suicide at least five times. This time she ran her car off Lookout Mountain at ninety miles per hour, with the help of two bottles of Demerol. I was told you could see the fireball in Longmont. Totally incinerated. Good thing she wanted cremation. There won't be a funeral. No relatives left. An electrical tower collapsed in that fire, which helped us explain it as an energy grid problem to the press without mentioning her name right away."

Her mouth opened in amazement. She'd been listening to a man made of stone. Stronsky chuckled, a painful reminder to Inez of her own chuckling after she'd heard Dolly's 'story.' Oh God, if she could only take it back.

Inez focused inward, while Bradley coldly gave his personal account of Dolly's psychological state. She had no interest in learning what a heartless self-serving lawyer thought of Dolly's mental health. The woman had had one goal that Inez knew of and Dolly remained as loyal to that goal as she could.

"And that brings us to the last question," Bradley said. "Why didn't she leave her estate to her granddaughter?"

His elbows rested on her table, while he clasped his hands together. "There is absolutely nothing," he said, "to confirm Dolly's story that her granddaughter is in Afghanistan or that she married a Taliban soldier or that Kadija Campbell needs money. To the contrary, I met Kadija Campbell when she was a freshman at Colorado State. As her grandmother's attorney, I made sure her tuition was paid, her books and housing taken care of. She was in graduate school for a year after getting her Bachelor's and then she moved on. Later we discovered she'd vanished off the face of the earth. We believe she's dead and had hoped Mrs. David would be lucid enough to file papers to that effect by the end of this year.

"I don't know why Dolly made you her executor and I don't know what you said to get Dolly's trust, but she didn't want us to handle her wealth alone anymore."

If Dolly was anything, Inez thought, she was lucid and if these two men were the only people working on her behalf, she'd been wise to seek additional oversight.

Stronsky continued piling documents in short stacks equidistant from each other on her table. For Inez, however, thinking was a solitary process. The dining room had become claustrophobic, with multiple mirrors reflecting an infinite number of intolerable guests.

She suddenly realized Bradley was nothing, if not a mountain of information. Leaning forward she asked, "Couldn't Dolly's granddaughter be working for some agency like the CIA or some similar organization somewhere."

Bradley interrupted. "Dolly David's contacts were considerably better placed than yours. She was given assurance by the President of the United States that Kadija was not and never had been a U.S. government employee or volunteer therein and, therefore, was not being deployed for any mission, covert or otherwise."

Stronsky slid a single sheet of paper across the table with the presidential seal embossed at the bottom. Inez read it, remembering that Dolly had recited a list of government agencies, never mentioning the White House.

She sat baffled by her own reaction after reading the irrefutable evidence in front of her. Dolly's suicide plus the lack of compassion from these two excuses for men, gave her story a certain veracity, if not heroism, in the face of long odds.

Inez put the paper down and looked squarely at Bradley. "You have evidence then that Kadija Campbell is dead?"

"I do," Bradley answered smugly. "But it's circumstantial. There's no body and not enough blood for tests. We'll wait another year to establish her as legally dead. That's just one of many options we'll need to discuss with you."

"Well, I feel saturated with all this information. I'll need time to process it. There is one thing I'll need soon, though," Inez continued, "copies of those investigative reports Mr. Stronsky referred to. And yes, I'll need hardcopies. Those investigators, I imagine, were paid from Dolly's account?"

Was it plain old-fashion rage she saw in Bradley's eyes? She let several awkward minutes pass, waiting politely for his answer.

"Dolly's real estate holdings alone are worth just under a half billion dollars."

Inez considered herself a sophisticated woman, but could feel her eyes bulge from their sockets.

"She was the last surviving relative," Bradley continued, "of John Fairchild, of the Fairchild Airline dynasty? And then, of course, there are her shares in Martindale, Inc. One more reason not to advertise her death. Her death in the same year as her husband's could send stocks down. The whole portfolio is around fourteen billion."

Inez's eyebrows rose automatically. To compensate for her embarrassing knee jerk reaction, she suddenly frowned and hoped Bradley hadn't noticed.

"I understand your need for time," Bradley said with his eyes on the table, "and you'll get that. But there's one thing *I* must insist on." His voice boomed, as he lifted his head. "You must contact a security company today to turn this house into a fortress as soon as possible. I'm worried about you being held for ransom or worse. As primary executor, you'll be able to charge Dolly's account for all renovations related to any security measures you need. Or a call to Stronsky here, when you're ready of course, can put him in charge of the whole project."

"Sounds like you believe the cloak and dagger stuff Dolly spoke of."

He unbuttoned his jacket, as he spoke. "Our inability to prove anything she said, doesn't mean everything she said was untrue. It simply means we can't prove it."

Still seated, Bradley stretched his arms out and locked his hands behind his neck, like a professor, comfortable in his own classroom. "You know, he said, "you probably don't recognize our names, but Colonel David and I founded Martindale Incorporated in the 1970s.

It's a global enterprise. Each division has its own research arm. We have architectural, construction, geological, and legal offices in London, Dubai, Denver, Beijing, Berlin, and we have contracts with numerous industries from motion pictures to mining to military, to ....."

"Really?" Inez asked. "So wouldn't Colonel David, with so many places and ways to gather information, have known about the existence his granddaughter?"

"Pardon?" Bradley asked.

Inez shook her head. "Nothing. I may have misunderstood."

Stronsky's sudden hand signals were visible in a mirror behind him at Bradley's mention of the word military. Inez caught sight of it.

She stood up and pushed her chair under the table. "Well, thank you for keeping *me* informed." Then turning directly to Bradley she said, "How soon can I get those reports?"

Both men continued to sit, while Stronsky flailed his arms, expressing in pantomime his discomfort at having to repack his files.

Inez said, "Leave them here then."

Bradley got to his feet quickly. "Tomorrow morning by special carrier, you'll have those reports. On the other hand, we can't leave documents concerning Dolly's estate here until you've secured a safe place inside your home."

"But aren't you giving me just copies? What you have in your office are the original papers. How secure do copies need to be?" she asked. "Why not take your originals back to the office and leave Mr. Stronsky's copies here with me." She was initiating a pissing contest, the kind little boys like to win and she knew it.

Bradley picked up his box from the floor and crammed it under his arm, making Inez feel respected by someone who understood the importance of being a gentleman.

"It's been delightful, Dr. Buchanan," he said. "Call me, if you have questions now or in the future. There are time factors, however. Courts get angry when vital documents aren't changed in a timely manner. "

"Yes, time does matter," Inez said. "If what Dolly suspected is true, we only have until the end of this year. That's if you believe what she said."

Bradley tilted his head back. "So, do *you* believe Dolly's claims?" Before she could answer he added, "Sometimes decisions must be made without the benefit of certainty."

Without a word, yet seething over his smug attitude, she walked to the door and opened it wide.

5

Stronsky slid behind the wheel of their company car, while Bradley flung open the door behind him. He threw the box on the back seat next to the far door and sprawled along the seat beside it. He intended to take a nap. He too, was tired of concealing his next move from a woman whose temperament was obviously volatile for no reason he could think of.

"Changed your mind about your retirement date?" Stronsky asked. He hadn't yet put the key into the ignition. "I'm asking because it seemed in there like you planned to be around to answer any questions that woman …"

"My plans haven't changed."

"Glad to hear that," Stronsky answered, "'cause I've decided to go with Harwood. He's doubled my salary. Yet it wouldn't be right, if you changed your mind. I mean I'd certainly stay, if you wanted me to. But I've spent some of his advance money already, if you know what I mean."

He knew what Stronsky meant. Bradley quietly stared at messages on his cell. His secretary was considered the best in the Denver office, highly skilled, innovative, and amoral. There'd been a bidding war among Martindale's top litigation lawyers in North America because Stronsky wasn't keen to leave the U.S.

Half-heartedly Bradley wanted to work past seventy, but only if he could recruit a voluptuous blonde from the secretary pool and turn her into the next best thing. He was fed up with gay secretaries, overweight black case managers, fast-talking Hispanic couriers, and buying expensive Hanukkah gifts for rich clients. He yearned for the old days, when office personnel were all alike, white and perky. But he especially hated the upturn of Democrats in the White House and having to donate to their bleeding heart causes to get a small contract. Yet the sale of his shares in Martindale made leaving worthwhile. Let the next generation try to keep the company alive.

"You know, you almost blew it in there," Stronsky said.

"I saw your signal. She did, too."

"And what were all those mirrors for anyway?" asked Stronsky.

"Narcissism? Who cares? We're out of there. By the way, you've already verified Dolly's ashes and …?"

"Course I have. Already done. And we didn't get that woman's signature because she's an ugly dumb ass," Stronsky said.

"Don't get callous and resentful son," Bradley cautioned. "I bet she was quite a handsome woman in her day, not glamorous, but certainly above average looking. I'm partial to women of any race with aluminum colored hair."

"Ha! You had your glasses off most of the time," Stronsky replied. "Did you see her actually stare me down for putting my briefcase on her fucking table? Please! And she's got no clue what she's in for as an executor. She'd *better* hire her own attorney."

"Complete waste of Dolly's money! There isn't a lawyer in this city we can't control. And stay on top of who she hires to turn her house into a fortress," Bradley added.

They both laughed.

"That was a good one." Stronsky continued laughing.

"Thank you. But remember, the technology has changed. It doesn't need to be one of our own companies anymore. We can intercept anybody's signal. And I need the name of that person who knows 'everything there is to know about crime in Colorado,'" Bradley demanded. "I want that name by the end of today."

Bradley briefly caught sight of Stronsky's eyes rolling, when he glanced in the rear view mirror. "We'd have his name now," Stronsky said, "if you hadn't stopped me from leaving a bug. I'm sure she's already on the phone to him."

"Listen!" Bradley sat up tall to make his point. "Don't ever leave bugs in any house. I've told you that before and I'm serious enough to bring you up on charges of insubordination, if you do it again. We're not experts in that field. And she's smart. Once she knows what we're capable of, she'll figure out some way to interfere.

"You noticed she never once said, 'no, I don't want to be the primary executor.' Well, I don't trust that woman to leave well enough alone. It's in her eyes."

Stronsky responded with louder laughter. His crassness and constant insinuation that the two of them were equals had repulsed Bradley for years. He'd have fired Stronsky two years ago, if he hadn't been so close to retirement himself.

"You're giving that old biddy way too many props," Stronsky said. "Yet she did have you going there for a minute. I could tell. You thought she was going to give Kadija Campbell all of Dolly's money, didn't you? Martindale won't let that happen." Stronsky finally put the key in the ignition and revved the motor.

Bradley put his phone away, while giving thought to Stronsky's words, words unusually laden with innuendo today. He agreed with Dr. Buchanan. Younger generations had no manners. But if there were a God in heaven, he wouldn't have to see her face again.

6

BEGINNING OF SUMMER, 2009
DENVER, COLORADO

One minute after Inez closed the front door behind them, she vowed never to open it to them again. They reminded her of the clean shaven, sweaty, pink cheeked men who smiled while they foreclosed on her parent's first house and who laughed while they increased her uncle's debt.

Still annoyed, she marched to the closet under the stairs and pushed back winter coats, to reveal a small cabinet door. After opening it, she grabbed the pink wallet Dolly had given her plus a small penlight. Carrying her treasures into the dining room, she got down on the floor, penlight in one hand, to examine chairs and the table's underbelly. If anything had been left behind, she'd find it.

Finally content with her own due diligence, she carried the wallet to the kitchen table and sat down hard from mental exhaustion. Okay, maybe checking the furniture was over the top. But then again, maybe it wasn't.

"Oh, Dolly!" she said aloud. "Why me?"

And yet she felt relieved. After all, they'd left nothing questionable. Perhaps they'd told her the truth as they saw it. Yet absolutely nothing could make Inez accept their story that the bigoted old woman, who sat in her kitchen not long ago and revealed her love for her racially mixed granddaughter, would commit suicide.

The sharp sound of knuckles against glass jarred her from her thoughts. There it was again. She bolted toward the back door, pulling the sheers aside. Trace Mitchell, a man who should have been in Washington, D.C., the man she'd called long distance for information about Dolly's granddaughter, was pressed against her back door.

As she opened it, he gently pushed her aside, locking the door behind him. He seemed to be playing the role of super sleuth in some campy play.

❧

Pressing his index finger against his lips, Trace whispered, "Got company?"

There was haughtiness in her answer of 'no', that he hadn't heard in awhile.

"Everyone's gone," she continued. "But why are *you* here? Good to see you, though."

He darted through the kitchen, hoping she wouldn't notice his crumpled suit and tie, the result of sleeping on the red-eye from D.C. to Denver. Inadvertently, he reached for his invisible hero's cape, but stuffed his hands in his pockets instead. He spied the corrugated box of legal paper on the dining room table and said, "Did they leave anything besides papers, anything else?" he asked.

There was no response. He turned to face Inez, wondering if she'd think he was was acting immature for her age. Maybe she was about to tell him so. Then he'd have to wait to share his success with her. It took him a minute to recognize that she was already beaming with pride over him.

"You taught me well, Professor Mitchell," she finally said. "I've already checked the chairs and the table where they sat."

"Did you? Really?" he asked, wondering if he'd created a monster, a criminal scrutinarian, a person who could see criminal intent behind every piece of furniture. The newspapers hadn't helped any by describing her as a modern day Miss Marple.

"Why?" he asked. "Because you felt queasy about them? You don't mind if I check, too, do you? Isn't that what teachers do, test their students, see if they've learned the basics?"

But Inez's instincts were better than average. He could concede that easily. If she thought something wasn't right, it probably wasn't. He watched her smile disappear, however. Not even retired teachers, he took note, enjoyed being tested.

Backtracking from table to chairs, he let one hand brush lightly over upholstered surfaces. He even crawled around baseboards and reached over doorways, hoping his thoroughness would increase her feeling of being specially trained.

When he opened the front door, a small wire in the lock caught his attention. Trace turned slowly and looked at Inez. She was less than three feet behind him. Not bothering to take the wire from its resting place just yet, he caught Inez staring at his prematurely graying hair.

"I planned to call you today," she said quickly. "Why aren't you in D.C.?"

Feeling a slight rush of adrenaline, he plastered his face with a fake smile. Sure, he knew she'd seen her share of guns and knives in inner city schools, but she probably hadn't seen this before. Unceremoniously, he yanked the wire away, closed the door, and held it out in front of him so Inez could see.

"Let's go to the kitchen," he said. "You can make me a cup of your tasty pecan coffee."

Once there, he turned the faucet on and dangled a tiny half-moon shaped disc at the end of a thin one-inch wire. He mouthed the word 'microphone' so Inez could see. First he took pictures, front and back, with his phone, emailing them to his office. Then he took out a lighter and watched the disc completely melt into smoke and air before dropping the wire down the drain under running water. Inez stared at the whole process.

He spoke gently, not wanting to scare her. "These things still work when they're wet. They have to be melted. No wonder those men sat out front so long. These devises are not known for their good reception. They're better with a dish nearby to bounce signals." He turned the garbage disposal on and off.

"Let me welcome you to the world of high finance because that's who uses this junk: bankers, gamblers, off-shore investors. Wires like that one disintegrate after four hours. I was half joking with you when I came in here. I saw them leave your house and sit in their car. You're right to suspect them of something."

Inez whispered, "They're employed by Martindale, Incorporated."

"Whew! That's global finance, all right." Trace answered. "Dolly David's husband and Alan Bradley created that company. Did you know that when you asked me to look into Kadija Campbell?" Mitchell asked. "Their political contributions got them contracts everywhere on the globe."

"No. But now I know that Dolly had an estate worth fourteen billion."

"No way!" Trace blurted.

"You're right, no way, because nothing that woman had on the day I met her said 'rich lady'. She wore no jewelry. Everything she had on said high-end thrift store. Well, I did think a maid put cream and sugar in her coffee for her daily. She had no kinetic memory for that simple a task. But tell me this, how does an elderly rich lady with a history of suicide attempts get her hands on a flask of liquor, a gun, two bottles of Demerol, and leave her home without a driver any time she wants? Wouldn't she have to walk past somebody she hired to take care of her? And yet it's her granddaughter I'm concerned about now. Did I say Dolly made me primary executor of her estate?"

"WHAT?"

He watched her snatch up her airtight canister of coffee beans with a vengeance. It was an act of pure annoyance with herself. So he decided to sit quietly at the table and wait patiently for what had become a very loud process for making coffee. She slammed cups against saucers and ran the water at full throttle. Although Trace tried, he couldn't hide his worry for her.

Finally, he said, "That's got to be what Martindale wants, the control they had before you showed up. Whichever man jammed that bug into the front door frame probably wore a receiver. Did you notice which one had something strange in his ear?"

"The secretary did. I thought it was his phone. Worse yet, I failed your test." She sighed. "Are you saying Martindale controlled all of Dolly's money?"

"Does poop stink?"

"You're taking advantage of my affection for you, young man. But I do understand your meaning," she replied.

"Yes, ma'm."

"They think I'm stupid, don't they?"

Mitchell rose from his chair, leaned across the kitchen table, lifted her face up to his and kissed her check. "Yeah, that's what they think."

Reluctantly, Inez beamed.

"And how's Sheila?" she asked. "Have you picked a day so I can go buy a dress for the wedding?"

Trace took a deep breath. "No. But first, let me tell you what I discovered. When the Associated Press reported Dolly David's suicide, I rechecked everything you'd asked me to find out about Kadija Campbell. I don't believe in coincidences.

"I disagreed with Larimer police. They focused on foreign students Kadija dated, thinking one of them killed her and fled the country. They investigated Sampati Jagjit, but nothing came of it. He'd become a Poudre Valley hero as a crop duster before attending CSU. However, I thought Kadija committed suicide because she'd been turned down for jobs with CIA, FBI, and all U.S. Military Intelligence Units.

"I looked for evidence supporting my conclusion. Her applications and FBI background checks were all there. But as I re-checked, I noticed how neat and tidy and in chronological order everything was. When I finally realized the files had been sanitized, I checked through redacted and misfiled materials and voila. Kadija couldn't have been murdered in Fort Collins."

Trace grabbed what looked like a homemade oatmeal cookie, laying by itself, off the counter, bit into it, and kept on talking.

"It finally hit me," he said. "Why would a girl this bright, taking Farsi at night during her freshman year, get turned down for intelligence work? Hell, my GPA was nowhere near hers. She quit Farsi early on and I assumed it was because she was depressed over her rejections. She did have one bad reference, but that couldn't have worked against her. I'll explain that in a minute. I'm thinking now that she knew she didn't need Farsi. She knew she needed another language. I think one of those intelligence agencies hired her and made their own application look like the others. All I know is she didn't die in Fort Collins."

The buzzer on the coffee machine went off and Inez got up to pour two cups.

"Did you like that cookie?" she asked, as she reached inside the refrigerator for a whole plate of them.

"Yes, I did," he answered, before biting into another. A moment later he said, "Her name is on a list I almost didn't find, a list of Americans who died from bacterial infections in Saudi Arabia in 1995."

Inez gasped.

"Everyone had been injected with tainted penicillin," Trace continued, while deciding which cookie to try next. "The list had been redacted from the files of a doctor arrested because of his illegal prescription drug trade.

"But there are problems with this list. There's a notation that the bodies were returned to their last known address. I knew a guy on this list, who died a month ago in Turkey. I don't doubt there're dead people on it. But not only is there no record of Kadija's body returning to the States, there's no record of a passport ever being issued in the first place. You okay?" he asked. Inez looked purple, drawn, and deeply saddened.

Inez spoke slowly. "If this list was at the FBI in Washington, D.C., doesn't that mean she once worked for them?"

"Not necessarily. The FBI does background checks for all government agencies."

"But wouldn't the President of the United States know about this?" asked Inez.

"What do you mean?"

"Those two men showed me a letter from the President saying that she never worked for the government."

Trace couldn't help himself. "They did, did they?" he beamed. Then he turned sideways in his chair and stretched his arm over its back. "Here's what that kind of letter tells me. If Kadija is alive, she's no longer Kadija Campbell. She's under deep cover. Only her case handler knows who she was before her mission. That's typical CIA protocol. Another thing CIA does is produce verification letters from people in authority saying the person in question never worked for them."

His smile disappeared. "I didn't mention this before," Trace said. "But in a letter of recommendation, Colonel Tucker David called his granddaughter a bastard child who had no business being born. He warned that her fidelity to the United States should be questioned."

Inez's forehead furrowed. "Wouldn't that prevent her from being hired?"

"It's clear the Colonel's comments spoke more to his own prejudices than to his granddaughter's fitness as a spy. Besides, sometimes what really matters about a resume is who reads it. Colonel David was attached to the White House for several years as an advisor. But it was a different administration that Kadija applied under."

Inez listened. Finally she asked, "She's alive, isn't she?"

"There's no proof either way."

"And she's working or was working under cover in Afghanistan. If she died there, wouldn't the CIA have sent Dolly one of those, "on behalf of a grateful nation" letters?"

"Maybe. Maybe not. In the beginning, they might simply have added a star to their wall in Langley."

His own words shut him up for a minute. He remembered one of the few times Inez talked about her own childhood. She'd said she always had a ferocious appetite for spy stories, constantly wishing for the opportunity to be chosen for such work. She'd said she could have gladly shown them how long an only child could live without human contact, exist on little or no food, and endure torture. Yet she'd never felt different from other girls her age, raised by a generation who believed in corporal punishment for children and the self-sacrifice of all citizens. His reminiscing was interrupted by her eyes staring at him.

"Kadija disappeared fourteen years ago from Fort Collins," Inez added. "Dolly could have had her declared dead before now. But she didn't. I bet Dolly had good reason to believe Kadija was alive and working as a spy."

"You're guessing."

"We know that the Colonel knew enough about Kadija to write a bad recommendation letter and send it to intelligence agencies and that Dolly believed that the call she received from Kadija earlier this year was real."

Trace added, "Bradley must know whether Kadija is alive or not. Martindale contractors are still in Afghanistan and throughout the Middle East wearing guns and doing construction work the military used to do. Though it's not official, it's no secret Martindale works hand in hand with the Company."

"Why would Bradley want Kadija declared dead, if she wasn't?" Inez asked. "Because he certainly wants her declared dead."

"Let's slow down." Trace responded. "Remember what I told you about brainstorming? It has no place in criminal investigations. Trained investigators rely on measurable evidence. Even if we knew her new identity, we can't seek any more information about her. Prying into her life is over. The U.S. doesn't want her found. Besides," he pushed back from the table, "I can't help you with this anymore. I'm not going to be working for the FBI any more. I'm moving back to Colorado. CBI accepted me back. I prefer life here. I mean, there's no room for me in Sheila's life."

Inez sat very still as he talked. Who was he fooling? She knew how he felt about Sheila. He, too, waited for her sage advice. She always had advice.

"You've got lots going on right now," she said suddenly, "and I certainly don't want to be an added burden. Anyway, you two will work this out." Inez smiled and stood up.

"Meanwhile," she continued, "I've got homework to do. I've got documents in the dining room I need to read and tomorrow I'm expecting more. Becoming an executor of an estate is like becoming an astrophysicist. You have to read one page at a time and ask questions, not necessarily in that order. So I'm going to be busy too, for the next few days."

"Oh," she continued, "I almost forgot. This is Kadija's wallet. I might take a short trip to Fort Collins to form my own impressions of the girl."

Trace blew air out like a man exasperated by what he was hearing.

"Did you even listen to what I said?" Trace told her. "The United States Government doesn't want her found." Inez had already walked out of the kitchen. If he had his way, he'd sit in her kitchen all day arguing with her. He enjoyed the warmth in Inez's house, particularly since his mother died.

He picked up the wallet, turning it over and over as he sipped coffee. "These symbols," he said absently, "I don't think they represent anything on CSU's campus. Gamma Tau Tau."

Inez walked back into the kitchen and snatched the wallet from him. "Let me see that. Can't be. She must have gone to Catholic School. I'd forgotten all about this. I can't believe it still goes on."

Trace watched her quizzically. "You going to share?" he asked.

"I went to St. Rita's years ago in Washington, D.C. Black girls sat together in the cafeteria out of fear, alienation, and friendship. The same thing was going on at other Catholic schools in the District of Columbia. Besides enduring the insecurities of puberty, those were days when anything could happen to you for no other reason than you were black. Anyway, we called ourselves the Girls of the Tan Table, G-T-T because the table had a tan Formica top and we were tan too. I bet Kadija went to Catholic school. The concept must have spread. I guess I'll start with her high school then."

"WHY?" Trace asked. "I get that this is important to you, but people were maimed and killed the last time you played amateur detective. When you focus your energy on something you get others to focus their energy on it too. Then unusual things happen. Let it alone!"

"We all have that power. It's called passion. I was afraid you might take that attitude." Inez stood tall and swallowed hard.

"I'm sorry Inez." It was an indictment and he knew it. "You didn't deserve that. But I haven't been sharing information with you so that you could transform yourself into a detective. I know you don't do your newsletter anymore, since Billy Needham was killed. I guess I thought you'd enjoy hearing and reading about crime from time to time. It's got to be lonely here without a hobby. You don't have family and I ..."

He stopped suddenly realizing that he might as well call her 'an old spinster' and be done with it. But that wasn't how he felt at all. He'd seen her with tears in her eyes whenever someone got the recognition they deserved. She was always happy for somebody else. But he knew the truth behind such tears. He knew she was also sad that there was never anyone to recognize her own contributions. She was very much a woman alone and in that respect, was very much like his mom. He never wanted Inez to feel that sad. He'd do anything to prevent that. And yet she wasn't facing the truth.

"... I love you Inez, but if Kadija is alive," Trace continued, "she could be anywhere. But more than likely she's dead."

Inez stiffened her back. "I believe the very last thing Dolly wanted to do was to beg an uppity old black woman like myself for help. She guzzled down alcohol and carried a gun in her purse in order to ask me. She may have made bad decisions throughout her life, but she wasn't stupid. I think she did her homework before coming here.

Kadija is in Afghanistan and she'll be killed at the end of this year, if no money is offered to her kidnappers."

Inez fiddled with the girl's wallet. "But before I pay the ransom and walk down that path to treason, *I* need to have some feeling for her, too. Being half black isn't enough. I need to know what she's made of. That sounds arrogant perhaps, but I need to know her as I would any other human being."

Pulling the lining away from the wallet, her fingers found tissue paper and remnants of a newspaper clipping. The latter crumbled into tiny pieces, as she let them fall onto the table.

Trace watched Inez's enthusiasm and said, "Perhaps CBI could verify Dolly's death. I don't trust Bradley's version of what happened any more than you do."

He wasn't smiling, but Inez was. "I'll never be able to thank you enough." And in the same breath asked, "Know what this is?"

"Cigarette paper? She made her own marijuana joints?"

"No, no. Ages ago hairdressers put tissue at the end of a strand of hair before wrapping it around rollers. There's hair inside these pieces of tissue." She opened them. The hair inside one was black, thick, and wavy. The second one held wiry crimped hair, the color of wet sand. Inez pulled out the photo from the wallet and placed it beside the tissue packets. "The wiry hair must be Kadija's, but I'm no expert."

"Vaboom! You didn't tell me she looked like that. Her application photos are quite different." Gathering all the things from the table, Trace said, "Maybe an expert *should* take a look. Hand me some plastic bags."

"You can't take both pieces," Inez said, holding one clump of hair out to him. "Here." He recognized that he'd given in to her desire to learn more, but he'd gladly admit that he had a hard time saying no to her." Take this one. There may be a time when the other is needed to identify its owner."

He carefully scooped up the tissue, hair, and what was left of the newspaper clipping. Yet he felt the need to give her one last caution.

"I'm not going to be able to help you as often as I did last year. Remember, I'm starting my career over again. What I will do is keep researching the two men who came here. And you keep me posted on what you find out. But Inez, you must understand. The government may tell you to stop interfering, because the security of an individual or a whole nation is at risk. If that happens, you'll need to walk away from this."

With wide eyes, she looked at him and nodded yes.

7

"I appreciate you meeting me here, Sophie." Inez tried to hide her excitement. She'd always wanted to see inside this place, but had never ventured in before, there being no reason to try their fare. "The Drink Emporium is close to my house," she said, "so I walked."

Smells of bubble gum, chocolate, whipped cream, coffee, and strawberries made her slightly giddy the minute she stepped through the door. Smooth enameled surfaces of every pastel color in the rainbow sparkled inside. It represented a childhood she'd only experienced in books and dreams about middle class children.

"Thanks for inviting me," said the large woman, who was conspicuous in the otherwise empty restaurant. She remained seated at a table against the back wall.

Sophie had a harsh look, created with dark purple lipstick and straightened hair stretched back till it reached a rubber band at the base of her neck. A small tarnished metal hoop was lodged in a man-made hole through one nostril. On the shoulder of her red cardigan was a tiny blue flower that could easily have been overlooked as lint. Was that the flower she wore to identify herself?

A pink embroidered bouquet of pansies was positioned prominently on the collar of Inez's white linen blouse, while her loose fitting collarless jacket gave her all the confidence she needed.

"Looks like we didn't need a flower after all," Inez observed. "If we're the only people here, I wonder how they stay open. But there must be a waiter somewhere, since you have a drink already."

Sophie had the tired look of someone who had been here lots of times. Perhaps, thought Inez, that explained her tiny flower. Or was it a sign of passive aggression, even before their meeting started?

"I'm just happy you could come," Inez said smiling. "Not many people in your graduation class still reside in Denver."

Sophie appeared hesitant. "Finding a decent paying job here ain't easy, I mean isn't easy," she replied.

"So what job *did* you find after high school?"

Inez's eyes, meanwhile, danced over plastic milkshakes dangling from the ceiling, ice cream sundaes and floats that jutted out from walls. None of its sugary fare appealed to her. Yet she correctly assumed Sophie wouldn't turn down an offer to meet here amid what an online reviewer had said was glitz for the tongue.

Wondering why the young woman hadn't answered, she suddenly looked at her. Was Sophie searching for the correct verb or was she about to tell a lie?

"That cab parked outside, I drive it," she finally answered.

"Sounds exciting." Inez meant that comment. She didn't know any cab drivers personally. But she also wondered about the sad story Sophie's unemotional expression reflected. The young woman seemed too proud to reveal any of it to a stranger.

"Ma'm," announced a waiter, entering through the back door with an empty trash can, "if you haven't tried the Grapa Frapacino, you should."

"Sounds like the very thing I was looking for," Inez graciously fibbed.

"One Grappa Frapacino coming up," he replied.

Inez turned to Sophie again. "You have any questions about why we're here?"

"You found Kadija's body?"

Inez was taken aback. "No."

"That's what I thought this was all about," Sophie replied. "I even told a friend about our meeting. Everybody on my block had heard about you from the newspapers and that other crime mess you figured out. Anyway, I guess I was wrong. So why do you want to talk about her?"

"I want to *find* Kadija Campbell. The more I know about her the better I'll be able to track her down."

Sophie let out an exasperated chuckle. "You must be the only person alive, who thinks she's not dead."

Saint Michael's yearbook had linked Sophie and Kadija as best friends.

"You must have known her when she went to CSU as well," Inez said. "Did other students at your high school follow her disappearance in the news?"

Sophie didn't answer right away, but sat up taller. Reaching under the table she pulled down on her skirt. "You know she was crazy, right?"

"No, I didn't know that."

"See, I went to the University up in Boulder for a year. We were still friends on and off. But it was Kadija's senior year in high school when she went crazy. And she never got any better after that. That's why she had no friends. People thought she went crazy 'cause her mama died, but her mama had been dead a few years.

"See, I can tell you exactly when she flipped out. I was with her. It was when some big shot from back East came to that public school behind ours. She and I usually met up on Oneida Street and walked the rest of the way to St. Michael's.

"The school year had just started. We were seniors then. I don't even remember what that other school did that was so important. Anyway, we wanted to see what the commotion was, 'cause cars were double parked all around it. But Kadija went crazy and started throwing up. Of course, that was after she started screaming."

"This may be hard," Inez said, "because it was so long ago, but do you remember what you saw just before Kadija screamed?"

Again there was a long silence. The waiter had already brought Inez's purpley-brown Grappa Frapacino, a concoction in which Inez could see the sugar hang in suspension.

"All we saw were long lines of people walking around the school. We found out later most of them were Secret Service. I tried squeezing in between and around 'em. I was much smaller then. Kadija was right behind me. They all had these long wire coils that came down from one ear and went inside their jackets. Kadija kept pointing to the wire and started screaming, then threw up. We were stupid anyway, to wear our school uniforms. We looked like we didn't belong there."

"Then what happened?"

"The police came. They wanted to lock her up in a hospital for crazies 'cause she wouldn't stop. I was scared. I'd been to juvie and getting sent to a hospital lock-up was the same thing, far as I knew. The police told me to go home and change clothes, 'cause there was some of her puke on it. But they put a blanket around Kadija and put her in a police car. She was out of school for a month."

"That is bizarre," Inez confirmed. "Would you like another drink?"

"Oh, yes, please," she answered. "They're awfully good. Thank you very much."

Inez raised her hand and the waiter filled Sophie's glass. Inez, meanwhile, took out the pink wallet, hoping it would help the girl recall more incidents.

"Remember this?" Inez asked.

"Is it Kadija's? No, I don't really remember it."

"I noticed from this," Inez said, while holding the wallet so the Greek letters were visible, "that you all sat at the same cafeteria table."

Sophie was quiet.

"And that you called yourselves the Girls of the Tan Table."

"How'd you know that?" Sophie asked. Inez could see her eyes get smaller as she tilted her head. Then Sophie spoke again. "We were much younger then, maybe seventh grade. Sister Margaret made us stop sitting together. Somebody squealed, 'cause those nuns sure didn't act like they cared about us much. I know it wasn't Kadija, because she wanted to continue doing it. She wanted us to hire a lawyer and go to court. Even marched in front of the church in the rain with a sign. All Kadija wanted was to start a girls club, but the nuns said it was a gang, a black girls' gang."

Sophie suddenly laughed. "By the time it was over, I thought Kadija was going to start her own religion. Her mom died not long after that. That's probably why they didn't kick her out of St. Michael's."

Inez put the wallet back in her purse, realizing its significance. Gamma Tau Tau had probably been Kadija's first adventure into political activism, with bad results.

"Did she have other close friends besides you?" Inez asked.

"Oh yeah, plenty, up until we were all in twelfth grade. That's when she went crazy. She didn't have *any* friends after that."

Inez was puzzled. "Because of her reaction toward the Secret Service?"

"She freaked out, grabbed a woman's wire out of her ear, almost cut her ear off. But see, I don't think anybody at school was as bright as Kadija. She collected mushrooms in third grade, magnets in fifth, memorized maps and capitols of countries we'd never heard of, taught herself sign language for fun. Yet she always had time to party with the rest of us.

"When she came back from the hospital, she was weirder. Didn't go out, was always busy, stayed in the city library downtown till it closed."

Sophie set her straw aside and took a giant swig of her drink, before wiping her napkin across what was left of her lipstick. Resentment hung on her face and in her voice. "Kadija knew she was going to CSU and knew what she wanted to study. She wanted to work for the federal government, she said. You knew her mom was white, didn't you?"

Inez nodded. "And what about her dad? Did Kadija ever meet him?"

"She knew he was black, that he was killed in Viet Nam. She told me once she'd never seen his picture because her mom destroyed them all. I was surprised she didn't want to go into the military like her dad did. But you know what she told me? Maybe you can figure this out. I never have understood it.

"When I asked her why she didn't go into the military, she said she already knew what it was like to be on the martyred side of justice. And I thought she was referring to the time she was almost kicked out of school because of the Gamma Tau Taus. Then she said she didn't have what it takes to be a Dr. Martin Luther King. She didn't have his patience and that was why she couldn't join the military or enter a religious order. They were all the same, she said. You understand any of that? I can't figure it out."

"I'd need some time to think about it," Inez answered.

Loud male voices entered the Emporium. Inez ignored the sounds, remaining fixated on what Sophie had shared about coiled wires and Kadija's change in behavior. She glanced once in the direction of those voices, not really seeing them. Their very presence, however, reminded her to ask one last question.

"Did you ever meet the guys she dated in college?"

Sophie sighed loudly. "That's the same as what the police asked. I told them, what I'm going to tell you. I drove to Fort Collins once to go to the movies with her. Found her in the parking lot with some foreign guy."

"Let me interrupt a minute. What exactly did that boy look like?"

"Black skin, almost blue it was so black, water colored eyes, hair almost as straight as hers was kinky. He walked away when he saw me. Oh, and he had this little red thing going on here." She pointed to the space between her eyebrows, as she took another sip.

"I even jokingly asked her if they were lovers. He could have been from Mars for all I could see in him," she said. "And what did she say? 'What me and my Mo Jo, my Mowgli or some such shit? Then she said no. But he kept turning around, as he walked off, and I knew he wasn't lookin' at me. Hey, all those foreigners look alike to me."

Inez took a deep breath. Sophie had awakened similar events in every woman's distant past. Shapeless faces dancing atop the faces of others, all involved with inevitable rivalries between young girls competing for young boys. Sophie and Kadija must have had their share of rivalries.

She cleared her throat, however, to address the more profound problem in Sophie's attitude. "We're not able to make discrete differentiations among people without practice. Like learning to read, we develop skills over time, only if we practice. And also, observations of this type require fieldwork, to distinguish between say the Japanese from Chinese, Mexicans from Filipinos, Irish from Germans. Intermarriage makes the process even harder. And you can still differentiate attitudes in a single family. But you'd have to be intellectually curious, of course. Are you intellectually curious?"

Sophie leaned closer. "That guy she was with could just as soon have been one of those men who just stepped in here, for all I cared." she said, with more than a tinge of defiance.

Inez looked at the men again. They had all taken seats in front of the plate glass window. What caught her eye was a pair of red tennis shoes among them. She'd seen the shoes before, but where? She got an idea.

"Come around to this side so I can take a selfie, Sophie." Inez had already pulled her chair to the side and was snapping wildly.

Suddenly, the sound of several pairs of shoes hurriedly scuffled out the front door.

How odd, Inez thought, but the whole maneuver put a smile on Sophie's face.

"You want a lift back to your place?" Sophie asked.

"How nice of you to offer."

Inez paid the bill and once outside, noticed the same group of men in a huddle at the far corner of the block. They stood tall in clean pale dress shirts partially buttoned with no ties. All wore slacks rather than jeans. There were no red tennis shoes among them, however.

"Don't worry, Dr. Buchanan. I'm bigger than they are. They won't try anything."

Inez wasn't the least bit afraid. She'd taken enough big people to the principal's office, whenever necessary, without putting her hand on any of them.

As Sophie drove, she asked, "So what makes you think she's alive?"

"Maybe it's more a hope than an idea, but it's not unusual for me to act on my hopes. In this case, if she's alive she might also need help."

When Sophie drove away, Inez intended to enter her home as cautiously as Trace had trained her. But in the dining room, she stopped. Sunlight, reflecting off a multitude of mirrors, had changed. Some were tilted differently. She stood still and listened, but heard nothing. With her heart pounding, she walked swiftly to the refrigerator.

Inez took a spoon from the counter drawer, opened the refrigerator and pulled out the bottom section. Bending over it, she lifted a tray of lemon gelatin resting on top of the tray that held Dolly's Glock. It was still there, untouched. Instead of scooping out a spoonful of gelatin, she closed everything with shaking hands.

Her house had been violated and Dolly's statement echoed in her mind. *"Would you believe me if I told you someone broke into my house, … and that I have no way of proving it?"*

Was this the same thing? The red shoes came to mind, this time with a boy inside them, a boy with an African accent. Could he have placed the bug Trace found? Had the boys at the restaurant been inside her house? Did they have any relationship to Dolly, Kadija, the Taliban, or Martindale, Inc? Who were those boys working for?

8

THAT SAME AFTERNOON, 2009
DENVER, COLORADO

"Saaiq?"

"How did you get this number?"

"I'm a clever boy. I can get any number I want. Keep telling your people that, so I can ..."

"Never ... EVER ..."

"My team planted your seeds, but ... G recognized me or recognized my shoes. G may have even taken a selfie with my team in the background. Could be, she knows."

"You're on your cell?"

"Yes, but everything's encrypted."

"Hang up."

"NSA isn't your problem. You're probably in Afghanistan. But I'm in Denver. I can take care of G, right now. Say the word ..."

"You fool! We put you there to study. And we'll continue to need your help from time to time. But you wait for my word. Call me again and you'll regret it. Just wait for my call."

9

"Sit up straight," the driver ordered.

He wondered if his New York City English and speed through the chaos of Bagdad's streets would give him away as a former New York cabbie. "Line up with my mirror. I need to inspect you."

She was a rookie and too flippant an American for his taste. He knew he had to scare the shit out of her. As he kept an eye out for military convoy trucks, he watched her slide to the middle of the back seat, while using safety pins, which she held in her mouth, to adjust her clothing.

"Guess that's the end of your Uday. But if we see him again, and we may, we act like we've never seen him before. From now on your name's Abida. You got that?"

Preoccupied with dressing, she mumbled. "S'on the passport."

"Aye! Why do they do that? Don't ever touch that passport again. The Company *never* gets it right. You believe yourself equal to me for one second and you're dead. Hand that thing to me before you get out of the car. And you've forgotten your mascara. It runs down your face. That'll never be allowed inside Wanted's compound." Was he expected to train her as well?

"Wondered what that cream was for," she muttered.

She removed fabric from around her head, releasing wiry black tight ringlets that bounced against her face. It was a sudden contrast to her peaches and cream complexion. Then she applied the cream. It was hard to take his eyes away. He'd never had an assignment with a woman. She was too young, too seductive. And if he didn't address his posture, he'd run the risk of being mistaken for her father. He wasn't that old. But her cheeks were red, her lips naturally full and he needed to focus on the road.

"Work quickly," he ordered. "We're approaching the parking lot. Signs to Mad Man's International Airport are more frequent now."

"What! We escape by plane? If Mad Man permitted people to board planes, those agents back there could escape, too."

"Don't concern yourself with problems you can't solve. We're not onboard yet. CIA's done this since before you were born. Let me tell you about our assignment in case we're separated."

"Ah, yes. My bad, oh holy husband. Should have known better than to *think*."

The driver smirked. If she thought she was over acting, she wasn't. "And don't forget your place in this world again."

"If no one's told you," Abida said, "I'm good at what I do. It's the reason I'm here. You waste time demeaning a woman. Now tell me about the airport, first."

"Tell you what? You dance to my moves and I play by ear. Praise Allah, you're so good at what you do."

"Beast!" she said. But he watched small lines deepen around her mouth. Was she being playful or calculating?

"I tell you of our mission, first! If all goes wrong, you must pick up the pieces and finish what you can. If all goes well, we'll be in Khartoum before midnight. There, you must do anything to assure your position within Wanted's family. 'The Company' expects you to become one of four servants. When the family moves, it will cut that number to three, maybe two. I am your husband, Malik, and …"

"Oooo, I've never been anybody's wife."

Malik ignored her and continued talking. "I have brought you back from your ill father, who is close to death but lingers on. Global positioning, meanwhile has not yet found Wanted. He left Khartoum three weeks ago, after the Prime Minister told him to leave Africa. Meanwhile, I've been training with members of his new organization called Al-Qaeda. We live inside his compound, knowing that whenever he returns we will all swear our allegiance to his cause and live with him wherever he goes."

"Yes, Malik."

"The cold cream goes into the bag you'll carry onboard. When dissolved in black or green tea, it becomes a tasteless, odorless poison. It may be vital to your position in the compound. We will not discuss these things on their premises. I don't trust Wanted and I don't think he trusts any of us. Nonetheless, we must at all times be adoring members of his household, even if and when I'm told to kill him."

Malik drove into a parking space midway between the perimeter and the main terminal. From the back seat, Abida handed him her passport. She'd already stuffed bags of clothes under the front seats and Malik set the detonator for eight hours into the future, guessing it would give them enough time.

Hurriedly, they walked across hot asphalt until they were inside a modern, massive stone and steel terminal. They stood patiently in line at their first counter. Malik did the talking in Arabic, while Abida's eyes never left the floor, their bodies touching. Her travel bag hung from her arm. Through the large windows he saw only three planes now. People arrived by the bus full, enough to fill four times more planes.

His body towered over hers and was twice as wide. Holding her slender elbow with his massive hand, he ably maneuvered her past the scrupulous eyes of military officers in Mad Man's Army. He'd walked past soldiers too often to feel self-conscious, three years in this part of the world and two in Africa. Women observed but never accompanied him, telling him he looked like a darker more menacing Omar Shariff. Their comments and stares would leave him puzzled.

When their counterfeit Iraqi passports were stamped at a second counter and returned to Malik, he escorted Abida down a flight of stairs, past metal detectors no longer in use, considered irrelevant under Mad Man's increased surveillance program.

The lower level contained massive crowds. Frantic people pressed against them and yet there were hushed tones. The crowd actively listened for directions given over loud speakers that called one family after another to be interrogated before given permission to leave.

All the while, Malik, still gripping Abida's elbow, deftly circumnavigated the masses in an effort to discover all the unlocked doors leading outside. He kept one eye on the 747, its engines still at rest. Across its fuselage the words, 'Royal Jordanian Airline' sparkled in sunlight. Salivating over his awaited prize, he watched two other Iraqi planes idling and ready.

Although Abida was an inexperienced unknown in his equation, he was surprised that her body felt relaxed beside his. She even anticipated the direction of his movements. After an hour of making visual observations, they let themselves be jostled within the belly of the crowd. From his gauze tunic to the sway of her hips to their Iraqi made sandals, there was nothing North American about either of them. Malik liked that very much.

Occasionally a man would stand on a chair, waving a ticket for a particular gate. A few people would follow him through a designated door and down a stairway to an awaiting plane. Voices from the dense throngs slowly rose into louder outcries, when that same man returned to escort only a handful more.

With equal regularity, two or more soldiers would grab a man somewhere near the perimeter of the waiting area, sometimes lifting him off the ground, while his wife, children, and extended family followed them down a hallway, screaming.

A single bead of sweat trickled down his neck, as Malik watched the blades of the 747 move. Within minutes another man stood above the crowd holding a blue card beside a door without markings. The heat of the day added to the rising hysteria of the multitudes. Malik elbowed their way toward the man to flash his own similar card. That man pushed them through an exit, where prostrate women overcome by heat, blocked the doorway for air. A few behind them possessed the same colored card and they, too, stepped over others to leave.

As he walked, Malik turned his head several times to count those behind him. A total of eighteen men, women, and children walked briskly, but there was no way to count passengers already onboard. He'd been given no final number, no list of names and yet he had a duty to perform, and a dilemma to solve.

In the distance, a topless Humvee sped toward them. It had to contain Mad Man's last minute deployment of troops to stop stray CIA agents leaving the country. Malik and Abida began to jog, reaching the top of the stairs before the others. But two soldiers, their rifles pointed at them, jumped from the Humvee and shouted to halt or be shot. Everyone froze with the exception of Malik who, with a smile and using both arms, waved the soldiers up the boarding stairs and closer toward him.

Two soldiers with rifles ran up the steps, past Malik, and into the awaiting airplane. One other soldier remained behind the wheel of the Humvee. Other passengers walked more slowly, hesitant to climb the stairs at all.

With the smile of a showman, Malik whispered, "Save me an aisle seat." Carrying only her travel bag, Abida moved onto the plane, behind the two soldiers.

Speaking rapid Arabic and smiling, Malik ran back down the stairs to stand in front of the Humvee. He explained to the soldier, seated behind the wheel, how happy he was that they had arrived so soon, but that the Humvee had to move fifty meters to the left to allow the plane room to taxi toward its proper position. When Malik pulled up the vehicle's hood in one arm jerk, the wide-eyed driver could no longer see ahead. Observers from inside the airport were also hampered from viewing events.

A tall blond man wearing an antique colonial khaki uniform had walked to the back of the Humvee, where he shot the driver at the base of the brain, using a silencer. Another man in a Western style suit, still holding his carry-on luggage, grabbed the slumped driver with his other arm. Those two men pulled the body out of the vehicle and held it upright, while Malik lowered the front hood, jumped into the driver's seat, and drove the Humvee about a hundred meters forward.

Holding the dead soldier between them, the two male passengers ascended the stairs. They all watched out for people at a distance. Only someone with binoculars would be able to see that the man was dead from his injuries. Malik hoped people in the tower had other things to look at. They were all too far from the terminal to be seen clearly by the naked eye. He could only hope the dead man would be considered a drunk.

Malik was close behind them when he reached the top where he began separating the stairs from the plane itself. This was a challenge, since the plane had already begun to taxi. No sense hollering for assistance. No one could have heard him over the engines. One cable proved unusually resistant, slowly peeling flesh from between his thumb and index finger. Pain spread through his left arm, but he managed to get the titanium cable over its hook.

Straining his back muscles, Malik closed the plane's door alone, which gave him pause. Where were the flight attendants? What happened to the first two armed soldiers who boarded? Was Abida unharmed? He had, of course, left her fate in the hands of other CIA agents. After locking the plane door, he turned around and pressed his hands together to stop the bleeding. He flattened himself against the closest wall to take inventory.

The cockpit door appeared locked. Thankfully, no partitions stood between first and second-class. It was a large practically empty plane with about thirty or so passengers in three sections. Five were adult females. Four of them wore hijabs, including Abida, who sat near the middle of the plane. Malik nodded to her, to keep her calm, but her eyes were closing. Only a retarded female spy, he thought, could believe herself safe enough to sleep through take off. The plane continued to taxi backwards.

Everyone pretended to be at ease. This was no group of ordinary tourists. The air-conditioning helped. A British man dressed in tweed sat with two giggling children in the front row. Malik recognized a Muslim from his past, reading alone in one of the back rows. He determined that his presence, though annoying, did nothing to disturb security. In the seat behind Abida was a Pakistani, he suspected, wearing a white turban. Several Americans dressed as businessmen, perhaps twelve or thirteen, were scattered in seats throughout the plane, while either a French or Israeli teenaged girl sat alone, plugs in her ears, listening to something that made her body move erotically.

Malik felt uneasy. Where were the dead humvee driver and the two other Iraqi soldiers with rifles? One of two men seated together in front lifted his feet slightly, recognizing Malik's need to count bodies. Under his feet, Malik saw a uniformed dead body and yet another squeezed under the next row of seats. But the man was sweating, as his eyes shifted to a man seated across the aisle from him. That man, Malik realized, dressed in a European style suit, was dead, his padded headrest stained in blood.

From where had the bullet come? As if answering his question, a tall man dressed in the robes of an Arab businessman leaned out from behind the drapes at the far end of the aisle and waved to Malik to join him. It was the same ploy Malik had used successfully most of the day. Malik stayed put, his mind racing through possible outcomes.

All the passengers, he'd been told, would either be CIA or MI6, along with their families in some cases. That was inconsistent with the ratio of white men and women to men and women of color. Without a minute's more hesitation, he reached under his tunic, rotated his gun from between his legs, and soundlessly shot the man in robes behind the drapes at the far end of the aisle. Sensing movement on his left, he confidently shot all three Iraqi women seated together, women who had dared to look directly into his face. Abida, he knew, was the only non-white woman working for CIA in the entire region. He then shot a man pretending to be a black American businessman, a man who appeared more African than African-American, dressed in an embroidered dress shirt under his suit jacket. He also shot the Pakistani seated behind Abida and an Indian man seated behind him.

"Fasten your seat belts. Now!" The voice of the plane's Captain was breaking up, distorted through heavy static.

Malik immediately stretched flat on the floor in the aisle nearest him. Holding his gun in one hand, he grabbed the bolted part of a seat with the other. Was there anyone he'd forgotten? He'd find out soon enough. Massive muscles in his biceps became rigid as the entire plane suddenly pointed straight up toward outer space. From under the rows of seats, one dead Iraqi soldier slid past him on the floor. The only thing stopping the body's forward movement was the door to the cockpit.

On his belly, Malik inched toward Abida's seat. The plane leveled off, her chin bounced hard against her chest. Had she been drugged? Perhaps the man seated behind her, the Pakistani he'd shot, had used chloroform. Would Mad Man have ordered that? Maybe, if he wanted every American paid spy dead.

"By my count," hollered a blond man with a British accent, "you got them all."

That man was now out of his seat and flat on the floor behind Malik.

"The pilot and your sleeping beauty there," the man continued, "shot the first soldiers that came onboard. They stuffed both under the seats before you got on the plane. But it's my guess one of those soldiers didn't die of his wounds and crawled to the galley to shoot the agent seated across from me. He must have found a thawb in the galley usually worn by the regular stewards and threw it over his head to hide his uniform.

"You single-handedly identified and killed all the people Mad Man keeps at the airport to infiltrate flights he deems suspicious. I've never seen such accurate shooting. How could you have seen pictures of them before today?"

Malik hadn't seen any of the men and women he killed, before today. He turned his head just enough to recognize the British man as the one who shot the humvee driver with a silencer. The two children seated up front began to cry softly. Air pressure was building in everyone's ears.

Malik turned on his side and forced a faint smile. No one at CIA had ever congratulated him on a job well done. The culture at MI6 was obviously different. Malik was relieved that this part of his mission had ended well.

The man smiled back and said, "Guess there's no reason to stay down here on the floor." And with that, he jumped to his feet. A short pop and then a red spot appeared immediately in the middle of his forehead, as he fell backward, knees bent in the air. A gun with no silencer had made the shot. Several passengers jumped, including Malik.

It was the kind of shot trained agents make with consistency and had come from over top of the right side of his head. Malik knew the shooter. Stunned, he sat motionless.

"Allah, be praised, my brotha," came a booming voice across the plane. "Your name is Malik for this mission. Hope I remembered that correctly. No matter, my brotha. You'll one day thank me. That man walked both sides of the street. I should know.

"Everyone stay seated! Everyone! We're all employed in one way or another by the same company here and what I need most is transportation. Don't get up yet, Malik! Put your gun away, slowly, then you can slide into your seat. Continue looking forward, toward the cockpit. That way I'll know I can put my gun away."

His voice brought back memories. As teens attending different high schools, they'd recited morning and evening prayers together. They'd eaten together during Ramadan, because no one could find their hiding place. As eleven year olds, they'd run through the New York City Library with security guards in pursuit. They'd each been whipped for that behavior by a grandfather who would not tolerate disobedience in their new country. They'd graduated from the Farm outside Williamsburg at separate times, the only first generation Muslims to graduate. How long had it been since he'd heard the voice of his fourth cousin? He couldn't remember and he wasn't happy at all about it.

Malik returned his gun to its thin leather strap. Slowly he edged closer to Abida's feet. Lifting himself up onto the seat beside her, he kept his head bent below the top of the headrest, catching only a quick glance of his cousin's silk suit and trimmed beard.

Curious about Abida, he leaned closer. Her eyelids popped open and he pushed back quickly. Her veil still covered her face, except for her eyes, which revealed exceptional self-confidence. Hadn't she warned him she was good?

"This is the Captain. In an hour, we'll land outside Ammon in an area with no runway. Expect the landing to be difficult. The ride on the ground will be bumpy. When we stop we'll take the dead off the plane and leave them in a shallow grave there. I ask everyone who can, to help carry those bodies and their belongings through the door at the rear of the plane. Working quickly, we can reach Khartoum in just under four hours, a delay of only thirty to forty-five minutes. Thank you."

Malik recognized the voice. It was the young man he'd driven to the airport. Had Abida known she would see her Uday again?

"I know what you're thinking," she said.

Malik started to interrupt her, but didn't. Exhaustion made him sink deeper into his seat. He closed his eyes knowing he couldn't stay seated for long. He had to help move the bodies to their burial place.

"Of course, I knew I'd see him again," she whispered. As she spoke, she tore cloth from one of her own undergarments she'd pulled from her bag. "I recruited him. Was his case manager and he was mine. He's got an incredible skill set, don't you think? Perhaps the man in the rear of this plane is similarly talented. Your decision not to kill him tells me you've known him a long time. That man and myself are the only people of color you didn't shoot in this passenger compartment. It must not have been an accident that the door to the cockpit was locked. It gave you one less person of color to decide on. And we certainly need our pilot."

She wrapped the cloth tightly between Malik's index finger and thumb to stop his bleeding. He said nothing, keeping his eyes shut to better hide his pain. He could forgive her sarcasm, but not the insinuation that she was more than an assistant. After all, she was only someone to dress his wounds and keep him well. Did she think she was someone who was supposed to know as much as he did about his mission? That question made him wonder why his cousin was on-board as well and how CIA ever experienced any successes with its duplication of duties.

Malik was only certain of two things. First, that a spy's greatest asset was being alive. And as far as he knew, this plane contained all that CIA had left in the way of human assets trained to infiltrate and collect intelligence on the ground in the Middle East. He'd waited for this opportunity for a very long time. His second certainty was that revenge was now more than a dream.

10

"It's so kind of you to see me without an appointment," said Inez. She marveled at how easy breezy her voice sounded. Stronsky would never have guessed that it had taken hours to try on every dress she owned, determined to resemble a sweet old grandmother with two breasts rather than a monstrous spinster schoolteacher with only one.

"I do appreciate this," Inez continued. She stared at the scraper held in the hand of an office maintenance man removing the letters 'E' and 'Y' from the glass door. While doing so, she bumped into a large leather chair and decided to sit in it, since Stronsky had already shown no prior knowledge of etiquette.

Two massive mahogany desks had been pulled together to make one. Inez considered it the right size for the giant who lives at the top of the beanstalk, but certainly too big for Stronsky. Had he just moved in? She watched him practically stretch his arms out of their sockets to reach the stapler and tape dispenser, while avoiding her eyes. She was entirely empathetic, seeing a similarity in her own plight.

"Didn't they tell you downstairs that Bradley retired?" Stronsky asked.

"Yes. But I didn't want to see him." That wasn't quite the truth. "I came to see you about these reports on Martindale's investigation into Kadija's disappearance. Remember? They arrived the very same day, Mr. Bradley promised they would."

As she spoke, she pulled two file folders from a large flowery tote bag and with a twinge of drama placed her bag on the carpeted floor beside her, where she strongly felt it belonged.

"But because I no longer work for Mr. Bradley," Stronsky explained, "I can't possibly comment on those papers. A new attorney has been assigned to you. In a few days he'll call and answer any questions you have."

"That's totally unacceptable," Inez replied with a courteous smile. "Various investigators said they reported directly to you, calling you by name. See here, it says your name, Mr. Joseph Stronsky." She held up a single sheet of paper, as if expecting him to read from that distance. "I need a full picture of what happened. Yet there are several discrepancies, when I compare these reports to what Dolly David told me."

Stronsky pushed his chair back and frowned. "Perhaps if I get my secretary to set an appointment …"

"Isn't that interesting," Inez beamed with enlightenment, "a secretary with his own secretary. Does your secretary have a secretary, too?"

He tapped frantically on a phone he removed from his jacket. "As a matter of fact she does."

Inez leaned sideways to get a better look at his ears. "I see you're not wearing that gizmo on your ear now. The one you wore to my house was quite conspicuous."

"I'm sure I have no idea what you're talking about, Dr. Buchanan. I wear a phone whenever I have files to carry in both hands. Maybe that's what you saw." He kept up a barrage of short taps to his phone.

"Well," Inez replied, while she watched his attempts to locate some other scapegoat, "I hope my attorney won't need to subpoena information from your attorney. But since we're both recording each other as we speak, I guess they'll have some data to work with?"

After another deep breath, Stronsky tossed his phone onto his desk and asked, "Just what *are* these discrepancies according to what you heard from Dolly David?"

Inez focused on the folders in her lap. "Dolly told me her husband disowned their daughter and as a result, never knew his granddaughter. But that wasn't true, was it?" She paused, waiting to see if Stronsky would volunteer information about that nasty letter of reference Colonel David wrote about Kadija. Inez had no desire, however, to reveal that she knew about such a letter, since that might reveal Trace Mitchell as her source. But Stronsky was a cold fish. He stared back at her without saying a word.

Inez finally continued. "One of your investigators interviewed Colonel David after identifying him him as the man who had visited Kadija. The investigator even took pictures. But he wasn't supposed to do that, was he? He was just supposed to report back to you. Is that why you fired him?"

"No. No. No," Stronsky insisted. "It wasn't Colonel David. We don't know who that man was. He looked nothing like him, puffy eyes, broken tooth, slurred speech. The investigator made a terrible mistake and we fired him for it. I know it's all there in the file. I filed it myself."

"Yes, it was filed and yes, Colonel David looked like he'd been in a fight, but it also looked like the investigator was being fired for insubordination, not for any lack of skill in identifying Colonel David."

Stronsky shook his head. "That's absurd! That so-called investigator jumped to erroneous conclusions and that's not what we hired him for."

"So when *did* the Colonel visit his granddaughter?" Inez asked.

This time Stronsky held both hands in the air while moving his head, as if the question was the most ridiculous he'd ever heard. Was that going to be his way of explaining discrepant information in each of the reports?

Disheartened, Inez decided to continue anyway. "I'm not asking too many questions at once, am I?" Inez then sat quietly, to give him ample time to squirm as well as time to think. He looked at each framed photograph on his desk and each stray paper clip.

Finally he said, "Without copies of those files in front of me I can't possibly expound on anything you're asking."

Stronsky was good at avoidance and that was the difference, Inez noted, between youngsters and adults. Adults have more resources to help them avoid what they can't face.

"I'm just realizing," Inez said thoughtfully, "you were awfully young when these reports were made, weren't you?"

Stronsky made no reply, but his color changed to raspberry. It was time to change the subject.

"Wasn't Colonel David a founding member of this company?" Inez continued. "I ask because his name appears on older Martindale stationary and then it doesn't and then it does again and then it doesn't. I'm sure, with your steady eye for detail, you've noticed it, too. Was he a lawyer or an engineer?"

Stronsky finally stood up and took a deep breath, as if deciding to start this conversation again. Slowly he sauntered toward his twentieth floor window. The significance of his view, Union Station crowned with snow-capped mountains in the background, was not lost on Inez. The height of his office was a measure of his success within the organization.

"How long has your office been on this floor?" Inez asked.

"Why?" He didn't bother to look at her, but the sharpness in his voice revealed his agitation.

"Because," she sighed, "it still strikes me as odd, when I don't see minorities in business suits in downtown office buildings here. I'm originally from Washington, D.C. where diversity is more common. You've felt the sting of discrimination, haven't you?"

"You're telling me you know I'm gay. Well, everybody in this building knows. And you're wondering how somebody like me worked his way up in an organization like this one. I can tell you it took a very long time, Dr. Buchanan. And you're right. Being gay incites the same wordless discrimination that's heaped on ethnic and racial minorities. And this is the kind of office you get when you keep fighting and undermining and backstabbing until you get here. I went from being totally incompetent to the best in my field."

Still staring out the window, he continued to speak slowly. "Colonel David was a cruel, homophobic, womanizer. I'm sure there is some psychological name for what he was, but I never learned it. More to the point, he was neither a lawyer nor an engineer. I never knew him personally. He wasn't on the board, when I came to work here and I'm sure he'd never have hired me. For one thing, the only people he hired and fired were lawyers and engineers, not secretaries. He and Bradley determined what cases the company would take and what oil-drenched foreign countries we'd enter. From time to time the Colonel had to divest himself of holdings that could have appeared to the public to unduly influence his decisions or his advice to the U.S. President. So we'd drop his name off the letterhead and he'd go away for a while. Then he'd come back."

He suddenly turned around and faced Inez, who looked up from taking notes with her pen, wishing she knew more about the contraptions on her phone, so she could stop using her pen. She met his disapproving eye and realized he still didn't like her. Oh well, she thought.

"Bet you'd have gotten here quicker," Inez offered, "if you'd stood your ground, walked your talk more. But you're you and I'm me. I do appreciate your honesty though. I have just one last question. Actually, it's more an observation. You signed off on several projects overseas when you sent investigators looking for Kadija in India and later in Afghanistan. But you never went overseas yourself did you? There's no evidence here that you verified any of the reports made outside the U.S. I suspect you feared what might happen to a young gay man abroad. I don't think anyone could blame you for having such fears. What I don't understand is how you can purport to know if Kadija is dead or alive?"

Stronsky strutted to his desk and with one finger tapped his phone. Was he turning his recorder off or turning something on?

"We aren't the rubber-stamping, oil-eating dragon we've been demonized to be. And now we have new leadership at Martindale, Inc. We're recruiting from all over the planet. We don't make decisions in vacuums anymore. And not every problem has a military solution."

Inez smiled. "For your sake, I hope your perception of change around here resembles what you're hoping for." She realized that was as close as she was going to get to any recognition of his malfeasance.

He perched on the edge of his desk, but as he was a short man, it could not have been a comfortable position. He wrote on a torn sheet of paper before handing it to her.

"You may want to talk to Bradley after all," Stronsky said.

"Oh?"

"Here's his private cell number, but it's no guarantee he'll talk to you. He served under David in Viet Nam. Rumor was, back in the day, that Dolly David's money convinced Bradley to help form this company. He and the Colonel are made from the same cloth you know. That may be too harsh."

"You win, Mr. Stronsky. I'll try to get my questions answered by Mr. Bradley. But if I can't, I'll be back with a lawyer. And that brings me to one last thing. Dolly's homes are included in her estate holdings, right?"

"Correct."

"Who has those keys? Dolly seemed to know more than what's in these reports, so I thought I'd ...."

Stronsky sneered. "We had good reason to ignore everything she said. Her psychological state was ..."

"I get it! Martindale wouldn't have to pay attention to how she wanted her money spent, if she was crazy. I'd still like the keys." She regretted saying it the minute it left her mouth. Inez knew she'd hit a nerve. His eyes had turned into daggers.

Still staring at her, he spoke into his phone, "Meet Dr. Buchanan in the lobby with a set of keys to all the Davids' homes."

She got off the elevator below ground and walked briskly to her car in the dimly lit parking facility under Martindale's offices. As soon as she reached it, she pulled out her cell phone from the tote bag she carried.

"Trace, I've got 'em. Meet me at the Park Hill address in fifteen minutes." She dropped the phone into her bag and opened the car door.

"What's that cha' got, lady?" asked a male voice behind her. She didn't need to turn around. A mixture of cheap after shave lotion and whiskey crowded in on her between parked cars. Her frantic fingers searched the key ring she already held in her hand and pressed the alarm.

The man backed away, but not before yanking the tote bag off her wrist. She fell hard on one knee, but listened as he ran away. He must have pushed a man to the ground, a man who had been in his path, a man who cursed him back loudly.

Although Inez's wrist burned and her heart rose to her throat, she felt no pain in her knee. She stood, but the man was far ahead of her now. She still held her car keys so the noise of the alarm travelled with her.

There he was at the top of the ramp, pausing and looking from side to side. Suddenly he pulled a set of keys from the bag before hurling the bag down the ramp behind him. Was that what he wanted, the keys to Dolly's properties?

Inez hurriedly gathered up her spilled belongings, her wallet, and phone, even her own house keys. When her wits returned, she stopped the alarm on her key chain. Cars in the garage honked, yet she refused to cave-in under their impatience. She hobbled to the curb near the parking attendant's hut, noticing her knee for the first time.

The woman inside busily made change for drivers leaving the lot. She hollered out, "You all right, lady?"

"No! I'm not," she replied. Inez first called 911 and then Stronsky.

"Oh, I'm so sorry you missed him, Dr. Buchanan," said his secretary. "He was called out of town. A limousine arrived just a minute after you left to take him to the airport. I think he was just as surprised as we were that he had to leave on such short notice. It will only take fifteen minutes or so to have those keys copied. And I'm so sorry about your catastrophe. I hope the security guards are down there helping you. I'll have those keys waiting for you at the main desk."

Sitting on the curb, inhaling exhaust fumes, she felt victimized, all right. What security guards? Where had Stronsky gone? Was his secretary lying? Could any Martindale employee be trusted? Inez made a third call to the one person she did trust. She wanted Trace to know she'd be very late. It was thoughtful of him to offer to meet her, in front of Dolly's mansion. And on top of everything, her knee began to throb.

She put her phone away, as the first police car drove down the ramp with its lights flashing.

11

I t was a little past noon. Inez stood beside her car across the street from Dolly's mansion. The pain in her knee told her to go home and put ice on it. But the opportunity to step inside the kind of house found on the pages of Architectural Digest was a stronger motivator than good judgment. Besides, she could see that some careless employee left a window opened on the second floor. As executor of Dolly's estate, Inez intended to close it and to make sure those windows were kept closed.

Over several decades, Park Hill had grown into a community with both large and small homes on the same block. Albion Street was no different. The David's house occupied a third of the block, giving insight into Dolly, who'd been born a Fairchild eighty years earlier. The Fairchild Mansion, as it was listed in legal papers, stood on three acres of land at the beginning of the twentieth century. But by the time their only daughter, Dolly, married, they'd sold off most of the land and built a house next door as a wedding gift. In the early fifties and after her parents died, Dolly remodeled both homes into one dwelling. Inez had already read about its archectural history and had no intention of waiting for Trace, when she held the keys in her hand.

After hobbling up flagstone steps to the wrought iron gate, she unlocked it without so much as a glance over her shoulder. An

outdoor plaza lay before her, its floor covered in stone tiles reminiscent of Mexico, its knurled shade trees manicured in concrete tree
boxes. A severely cut hedge grew around the entire property providing no privacy at all. Awe struck, Inez imagined movie stars and
politicians of the day, dancing to band music in what seemed like a
private park.

Wanting desperately to see as much as she could before Trace arrived, she limped to the front door and opened that as well.

A horrific odor greeted her like a spongy invisible wall. Dead pets,
Inez thought. Having more than one pet was an overindulgence of
the elderly and was one of the more gruesome items of gossip in Park
Hill. Finding a pet stuck in the crevices of a house, after its owner's
death was not uncommon. Inez merely pulled out a small package of
tissue from her purse and without folding them further, held three
over her nose, and stepped inside.

She moved cautiously, to avoid disturbing anything resting in
what she considered an object's historic position within the house.
The hallway opened onto a sprawling living room filled with low
couches and tall gilded floor lamps. Sliding glass doors along the far
wall looked over a wooded yard with a swimming pool. Sun from the
West created a bright-carpeted movie-set from the 1950s. As she took
one step down into the room, she saw a huge portrait over a marble
fireplace with no mantel.

Several things were striking about the picture. The canvas had
been slashed across the neck of the portrait's subject. The bottom
part hung away from the frame. The face of a remarkably angelic
looking young woman was intact. Her hair was blond, eyes blue,
wearing a peculiar expression that made her seem impish if not mis-
chievous. Inez walked closer to see the nameplate that read, Dolly
Fairchild. She speculated for a moment as to Dolly's age at the time of
the painting, but found herself enticed by other objects and unique
spaces around the room.

A large doorway was hidden in part by an equally large painted
Japanese screen. Looking past the screen revealed a bedroom where

a dining room ought to have been. Against that doorway rested a machete, likely the tool used to slash the portrait.

Without touching it, Inez wandered behind the screen, where a queen-sized bed stood in the middle of the former dining room. Whose machete was it? And did it belong to the same person who took guns and other weapons from empty gun cabinets along the walls? This must have been the Colonel's bedroom with his war photos and souvenirs.

And was it her imagination or was the odor getting stronger? A narrow doorway from the former dining room suggested a way out, but the odor was even more intense, as she stepped into the kitchen.

Her insatiable curiosity dragged her further into the house only to see the bodies of two huge mastiffs stretched across a ceramic tiled floor. She decided not to take another step forward which would have been treacherous over such large limbs.

From where she stood, she could see the far side of the kitchen, where bay windows looked onto an empty swimming pool. Under those windows sat a whitewashed wooden table with three chairs. Inez imagined joyous mornings seated at those windows, where a family ate and planned its future together. These were symbols of family life that she'd never experienced herself. However, it had been Inez's observation that the possession of money could cause as many bizarre behaviors in families as the lack of it.

So overpowering was the smell, she hurriedly retraced her steps to the front door she'd left wide open. Consequently, the odor was all but gone in the entry hall. From there she enjoyed a panoramic view of the place.

Each room she'd visited so far boasted coordinated colors, fake flowers, and showroom drapes, all telltale signs of a professional decorator. Nothing was well worn, yet nothing appeared new. You'd expect Frank Sinatra to suddenly appear.

Trace, however, still hadn't arrived, which gave her time to focus on the second floor. A black marble staircase at the end of the entrance hall was the kind Fred Astaire toe tapped down in Depression era movies and film noir women climbed, wearing real furs in black and white movies.

Small windows along the wall created dappled sunlight along the ornate wrought iron banister. These windows looked out on bungalows and two storied homes across the street. Had the mansion's occupants resented the prospect of having neighbors?

As she took in the atmosphere along the bottom steps, a barely noticeable breeze, probably from that opened upstairs window, blew past her. She felt a chill. Mirrored closets as well as bedroom and bathroom doors at the top of the stairs moved hesitantly in that same breeze, until they came to rest at odd angles. Someone must have opened all the upstairs doors, which never came to a resting position, but slowly opened and closed, opened and closed.

It was then in a bathroom mirror that Inez saw the image, a red Halloween mask, a monstrous mask, that glided away, as slowly as the door opened and closed in the breeze. Inez felt her heart drop. What was that? Her foot paused on the next step. The door moved again. In the mirror was ... was it human, with one eye open, the other bashed into its socket, the whole head attached to a wrinkled neck that sat upright?

Inez looked away, falling back against the railing, trying hard to catch her breath. But each breath created a short scream followed by another short scream.

Suddenly Trace stood at the front door and seeing Inez on the staircase trying to breathe or scream or do both, rushed upstairs to her side. She pushed him away, trying to set him in the right direction, pointing to the top of the stairs. Finally, Trace climbed in that direction. Inez heard him say something, but she couldn't make it out. She couldn't hear herself scream anymore, and she wondered why.

Another young man, clean-shaven, stood at the front door pulling on a pair of plastic gloves. Unlike Trace, his clothes were unwrinkled and his hair lay down flat. Inez had to tell him too about what she saw, but she still couldn't hear herself speak. That's when her knee gave way and everything faded to black.

12

TWO HOURS LATER, 2009
PARK HILL, DENVER

There was no doubt in Trace Mitchell's mind that the nude body in the master bathroom had once been Dolly David. His assistant, Schaffer was still inside the huge mirrored tub room taking pictures and tap dancing over evidence that lay splattered over black and white marble floor tiles.

Meanwhile Mitchell opened drawers in Dolly's bedroom hoping to discover why she died inside her home rather than on Lookout Mountain where her ashes had supposedly been found. He hoped to erase the mental image of her decaying eighty-year old body propped up with leather military belts on a whitewashed chair in the bathroom that belonged to a set in the kitchen. Even her white hair was dark red with blood.

Not quite an hour had passed since an ambulance transported Inez to the hospital. She'd fainted and fallen down the stairs. Mitchell's heart had almost stopped at her listless body. X-rays were essential for a woman who had been pushed to the ground earlier that morning. However, by the time paramedics whisked her away she was talking and seemed more embarrassed than anything else.

Mitchell had to take a deep breath. Inez wasn't supposed to die. He'd felt the same way about his own mother, a woman who had quietly kept her whole family focused on improving the quality of their lives together. Inez was the same way. Some people didn't have one person like that in their lives. He'd had two.

Yet Mitchell was grateful that Inez was at the hospital. He wasn't going to tell her what he'd found. This wasn't anything civilians should see.

He heard Schaffer request a mobile lab on his phone, something he should have done a half an hour ago. Mitchell's concentration was gone. Dolly had been around the same age as his own mother and it was hard to get the image out of his head.

Schaffer walked into the bedroom, stood beside him and said, "You alright? You look purple."

It took Mitchell a minute to realize Schaffer was talking to him.

"So what do you make of it, so far?" Mitchell asked, as nonchalantly as he could.

"We're looking for somebody with anger issues," the young man smiled. "Somebody who's been in the military, maybe Special Forces, someone who's been water boarded himself or knows someone who has."

"Maybe," Mitchell quipped, "or someone who didn't want her identified. Hardly anything's left of her face. Call headquarters and get arrest warrants for Alan Bradley and Joseph Stronsky. They supposedly buried Dolly's ashes beside her husband's. I want those assholes to tell me who's really in their urn and who died on Lookout Mountain.

Schaffer was already on the phone when Mitchell ran downstairs and out the front door. Escaping the smell was his first concern. The only thing he'd eaten that morning was a banana and he was thankful he hadn't had more.

He lifted his phone to his ear and pressed one button. "Boss, Mitchell here."

"What?"

"See if you can get somebody here from CIA, Middle East desk, if you can. I know they're not going to tell us anything, but I'm not going to ask them much, either. I just want them to see this crime scene. Maybe they'll volunteer something we can use."

"So when they tell me to shove it up my damn ass, I'll just say a former FBI fledgling told me to call 'em, right?"

"Call 'em anyway, boss. Okay?" Mitchell shut off his phone and wondered about Inez. How could an old retired schoolteacher, manage to get involved with yet another murder.

The whole thing was creepy. Why wouldn't a house this size have an electronic alarm instead of two dogs? And where were the people usually employed to care for a place like this?

Schaffer came out of the front door and sat on a cement box under a tree beside Mitchell.

"While we're waiting for forensics," Mitchell said, "you could be canvassing this neighborhood. Call headquarters again. See if they'll send you some help. Ask the neighbors if they know who worked here and when they last saw anyone around."

"On it," Schaffer said before he got up.

Mitchell caught the smirk on his face. Times had certainly changed. He'd never have done that in front of a veteran agent. But he forgot about Schaffer the minute he saw the forensic truck turn the corner. There was a lot he needed to know before going to the hospital to see Inez.

13

Uday lied about the landing outside Amman. "Bumpy" didn't half describe the near death experience they'd survived. That they were alive at all was due entirely to Uday's piloting. What name would he be using now Abida wondered?

Worrying about Uday reawakened her brain. In all their days at Colorado State University she'd never once gotten into a plane with him. Too scared. For the past twenty minutes, she'd listened to her own Hail Marys plus the whispered chants of passengers not wanting to reveal the identity of their own sacred entities. All that, while the plane went into free-fall to avoid radar at Queen Alia Airport.

At the beginning of the descent, Malik went silent. Temples pulsing rapidly, he squeezed both armrests, while his veins protruded across the back of his hands. Hours before, he'd acted like an impulsive young killer. How old could he be?

When the plane stopped, he unlocked his seatbelt, jumped up, and said, "Come on! Collect that gear so I can toss it. The men'll take care of the bodies," then darted down the aisle.

Abida wasn't ready to consider him a total jerk. After all, he'd been the designated proprietor of this rescue mission. CIA held him responsible for failures in boarding and deplaning. And although she'd heard that female proprietors were occasionally appointed, she hoped never to be worthy. She'd heard proprietorships, she'd heard were never given as rewards.

Quietly she got up to travel sideways down the row behind her until she reached the dead Pakistani. She wrenched his briefcase free from under his body and quickly traveled down yet another row.

"Don't bother," said a man of average height. Thick curly black hair fell over his forehead. He could have been Israeli, Spanish, Mexican or any nationality CIA or MI6 wanted. Although Abida's eyes surveyed every inch of his tailored silk suit, his voice made him instantly recognizable. It belonged to the arrogant guy who shot over her head, killing the man in uniform behind Malik.

"I'll get the luggage on this side of the plane," he said. "Help your partner." He grabbed the briefcase from her before she knew what he'd done. Her face must have registered surprise, anger, or both. How did he know she was Malik's partner in this upcoming mission?

"Go on!" he shouted.

She stood steadfast, embarrassed by her failure to hold on to it. By now she should have developed an instinct for workplace zealots, who could destroy her just as quickly as the enemy. She knew nothing about this man except that he was still alive, because Malik knew him. If he thought she was going to be scared of him, he needed to travel through Five-Points on a dark night in search of the right party. Finally he smiled, thinking what? That she'd be charmed by his narcissism.

"We're on the same side," he added. "Go help Malik. Everything's going to be fine."

Everything was not going to be fine, but she wasn't veteran enough to know exactly why. She knew she didn't have enough information. She knew stopping here was out of the ordinary. And why hadn't Malik killed this man? He'd killed a third of the passengers in less than a minute. Nobody knows what he or she is doing at that speed. Cautiously, she walked to the back of the plane, looking between rows for anything that belonged to the dead.

Taking her time, she looked out windows on both sides of the fuselage, without seeing any sign of life. Queen Alia Airport was twenty miles past Amman and they were certainly thirty to forty miles past that. They'd lost an hour between Iraq and Jordan and if she weren't careful, she'd find herself inside another nightmare.

A quick glance back at the well-dressed man made her wonder where he'd started his day. Was he really an executive from Headquarters or was he pretending to be something he wasn't, like all the other spies on this plane? She really didn't give a damn what he was, as long as he didn't interfere with her mission.

She watched that nameless man peer inside the opened briefcase of the dead Pakistani, before she turned to look out the plane's wide back door. Abida's attention was drawn toward two men and the teenager standing near Malik on the ancient tarmac. Each held the feet or arm of a dead body they'd dragged outside. Abida noticed the steadiness of the young girl and realized she'd likely done this before, maybe with people she'd known. Her thickly mascaraed eyes were like those of a zombie, dead on the inside. Abida continued to watch until the young girl set down the body she carried and walked toward her.

"Oh, it's you!" gasped the flirting teen, as if eyeing a movie star.

Though she looked in Abida's direction, Abida realized the girl's eyes were focused on someone else and turned to follow her gaze. Behind her stood the dark mahogany skinned, blue eyed Uday in his uniform. His closeness made her heart swell. Unsuccessfully, she fought to keep the muscles of her face and chest motionless.

Ignoring all other passengers, he smiled. "Your plans have changed," he said. "Several governments know about this flight. Headquarters believes it's unwise for you two to arrive in Khartoum onboard. You both must get to Khartoum quickly. Just not on this plane."

"What?" she asked breathlessly, his words slowly invading her imagination. The plane's cabin began closing in around her. Who was he anyway to talk to her like this? They weren't supposed to know each other. She opened her mouth to speak. "You don't expect me to walk to Khartoum, do you?" Those were the last words she would remember.

$$\mathcal{Q}$$

When she opened her eyes she could see Malik's throat from her position beneath his chin. He cradled her head on his thighs as he stretched his head back to watch what she'd always called a Disney sky. His body smelled of sardines soaked in ouzo and perspiration sat atop his brow like opaque beads. No mutual pheromones here.

Garbage can odors and men's socks crept into her space. His closeness made her roll her head away from his chest to find pure air. Lazily, she gazed across a hot copper desert, crumbling sandstone, and a large misplaced mound of dirt. As her eyes focused and her memories congealed, the misplaced dirt turned into dead bodies, hidden by a dusting of sand, dried brush, and scorpions.

Malik's face and shoulders shielded her from the sun's rays. But the minute he moved, a beam of light forced her eyes to shut.

"Ah, ah, ah!" Malik shouted. "You can't go back to sleep. I've been waiting too long. We've got to find shelter, away from those bodies."

"What h-happened?" Her mouth moved slower than she wanted. "Where's the plane?"

"You've got this huge dark blue bruise, right here." He pointed to his own chin. "Where your boyfriend let you have it with his fist. That's been over an hour ago."

With a body that ached all over, she would not have thought his words could have stabbed her so deeply. Uday deliberately left her behind with no goodbyes? No one could possibly have ordered him to hit her. She couldn't help it. Tears spilled over the rims of her eyes.

Seeing this, Malik moved his knees, letting her drop to the sand as he got to his feet beside her. Standing, he continued to cast a shadow over her. With a slight twist of his torso, he relieved his bladder right where he stood. In disbelief, Abida turned her head.

"I'll say this about your guy," Malik added, as he restored the folds of his pants over his crotch, "he probably won't do that again. Come on! We'll die here. I didn't risk my life to rescue you and that damn Indian just so he could kill us here. Guess I shouldn't be so negative, huh? I owe him my life. You were right. He's got a hell of a skill set."

He grabbed both her hands to pull her up from the sand, while she viciously smacked at them, resisting the touch of his urine damp fingers. Where the hell were they anyway? It was time to get her act together.

Where she'd slept, she discovered the bag she'd taken from Malik's car to carry onto the plane. It had been half buried beneath them. She kneeled to rummage through it, its mere presence making her forget about her bastard boyfriend and her hurt feelings. These were the tools of her trade, the things that would keep them alive. They'd both wanted separate careers anyway.

"Either we've got all the time in the world," Malik ranted, "because, Wanted still hasn't returned to Khartoum or we have no time left, because they're packing to leave right now, while we waste time in this forsaken desert. Nobody, I mean nobody, not the CIA, Interpol, Mossad, MI6, and certainly none of America's satellites have been able to keep eyes on this guy. He's cagey. Only men who fear him are by his side. Well, I'm cagey, too and I pretend better than most. I'm sure he likes me." He kicked up sand with his foot like a pouting brat, causing Abida to cradle her bag like a mother would a child.

"We could fail, you know," he continued, "before we even get started. The least Headquarters could have done was ask me about this change before they went ahead with it. Bet your boyfriend won't forget to ask next time. Nobody realizes how dangerous Wanted is."

"Just who the hell have you been talking to?" Abida finally asked. She busily examined items in her bag. Her jaw still hurt and her head throbbed. It was all she could do to ignore her own pain.

"You're not questioning my judgment are you?" he asked. "I realize there's no one around to listen, but you'd better get comfortable as my devoted Muslim wife. One slip in attitude could get you stoned to death."

"Yeah, it's always the squeaky man, who gets the grease."

"Is that feminist humor? You've never seen a woman stoned to death, have you?" he yelled. "And the fedayeen are everywhere in Jordan."

"Pleeeease."

"You really don't believe me."

"I believe," she said, awkwardly getting to her feet, "that most fedayeen were expelled by Jordanian forces as long ago as 1971. If I had to be kicked off a plane, I'd prefer it to be in Jordan rather than Syria or Egypt. You may want to catch up on your political history. And if I'm not mistaken, that short line in the distance over there, moving like a caterpillar …" She pointed with a steady finger, "… is a train, heading north. Carrying phosphate most likely, to Aqaba. Why phosphate, you ask?"

"It's Jordan's largest export!"

"Bravo." She beamed at him, as one would a child. "I bet we could stop that train on its way back. That's a six-hour delay maybe, but we can survive six hours, can't we? Painful as it is to admit, this bruise may actually help us with a believable story."

She kept her flip-flops on and took giant wobbly steps toward the distant caterpillar. "I'm thinking it's a good six kilometers away," she speculated. "You coming?" she asked.

He had nothing to carry, but his customized silent gun and an extra round of ammunition, both strapped under his tunic. "I need to be in front. And if you mock me again, I swear I'll smack the saliva right out of your mouth."

She shrugged. "Whatever thrills your gut!"

"My wife! My miserable wife! May Allah convince you of our need! May your children's children prosper because of your concern!" On one knee, Malik shouted at the slowing train. Abida's head rested against his sweaty chest.

He waved at men he couldn't see, because Abida assured him company officials occupied the first orange cars, now stained black from the engine's smoke. As the never-ending cars of phosphate came to a stop, officials, wearing western suits and well wrapped keffiyehs, jumped down and walked back to where they lay in the sand. Malik waved for them to come closer.

He would not disappoint. Eagerly, four men listened to his highly animated story about his uncle, who kicked them both out of his sports car. They had all been riding to Aqaba to buy fish for uncle's birthday, Malik explained. On the way, his uncle said that his wife was too beautiful for his nephew. Tears covered Malik's face, as a listener fiddled with his phone. Another man took out a camera and photographed Abida's sprawling figure, while the desert wind pressed her burqa against every part of her body.

Before his uncle drove away, Malik continued, he knocked his wife to the ground and kicked her, pointing to Abida's bruised chin as verification of his word. Then he beat his nephew, with a crowbar. Though Malik pointed to his own shoulder, he never removed his tunic. When they regained consciousness their money was gone. He had to find his uncle in order to get his money back.

It worked. The railroad inspector took their description of the uncle and his car. Not only were they invited onboard to eat and rest, but an unknown benefactor gave them money to search for the uncle once they arrived in Aqaba.

Added to the dinar they'd been given on the plane, they'd become wealthy by Jordanian peasant standards. Abida took a copy of the Qur'an from her bag and with a pencil transposed a current map from memory over one of the historical maps in the book, detailing a route from Jordan to Sudan. Malik studied it in silence.

"What are we planning?" she asked. Malik's 'take charge' attitude in the airport, on the plane, and in the desert had impressed her. But they were a team. Surely he understood how important that was to their success. She was about to repeat her question, thinking he was too deep in thought to have heard, but he suddenly leaned close, grimacing an inch away from her face, and replied, "Speed. We need speed."

Was he angry? Had he no idea why CIA thought she was an asset? Or was he simply unable to have a civil conversation with a woman?

The train slowed. He grabbed her wrist, pulling her to the compartment door, making sure her bag was securely wrapped over one shoulder. Train officials in the corridor once again wished them speed in finding the uncle.

Abida had removed her hijab from her face to flaunt her bruise and smile graciously. She'd enjoyed the elegance of their wood paneled car and seven-course meal. Standing by the opened door of the train as it continued to slow down, she happily inhaled salt water from the approaching gulf. Because she'd grown up in a land-locked state, it all smelled as exotic as the very pages of National Geographic magazines.

She fell hard onto the cement platform and thanked God her instincts had forced her arms out in front of her, preventing her forehead from reaching the hard surface. In shock, in slow motion, and amidst the clamor of hundreds deboarding she managed to roll over on her side. Yes, she'd felt the shove of his large hand on her back.

14

END OF SUMMER, 2009 PARK HILL, DENVER

Inez sat quietly on her sofa till after midnight, wondering if the police really were looking for her purse-snatcher or had the sight of Dolly's body spurred them into action? She'd never be able to erase the image she'd seen.

She replayed her entire day over and over. With her feet resting on an ottoman, her knee wrapped in foam bandage strips, she once again watched Mitchell enter her hospital room, stare at his shoelaces, and tell her how light must have played tricks on her vision. Finally, he confessed what she already knew, that they'd found Dolly David murdered in her bathroom.

Inez wasn't stupid. She knew he wasn't giving her the details of her death, but what he did tell her made her cry unashamedly.

Even now as she rested, tears ran down her face for what Dolly must have endured. Inez closed her eyes, immediately feeling a heavy blow to the side of her face in the darkness, felt her whole body lean forward, felt the humiliation of being unloved. She opened them quickly to destroy the image. Had it been a memory or foreshadowing? Inez had no desire to know. Breathing hard, she once again disciplined herself to stay away from unknown worlds and mentally began her day parking her car in the underground lot of the Martindale Building. But this time her heart began to fill with an even greater determination to see Dolly's mission through to the end.

The nagging question, of course, was where to start and who was she anyway to think she could succeed at something she had no training for. Was Trace right?

She wiped her face with the hem of her robe and instinctively began brainstorming, when her cell phone rang. Inez jumped. No one ever called this late.

"Doctor Buchanan, this is Sophie. I was driving past your house earlier today and saw you being helped inside by paramedics. Hope nothing's serious. You gonna to be okay?"

"Yes, the hospital discovered I have no broken bones." Beyond that statement, Inez couldn't get in another word.

"So," Sophie continued, "I decided to drive by again just now and noticed you had a light on in the living room. I thought I'd call. I'm parked out front and wondered if there was anything I could get you, take a prescription to an all night drugstore, get you some ice cream and soda. That's the kind of thing that puts *me* to sleep."

"That's so nice of you." Still seated on her sofa, Inez pulled the curtains back to see. "Would you like to come in? I can offer you tea or pecan coffee, but you'd have to make it yourself, I'm afraid."

"I know how to make tea."

"Very well then. It'll take me a minute to open the door."

Though surprised by the attention, Inez was thankful for the company. She described the incident involving her knee, which elicited additional purse-snatching stories from Sophie. Suddenly the young woman stopped in the middle of one such story.

"You know, I don't talk like this at home. Mama'd say, 'Don't you be talkin' like you white.' She never said that when we listened to Oprah. And I lied about going to college. I haven't been back for over a year. But if I could talk to somebody like you, I'd probably talk like this all the time."

Inez smiled. "We can do that."

"Can we? Because I was thinking maybe you needed somebody to move in here with you. All this house and all these empty rooms, I'm sure you …"

"The answer to that is no. I *need* my space."

Inez smiled at the young woman's gumption for asking, as they waited for the water to boil. Even her nose ring had become less obtrusive. But as they sat in the warmth of the kitchen, Sophie pulled a gun from her side jacket pocket and with her elbow propped on the table, waved it around haphazardly.

"You sure about that?" Sophie asked.

Inez was shocked, disappointed, but more than anything, she was angry with herself for being so stupid … again. Inez reared her head, stretching vertebrae in her neck and back. Her strength was returning. She'd misjudged the emotional stability of yet another woman at her door. A black woman this time, as if the lesson hadn't been nailed home deep enough the first time.

She had to keep focused and not let this turn into a physical brawl. She'd surely lose. Billy, her comic prince, came to mind. He'd easily been the skinniest student she'd ever taught. But he'd been endowed with elaborate intellectual verbal strategies that inevitably kept him alive.

Yet how could she consider herself intelligent, endowed, or wise after making the same mistake twice? She had to be the most expensively educated stupid person she knew. And with that thought, laughter started from her diaphragm and exploded out through her throat. "The moon," Inez said, between hysterical fits of laughter, "must be in the seventh house."

"What does that mean?"

"It means, that it's still the dawning of Aquarius for me, a time when innocence and confused thinking ruled. I'm still back there, because I never accepted the notion that only crazy people can act normal. It's normal people, who are too afraid to ever act crazy that are scary." Inez's jaws hurt. "Why can't I remember stuff like that? No-o. Instead, I remember the properties of lithium sulphide and who signed the Treaty of Versailles."

She almost fell off her chair laughing. And although she recognized her own nervousness, she couldn't stop. Sophie, who wasn't smiling at any of it, placed the gun on the table in front of her, so as to pour tea into the two cups that sat on the counter.

Inez suddenly inhaled, and stared at the metal harbinger of death. Cautiously, she picked it up by its neck and asked, "Are there bullets in this thing?"

"Naw. I usually take the bullets out before I go inside. I don't like to leave my gun in the cab, loaded or not."

Inez's eyes widened, taking in the emotional panorama stemming from the gun itself. She watched Sophie set a cup of hot water in front of her with a tea bag in it.

"Does that ever happen to you?" Sophie asked. "You think maybe something is the right thing to do, but then you think maybe it's the worse thing to do. So you wind up taking a chance one way or another. I guess I should have asked, if it was okay to bring my gun inside. I just didn't want to hear you tell me 'no'."

"This," Inez said, still holding the gun by its neck, "is a problem. You almost had me scrambling for my own gun. Then we could play a game of 'who gets tried for murder'."

Sophie's eyes got bigger, as she settled back into her chair. Inez, however, hadn't even begun to rant.

"You act like no one taught you any manners, like no one took the time to take you to Sunday School. No, wait, you went to Catholic School, where the nuns dared you to mess up. So what are you trying to sell me; that you were too poor, too black, too neglected to know better than to flash a gun in somebody's face? You want me to believe you don't know the difference between right and wrong? And didn't you tell me you'd been to juvie?"

"Thought you'd remember that. But having a juvenile record had no bearing on my application to carry. I've got a permit for that concealed weapon and I've got my certificate saying I'm a registered sharp shooter with the National Rifle Association. Wanna see 'em?"

As noiselessly as she could, Inez sucked up a small amount of hot liquid from her cup, all the while staring at the woman. She had little patience for young adults who paid no attention to authority. "If you tell me something stupid like the ghetto made you do it, I may just use this gun on you."

Inez still held the gun, hoping her fingers wouldn't betray her lack of experience with firearms. It was obvious Sophie knew nothing about Emily Post, the Girl Scouts of America, or the Jack and Jill Clubs.

"I'm sorry," Sophie said. "I really am. I do the wrong thing more often than I should and I'm never sure why."

Exasperated, Inez answered, "I'm not a retired psychologist. I haven't got a clue why you do the wrong thing or why you make bad decisions, because you've got brains enough to know that you're going to regret it."

"I said I was sorry. Guess you were one of those teachers who made sure nobody did the wrong thing around you. No wonder you don't have awards and certificates on your walls. You don't have anything to show for years of making your students so nervous they didn't even want to come to school. You must have had the quiet classroom, the one where everyone was afraid to talk, the one where everyone walked single file down the hall because they were scared."

"No! I had the classroom where students could hear themselves think, where students were proud of themselves when another teacher caught them being quiet and orderly, where they were so proud of themselves they were afraid, yes, afraid to fail!"

"Guess you want me to leave now, huh?"

Inez had never been her students' friend. Their peers were their friends. Inez had been their teacher and was proud of it. She decided then and there she probably wasn't going to be this woman's friend either.

"I want to see that permit you said you had, before I decide whether to call the police."

Sophie looked surprised, but quickly got her wallet out and unfolded a piece of paper, flattening it with the palms of her hands on the surface of the table and sliding it over.

"You noticed I didn't aim it at you," Sophie added. "I may have been just trying to show off," she explained. "See, I knew Billy Needham."

Inez was sorry her head jerked inadvertently, while reading the permit.

"I lived near him," Sophie boasted. "One proud peacock, he was. Going to college at night, working part time for you, and part time at the liquor store. He knew he'd be important one day."

Inez barely blinked. "He was important every day I knew him. What's your point? Are you going to waste time trying to teach someone my age how to feel guilt?"

Sophie's bottom lip quivered and her words were spoken in staccato. "Thought you might need somebody like me. I got better skills than Billy ever had." Her eyes glistened under the ceiling light. "I was letting you know I had a piece of my own. Better than what Billie carried. Any female cabbie without a gun might as well be dead. And I've been practicing. I'm a damn good markswoman."

Inez felt sorry for her and sorry for herself and sorry for the kind of sorry world they both lived in and sorry for the conversation they had fallen into. Obviously, Sophie had strong reasons for pleading her case. Inez had heard it all before.

Her knee throbbed. A look at the wall clock told her four hours had passed since her last pain pill. And yet she asked the same nagging question she'd asked herself all the years she'd ever taught school, "If I don't teach her, who will?"

It took another deep breath before Inez began to speak. "Billy and I edited an underground newsletter. Teachers and parents became whistleblowers, by reporting their school or district whenever they caught someone using money allocated for students, in other ways. We were like vigilantes, making cetain that money was going into classrooms and not toward easing the paperwork of administrators. We both loved tracking down hidden reports on the Internet showing us where money was being siphoned. We were helping more people get an education.

"Billy didn't wear a gun for me and I never saw him with one. When he was killed, I lost my taste for newsletters. I'm still reluctant to use a computer. But I'll have to in order to help Kadija. Ever wanted to help somebody and you couldn't? It's the most painful experience you'll ever have."

Inez was tired. Looking at the stoic expression on Sophie's face as she tried hard to blink away tears, made her more tired. Yet before the night was over Inez wanted to discover who the Taliban were and where the CIA would likely assign a woman of color. Plus, if Colonel David could lie about the character of his granddaughter she knew she'd discover evidence of his grander deceits.

She lowered her eyes finally. "Would you do me a favor?" Inez asked.

Sophie's smile lit up her whole face. With both hands on her hips she said, "Try me! Test my juice! See if I don't satisfy!"

"No. You don't want to act smart with me," Inez answered, "because I'll call the police in a heartbeat."

"Okay, I mean yes, ma'm. I'll do it."

"Thank you. Would you to go to the basement, the door is over there, and bring up my laptop? Here's your gun permit." Inez still held Sophie's gun in her left hand.

No one could take Billy Needham's place. Besides, now that she wasn't doing the newsletter, she had no money to fund an assistant. With her right hand, she took a pill from the pocket of her robe and swallowed it down with tea. It made her think of lemon and lemon made her think of Dolly's gun, right beside her in the refrigerator.

If only Dolly had kept it. Maybe ...

The young woman returned and slid the laptop across the kitchen table. "What should we do first?" Sophie asked.

"It's late," Inez answered. "And thank you. I guess you want your gun back. I'll walk you to the door and give it to you there. You have everything you came with?"

Painfully, Inez got up from her seat, holding the gun at her side.

Visibly upset, Sophie found her purse. "I guess I was hoping that ..."

Inez interrupted. "I'll think about what we've said. Lots happened today, I mean, yesterday. Who knows, once I've had a good night's sleep, my perspective may change."

Inez opened the front door and handed the gun back.

"I'm afraid to say anything," Sophie sulked, "for fear I'll say or do the wrong thing. Is it okay, if I come back tomorrow and check on you?"

"You mean practice your insults?"

"I ..."

Inez wasn't smiling. "Learning can't always be sweet and engaging. Stern teachers know that self imposed discipline is your best ticket to success. Good teachers model it so you know what it looks like when you see it. As long as I don't see your gun, we're okay. If you've got to bring it inside, it's got to be empty and concealed. And that's a rule I'm writing in stone."

Inez watched Sophie run to her cab, not expecting to ever see her again. Soon as the light went on inside Sophie's cab, she honked three times, with no regard for Inez's neighbors. Closing her door quickly, Inez knew Sophie was never going to be her Eliza Doolittle.

15

Inez grabbed her floral bag, the one she'd taken to Stronsky's office and walked back to the kitchen table. Excitedly, she opened her laptop. It hadn't been opened in close to a year. There were so many words to google. As she pulled files from her bag, a piece of torn paper fell to the floor. She picked it up, remembering several things Stronsky had said when he'd given it to her.

> *"This is his private number, but that's no guarantee he'll …*
> *They seemed to be made from the same cloth … may be too*
> *harsh"*

Could Stronsky have killed Dolly? No. Dolly's killer was angry and Stronsky had no passion in him. What about Bradley, a man with manners and passion? Could Dolly have made him angry enough to kill her? Inez wasn't sure. He'd used such caustic words to describe Dolly, like incinerated and yet they had a similar respect for etiquette.

She grabbed her phone and called him. A whispered voice answered, "Hello?"

Inez was struck dumb. The wall clock said 2:00 am. What was she thinking? Hang up.

"It's you, isn't it?" The way he said it made her flesh tremble. "Stronsky said he'd given you my number. Why was a warrant issued for my arrest? I can't reach him to ask."

"I'm sorry it's so late," Inez said finally. "I … need to talk to you about Kadija Campbell, but I … guess you haven't heard about Dolly David."

There was a long silence before Bradley spoke again.

"What about her?"

"Her beaten body was found in her home on Albion Street."

There was no sound on the other end after that. It didn't matter, Inez told herself. She had a lot of work to do. Yet, why was there an arrest warrant? Did police think Bradley had something to do with Dolly's death? But they'd been lovers for several years. And where was Stronsky? He and Bradley obviously didn't travel in the same circle of friends, but where would he go after leaving his office?

16

NEXT MORNING, 2009 PARK HILL, DENVER

Sunlight landed on Inez's eyelids, popping them open. An ice-cold keyboard propped up one of her arms. In slow motion, she pushed away from the table, stood against it, and tied the sash of her robe tighter around her waist. Splotches of sunshine throughout the kitchen and a cold draft across her shoulders, made her suddenly aware of the wide open back door.

Astonished, she closed it, looking for evidence of a break-in. Even a stupid robber would have closed the door. And robbed of what? She remembered what Trace had said the day before.

I checked the video on your place ...

She paced throughout the entire kitchen realizing her phone and computer were still in the same place and that her knee was no longer swollen. She must have forgotten to lock the door and the wind pushed it open. Just one more symptom of growing old.

Slowly she managed the stairs. A shower was a great idea. Inez walked with cautious steps, still favoring her injured knee, while an image of Dolly bombarded her thoughts. Where were the people she had employed? Why had she been alone?

Sheets of hot water finally rinsed yesterday away including her professionally wrapped knee bandages. It felt glorious.

She paused for a moment. This was the first shower she could remember taking without dwelling on the amputation of one breast to cancer. Instead, she was worrying about someone else, and it made her more determined to bring Kadija home without wasting time. Inez dressed quickly with no regard to whether she was lopsided or not and carefully descended the stairs.

Someone pounded on her front door. When she reached the bottom step, it sounded as if the door was about to shatter. Trace's voice rang out.

Inez opened the door

"I was about to break it down before I remembered your damaged knee! I'm sorry."

Trace's face was pink all over. He stepped inside hesitantly, as if he expected Inez to smack him.

Trace continued, "I was worried. I've been wondering whether home grown terrorists live in this very neighborhood. My partner thinks I'm just spooked after finding Dolly's body because there's no evidence of terrorist activity anywhere around here."

Her mind passed over his words, as if they were irrational. But she sensed an attitude in his voice of someone who had taken it upon himself to become the caretaker of the addled elderly. She didn't like it. "Maybe," she said, straightening her back, "you're just trying to form a hypothesis that explains the evidence you've already collected. Wouldn't it be funny if you were right about a terrorist group around here and your partner was wrong?"

"As long as forming a hypothesis doesn't turn into brainstorming we may be on the same page. By the way, you look like you're feeling much better today."

"My knee feels great, thank you. Rest and pain pills seem to cure anything."

"Good. Then how about breakfast at the Krameria Café?"

"I'll say yes to that, if you tell me what more you discovered at Dolly's."

Instead of searching for a jacket to hide in, Inez grabbed a small purse just big enough for keys and a wallet.

"First off," Trace said, "we can't find Dolly's maid anywhere. According to neighbors, the two of them went everywhere together;

Vail, Las Vegas, San Francisco, and Dolly would never bother to tell friends or neighbors that they'd gone. Nobody missed her, thinking Dolly was on one of those trips. The maid has a son who filed a Missing Person's Report on his mom nearly a month ago. It got lost in the system, because he hadn't listed his mother's employer. We made the connection only after Dolly's neighborhood was canvassed and we got her full name, Casema Meda. We'll try to pick him up for questioning today. He's got a record and he's not easy to find, either."

When they were both inside his unmarked car, Trace changed the topic. "Not everything's back from the lab yet, but DNA from that hair sample inside Kadija's wallet identified Sampati Jagjit, a student who attended CSU. I believe I told you Larimer County thought he'd killed Kadija and fled the country."

Inez added, "I remember his name from an investigator's report. But keeping a lock of his hair suggests they were more than friends. He might be the same boy Sophie described, but I'm not sure he's the man in the photograph who Dolly said was Kadija's husband."

Trace continued. "FBI says Jagjit's passport and photos vanished, which is why I believe CIA may have recruited them both. And who's Sophie?"

Inez sat quietly in the passenger seat, thinking about what Trace had said, ignoring streets filled with people doing errands, and wondering where Google would take her, if she altered her search words. Maybe she could locate people who knew Sampati?

"So who's Sophie?" Trace asked again.

"She's Kadija's friend from high school," she answered.

By the time Trace had driven two blocks, found a parking space in the lot across from the café and opened his car door for her, Inez had shifted her thinking.

They were seated with coffee in front of them when Inez decided to tell Trace about her online investigations rather than the back door she'd found open.

"Last night," Inez said, "I read about the Taliban. Jagjit was from India, not Pakistan. I'm sure he's Hindu, not Muslim. Sophie mentioned a student Kadija dated who wore a bindi in the middle of his forehead. Plus, I cross checked with missionary organizations in and around the Fort Collins and Greeley areas. There's a church in Greeley that sponsors more than one Hindu orhanage. The origins of the Taliban come from Pakistan and Afghanistan, not India. How did Dolly know anything about the Taliban?"

Trace drew in a long breath before exhaling. "Perhaps you're reading too much into what Dolly said."

"Maybe." Inez looked at him over the rim of her cup. Since he hadn't experienced Dolly David at all, he'd never know what she considered important.

He cleared his throat. "I guess it's as good a time as any to tell you this. Stronsky's body was found early this morning, frozen in a Kansas cornfield. Our scientists are trying to figure out what caused his organs to freeze between the time you saw him in his office yesterday and 2:00 am this morning, when he was found. Troopers speculate he'd been dropped from a plane."

Inez knew she was breathing, but everything around her had stopped. Stronsky was a weasel of a man and yet it was always shocking to her how life could end so suddenly. "That's terrible," she heard herself say. Gradually she began to notice the clanging of spoons against coffee cups and other small sounds of a cafe.

"Stronsky recorded our conversation on his phone," she said absently.

"Did he? Nobody found a phone on him. Why did he do that?"

She shrugged her shoulders. "Actually, I recorded it, too. I knew his answers might be important enough for me to check them again later. I don't know why *he* recorded it."

"Shut my mouth! And I thought you went to Stronsky's office just to get the keys to Dolly's place. I'll need your phone then. I won't need it for long. You'll get it back later today. What are you thinking? That what he said to you got him killed?"

Inez hesitated. "I don't think so. I asked him questions about the investigation he did years ago when Kadija went missing. You'll understand, when you hear it. Could someone have bugged his phone or his office?"

"Do bears pee?"

She was becoming insensitive to his remarks concerning urination and cautioned herself against letting him get away with it too often. As she searched through her purse for her phone, she asked, "So is that why you issued an arrest warrant for Bradley? You already knew what had happened to Stronsky?"

Trace held both his arms up in the air. "Am I leaking information out my pores?"

Inez wasn't amused. "I called Bradley early this morning," she said. "That's when he told me about the warrant."

"You WHAT!"

Everyone in the cafe turned in his direction.

"Let's get out of here," he said, changing colors as he stood.

Paying quickly for both coffees, he still clutched the café's cup in one hand, while he jogged to his car. Inez couldn't possibly keep up. When she finally approached, he was inside sitting quietly. She knew she had trampled over his sweet-little-old lady-who-dabbles-in foreign-intrigue image. Inez sat beside him quietly because once again she needed his information more than he needed any knowledge she might provide.

Minutes passed before Trace took a swallow of coffee, then spoke. "We've been looking for that son of a bitch, Bradley, ever since I laid eyes on Dolly's dead body."

"Why?"

Trace began again. "What I meant to say was, WHAT THE HELL were you thinking? We don't know when he left his keys inside Dolly's house, but we found them there. That set with his name on them included the keys to his car, her home in the mountains, his former office at Martindale, Inc., keys to his own house, and a Porsche medallion. There was no Porsche in either her garage or his. He lived for a short while with a woman who left him over ten years ago. There's no wife and no kids. Not only was he a lawyer and part founder of

Marindale, Inc., there are strong indications he was a CIA operative during the Viet Nam War. So where was he when *you* called him?"

Inez let all that information soak in before speaking. "I don't know. But Stronsky said ..." She went silent, picturing Stronsky sitting on the edge of his huge desk, handing her the piece of paper with Bradley's number on it.

Now she knew what last night's robber had stolen. It should have been sitting on the kitchen table beside her computer or at least beside her phone. And if it had fallen to the floor, she'd have seen it, when she stood up and certainly when she walked around.

She felt Trace staring at her, so she finally said, "Stronsky gave me Alan Bradley's private phone number." She made no reference to the piece of paper it was written on. "When I called him, he didn't seem to know anything about Dolly's death."

Trace did a cackling impression of an evil villain, even twirling the imaginary tip of a moustache.

"Remember," she added, "he was the one who told me Dolly was killed on Lookout Mountain."

"Oh, I didn't forget."

"So the murderer must have fooled Bradley too, don't you think?" Inez continued, "Anyway, it's a 303 number, the last one I dialed, so you'll be able to retrieve it off my phone. And one more thing," Inez wasn't feeling nearly as self-confident as her voice might have suggested, "I need Dolly's holdings audited. I need an accredited organization to do the auditing one that won't be influenced by Martindale, Inc. Obviously, that means the United States government can't do it."

"Don't you worry about any of that. I've already ..."

Inez interrupted him. "Listen Trace, there was a time when the Feds hired Martindale for everything. But something changed recently because they haven't received nearly as many government contracts as they did years ago. Maybe it's because there's no Republican in the White House now, I don't know. All I'm saying is the Feds may not be as objective about Dolly's money as they should be. Stronsky felt Martindale had changed from the days when Colonel David and

Bradley ran the place, but in light of his murder, Stronsky's perceptions may not have been accurate. I can't think of anyone I can trust to do an audit. But I'd appreciate it if you'd give it some thought and get back to me."

"Have you ever been to Disneyland?" Trace asked.

Inez didn't answer. If Trace thought he was being funny, he wasn't. Instead she asked, "I don't suppose the CIA is ever going to disclose where or even if they sent Kadija anywhere?"

"Right, they're not." Trace's voice was suddenly hostile. "They didn't even think viewing Dolly's crime scene was important. They even seemed offended because I thought they might know something about waterboarding."

Inez remained silent. Trace had just made a career-halting mistake. *Waterboarding? Was Dolly waterboarded?* Now was not the time to think about that or to give Trace a reason to be concerned over his slip of the tongue. He obviously felt safe around her, but he should never have jeopardized anyone else with his knowledge. And yet ...

"Guantanamo," Inez said, "employs Martindale personnel. Martindale, Inc. might give you the information you're looking for, even if the Feds don't."

Neither one moved. Trace stared at the dashboard for what seemed like forever, until he took his notebook out. "I wasn't trying to be sarcastic, when I mentioned Disneyland. You should disappear for a while. As Dolly's executor, you may wind up being at the very heart of this mess. Thanks for the tip about Guantanamo by the way. Guess I don't need to tell you that this shouldn't ..."

Inez's eyes looked far away. "Didn't you say you put surveillance cameras on my place?" she interrupted.

"Just the front? Why?"

"Just curious. I guess you did that because there's no alley in back. You didn't think anyone would bother to cut across another person's back yard to get to my place?"

"Yup," Trace answered. "I know Dolly David asked you for help, but you can't keep putting your life in jeopardy because ..."

"Finding who murdered Dolly and Stronsky," Inez said, "is your job. My job is to bring Kadija home. If she's already dead, I'm bringing back what's left."

"Dr. Buchanan, no government official can let you go where war is being waged. And there's a reason I'm called an agent and you aren't. Training! Experience! Investigative knowledge! You don't have that. "

Inez's voice got louder than his. "Don't you, 'Dr. Buchanan' me. I can't think why Kadija wanted to be a spy. With a grandfather who hated her and a grandmother who couldn't even help her daughter much less her granddaughter. There's only one person in all of this mess who deserves protection and that's Kadija. I can't help but have the deepest respect for our country's spies. So many become martyrs for the cause of personal freedom. I think Kadija and Sampati may actually be some kind of CIA research project. There's no history of that agency using people of color as trained field operatives. Somebody has got to help them, actually help them. Have you ever tried to help someone and you couldn't?"

Inez's heart pumped faster just thinking of their vulnerability. She glanced out her side window at people walking along Krameria Street, hoping to gulp back her emotions before Trace could see them spill over. Surprisingly, she spotted a very white man with no eyebrows, wearing a tattered skull cap.

Turning back to Trace she said, "Our goals are very different. I'd rather walk home from here." She was already out of the car.

Trace fumbled with his own side door. "I'll be back with your phone later today," he hollered, having given up on getting out with her. The noisy helicopter overhead made him holler even louder. "WE CAN TALK THEN."

She waved to him as he drove away. Treading quickly, she realized the man she sought was walking slowly and was dressed in dirty worn clothes.

Still behind him, she whispered, "My back door, in an hour." He turned around and swiftly grabbed her under her arms, lifting her onto her toes. He had the height of a basketball player. She wanted to scream, but when she looked into his face, she was even more certain that this was Alan Bradley, Esquire.

"Follow me." He had mouthed the words without making a single sound, inches from her face. Other pedestrians barely looked their way, thus was the liberal nature of Park Hill. He set her down and walked away, as another helicopter passed overhead. She stood where she was for a moment, letting her heart slow down. He walked toward the bus stop on Colfax. He never looked back, this man, who was her only link to stealth bombers, black hawk helicopters, AK 47s and Martindale's soldiers of fortune, all capable of saving Kadija from the likelihood of death. She was more than ready to follow Bradley anywhere.

17

JUNE 1996 AQABA, JORDAN

On all fours, Abida angrily turned her head left and then right in search of Malik. Trains arriving in Aqaba continued screeching to a slow stop, smoke and soot pouring out from around their tracks. Several women further down the platform had been pushed out of trains as well, along with their children. Some jumped and laughed about it. Their men, like Malik, jumped shortly after them. Most passengers weren't waiting for any of the trains to stop. They were all in an absurd hurry. Abida felt better though she was still shocked by what Malik had done. Some who jumped had already hailed cabs. Others raced toward long lines of people standing and waiting at outside stands with government officials directing people forward.

Malik grabbed her hand and pulled her to her feet, before she could open her mouth to complain. Jogging with others into the streets of Aqaba made her become more adventurous than cautious. They were on their way to long lines, where they too, would be processed before crossing the border into Israel.

She was grateful, when he slowed down. Keeping up with him was hard. Still holding her hand, Malik kept slowing until he was behind her. His large palm covered the middle of her back briefly, but she flinched away from his touch, remembering what he had done on the train. She ran with more deliberation now, making sure of her balance. She no longer totally trusted his guidance. Turning her head slightly, she meant to yell to him to stop and rest a moment. But in that same instant, she was off balance.

Abida felt his hand on her shoulder, felt her body being thrown in front of several fast motorcycles. Time hung in midair as one foot slid from under her. The noise of metal scraping metal and people screaming made her picture her own death right here, right now.

She felt no pain, but rather a jarring motion in her head as everything collided in blurred images. Motorcycles tilted over. She whirled in centrifugal space before coming to a final stop seated on the ground. Unsure where she'd been hurt, she watched as a motorcycle skidded across asphalt without its driver. It was careening toward her. There was nothing she could do, but wait for the inevitable.

Her tight curls flew into her eyes, her vision blurred even more, her stomach cramped, and her ribs made a funny noise upon impact. Her abaya ripped. Before lifting the bike up and off of her, Malik pulled the niqab around her exposed cheeks and hair. With her garments torn at her ankles, Malik once again on his knees, cried loudly to Allah, while holding the cloth together with both hands, so no one would see any part of his wife's body.

Abida had had enough. He was again making decisions with no input from her. Every deep breath she took caused pain along one side of her body. And the anger and frustration in her brain created a throbbing headache. Carefully, she brought her hands out from under her for support and eased her upper body into a less painful position. Malik never glanced at her through his tears, which frustrated her more. She was determined to let him see how she really felt about him.

As her eyes narrowed, her mouth opened, ready to holler obscenities at him. But money, slowly at first, began showering down on them. Malik's tears vanished quickly. The money included U.S. fifty dollar bills from scared North American tourists who envisioned themselves locked up inside official offices and jails in foreign lands for lengthy periods of time. He scrambled quickly to his feet to pick up each bill.

Dutch was the predominant language heard among the bikers. Using broken English and superb Arabic, Malik quickly revealed what he wanted in return for not making a fuss with authorities.

Within the hour, Malik and Abida sat atop a brand new BMW with an extra tank of gas strapped to it. There was no time for Abida to voice her concerns about the way she was treated. Seated painfully with her arms stretched around his waist she knew he couldn't hear anything she said. As seemingly well-off Iraqis they had no trouble crossing into and out of Israel's borders thru Eilat.

Though her face was swollen, her chest in pain, Abida watched with some appreciation the beauty of the Grand Canyon of the Middle East through squinting eyes. The orange and umber colors of the spiking rocks resembled pictures she had seen of the Grand Canyon in the United States. But the winds against her face finally made her close her eyes completely. Using Malik's back as her pillow, she slept.

Malik made a surprising stop in Taba at a shop selling blankets and robes. He got off the bike and ran into the store leaving her to stand bent over in pain. When he came out he carried a robe and a blanket, put them around her entire body and strapped her to the bike. Then he ran back into the shop and bought one more blanket, which he tied to the motorcycle to make a brace for her back.

Traveling less than a mile down the road, they stopped again. This time Malik bought bottled water and pieces of roasted lamb which they picked over before driving across the Suez Canal Bridge and on to Cairo. Abida had only seen the pyramids in magazine and textbook pages. This was as close as she'd ever get to them at speeds reaching over 200 km per hour. She smiled. Her mom never got this close. They rode through the night like mad Bedouins. She especially enjoyed those parts of the road that were smooth asphalt highway without bumps or irregularities.

Abida refused to open her eyes, nodding off for minutes at a time, until she felt the bike swerve. Malik was drifting into traffic, unable to stay awake himself. She screamed at him until he stopped driving.

He made her drive off-road. She drove the bike behind several huge boulders with his help steadying the machine. Somehow he had the strength to wrap them both in blankets over the sand. Through the night they huddled for warmth in the open desert beside a very small fire he'd made.

But Abida couldn't sleep. Everything in her body hurt. Besides, she still hoped for an opportunity to scream at him about his recklessness toward her life. But as soon as his head had hit sand, he was asleep.

What hell had this man come from, she wondered? He spoke English like a New Yorker and Arabic like a Saudi Prince. His skin, like hers, looked like roasted chestnuts in sunlight. He had the strut and arrogance of a teenaged Iranian with little knowledge of Middle Eastern or African history. And he had the stomach muscles of a forty year-old stretched outward by beer yet hardened by sit-ups.

Awkwardly, she propped her torso against the motorcycle. Other positions were too painful. He was also a bully, which suggested to her that he'd learned from being abused himself. Had he personally experienced Wanted's terror? Is that how he got assigned to this mission? He said he'd been training with Al Qaeda. Was he really supposed to kill Wanted or was his mission the same as hers, to report on Wanted's activites?

Maybe he had family members killed at Mogadishu, Riyadh, or Khobar Towers. And maybe Malik had really broken her ribs with his obsession to reach Khartoum. Anyone could easily be swallowed up whole and eaten alive by the very things Americans believed to be important to them. Maybe that was at the very heart of espionage, that spies were expected to give up the very principles their country was founded on in order to keep their country's freedoms safe?

Stone hills along the horizon gave the land a sense of immutable peace. They weren't high compared to Pike's Peak or the Sangre de Cristo mountain range, but she'd never seen those mountains in person. Her mom had always been too busy working several jobs at once in order to give her the things she wanted her to have. There would be time later for us to travel she'd say.

But this mountain range had its own kind of beauty, a beauty that existed *because* they were so far from home. And yet no matter how far away Kadija travelled, she could always feel her mom's arms and breath against her skin, propping her up and nourishing her thoughts. It was the reason she felt she could endure anything.

Next morning she had no memory of sleep. Malik had to help her stand and then sit on the bike, her body had cramped during the night. By late morning, as they rode through Luxor her tongue had loosened enough to criticize his total disregard for team effort. Malik refused to answer, to stop, or even slow down. But he did remind her that they should have been in Khartoum yesterday and that nothing else in all the universe mattered more. If Wanted had already left with his family, it would mean no one would find him again and their mission would be over.

She felt him tremble as he spoke, even as his chest expanded. Abida found herself conceding that he was a gifted actor and accepted his need to improvise on the spot. He in turn told her how much he appreciated her knowledge, which added believability to his impromptu lies. He even apologized for her broken rib, in case it actually was broken. Perhaps, he offered, it was merely bruised. Kadija found herself thinking that if only her mother had at least dated.

Maybe she had but never let her daughter know about such intrigues. That would have been just like her.

She had never seen how male and female relationships were supposed to work. But if she lived through this experience she'd be able to write a thesis on it.

Her anger had dissipated. In its place rose fear as they rode closer to Aswan. They were too close to Khartoum to screw up now.

In Aswan, they had to obtain exit papers from the Egyptian Government in order to board the ferry to Sudan. They'd have to convince one official after another that they were Iraqi citizens with passports that said so. Together they'd prepared a partially true story about a wealthy man residing in Khartoum whose name Malik incorrectly pronounced each time he said it. This man had promised them jobs to work for his family. What they wouldn't share with officials was that the Sudanese Government told Wanted he could no longer live in their country.

Not until they were finally permitted to board the ferry did anyone ask to hear their history. The Sudanese ferry captain was a curious man, first about the motorcycle they'd stored in the lower freight compartment, and then about the couple themselves. He claimed to want their passports to determine if they were able to afford a cabin.

Malik was adamant. After Egyptian officials had played hide and seek with his passport six times in three hours, he refused to hand them over to the ferry captain. The accommodations were not worth the additional price. The only disadvantage in not having a cabin was their proximity to inquisitive American and European students.

For Abida there was no filthier experience than staying on deck. While male and female tourists from all over the world squeezed in among natives, it was obvious that some people, regardless of origin, hadn't bathed. Some carried their wriggling small animals in their arms. She saw geese, a dwarf mongoose, and larger animals like chimpanzees carried in smelly backpacks. Some travelers were unable to reach the blackened latrines in time.

Her body sweltered under her garments and only the top deck provided enough light and air to breathe. She huddled close to Malik, because the air around them was putrid and far worse than his sweat.

As the sky darkened, the smell became tolerable. But she could also feel the fingers of someone seated behind her through the wooden slats of their bench. Turning quickly caused a sharp pain in her side, but also gave her a quick look at an elderly man who was poking his fingers between those slats playfully seeking sex.

Without a fuss, Abida quietly got up and sat on Malik's muscular thighs. His eyes remained closed so she felt comfortable resting her head on his neck to feign sleep. The cool buckle of his gun holster against her painful ribs offered a sense of security. Keeping an eye partially opened, she became alert to those men who dressed differently from others, who whispered in dark corners, and those who watched others more closely. When the ferry captain sat amidst a small group of men, Abida noticed him pull a rifle from beneath his thawb, then whisper to a man while looking their way. She whispered as much in Malik's ear, wondering if he really was asleep.

"It's the bike," he whispered back.

"Let them have it," she replied. "We can take the train."

He opened one eye, then closed it quickly. In that instant, Abida knew Malik had bonded with that bike. He wouldn't give it up easily.

While still using her one eye to stay vigilant, she noticed a Sudanese man push aside the Indian family seated across from her, seemingly in order to sit down. He had the calm disinterested look of someone who worked in an office, dressed in a blue plaid western shirt and khaki pants. Perhaps because he held a sheet of paper in one hand, the family thought he had some authority. Separating a family, as he did, was an ominous gesture, yet he sat for almost half an hour saying nothing, as if patiently waiting for the end of his journey. The sky would become brighter within the next few minutes, but when Malik opened his eyes, perhaps sensing discord, the Sudanese man finally spoke directly to him.

"You spy. I know."

18

END OF SUMMER, 2009 DENVER, COLORADO

The minute Inez put her foot down on the bottom step of the Number 15 bus her students' laughter echoed in her ears. Memorable field trips to the Capitol and Main Library flooded her brain. Automatically, she walked to the back of the bus, as she always did, to better keep an eye on her entire class. This time it was to keep an eye on Alan Bradley, seated behind the bus driver.

Although Inez hadn't taken a bus in years, she kept her balance as she walked. There was obviously an artisan at the wheel. The female driver, putting her foot gently on the gas pedal, weaved in and out of double parked cars and darting teens who, already late for class at East High School, played tag in the street.

Through greasy plexiglas windows she watched people run to catch the bus. These were people who looked as if they worked in banks, legislative offices, and boardrooms. But Inez had known the parents of some of her former students. Some were homeless, while some sought employment downtown. They'd put on clothes from plastic bags kept in the trunk of a car with no gas in it. She knew there were passengers seated around her silently praying for just one last break, hoping to pass themselves off as reliable hardworking people like the other passengers.

Inez sighed deeply. She fingered the transfer held in her lap. She'd only requested it because Alan Bradley had asked the driver for one. Following him wouldn't be difficult. But where were they headed? He hadn't trusted her house as a place to talk and he was probably right to be cautious.

When the bus neared Tattered Cover Bookstore, he stood. Inez dutifully did the same at the back door. The bookstore would not have been Inez's first choice for a place to talk. She quickly realized it wasn't his either, since he walked briskly past the store to the southbound bus stop on Josephine Street, where another bus waited.

Before getting on, they both paused while he watched the bus marquee change its lettering. It finally stopped on the sign that said Cherry Creek Mall. He boarded immediately, never once looking in her direction. Genius, she thought; a pleasant but very crowded place with coffee and chairs to rest her slightly aching knee.

❦

Inez hadn't been inside a mall for several years. She remembered being fascinated by the hubbub and theatrical colors when she was younger. Hardly anyone was shopping now. Suddenly she focused on his reflection in the window of Allie's Boutique. While Bradley had walked from one end of the mall to the other, Inez window-shopped slowly, exercising her knee with caution.

Turning to face him, she smiled. His clothing, a grease mechanic's stained shirt and frayed pants, blended well on Colfax. But they'd have to stay out of Neiman Marcus, Inez mused. "Let's order coffee," she suggested.

"Sounds good. And then let's go upstairs so I can see who's approaching, before the police actually reach me."

He spoke and acted like a man who'd done this before. His ease with their situation showed. Eventually, they found an unoccupied loveseat to accommodate his long legs. With coffee in hand, they sat on its edge.

"I was hoping," he said right away, "that we could share information, ask each other the questions we've been dying to ask. Before I'm arrested." He paused a moment to stare into her eyes. "Or maybe we could just snuggle up here on the couch together. I am prepared to turn myself in, if I'm not arrested soon."

Interesting behavior she thought. "You still have the phone you answered early this morning?" she asked. "I gave mine to CBI this morning."

"I see you don't respond to flirting. No, I don't have it," he said with merrily flashing eyes. "I slipped it into the pocket of a man at DIA as he boarded a domestic flight."

She smiled uncomfortably assured that civility was their only common denominator. Flirting, she thought. Is that what he thought he was doing? All she wanted was his cooperation, not his friendship.

"With so little time," she said, "I'll start. Police found Stronsky's partially frozen body in a Kansas field this morning."

"Oh, my!" He pushed his tongue against the inside of his jaw. "He was such a dirty little queer, I'm surprised it took so long for someone to actually kill him."

Inez scrunched her face at the anomaly seated beside her. "What are you saying?"

"That he'd do anything for money: sell out his friends, take bribes, lie about anything. He bugged your house when I specifically told him not to. That's why, when I decided to talk to you, I knew we couldn't meet there."

"That bug," Inez said, with more than a little pride, "was found and tossed some time ago."

Bradley chuckled. "That bug?" he repeated. "The man was amoral, Dr. Buchanan, not stupid. It would have been unlike him to place one bug where two or more would have been better."

"I'm Inez, by the way." She wasn't ignoring his criticism. She had more pressing things to talk about before police found him.

"And I'm Alan."

"Well Alan, CBI thinks you killed Dolly. They think you left your keys in her house, maybe on the day you killed her."

She watched him stare into her face without even a raised eyebrow. She'd already taken note of his willingness to share his first name with a black woman. That his sense of etiquette extended to racial minorities set him apart from a great many men. Slowly, he slid back into the leather loveseat. Inez had to do the same, if she was going to continue to talk to him discreetly.

"And I bet you think I hated Dolly enough to kill her. Well, I hated thinking that she killed herself on Lookout Mountain. That's what I hated."

He took a sip of his coffee and focused on the crowds loaded with shopping bags. Occasionally they'd bump his head, but he seemed very understanding and smiled back. Surely he wasn't about to explain that he loved Dolly, but that would explain his keys.

Inez again noticed his clothing. Theatrical props owned by a professional spy? Somehow his shirt sat funny, protruding somewhat under his arm.

Finally he looked at Inez and said, "I was ten years younger than Dolly and fell in love with her the very first time we met. I've loved her ever since. Her husband was amused and kept me around for the humor in it. Perhaps I'm being too modest."

A woman parked her expensive perambulator in front of them, occasionally looking at the baby inside. Not a subtle way to ask for a seat, but Bradley inched closer to Inez. This time he spoke louder.

"When I first met Colonel Tucker David he was a Captain and a serial rapist. That's a recent term. Psychobabble hadn't been invented then. He married money and thought I'd be willing to watch his back, while he spent it. Hell, I was so young I thought all men engaged in good clean sport-fucking."

Bradley seemed to fear nothing, certainly not being overheard. The woman with the expensive baby buggy had misjudged them and pushed it farther down the mall. Bradley did have a movie star quality about him. He didn't look particularly famous, but his demeanor hinted at stardom somewhere in a world of bad-boy white society.

Inez chose to ignore his off-putting behavior. "So why did Colonel David hate his granddaughter?" she asked.

Bradley pushed his head back, as if needing more space to stare at her, "You've just jumped a generation missy."

Shrugging her shoulders and ignoring his, 'missy', she replied, "Does it matter? He wasn't ever cured of serially raping, was he?"

Bradley rubbed his face. Maybe he was noticing how young the men were in the mall. Or maybe he was only now recognizing how abuse travels through generations. Bradley too, must have come from a family with money. Inez speculated it was a CIA requirement for the job, so you wouldn't accept money from an enemy.

"This may take a while," he said, "but I want to explain Colonel David to you for two reasons. First, as a reward for believing that I'm not a murderer and second, because, believe it or not, you have information I want."

His hands flapped, pointed, and cradled air as he spoke. Inez ignored his previous arrogance. She could relate to their shared graphic method of instruction and was grateful he'd sought her out.

"I didn't know Tucker David when he was first assigned to the Philippines," Bradley explained. "I was in law school. Dolly told me she loved David's attention at first and only after they married, did she notice his proclivities. The women he became addicted to however, flew under her radar. David fed on minority women who needed his approval for advancement.

"As the story goes, the fiancé of a woman he repeatedly raped received a full ride to West Point. David meanwhile had the young man's girlfriend discharged for insubordination when she threatened to expose him. The girl went home, explained to her family what David had done, and promptly committed suicide. Her mom waited until the young black man had graduated from West Point before telling him what her daughter had confessed."

Inez put one hand up to stop him. "I think I know the rest," she said. "That was Kadija's father, killed while on a special mission in Viet Nam. Once he finagled his way into David's command he worked his strategy for revenge." She paused, then said, "It must have included seducing David's daughter, right?"

"Oh, you're good, quite good," Bradley answered. "That young man waited until he was certain David's daughter was pregnant, before telling him everything. And yeah, he knew David would send him to his death. He'd lost any desire to live when his girlfriend died. He sent David's daughter a letter asking for her forgiveness in using her the way he did. In it, he said he'd already forgiven her and her mom for the death of his former fiance.

"God, the whole thing was a mess. As much as I tried to stay out of it, he tried to drag me into it. Said he'd always need a lawyer by his side."

"Dolly knew about all this?" Inez asked. As Bradley spoke, it was as if they were both invisible, surrounded on all sides by lunch-frenzied, mall-happy humanity.

"Yeah, but I never told her," he answered. "Dolly and I carried on a discreet love affair for decades. But her husband had convinced her that their daughter cavorted with black men. And you know the kind of crime that used to be."

Inez listened attentively and quietly sipped her coffee, not wanting to distract him from his story telling.

"Tucker later cleaned up his act and we started Martindale, Inc. together. No, don't look at me like that. I know what you must think of me.

"Dolly was devastated, when her daughter was killed in a car wreck," Bradley paused for a moment before he continued. "Guilt ridden, she went to comfort the granddaughter she'd never met and found the letter the young man wrote years earlier."

Bradley put his elbow on the arm of the love seat and covered his face with his hand. The other hand propped his coffee cup on his knee. Inez thought he was sobbing and gently tapped his arm. "Be careful," she cautioned, not wanting him to attract attention.

What brought on his tears? He had described repeated rape and suicide in the life of minority women without even a downcast eye. Bradley reached inside his pocket for a handkerchief and wiped his eyes until they were red. Now he looked like a homeless addict. Was he crying over Dolly or what?

"Stop," Inez whispered. "People will think I'm your social worker."

He laughed through his fingers, Inez noting the quickness with which he switched emotions. Was it an act?

"Think before you answer this question," Inez said. "Did you ever believe Dolly might have killed her husband? He died earlier this year, didn't he?"

"Of course not! That's absurd. You talked to her only once in her entire life."

Realizing he hadn't given his answer much thought, she pressed on. "You're saying then that Dolly didn't know her husband had abused their daughter?"

Bradley stood up abruptly, his coffee splashing onto his dirty shirt. His back was toward Inez and she could see the raised outline of a strap under his shirt. A gun holster. She wondered if she should get up, too. And why was he carrying a gun, but Bradley suddenly twisted around and bent over her, his eyes pointing daggers into her face. "You're guessing! I thought you'd be more professional than that."

Inez barely looked at him, but patted the seat beside her. "Sit down, Mr. Bradley, Alan, I mean. We don't have time to discuss statistical reliability, otherwise I'd draw you a graph."

He sat on the edge of the loveseat again. Not wanting to anger him enough to leave, she sat quietly, too.

But she couldn't be quiet for long. "Colonel David went to see Kadija in Fort Collins, didn't he? It would have been inconsistent of the bastard to screw his daughter and leave his grandchild untouched. You probably drove him there."

Bradley slid further back and faced her, shouting, "If anybody took him there, it was Stronsky."

Inez nodded. "I believe the Colonel actually intended to rape Kadija the night he went to see her. He was going to make her beg for his recommendation to CIA, but she almost killed him. If she didn't beat him up, her boyfriend did, which explains why Colonel David didn't "look himself", according to Stronsky's written reports. The Colonel didn't want anybody he couldn't control to get the government's ear."

Inez continued, "But then someone, who knew the Colonel well, intervened to get Kadija into CIA. This someone must have worked for CIA himself at one time in his career, maybe in Viet Nam."

"Stop!"

"Then answer this," she went on, "could the Colonel be responsible for turning Kadija over to the Taliban? Is that how the word 'Taliban' got into Dolly's narrative? Paying ransom was never going to be off the table for Dolly, she had the money to do it, no matter how illegal it was to pay the enemy and no matter how crazy you made her seem. How do you contact the Taliban, Alan?"

Bradley stood up again and this time Inez stood up with him. His facial expression had changed. People swooped in to take physical possession of their love seat.

Bradley was loud in order to be heard over the din of the crowds in the mall. "You don't have anywhere near the government clearances you'd need for me to discuss any of this with you. And that's for your safety, not mine."

It suddenly hit Inez that Bradley's only purpose in talking to her was to discover what could keep him out of jail.

She stiffened her back with the bravado of an old retired schoolteacher, and turned to walk away. Bradley grabbed her wrist and pulled her around. "Whose ashes were on Lookout Mountain?" he whispered. "Does CBI know yet?"

Inez gave a strong kick to what she hoped was his shin. There were so many people no one looked down. Bradley bent over slightly and released her wrist. Her anger made her speak slowly in an attempt to control herself. "CBI doesn't even know who stole your phone number from my kitchen table last night," she replied.

Suddenly, Bradley stepped back and looked at her. Two smartly uniformed security guards rounded the corner. Was that why he stepped back? One guard turned his head to get a second look at Inez, his smile frozen in place across his face. Was she being unduly paranoid, she wondered?

The mall teemed with late lunch people. Bradley stepped closer. "Meet me at Loyola's College Library, tonight, seven pm."

"Why? My security clearance isn't good enough, you said." Something had frightened him.

"After I leave here," he said, "wait five minutes. Go to the ladies room. Stay there twenty minutes, then leave. Go home."

He walked downstairs and into the crowd. Inez couldn't wait, but went directly to the ladies room, where she sat on the toilet, trying to understand what made Bradley's question about the ashes important. Why hadn't he turned himself in to those security guards? And why did he feel the need to carry a gun if he really intended to turn himself in to the police?

And if Bradley had been CIA, could she really believe anything he said?

19

END OF SUMMER, 2009
DENVER, COLORADO

Following Alan Bradley's directions, Inez left the ladies room exactly twenty minutes after she'd entered. With surefootedness, she marched past salesladies waving blotter paper samples of Macy's perfumes. Gathering speed, she power walked through the men's department and out a side door.

Under a dazzling blue Denver sky, she suddenly realized how important it was to go home. Trace Mitchell planned to deliver her phone there. How wise would it be to meet Bradley later in the evening with no way to call for help? She looked up to see there wasn't a cloud in the sky. Only a single helicopter sped by.

She marched back into Macy's and straight through the mall. This time Inez went out the main entrance where cabs waited in a single line. A tip to the baby faced valet attendant brought the first cab forward with the wave of his hand.

Invisible currents of cheap after-shave lotion, the kind her eighth grade boys wore on their first days of school, wafted over her, forcing her heart to accelerate. It was the same smell as yesterday, while in the belly of the underground garage. It had been overpowered by alcohol yesterday. She swiveled on stout heels to see a man in his forties dressed in a light beige business suit. His clean-shaven face and well-worn leather briefcase said he was not likely a purse-snatcher. They looked at each other longer than usual. Had he recognized her? Or did he just have bad taste in after-shave lotion?

She broke off her gaze to plop into the backseat of the cab.

"That you, Dr. Buchanan?"

The voice was familiar. Immediately, she looked at the front mirror above the windshield.

"I don't believe in coinkidink," Inez said resolutely. "Too much like stalking."

Inez shifted her weight on the seat to get out quickly. She was ready to confront that clean shaven man with his unusual taste in after shave lotion.

"Hey, no! Close the door! PLEASE!" Sophie shouted. "Okay. I did see you get off the bus, but that was over an hour ago. I've been to Littleton and back since then. I hung around a while, waiting to see if you'd care to have a ride home. See, I'm offering you a free ride. Why turn that down? Besides, I've got a lot to say. I know that I'm sorry won't cut it. Give me another chance to redeem myself? Please."

Through the back window, Inez watched the man in the beige suit get into the cab that had driven up near hers. She'd never gotten a good look at the face of the man who grabbed her handbag, so how could she possibly identify him? She closed the cab door and shut out her paranoia.

As both cabs drove off, she finally focused on where she was. "Look here Sophie," Inez said. "I like you and all that, but I …"

"I know. I know. And I'm just thankful you see something in me to like."

Inez heard rejection in Sophie's voice and it stopped her from speaking again without more thought. Besides, Inez thought, no sense in being hasty. If she was Kadija's only hope in getting home, she might need an entire army of volunteers to make that happen.

"Are you looking for part time work, Sophie?"

The woman behind the steering wheel didn't answer right away. "You mean, working for you? Sure."

Inez sat further back in her seat. She hoped her comment about a job hadn't insulted her. She could feel the young woman looking at her in the mirror from time to time, her mouth open, ready to talk. Yet Inez was in no mood to chitchat and her face must have said so.

By the time they reached Colfax Avenue, Inez asked, "And do you still have your gun?"

There was no answer from Sophie and after a moment Inez understood. She'd been more than harsh about her having it in the first place.

"You want me to shoot somebody for you Dr. Buchanan?"

"No! Of course not!" Inez wasn't surprised. A misguided gang member had asked her that same question years earlier.

"Let's go to the nearest park and talk. That is, unless you've got other things to do."

Without warning, Sophie made a sharp U turn in the middle of Colfax, forcing Inez to grab hold of the upholsterd seats in the back.

"See, Dr. Buchanan, I've got time right now. City Park is coming up."

Dried leaves swirled around their cab. It only took one recent cold snap to change the colors of the park's tallest trees. That was good because the leaves told Inez she had to work fast. Winter wasn't far away and remembering Dolly's statements, Kadija would be just outside Jalalabad only until the end of the year.

Sophie stopped just inside the park beside one of its ornate stone gateways deliberately fashioned a century earlier to resemble New York City's Central Park. She turned sideways in her seat and eagerly asked, "What's the job?"

"I was about to say that I can't pay much, but actually I'd forgotten that I'm the executor of an estate with a focused mission. I can at least pay you what you already make and you can still use your cab.

"No way," Sophie said with the most infectious smile Inez had ever seen.

"I'm not going to start from the beginning," said Inez, "that would take too long. According to Kadija's grandmother, Kadija called her from Afghanistan and asked her for money earlier this year. Her grandmother felt this was a ransom request or a request for money that would save Kadija's life. It's against the law to give money to countries we're fighting and her financial and legal advisors successfully prevented her from breaking that law."

Inez paused and leaned closer toward Sophie. "If you work for me, there's only one answer you can ever give anyone who might ask you questions."

Sophie's eyes got bigger. "What's that?"

"Tell them to ask Dr. Buchanan." Inez paused to see if Sophie understood.

She nodded. "I get it."

"You can never," Inez continued, "repeat what I tell you or even hint at it. I'm trusting you with Kadija's life, but then you two trusted each other when you were younger, didn't you? That's why I'm confident you can be trusted now."

"Wait a minute." Sophie put a hand on the top of her leather seat in order to twist all the way around. "I don't know, I mean Kadija and I can't possibly be the same people we were years ago."

"You're not. But what you two shared back then, a determination to help each other survive, is exactly what needs to be shared now. Trust me. I know you're the right person." Inez placed her hand on top of Sophie's. "Remember this well, you and I must act at all times as if the people who are holding Kadija captive also know about us."

Sophie took in air, lots of it, then whistled as she exhaled.

"Since I'm not sure who's got her," Inez sighed, "we need to suspect everyone around here as well. I have my reasons. One thing is certain. Whoever has Kadija *must* believe the ransom will be paid. I can't believe that Kadija's captors would kill her rather than try to get their hands on the millions of dollars she represents. If what they really want is money, she should still be alive. The thing is, her grandmother had the money to hire an army, rent a plane, fill its gas tanks, and bribe officials to get her out of any hell imaginable." Inez grappled with her thoughts for a moment.

"Whew!" Sophie said. "She's got that much? She and her mom lived in a small duplex near me. When her grandma offered to pay Kadija's college tuition, Kadija didn't know she even knew anybody with that kind of cash. The first time she ever knew she had a grandma was after her mother died."

Inez listened attentively. So who told Kadija's captors about her grandmother's wealth? Why hadn't Bradley been able to bring Kadija home? Her continued meeting with Bradley was absolutely necessary.

"Are you free around six tonight, Sophie? And, can you bring your gun? I've got one too, but I'm not sure I know how to use it. Maybe you could teach me by tonight."

"Holy Shit, Dr. Buchanan!"

20

JUNE 1996 ASWAN, EGYPT

Under a predawn sky, the Sudanese man again said, "You spy, I know."

Still, Abida wondered if she'd heard him correctly. To a certain degree, his English was incomprehensible, his words drowning in the beat of his own native cadence. The clamoring motor of the ferry itself was of no help either. His voice, neither loud nor whispered, was in no way accusatory or angry.

Being a female in a predominantly Muslim area, she had no reason to respond. The man never looked her way, although she was still on Malik's lap. She merely continued, as Malik did, to casually glance at him, along with the other people on the bench beside him. No one in the immediate vicinity seemed to understand his English either.

"No fool," the man continued, after a moment's pause. "Paper from Amsterdam." He held a crumpled typewritten paper up to the level of Malik's eyes, a definite gesture of disrespect. "No stamp on passport."

Malik snatched the paper from the man, perhaps too eager to make sure others couldn't read it. He read it silently to himself. Abida averted her eyes from it altogether. In a few minutes, Malik spoke in Arabic, matching the man's quiet tone. "You took this paper from my motorcycle? Why? Did I drop it somewhere?"

A woman seated beside them slid sideways and gently pulled at Abida's abaya, wordlessly indicating a place for her to sit on the bench rather than Malik's lap. She smiled at the elder woman, showing her appreciation, then slipped from Malik onto the bench.

Their small section on the upper deck had become hushed as people watched Malik and the Sudanese man speaking softly. It wasn't her imagination that more men began to congregate nearby. However, they did not seem organized or part of the same group. Some wore izaar, while others wore the thawb or Western style pants and shirts. Perhaps they crowded closer because the ferry was nearing the dock and they wished to see people they were to meet. The man's Arabic was as difficult to understand as his English.

Malik leaned all the way over toward him and began to whisper while keeping one hand on the gun covered by his tunic, his way of calling attention to it. Meanwhile, the ferry conductor, on the other side of the deck, rose from his seat. His rifle remained at his side while he shouted several times, "Wadi Halfa!"

Abida had memorized the faces and dress of men who had been seated around the conductor during the night. Those men wore loose fitting white garments that hung from very slender bodies. All wore beards and did not appear interested in Malik nor the man across from him.

Malik rose from his bench in slow motion and the man across from him rose, too.

"Sukran gazelan!" Malik shouted for everyone to hear. He grabbed Abida's arm, pulling her up and directing her swiftly past the standing man and down to the next level. Many passengers were already in line to claim their cargo and depart. Like a dutiful Muslim wife, Abida said nothing, but followed his lead, knowing he had no more idea what would happen next than she did. Africa, she knew, was not supposed to be difficult to enter or exit. But every government's particular interests differed. If they were going to be stopped and questioned here, it would more likely be the result of bandits than the actions of the government.

She wasn't afraid of the unidentified man, believing he was likely working alone. He had not followed them to the next level and she couldn't find anyone else seeming to take his place or join him in conversation. She braced herself for anything since she was in the company of a man wearing a gun and unafraid to use it. Based on previous experience she felt their chances of survival were good and her side felt much better this morning.

After standing an hour in a line, from which they took turns using the latrine, the first of the cargo was released. It promised to be an agonizing process for the hundreds onboard. Soon it became evident that some passengers were paying the ferryboat captain to have their merchandise taken off sooner. One glance at the captain with his rifle by his side told Malik and Abida they might be among the last to leave. There'd be no witnesses left on board to confirm the theft of their BMW.

The troubled look on Malik's face told her he was improvising again without her input. She had to stop him, but people in line stood too close. No matter what language they used she was certain someone onboard would understand. His eyes took their time wandering over the entire deck, until they landed on her face. Abida grabbed his hands and wordlessly shook her head, 'no!'

But he swallowed hard and said, "Aintfay."

She rolled her eyes up into her head in disbelief, so he repeated it louder. "Aintfay!"

With a stiff index finger, she jabbed his chest again and again. His face registered no expression at first until his eyes locked onto her stabbing finger. Each time she poked him his eyes grew wilder. Abida stepped back as his chest grew and his face turned red. In Arabic he asked why she couldn't understand, his opened hands changing into bulging fists.

Was he going to hit her? What would Langley say? That he had to inflict Sharia Law to maintain his cover? That he responded appropriately towards a woman who was supposed to act as his wife? Suddenly his body crumpled over his gun and onto the floor. She knew he was acting. Immediately, she pleaded with men standing nearby to help carry him down the plank to their motorcycle where he could rest. It all sounded reasonable, but the rude Sudanese man appeared from the galley area and followed them staying several steps behind. He waited menacingly at the rear of the bottom deck on which cars, industrial machines, and motorcycles were chained together.

Her husband's pills, Abida explained, were inside a bag attached to his motorcycle. She bent down pretending to search them out. The volunteers were anxious to return to their place in line. When she stood up again, the men had already propped Malik against a nearby bicycle and pushed their way back up toward the line. Over the tops of vast amounts of cargo, she could see the Sudanese man slowly edging his way toward them.

"You see him?" Abida whispered.

"No. You be my eyes." Malik had already taken his gun out from under his tunic and remained on the floor, next to the motorcycle. "As soon as I shoot, the captain and his friends may come running. Prepare to swim ashore."

"I don't think so," said Abida, confidently. "You haven't shown your passport to anyone on this ferry. He knows you have no stamp from Amsterdam because he saw your passport in the only city he could have, in Aswan. Certainly no one followed us from Aqaba. We were too fast. Anyway, he has stopped walking. He knows I'm talking to you. I think he wants money. If he wanted to report us, he would have talked to a ferry official by now. One option is to pay him off."

"You can't be serious. Is anyone else around?"

She watched bickering families standing beside their property, feeding goats, polishing dusty furniture. "People are preoccupied with getting off this boat. They're not looking at us."

Malik jumped straight up from the floor, waving to the man to come closer with his outstretched left arm, his gun hidden behind his back. The man didn't return the smile, but walked toward him. Abida heard no gunfire, but saw his plaid shirt suddenly turn bright red across his chest. The man was still on his feet but Abida, rushing to his side, began unbuttoning the bloody shirt. Malik pulled it off and dropped it. He then pushed the man forward and over the railing.

No sound of water splashing was discernable on board it seemed. Malik put his arm around Abida's shoulders, puffing himself up to look like three people standing at the railing.

After some time had passed, Malik cautioned, "Let's move away now in case he floats."

Seeing the shirt on the floor, he picked it up and twisted it into a ball. Both looked for a place to hide it. It was then they realized they were standing beneath the cardboard covered boom of a large excavator destined for some costly industrial project. Above the engine, standing 25 meters above the floor, was a smoke stack on top of its cab. It was easy for Malik to reach it by climbing the tractor-like machinery past the hydraulic pump. When he climbed down, he sat on his bike and noticed it had been chained and locked.

The captain peered over the railing of the upper deck. He looked down on families seated atop their farm equipment and animals. Some waved money in the air, whatever they could scrape together, as a bribe.

The captain would send a skinny boy down to the lower decks to collect those bribes. The boy's prominent ribs and bloated stomach extending over his pants, told his story. Yet he was a climber with enough energy to grasp hold of overhead pipes and swing from hooks that dangled from the ceiling. The boy never walked down stairs or planks. If the captain liked the bribe he sent the boy down again with the key to open the lock.

Finally understanding how the process worked, Malik waved money, too. The boy hung by knotted knees from a ceiling pipe and snatched it from Malik's hand. The youngster became momentarily distracted by the unusually large piece of equipment next to Malik's motorcycle. The conductor had to call to the boy to remind him of his job.

Abida modestly sat on the back seat of the bike behind Malik watching the boy carefully.

"Let's hope your bribe won't be so large it makes the captain greedy for more," she whispered. Her mouth rested on Malik's broad back. "Or too small to be taken seriously? We should have made the decision about the amount together."

Malik said nothing and didn't move. Abida got off the bike from time to time to casually glance over the side railing, hoping the dead man's body had not yet come to the surface. Increased debris made it difficult to see anything.

The conductor's face revealed nothing, obviously concerned with other matters onboard that kept him away from the railings. Finally, the boy reappeared, this time with the key. He went by way of the ceiling above the excavator.

Only after he unlocked the chains, did the youngster climb the excavator itself. The machine's arm rose high above two decks, while its boom hung over a side railing. An attached bucket was at the end. The arm and the bucket, unlike the boom, were wrapped in plastic.

By now, the bottom decks were congested with people pooling money for bribes. Abida, continued watching the boy. But Malik directed her to sit securely on the motorcycle and hold on tight as he inched the bike closer to the planking that would get them off the ferry and onto shore. It wouldn't be easy. People and poultry blocked their way.

No one could have heard the boy's key drop into the smoke stack, but Abida saw it happen. She also saw those unable to pay bribes begin to tear away parts of the ferry's engine and use them as tools to break open their locked belongings. The captain disappeared off the upper deck while the boy disappeared behind the short walls of the smoke stack. Suddenly he stood up wearing the Sudanese man's shirt around his neck. Like Spiderman, he kept reaching for the next ceiling pipe and swung from it, using the shirt of the dead Sudanese man as his cape.

"He found it," Abida whispered. "No need to look up."

Malik didn't, but asked, "What's he doing with it?"

Before she could answer, a woman standing in front of their bike, pointed to something above their heads. She consulted with a man standing next to her.

Malik started his engine with a roar that frightened both the women and children in front of him. Men backed away surprised. With an aisle cleared, he drove his motorcycle to the end of the bottom deck, then turned the bike around and drove up the narrow planks to the next level where the captain had been standing and then to the next level above that.

"Hold on tight," he instructed, as he rode to the very back of the top deck and peered over the side.

With her heart in her mouth, Abida asked, "Can you do this?"

He didn't answer, but revved his motor until nothing else could be heard.

"Wrap your legs around my waist and lock your hands around my chest. Don't let go for any reason!" he shouted.

His instructions gave her no room to consider modesty. If she lived through this ordeal, would she be stoned to death? She raised the bottom of her abaya high above her knees.

Across the deck he rode at top speed, the sun at his back, eyeing the excavator's boom, arm, and attached bucket below. They were both wrapped in plastic and would provide a perfect ramp. Abida turned her face away. He drove his motorcycle through the small section of deck that had no chain railing.

High into the air they traveled and for a fraction of a second, only his two hands touched the bike with Abida on his back. Within that fraction of time, Malik forced his arms, then his whole body to go downward, making the bike nosedive.

As their full body weight landed back onto the motorcycle, it hit the encased boom. All that weight pushed the arm into the air suddenly turning it into a ramp from which Malik's revved up engine and wheels propelled them into the air, this time over the water that separated the ship from the shore. Gravity took over and they dropped onto land beyond the dock.

They crash landed on one side. Abida screamed with pain as the motor continued to run. Like a competing weightlifter, Malik brought the motorcycle with Abida still on its back seat, to an upright position.

Passengers, from the top deck all the way down to the mouth of the ferry, stood speechless. One or two cheered.

Leaving thick airborne dust behind them, they headed straight for Khartoum at reckless speeds. Abida had never been so close to death. Skin on the inside of her right leg was raw and blistered from the hot fallen motor. Unable to speak, she sobbed and trembled violently against Malik's back. But nothing could have made him stop.

※

"You're so young!" Madam Wanted said, while pulling at Abida's niqab.

She was a delicate woman, many months pregnant, and very commanding in her short stature. As the oldest of Wanted's wives, she and her children occupied the central portion of a large sitting room, along with the younger children of his two other wives. Servants stood over cabinets and tables packing belongings into large crates.

"I'm sorry you had to travel so far and I'm particularly sorry about your accident with the hot soup that spilled down your leg," she said to Abida. Malik's lie had travelled quickly from one side of the compound to the other.

"My husband hasn't told me where we will fly, but we won't be able to take as many with us as we originally hoped. Unfortunately, I must leave behind even those servants who have become my close friends. He needs the room for his soldiers. Your husband will be among them, of course. My husband thinks very highly of him, but I do believe that if you two had come just one day later, your husband would have missed us. My husband is not a man who waits well. Please sit here beside me for the moment and let us talk."

Abida hung her head, to assume mutual fault for her husband's tardiness.

While her head was bent, she was able to assess two servants out of the four who packed clothes and dishes, but who never took their eyes off her. Had they already been told whether they would or would not travel with their mistresses?

"Servants who cannot come with us," Wanted's wife continued, "will find that there are families here in Khartoum, so I've been told, who will take them into their homes as you wait for your husband's return."

Abida's heart pounded. Would she need to use the poison she carried in her bag to eliminate one or both of the servants? Seated at the first wife's feet, she looked through an opened window. A servant would be her first kill, if she couldn't think of another way.

About thirty-five men played war games with rifles in the weed-covered fields. She could pick out Malik in the distance. His size put him above most of the other men.

"May I speak?" Abida asked.

"Of course you may, my dear. I'm not so worthy as my husband, that permission must be asked whenever you wish to address me," said Wanted's first wife.

"Thank you," Abida replied, knowing she would never forget to ask permission. "I see you will not be taking your beloved garden with you. I know it's beloved because the roses under this window could only have survived because of careful tending." Abida paused to savor the warm smile given her for understanding the woman's plight. CIA's intelligence had been correct about the wife's interests.

"Shall I," Abida asked, "harvest those roses so that you may replant the cuttings wherever you go and shall I pack the leaves and stems for special teas that address sleeplessness, fatigue, sore throats, blistering gums?"

"You can do that? My family leaves early tomorrow. But my husband loves fruit and flower teas." The older woman rubbed the sides of her stomach as she spoke.

Abida smiled. "If I start now, I'll finish harvesting by sundown. Your teas can be enjoyed tomorrow, but most will need to be mixed for you, to avoid side effects."

The lady leaned back. "I see," she said. She motioned to a servant to bring a pillow for her back. The servant brought it and said nothing. Only her eyes were uncovered and she waited until Madam nodded that she may leave them.

"Harvesting means what exactly?" Madam asked.

"Removing the ripened fruit. For roses, I must remove the leaves, petals, and hips. For other plants in the garden, I must chop the stalks and the leaves. And for still others I'll dig a root ball, which can be planted again. Only if you go to the North or South Pole, will there be a problem planting roses." It was a joke she regretted making the minute it left her mouth. Would this woman have any knowledge of Poles? Would any servant have such knowledge? Her stomach churned knowing she may have made that one horrible mistake that could identify them as spies.

They sat quietly, while Madam Wanted watched Abida carefully. "No men are here. Take off your hijab?"

Abida did so immediately.

"You are African, part African perhaps?"

"Yes."

"But your parents are Iraqi?"

"Yes."

"You've learned many things, then." Madam Wanted waved her hand again. This time the gesture summoned a tall woman whose hijab revealed her whole face. Happiness surrounded the young woman's eyes and mouth. It was obvious to Abida that she'd been told that she would travel with her mistress.

"What will you need?" Madam Wanted asked Abida.

"Plastic and paper bags, if you have them. Newspaper if you don't."

Madam Wanted stood with the assistance of the tall woman. "This is Pakeezah. She'll provide whatever we can. I'll take a short nap in the next room to make myself look strong for tomorrow." Everyone smiled at her as she left.

Abida avoided looking into Pakeezah's dark eyes and oval face as they walked beside the whitewashed walls of the house and entered the garden together. Would Madam Wanted have enough influence over her husband to persuade him that both servants should come along? CIA had given her no personal information about Wanted and his first wife to make that kind of analysis. Yet she could tell that Madam Wanted had a lot of respect for her husband. Killing Pakeezah might plant even more suspicion in Madam's mind.

They were in the middle of a parched and dying flower garden, when Pakeezah abruptly stopped and turned around. With eyes as pointed as daggers she said, "Only one of us can go. My parents will beat me if I am returned to them. You already have a husband to protect you. Think very carefully about what you do and say, because my family will have their revenge."

Abida said nothing, but hurriedly tended to the dried plants. She thought deeply about what she needed to do. Being left behind was not an option. Could she really kill a servant? She'd have no problem killing an enemy of the United States.

21

END OF SUMMER, 2009
THE HIGHLANDS, DENVER

Trace Mitchell hid behind partially barricaded windows in a garage across the alley from The Hotchkiss Building. Over several decades, The Hotchkiss had become a ramshackle west side boarding house with rooms rented by the hour.

Mitchell knew the building. His dad had taken him to see it as a teenager. His father and grandfather had lived there when they first arrived in Colorado in the 1930s. Then, it was a small but elegant hotel with a polished wood paneled lobby. It was the place to stay, if you were up and coming.

Glad that his father couldn't see the place now, Trace eyed everything around him with discomfort. He was there to track down Dolly's personal maid. Through cross checks he'd found a missing person's report for a maid with Dolly David's address filed by a man named Freddie Meda, the maid's son. Mitchell had already spent the better part of the morning overseeing Schaffer's surveillance team.

Now he stood around with nothing to do, but feel sorry for upsetting Inez earlier that morning. Part of him was still angry with her though. She'd actually talked to Bradley by phone, while law enforcement searched everywhere for him.

CBI technicians meanwhile were busily working on Inez's phone, extracting her last conversation with Stronsky and hopefully connecting her phone to Bradley's movements.

Forty minutes had passed when there was sudden movement. Schaffer and two agents behind him held their guns out straight. Their person of interest had lunged through the back door with a cigarette dangling from his lips. There were no recent photos, only a tip about a skinny dude with a mom who cleaned houses. And the same man never smoked inside, only under the back porch of the Hotchkiss.

"CBI! Hands out so we can see 'em." The barrel of Schaffer's gun faintly touched the man's right temple before the two agents beside him pushed the man flat against the nearest sandstone brick and iron vertical beam.

Trace ran from the garage and across the alley. Two agents followed, ready to stop the guy if he tried to escape. Schaffer's team had already ripped away everything bulging from the man's body, which included a waist pack with phone, keys, and a lighter.

Surrounded, the skinny guy kept moving, wriggling from head to toe, finally collapsing face down into the sandy ground under the porch. But like a lizard, he began to scamper between their legs and kicked up enough clay and sand to create a thick cloud. Emerging from the sand and into the sunlit alley, he established his balance. But Trace and the other two agents had been waiting for him. They tackled him to the ground and piled on top. Holding him was not easy. Sand loosened their grip.

"Who the hell ..." the man shouted.

"Colorado Bureau of Investigation, Asshole! CBI!" Schaffer answered. "We sent you a letter, but you didn't respond. Thought we'd see what was up with that."

Although the man's mouth rested against asphalt, he managed to mumble, "Hadda' walk my dog."

"Funny."

"Ow'n know what the hell you people do."

"Well, first thing we did," Schaffer acknowledged, "was check to your outstanding warrants. If we were interested, we'd turn you over to Denver Police. But we're interested in yo' mama. If you'da read our letter you'da known that, homie."

They let him get to his feet, while he stared back at Schaffer.

Mitchell was uneasy about the way Schaffer had slurred his words to imitate the man's speech.

The man began shouting, "She's GONE, man! I filed papers over a month ago and where was you?"

"Freddie Meda! Calm down!" Mitchell interjected, his voice a beacon of maturity among younger, less veteran agents. "We're here now!"

He was frisked and wrist restraints put on him before agents lifted his skinny frame onto an upside down oil drum at the back basement door. According to records, Freddie was in his late forties. Dressed in a polyester wife beater and equally loose-fitting shorts, skin dipped in petroleum jelly and dredged in sand, he looked like the village idiot who'd been tipped off about agents looking for him. But if Mitchell could read Freddie's body language accurately, it might mean the difference between Freddie staying alive or being shot accidentally.

Mitchell directed agents to make certain no one entered the alley, while he noted that the windows in other buildings were devoid of onlookers.

"You see," Mitchell continued, "you forgot to write down the name of your mother's employer. Police informed you of that by snail mail since you listed no phone. It slows processing."

"Mom wasn't employed. The crazy bitch fired her after her husband died. Left my mom with nothin'. If I'da known her name, I'da beat her senseless. My mom worked for her since before I was born. Only name I knew was "Doll". Shit. After Mom sat upstairs broken up about it, she ups and disappears, right after I left for work one morning," his voice cracked.

"What work, Freddie?"

He turned his head to glare at the agent who asked. "Flippin' burgers, hot dogs, fries out front of that hardware store." He nodded toward a nearby intersection.

"In all the years your mother worked," Schaffer asked, "you're telling us you never knew the name of the family she worked for?"

"Hey, I was young when I first met 'em. My mom was maybe ten, eleven, when she started working for 'the doll' in the Philippines. They brought her here. Don't know what year, 'cause, like I say, I wasn't born yet. Fifties maybe."

"You're Filipino?" Schaffer asked. Mitchell winced.

"American. Born in America." Freddie replied.

Other agents questioned him, but nothing new surfaced. Mitchell finally asked, "What about Colonel David? You meet him?"

Freddie's response ricocheted off the sides of buildings. "NO! Mom worked for his WIFE! Washin', cookin', ironin', stuff like that. NEVER the old man!"

Mitchell scribbled responses into a notebook, noting Freddie's sensitivity to Colonel David's name. Freddie's warrants had mainly involved misdemeanors. But there were a ton of reports naming him a possible 'person of interest.'

"Don't you have a sister somewhere?" Mitchell asked.

Freddie's face wrinkled. "St. Paul. She had a good job. Mom and I was gonna go live with her. Died the same week mom disappeared. Ain't that somethin'?" Freddie's eyes searched the faces of the men standing over him, like he had his own questions to ask.

"How'd she die?" Schaffer asked.

"Fell off her front stoop."

Each man looked skeptically from one to another, but said nothing.

"Show us the room your mom disappeared from."

They lifted him off the oil drum and together walked inside the boarding house, which by all rights, Mitchell observed, should have been condemned.

Ducking to avoid frayed electrical wires, Mitchell yelled, "Halivan! Start the paper work on these code violations. They're jumping out at us."

"Yes, sir."

Halivan descended the stairs, while Schaffer, Mitchell, and three others continued upstairs behind Freddie. A whiff of urine and cilantro at their first landing made Mitchell's intestines quake.

"If you were at work, Freddie, who told you your mom was missing?" asked an agent.

Mitchell spied two grimy faced kids, just inside a barely opened door.

"Next door neighbor." Freddie answered over his shoulder. "Older friend of mom's. They'd bang on the wall with their canes. When mom didn't bang back, she called me at work."

The agent who inquired stopped walking to look at the numbers on the doors.

Freddie looked around, lips moving. Was he counting agents? They followed him through an opened door off the main hall on the fifth floor, when suddenly he stopped and announced that this was the bedroom his mom disappeared from.

Mitchell looked at his notebook again, checking the number on the opened door. "Mailbox said 'Casema Meda'."

"Yeah. People call her Cassie," Freddie responded. He pushed his chest out, as he said it.

Looking at a pink ruffled bedspread, Mitchell asked, "Did she sleep here or at the David's?"

"Weekends, she'd come home. Somebody'd pick her up here every Sunday evening."

"A family member?" Schaffer asked.

"Naw, usually somebody in uniform though: military, nurse, taxi driver's cap. I didn't pay much attention."

"Let me get this straight," Schaffer asked. "Saturdays she'd be dropped here and every Sunday she'd be picked up again?"

"No. Every Friday she'd be brought home here. She didn't like staying there all the time. When my sister married and moved out, we found this place 'cause it was cheaper and just us.

"So five nights out of seven she stayed at the David's home?"

"Right."

"Then what?" Mitchell asked.

"One Sunday, she sat on that bed with her coat and hat on. She'd keep this door open but nobody picked her up. Mom called that doll dame and all she said was she didn't need her any more, 'cause her husband was dead. Mom said she didn't sound like herself, and it didn't make sense. Her husband had been dead and buried for a month or more."

"Try to remember the date. It's important," Schaffer said."

"Got a calendar?"

It took awhile for an agent to offer his phone. Freddie put his finger on a number he liked.

"So how long after that did your mom disappear?" Schaffer asked.

"Next day, Monday. She was here when I left for work."

Meanwhile, Mitchell examined a TV set across from the bed. The other piece of furniture in that room was a dresser with a cracked mirror. Its reflection made the room appear as dingy as the glass. There were no windows.

An adjoining smaller room had an oversized brown sofa against one wall, a small fridge, a sink against another, and a window that faced new construction in downtown Denver.

"You live here, too?" asked Schaffer.

"Yep."

"Where do you sleep?"

"One guess."

"Where's your toilet?"

"Down the hall."

"Man," said Schaffer, "how'd you find this hell hole?"

"Maybe you carry your hell hole with you and don't realize you're looking through it every time you look at other people's places. Ever think of that?"

Mitchell turned his back on their verbal sparring, confident Schaffer knew better than to rough him up in his presence. Eager to block out the rancor that can come with indigence, Mitchell opened bags and dresser drawers. His own family's experience with poverty, though short, kept him forever alert to any misstep, any sliding downhill that might bring him into it again.

A small piece of carpet was neatly folded in one of the dresser drawers, while expensive looking nightgowns and bed jackets were tucked under it. The sleepwear looked like gifts from a family too wealthy to give any thought to their giving, but the carpet was another matter.

Without taking it out, he asked Freddie what it was. His feet were free, but Freddie took baby steps, his wrists still in restraints. Mitchell motioned to Schaffer to remove them.

Freddie still held his hands behind his back and looked from the small carpet to Mitchell and back to the carpet.

Finally he answered, "It's a prayer rug."

Mitchell waited for a better explanation.

"It's Mom's." But a minute later, words poured from him. "Mom was Muslim. Her parents were Muslim. The family she worked for wanted none of it. Mom used to come home from work every day when we was teenagers, 'cause 'the Doll' didn't want us Muslim kids in her home. Mom made us go to the Mosque and we did for a while. But soon as we got taller than she was, we stopped. I'm surprised that rug's still here, 'cause Mom stopped going, too. That was years ago."

Mitchell stared at it. "Think Freddie," he said. "Anything else in these rooms you remember from your days as Muslims?"

They stared at each other until Freddie asked, "You got a warrant?"

Schaffer presented Freddie with the document and to Mitchell's surprise he began reading it.

"What's this 'murder investigation' stuff? That why there's a platoon of you guys? You think mom's been murdered? How? You got her body? Where?" His voice rose an octave. "Were you ever gonna tell me?" He threw the warrant across the room. "Hell! You think I murdered her?"

"We don't know what happened to your mom," Mitchell replied. "But we'll keep looking till we find her." Then he added, "Your mom's employer, was murdered."

Freddie flopped down on his mom's bed and sat quietly, while Mitchell photographed the rug he'd spread open inside the drawer and draped over the sides.

"Who did *that* murder?" Freddie asked. His voice was just above a whisper.

Schaffer had gone to the bathroom down the hall to use it or scope it out. Mitchell wasn't sure which. Deciding he'd taken enough photos on his cell, Mitchell turned around to answer Freddie.

"Don't know. But do you remember my question? Anything else here remind you of your life as a Muslim?"

Still on the bed, Freddie rapidly rubbed his bare arms. Mitchell was impressed by both his lack of trace marks and concern for his mother. When Schaffer returned, Mitchell suggested they leave. If they needed more from Freddie, they knew where to find him.

Schaffer was already in the hallway, when out the corner of Mitchell's eye, he saw Freddie slowly pull back the top of his mother's bedspread. Intuitively, Mitchell raised his left arm, his right hand already on the butt of his holstered gun.

From under the pillow Freddie snatched something.

"FREEZE!" Mitchell shouted, his gun and Schaffer's both pointed straight at Freddie.

He held an eight by ten glossy photo, a head shot of a man with curly black hair, in his hand. "My brother," Freddie said, his frozen arm extended toward Mitchell. "It was taken when he was much younger. I last saw him in '84, when I begged him to stay, but he wouldn't."

Trace and Schaffer exhaled, holstering their guns in slow motion.

"I needed him then," Freddie continued, oblivious to his own near-death experience. "Mom saw him here in Denver around her birthday last year."

Mitchell grabbed the photo and glanced at it before handing it to Schaffer.

"What's his name?" Mitchell asked.

"Don't remember. He changed it lots of times. Whatever name he's using now, it's not Filipino."

The agents stood over Freddie like doctors watching disease spread. Something didn't feel right. Mitchell inched closer, then jerked the pillow all the way off the bed, revealing a small caliber Smith and Wesson, small enough to fit in a woman's purse.

Freddie jumped off the bed. "It's Mom's!"

"Please!" said Schaffer, after he quick-jabbed him in the stomach. Freddie doubled over sideways onto the bed. "Don't insult me."

"You're under arrest," Mitchell said. "We need to know about your brother, your sister, your mother, this gun, your early days in Denver. It'll help us find your mom."

Lying face down, hands behind his back, as Schaffer put restraints on, Freddie muttered into the bedspread. "Her permit to carry is in the purse that went missing too."

Schaffer recited his rights in a loud voice, which brought two agents into the room. When he finished, those agents escorted him downstairs, while Mitchell barked orders over the hall railing.

"Jackson! Get forensics out here. Tell them to pull these two rooms apart. Mackey, knock on doors from here to that hardware store. Make a timeline for Freddie and his mom. And Alvarez! Find out why this neighborhood is so damn quiet."

Mitchell then turned to Schaffer, who walked in circles through the two rooms. Schaffer was good at his job. Mitchell relied on his thoroughness. Yet there was tension between them. Mitchell knew if he hadn't returned from D.C. when he did, his job would probably have been given to Schaffer.

"Freddie smells," Schaffer said. Mitchell stood at the doorway and listened.

"He hated his mother's employer," Schaffer continued. "And he hated being a Muslim. So if he's got all this hatred, why tell us about his brother? Unless perhaps, he was reaching for the gun, realized he wouldn't make it and got lucky with the photo. Guess you know this brother isn't on any of his records. Only a sister. Maybe the brother was born in the Philippines."

"Possible," Mitchell acknowledged. "And it's possible that hatred you described fits the brother better than Freddie. Did you also notice there's no hairbrush, robe, no change of shoes, and no lamp. Her bedsheets smell like soap. I wonder if forensics will find her DNA anywhere? But those ashes on Lookout Mountain had to belong to somebody."

Mitchell wondered to himself why he couldn't find other workers in Dolly's home like a chauffer or gardener. Out loud, Mitchell said, "Alan Bradley is the only other person who would know who else worked in Dolly's home. Hell, he could have killed Dolly and her maid and nobody would be the wiser."

Schaffer stopped pacing. "I don't get it," he finally said. "You're suggesting Bradley's some kind of mass murderer. Yet he was a big man in my dad's era, a CEO of a corporation that did a lot for this country. They built roads, prisons, airports in foreign countries, acted as body guards, provided legal help."

"That's why," Mitchell explained, "he's going to be hard to catch. And let me set you straight about something. Working for Martindale, Inc. isn't the same as working for this country. That company works for its stockholders. Martindale has always had a network of shadow people who act like a hybrid between military and police."

Could Schaffer really understand what he was talking about? Mitchell's phone vibrated. Sheila's name popped up. Why now? Could his plate get more full? Silently, he read her text.

"Can't believe you left D.C. Not leaving Denver 'til we talk. C U @ the Brown."

Holding his heart in his hand, Mitchell looked up and said, "I'm going to be busy for a couple, maybe three hours."

"How do I reach you?" Schaffer asked.

"You can't."

Mitchell was already one flight down but continued talking. "And Schaffer, don't forget. Deliver Dr. Buchanan's phone to her by the end of the day. You'll have to pick it up from headquarters first."

He turned to the agents surrounding Freddie at the front door of the building. "You still here?" he asked.

"We're waiting on an equipped transport vehicle sir. We used unmarked vehicles for this stakeout."

Mitchell jogged to his car, feeling good about the arrest, and uneasy about his destination.

22

Trace Mitchell sat behind the steering wheel of his car in the Brown Palace parking lot wondering why. Hadn't they discussed it enough? He wanted a family damn it! And of course he was being chauvinistic. How could he have known models with a leg blown off still got jobs?

The whole thing was unfair. If *his* leg had been blown to pieces he'd be balancing himself on anything titanium too if it could him get back to work.

"How long you staying?"

Mitchell lifted his head to see the parking attendant standing beside his car. Without a word, he mashed his badge up against his dirty car window, a feeble move, but he did it anyway, knowing that if he stayed, he'd have to pay.

"Give me a minute!" Mitchell hollered, then pretended to be on his phone.

If he didn't watch it, he'd be sitting in the same place for the next two hours, arguing with himself. Yet the Palace Hotel was no place for a state employee to hang out. He reread her text, running his hand through his hair. The day was warm and sunny and he'd never be any younger than he was today. Finally, he opened both his door and his wallet for the attendant.

☙

Every native Denverite knew the Brown Palace was built in 1892 and was one of the first atrium-style hotels ever constructed. Yet he ignored its opulence, remembering the first time he ever saw Sheila Drisco. His mouth had dropped open and Inez told him later that he stared into the girl's blue eyes for the better part of a minute. He wouldn't let that happen again. But when Sheila limped off the elevator, cane in hand, he had to remind himself to stop it.

"Over here," Mitchell called. He could smell the cinnamon in her auburn hair before she reached him.

As she got closer, she asked, "What took you so long?"

"I've got two related homicides, maybe three, and I can't leave my team in the lurch."

"You eat, don't you? How about sleep? Still do that? Or have you changed that much since D.C.?"

"You're pouting again and … and …" He couldn't help himself. His banter was going nowhere. He put his arms around her waist and kissed her, right there in the lobby. The 'aw's' and 'ah's' from bystanders helped spur him on longer until she took over. He backed away slightly. Why did he do that? She kept both the embrace and the kiss going until they heard applause.

Finally, she released him and with her honey coated voice said, "When I kiss a man, I don't want him to ever forget it."

"You don't think I forgot, do you? I was just testing to see if …"

"Seriously," she interrupted, "we need to talk." She'd already grabbed his arm and was leading him toward the bar. When Mitchell realized her intent, he began pushing her back toward the lobby with his own hip.

"There you go pushing your weight around," she said.

"If I didn't, you'd leave me behind."

She stopped where she was. "You don't mean that do you?" Her eyes turned into wet glass marbles.

He gazed into her eyes and did a fast rewind through their past. Perhaps, he thought, she was doing the same. But it had to stop. He took one step backwards, refusing to be pulled into more heartache.

"I'm pregnant," she said, "and I want to have our baby and start our family, right here in Colorado."

For Mitchell, somebody had just sucked the air out of the lobby and left him standing there to fight for his next breath. During what seemed like an hour, he inhaled his weight in air and stuck his hands inside his pockets.

"Well," he uttered. "If you're asking me to marry you because you love me very, very much, well … I'll need some time to …"

She wrapped both her arms around his neck, cane and all. "Of course I love you very, very much and I can't wait to marry you."

An elderly woman with a quivering voice said, "This *is* the Brown. Anybody can afford a room for *one* night!"

They held back their laughter until the elevator door closed. Mitchell put the rest of the world on hold, while his mind fast-forwarded into bliss.

23

EARLY SUMMER, 1998
OUTSIDE KANDAHAR, AFGHANISTAN

Within the hour a blinding sun would peek above the curvature of the earth sending temperatures over the hundred-degree mark. Black sky had already turned deep blue.

Hoping to avoid the upcoming heat on their mutual day off, Abida strode quickly in the cool hours of dawn to keep up with Malik. She stood behind and to his left. Guards, meanwhile, scrutinized their pass to leave the compound for the entire day. Even in darkness they were recognizable. His marksmanship and bravado were known throughout the entire Al Qaeda camp.

Two years ago Abida would have let her body casually touch his to remind him of her existence. Time had changed them both. Now she gave full attention to her own survival since he regularly refused her assistence.

Having passed their first hurdle, they jogged through less populated alleys to avoid two common dangers. Armed men waiting on Kandahar's main streets for agents offering a day's labor would turn belligerent when work was not forthcoming. Another danger came from small wandering groups of religious police ready to enforce Taliban proclamations with a verbal warning, torture, or death.

Abida didn't speak, as they jogged toward the interior city. She was struck dumb by Malik's words. As they traveled, he confessed that for the past two years they'd had no case manager, no communication with CIA, and no safe house; that he'd even recruited a ten-year old boy to carry messages out of Kandahar, but had to kill him when he suspected the boy's duplicity. And now, when they both had intelligence concerning Wanted's imminent plan to bomb American embassies in Africa, there was no one to whom information could be relayed.

Abida stopped walking and threw her bag to the ground before plopping down beside it. Angry, bewildered, she pressed her hands against her face already covered by her burqa and furiously fought back her tears.

A sudden tangled cry to morning prayers stopped his depressing monologue as she wrung her hands in the air and cursed. Although the Taliban from neighboring Pakistan and local villages proclaimed that everyone had to attend a Mosque during prayers, Al Qaeda soldiers, composed of Muslim men from all over the world, were exempt. They prayed once in the morning and again at night in order to spend their entire day in military training against the infidels.

"Get up," he shouted.

She obeyed. No one stood on the street to hear them, but only one suspicious Taliban could get them killed.

Abida knew that Malik had already completed prayers that morning with two other elite soldiers. All three had been given day-long passes before they would depart for Africa by chartered plane.

Early morning wind swept sand across Malik's exposed face. She felt no pity for him. All the daily risks she'd taken to acquire as much information as she could for the benefit of her government meant absolutely nothing now.

Finally, she motioned for him to help her up. Their pace was slower as they approached Kandahar's central bazaar. They intended to buy fresh naan for their day's meal. Then they planned to journey to a park where Al-Qaeda, as well as Taliban and their families, picnicked together. Malik carried his rifle, while Abida carried food and Malik's torn tunic in a bag under her burqa. She intended to repair it while they talked. This was their first opportunity in months to speak alone.

Glaring light poured out into the darkness from behind woven cloth hung at a doorway shielding a baker and his family from customers. Other men baked around an open cauldron. Abida took in deep whiffs of grilled spices, flour, and oil. She felt comfortable speaking her mind amid the bustle of people, the fragrant smells, and loud morning conversations among all the merchants in the bazaar.

"Two whole years you lied to me!" she said. "I should have realized last year when you said you had to meet our contact alone. You said he'd been on the ferry with us. As hard as that was to believe, I refused to think you'd lie to me about anything so important. How can you be so arrogant, so selfish?"

Yet she was also aware of her own culpability. Hadn't she let him assume a traditional Muslim role even on those few occasions when they were alone?

Cloaked from head to toe in a blue cotton burka, Abida's vision was seriously obscured by the latticework cloth that covered her face and pinched the back of her head. At first, she hated wearing it, but later in their mission, taught herself never to cry. Tears rendered her totally blind under such a garment. She reflected as she walked that she no longer hated her clothing, Malik, or anything around her. By forcing herself not to cry, she'd made her emotions less intense.

From time to time, Malik turned around as he walked, sometimes walking backwards. "We're being followed. But that'll stop when we continue past the city."

Abida was not concerned. The park was half a kilometer across desert. Ambush was impossible. Besides, Malik believed himself capable of handling anything.

A half hour later they'd gone far enough. Abida squatted under the shade of several pomegranate trees and released her bag from a rope under her burqa. Malik leaned against one of several straight-sided boulders taller than himself. Always the soldier, he made sure his rifle had a line of sight back to Wanted's compound. In the distance was the Arghandab River and beyond that were mountains that pointed a route to Pakistan.

His AK 47, the rifle Wanted issued to all his soldiers, usually hung over his left shoulder. Guns were the norm for any man traveling through Afghanistan.

"You again fail to see what's important," he said. "When we left Iraq, I knew President Clinton's no-kill order was in effect. He'd hoped to jail Wanted rather than declare war against him. You could seize him, but not kill him. The Executive Branch hoped SEALS would vindicate themselves by dragging him through the streets wherever they found him. And of course, CIA wasn't trusted to do anything that controversial. I was told to wait for specific orders.

"But I had absolutely no intention of waiting. What I didn't know about until I was onboard that plane, were the sanctions CIA would inflict if I killed Wanted as we had planned. See, there was a time when my cousin Amir and I dreamed of his death and planned it together. But Amir's goals changed. That's the kind of boy he was. Even as teenagers, he liked wearing suits and playing bureaucrat. Amir made it plain that any CIA agent or collaborator who saw us anywhere ..."

"Us?"

Malik's eyes looked at her as they grew large, "Yes, us. Anyone could assassinate *us* on the spot and receive a monetary reward with proof of death. If I were as selfish as you say I am, I would have killed Wanted by now and we'd both be dead."

Two years had taught Abida much. Malik could rationalize anything to suit his own purpose. That was a fact. She considered herself a half decent spy even without a partner. And so, with outward composure and inward disdain, Abida ignored Malik's posturing and concentrated on threading her needle. In the same two years, she'd also become aware that they were nothing more than 'rookies' in CIA's vast field of international data gathering.

"You forgot that I was unconscious," she said bitterly. "Uday knocked me out and you never said a word about your fight with Amir, the man most likely to have been assigned as our case manager."

Malik threw his arms in the air. "What can I say? Never liked him."

"You're a fool, Malik, a bully and a fool. We should have aborted this mission eighteen months ago. I can't believe we stayed in Tora Bora on that God forsaken freezing mountain, you knowing all along that we had no way to disclose Wanted's location. Did you think the Company wanted you to make unilateral decisions without me, someone who'd memorized the longitude and latitude of the place? And for all you know, you may have killed your cousin on that plane. What was his name, Amir?"

"It's possible. I made sure he couldn't move when they threw us off."

Abida put her sewing bag on the ground. "Do you hear yourself? You're bragging, even now. You still think this mission is about you and your need for revenge."

He grabbed Abida's throat and with one hand pulled her up off the ground. She was in pain, but not afraid. She knew he wouldn't hit her again. What shocked her the first time he'd smacked her was how fast news of it traveled to the first Madam Wanted and possibly to her husband.

He released his grip. "See the restraint I use. I just hope that no-kill order has been rescinded by now. But whether or not I killed Amir, or whatever he called himself on that flight, that's not why we haven't heard from our employer."

"Spare me your theories."

"Think about it," he said eagerly. "You didn't graduate from an Ivy League College either. Most field operatives are recruited from those kinds of places, the white operatives, that is. They're the people they can trust, people so comfortably rich, so confidently capitalistic, they can't be bribed or seduced. At least that's the thinking of the already wealthy. And then there's the other thing. We're both," he held his fingers up to put quotation marks in mid air, " 'people of color'. Are you going to tell me CIA will trust whatever *we* tell them? Do you see a white man around here, who could verify our story? I bet they think I've embraced Sharia Law by now and that you've just discovered how really bad slavery is. They've probably torn apart everything from the Quran to Negro spirituals somewhere deep in the bowels of Langley, to satisfy themselves they've done enough research to confirm that we're double agents or worse yet, defectors."

"Stop it!"

"They're not looking for us. If we get back, we'll be locked up for years."

Abida put her hands against the cloth that covered her ears. This wasn't the first time he'd said these things and it wasn't the first time she'd analyzed the possibility that he was right. "I don't want to hear this. You've got your own agenda. CIA needs to know what we know. And we need to get out of here so we can tell it."

"How far do you think we'll get? We're in the middle of a kill zone."

"Well, you're out of here. You get to travel to Africa!" She couldn't hide her resentment.

Malik took a deep breath, "Time out! Let's not do this."

She said nothing. His sudden sensitivity was demeaning. She pricked her finger with the needle she was using. Being left on her own did scare her, but only a little. She'd thought about being left behind thousands of times. Malik sprawled on the ground next to her. A long while passed before they spoke again.

"I don't think Wanted suspects me," he finally whispered, "but the American Embassy in Dar Es Salaam was the best place we could have escaped to. I'd even cultivated a friendship with a tribal leader in Western Afghanistan, who may have helped us. When Wanted revealed his plan to bomb that embassy, I almost shit in my pants. Did he intuit my plan to escape or does he trust me more deeply than I could have realized? I don't know."

Abida stopped sewing again. She was convinced Malik would never become a team player or even understand the options she could have provided him. Several times she'd thought of killing him, of making some sorrowful excuse to Langley about him being shot in the line of duty, so she could continue her career in a different international arena. She had no doubt Malik had thought of doing the very same to her.

Yet there were the times she felt sorry for him. He didn't know *how* to respect women. He'd likely never felt empathy. Certainly he'd never talked to a woman about sex. He cried when they first had intercourse, saying that until then, he'd raped every woman he'd ever had sex with. Why CIA hired him was a mystery to her. Maybe he would say the same of her. Neither his race nor ethnicity could have been the sole reason he was hired. And yet perhaps he was right, they were both government guinea pigs, put in harm's way to see what would happen next.

"Wanted is cagey," Malik continued. "Whenever anybody arrives at the camp, he absorbs their facial expressions. I've watched him do it. First, he looks for recognition. I've worried that someone I know from Brooklyn will come here, donate money to him, and recognize me."

Abida smiled. "My life was so dull," she said. "No chance of that ever happening to me."

Malik gathered sand in his large sunburned hand and let it fall through his fingers. It wasn't like him to share his thoughts and she had learned not to share her own with him. She decided not to share her small adventure from a few months ago.

It had started with a pair of eyes that glared at her from time to time. They had been frightening eyes in the beginning, because she'd seen them before but couldn't place where. They belonged to an older man who came twice for jihad. From time to time he'd bring a friend whose face was older and more expressive. She'd asked Pakeesah about the two men. She told her that they were Wanted's close friends and highly skilled in warfare.

Pakeesah had turned out to be her most reliable source of intelligence about Wanted. Pakeesah also explained why learning the names of Wanted's soldiers was silly because many changed their names as soon as they arrived in Afghanistan.

When Abida finally realized that the first set of eyes had actually resembled those from a childhood nightmare in a grocery store, she no longer feared the man. And miraculously, he never appeared again.

"I do have fears," Abida said, as she sewed.

"Yes, I know. You're afraid I won't return from this mission," he responded, "that Wanted will hang me, and that you'll become a sex slave."

She reminded herself that he couldn't see her surprised look behind her burqa.

"You wonder," he continued, "how I know what you're thinking even when I can't see your body. You've forgotten I'm American. Compared to men here, I know more about their mothers, their wives, their sisters, their aunts than they'll ever know."

The faint sound of guns against ammunition belts interrupted them. Malik was already on both feet, cocking his rifle with noisy exuberance. Abida's directional hearing was not good beneath her burka, but she understood Malik's quickness. Mentally, she'd rehearsed this scene often over the past year, deciding never to reveal her most important decision to Malik. If he were ever killed, she'd forget her CIA training and do whatever was necessary to be killed as well. She had some time ago considered it an insurance policy against the possibility that Malik might be right about the Company's attitude toward her.

Two young Taliban soldiers ran from behind the boulders. Their sudden appearance took Abida's breath away. One carried a rifle close to his face in the same way Malik held his. The other young man wore a whip, his right hand resting on its grip.

These were the religious police that her best friend and ally, Pakeezah, had warned her of. Ever since that last morning in Khartoum when Abida persuaded Madam Wanted to take them both, Pakeezah always did her best to warn Abida of anything that might create danger for a woman with a husband away from home so frequently.

Pakeezah said she feared the religious police herself for their sudden irrational actions and had recently warned her, as they bathed together in the *hammam*, that such police sought superiority over Al Qaeda soldiers by finding fault with their women. No one could see the rivulets of water that trickled down Abida's temples. But could they hear her heart pound?

Following Malik's lead, she danced across the sand, staying on his left. They formed a circle, each waiting for the other to move. Finally, Malik asked in his best Pashto, "Are you from Taliban headquarters?"

The man with the gun stepped forward slightly, poking the end of his rifle at the ground "What's in that bag?" the youth asked.

There was no hesitation on Malik's part. He ignored the young man's question and repeated his own, while moving his rifle from one Taliban to the other.

The man holding the rifle speared the sand with his nozzle, then lifted the tunic off the ground. A needle and thread swung from the garment while the garment swung from the nozzle.

"You are a tailor." His statement was directed toward Abida.

"My tunic," Malik replied, "was ripped in combat."

"Women are not to sew in public." said the young man with the whip.

Abida's heart pushed against her chest just as hard as the young men's eyes pressed against her. Though she'd paid little attention to the Taliban, their decree banned tailors, not wives. There were to be no more shops run by tailors. Only her brain screamed out what little she knew of the decree. It had nothing to do with wives, as she had learned it. But she knew better than to speak.

In her nervousness or perhaps because of it, her eyes watered. Dust formed near the gates of Wanted's compound and moved in their direction. It was all she could see. Such configurations were usually caused by speeding vehicles. Abida wondered if she'd still be alive by the time the vehicle, assuming it was friendly, reached them.

"I'll return my wife to the compound," Malik answered, lowering his gun. "She is not a tailor, but I'll see she stays home to sew."

Abida was surprised at Malik's reaction. He'd never shown any ability to back down before.

The young man with the whip turned toward Malik, as if Malik was very important, and said, "Your words mock Mohammad."

Those were the last words that man spoke. Malik had always been faster than his massive physique suggested. His single rifle report could be heard across the vast desert.

The other Taliban held his rifle in both hands while his compatriot's body fell. "You are dead!" he finally said to Malik.

Malik did not lower his rifle, but said, "I have been dead for a very long time. Don't bother to tell me that this dead man has vengeful brothers, because I am a vengeful brother, who has not yet had his vengeance."

Abida fell to her knees in the sand, frantically grabbing the strewn contents of her bag. Carefully, she stuck the needle in cloth, then stuffed everything else inside, when she heard the second shot and then a third. Both shots startled her. She prayed it was not Malik who'd become a victim.

Slowly she rose to her feet and saw both Taliban on their backs.

"What have you done?" Abida cried.

"Preserved our family's honor," he said, grabbing the extra rifle.

They started running back to the compound, but had to stop, exhausted after only a few paces. The temperature was well over one hundred degrees outside the shade of the boulders and pomegranate trees. Waves of radiant heat rose from the ground making it difficult to determine distances.

A truck screeched to a sudden stop beside them. As dust subsided, Malik recognized his compatriots seated in the front of the cab. Climbing onto the back bed of the truck with Abida, Malik tried to explain what had happened to two dead Taliban soldiers they were leaving behind. Abida felt dizzy, the heat of the day drowning her in sweat. Yet, she felt she'd forgotten something. What was it? She couldn't ask Malik. He hadn't stopped talking since they got into the truck.

Five soldiers seated in back refused to listen at first. They'd been entrusted with one mission, to drive Malik and two others to the plane taking them to Africa. Now, with misgivings, they would return Malik's wife to the compound first.

When the truck got to the gates, they helped Abida down and immediately sped off. Malik stood up on the floor of the truck.

Without sound, his lips said, "Saalum Alaikum my love." And with his powerful right arm, threw his water canteen at her feet. She stood numb, neither scared nor sad over all that had just happened. After all, there were other maids and Pakeezah who could help her.

But there was no kiss goodbye. Perhaps it would have been sacrilege to kiss a man who'd been dead for as long as he said he had been. Why think of him at all? She'd do better planning her own escape.

Nothing good could come from this day. She felt the ache of catastrophe throughout her whole body. Taking a step forward to pick up the canteen, her legs buckled. As she fell, she caught sight of blood soaking the hem of her burqa. The third bullet. She'd meant to ask Malik about it, before her world went black.

24

END OF SUMMER, 2009
THE HIGHLANDS, DENVER

Approximately eight minutes after Trace Mitchell left the Hotchkiss Building, a short series of bass notes vibrated buildings throughout the entire block. The explosion was both deafening and fiery. Arson investigators would later determine that an incendiary device had been placed on the roof directly over Freddie Meda's apartment.

There was a sense of quiet just after the explosion as people realized they were conscious. Smoke rose while airborne debris and dust continued to fall. Children cried in slow motion and adults screamed the names of their children with agony in their throats. Sirens came much later.

Exiting the building at the time of the explosion, Freddie and Schaffer were thrown off the front porch, while flames crackled loudly, engulfing the top floor. A dad and two sons jumped from a window on the third floor to the porch, which miraculously held their weight long enough for them to scurry off. Two agents, four children, and three adult residents sustained minor injuries. Other residents requiring oxygen, blood, or an ER were taken to various area hospitals. Fifty-five minutes after the explosion nothing of the Hotchkiss Building remained standing.

Freddie was unconscious and left by ambulance in the custody of Denver Police. Schaffer, a bandage applied to his forehead, where glass hit him, left the scene in his own car anxious to report to headquarters. Remaining agents, in good condition, assisted first responders in search of the missing. Onlookers appeared from nowhere.

The explosion was opportunity knocking on Schaffer's door. He ran to his desk, once he reached his office, zealously ready to look more like a CBI supervisor than Mitchell. One thing he had to do while Mitchell was away was find Freddie's brother. It didn't make sense to him that Alan Bradley, an outstanding and loyal American, could be a murderer. It was time to show CBI just what he could do.

*

"What day is it?"

Schaffer heard Freddie's question from the hallway, so he pushed the hospital room door wide open and walked in. He carried two dog-eared folders in one hand. His own bandage was still attached to his forehead. A uniformed policewoman with skin the color of strong black coffee, kept staring at it from her seat.

Pulling off his bandage while pulling out his badge, Schaffer spoke to her as if she were his subordinate, "Come back here in half an hour. And don't go far."

She got up from her chair and left without saying a word.

A short physician darted through the open door and spoke loudly as he leaned over the prisoner. "You may experience a headache and problems hearing over the next twenty-four hours but all that should gradually go away. You've suffered a concussion and we sedated you long enough to get x-rays and determine the extent of brain swelling. Nothing was broken, only bruised."

"What day is it?" Freddie asked again. His eyelids fluttered.

"Same day," Schaffer shouted back, "but it's evening and dark out." Turning to the doctor, he said, "Thanks, I'll take it from here."

He expected the same rapid adherence to his orders that he got from the policewoman. But the doctor hesitated, then said to Freddie, "I'll be back in fifteen minutes." Turning to Schaffer, he said, "He'll need to rest then."

Schaffer made a point of slamming the door behind the man, in a show of superior jurisdiction, then took out his phone and fiddled with it before propping it atop a rolling table.

"I've been busy collecting data on this brother of yours. Had to get a court order to open his juvenile records. Thought this was just another rabbit hole you people like to lead investigators down. You know the kind I mean, 'My brother made me do it, my mother made me do it, my sister made …' You know the kind of hole I mean."

Freddie's eyes remained shut.

"But alas, we discovered you were telling us something we didn't know," Schaffer added.

"Morton," Freddie responded. His eyes were still closed. "That was his name originally. Morton Meda."

"Little late. But let's see if I can get your help verifying what else I discovered."

Freddie's eyes opened slightly. "Sure. I want to cooperate."

Schaffer spread the contents of a folder across the table. "Police picked up Morton several times between the ages of nine and fifteen. We have your mother's signature on several of those reports, but we couldn't find a birth certificate for Morton or a single place where your mom listed him as one of her children. There's a social worker's report here where it looks like she's listing three children rather than two and then Morton's name is erased. See?"

Schaffer held a smudged card up so that Freddie could see, too. "Why's that?" Schaffer asked.

Freddie squinted. "Morton's my brother, all right. Half brother. Born in the Philippines. My sister and I were born in Denver. We all have the same mother and growing up I assumed we had the same father. But, turns out, I never knew my dad. My sister Grace did. She always remembered everything. God, I'm sorry she's dead."

Schaffer's eyes never left Freddie's face. He'd already confirmed the death of Freddie's sister's and for a second time wondered about it being an accident. More importantly, could he wrap this Dolly-Stronsky case up singlehandedly? It had only been a dream until Mitchell told him he couldn't be reached. If he could leave Mitchell in the dust to fiddle with his old lady friend and liberal causes Schaffer could finally get the job he'd trained for his whole life. He pulled his chair closer to the bed. There was an outside chance Freddie and his brother were somehow linked to Dolly's incredible story about her granddaughter. All he had to do was keep Freddie talking.

"Come on, Freddie, stay awake," he urged. "We know Morton was sent back to the Philippines when he was fifteen. Your mom couldn't handle him anymore."

Freddie was breathing hard, but his eyes were shut tight. "All I know is mom wanted him to walk us to school, but he'd disappear. He never did what she asked. But I'm talkin' kindergarten, fourth grade maybe."

"So you don't know who raised your brother when he was in the Philippines or what he did there?"

"He lived with Mom's brothers. I can tell you she cried over what they were teachin' him."

"How did she know what they were teaching him?"

"Morton wrote letters in the beginning and she'd cry while she was readin' 'em to us. Grace told me Mom didn't read everything out loud. He'd write about using rifles and grenades and killing people."

"What happened to those letters, Freddie?"

"How the hell would I know?"

"He came back, didn't he?" Schaffer asked. "To the States, I mean."

"Yeah. I was twenty-somethin'. We was gonna hang together. He was thirty-somethin'. Guess I was hopin' for too much. He'd be one way one time and another way another time. Anyway, it didn't work out. Said he had to leave Colorado. Said he wanted to be a jihadist."

Schaffer began shuffling through papers in the other folder.

With his eyes closed Freddie said, "That was around 1984."

"He killed some people then didn't he?" Schaffer asked.

"I don't know. Police weren't lookin' for him. He talked jibberish mostly. Couldn't take him seriously."

"You mean," Schaffer asked, "he spoke a foreign language?"

"No. I mean, yes. I mean, no."

"He told you what he'd done, didn't he?" Schaffer asked.

Freddie's face scrunched in on itself. Tears rolled down his cheeks. "No!" he answered. "He was talking nonsense."

"In 1984 Denver had two horrendous murders. The FBI stepped in. CBI assisted. Before my time. They never found the murderer. Both victims were homeless and both were beheaded. What was Morton doing, practicing?"

Schaffer waited silently for an answer, his mind racing through the possibilities, while Freddie softly sobbed. He reached over to stop his phone from recording, then punched additional numbers into it. His division chief picked up.

"Will you be in your office in twenty minutes?"

"You got something, Schaffer?" she asked, "'cause I'm about ...'"

"I'll be there. It's important."

Schaffer put his phone in his pocket and continued to watch Freddie's tears roll from his closed eyes and down his neck. He watched with the same contempt he had for any murderer. Freddie might have fooled Mitchell into thinking he was a righteous citizen, but Schaffer knew better. He knew the Freddie's of the world and their families had no business in this country in the first place.

"Here's the thing, Freddie, when I said 'He came back, didn't he?' I was also asking about a time more recent than 1984. You said your brother was here around your mother's birthday. Remember telling us that?" Schaffer leaned over the bed, totally unafraid of someone whose feet were shackled to the frame. But he backed off a little. The antiseptic smell of hospital cleanser and the bag containing Freddie's sweaty clothes slowly hit him.

Freddie had quieted down and answered, "If I knew where the hell he was, I swear to God I'd tell ya."

"I believe you," Schaffer replied, "because I think that's why you're being so cooperative now. You think he murdered your mom, don't you?"

Freddie's eyes opened all the way and looked directly into Schaffer's.

Schaffer flashed a smile at him. Gothcha, he thought. "Could he have blown up your building, trying to kill you too?" he asked.

Freddie began to bawl loudly between erratic breaths. A machine in the corner of the room began beeping loudly. It startled Schaffer, unaware Freddie was hooked up to a machine.

"Why'd your brother come back here?" Schaffer asked quickly. "Did he become a Jihadist? Was he ever in the Middle East?"

A nurse's aide opened the door, left it open, and ran off to find somebody else. Schaffer knew his minutes left with Freddie were in the single digits.

"How old would your half brother be now? In his fifties, sixties? What does he want here?"

Freddie's watery red eyes stared in Schaffer's direction. His breathing was as loud as his sobs.

The doctor and a nurse appeared, the latter holding a needle.

"That's all for tonight, Agent," the doctor said. "He'll sleep until morning."

Schaffer scooped up the papers he came in with, hurrying to keep his appointment. Before leaving, he addressed the policewoman who stood in the hall. She squeezed a Vogue magazine tightly under her arm.

"I'll take that," Schaffer said, snatching it from her and throwing it down the corridor. "You'll need to stay alert. Only law enforcement goes in. Hold up any and all hospital staff until you've double-checked each badge. Be a shame, if he died on your watch."

25

Inez sat in the back seat of Sophie's cab wearing the very jacket she'd refused to wear earlier that morning. Now the sun was down. The air was cool. She had a reason to wear it now other than to hide under it.

Life was good. Inez hadn't said that in a while. Not only did she have a mission but an immediate destination for which she had dressed casually and it was after dark. Thank God for the little things.

How grown up Lodo had become. She enjoyed imagining that its streets still vibrated with countless cattle herds, as they did in the early 1800s. When she first moved to Denver she'd sworn she experienced ghost smells: fresh blood, slaughtered meat, and pungent summer mud surrounding Union Station. Opening the cab's back window, Inez inhaled downtown's new smells, a gust of musk, oregano infused cheese, and bourbon.

They sped toward Auraria's Campus, home to four separate institutions of higher learning, which included the University of Colorado and Metropolitan State University. Arriving on campus brought her back to her senses and opened the pit at the bottom of her stomach. Bringing Kadija home also meant carrying a gun in her purse and hoping Bradley would say yes to her offer.

Yet he wasn't the only egg in her basket. A former CSU roommate of Sampati Jagjit had contacted her on Facebook just before she left home. He offered to call or meet her in person with news about his friend.

"There's the library ahead," Inez announced. "Let me out here. Since I'm early I'll walk the rest of the way. You find a parking space that looks like you're here to pick up a passenger."

"On it! You care if this Bradley guy sees me?"

"Heavens no. He ought to know an old lady like me isn't going out at night alone."

Inez had already opened the back door and stepped onto the curb. "Wish me luck," she hollered.

Wearing a loose fitting jacket, a tailored blouse, a pleated skirt, and black tights, made her feel as confident as she had every day of her career. She clutched the strap of her crossover purse, while students ran semicircles around her on their way to meet deadlines and other obligations she once shared with a younger generation.

Having carefully walked the gauntlet she rested on a cement slab in front of the library. Twenty to thirty other students milled around the steps smoking, smooching, reading, or ogling. A cornucopia of nationalities, ethnicities, and ages surrounded her and she loved every minute of it. One thing surprised her. Only one other female there besides herself wore a jacket on a night that was turning nippy.

She also noticed Sophie who stood in front of the Fine Arts building. Where could she have found a place to park? Sophie pretended to talk on her phone, or maybe she wasn't pretending.

Trace Mitchell had not returned her phone. But that was okay. She often forgot to use the dumb thing. Besides, she told herself, looking at her wristwatch, she didn't need a phone to tell time. 7:00 pm exactly. Alan Bradley was late.

Both women settled into their respective vantage points, when Inez spied two cars, one black, one green, inching along the side of the library, in front of posted signs that read, "No Vehicles Beyond This Point." Pedestrians grudgingly moved aside to let the cars through. Their windows were dark, but Inez was certain Alan Bradley would jump out of one of them.

Occasionally she looked at Sophie who seemed not to notice her and that, Inez hoped, was good acting.

The door opened on the opposite side of the first vehicle and a young man in a military uniform jumped out, closed the door, and sprinted toward her. With one white gloved hand outstretched, he smiled and said, "You need to come with me."

As he spoke, the second car pulled around the corner and stopped behind the first.

"Why is that young man?" she asked without moving from the slab. Inez read "ROTC" on a tag pinned to his uniform and thought him slightly too old for that.

The man leaned closer, blocking her view of Sophie altogether. His smile was gone. "You want Alan Bradley to help you or not?" he whispered.

Inez processed the question instantly. If she was dumb enough to show up, she was dumb enough to go with him. Both cars were in front of her. She stood, but the man was still bent over. He put a hand on top of her head and gently pressed down. "Our car is very low," he said. "Don't want you to hurt yourself."

He had the sound of reason about him. So Inez took the necessary step in the same bent over fashion, but noticed, with some difficulty due to all the foot traffic around the car, that the young woman with the jacket she had noticed earlier was entering the second car. Defiantly, Inez stood up tall just before entering the car to look in Sophie's direction. She was no longer in front of the Fine Arts Building. What could that mean?

"Oops," the man said, pressing her head down harder. "Easy does it."

In no time, she'd been pushed inside and was sitting next to another man in military uniform. They were boys really, freshmen in college, she thought.

Somewhat surprised, she looked from one clean-shaven face to the other and got a glimpse of the driver through his mirror. Alan Bradley was not in the car.

"How far are we going?" Inez asked. "And where's Bradley?" No one said a word. "Did I make a mistake? He is going to meet with me, isn't he?"

Her questions were met with nose-in-the-air silence. Her blood thrashed against her veins.

"So you're not going to talk to me? That isn't very friendly! What must your mothers be thinking of you now?"

The driver snickered.

"There's a good boy," Inez said. "Why would anyone try to scare an old lady?"

"Sorry m'am," said the driver. "We're just volunteers sent to drive you to Mr. Bradley."

The man seated behind him smacked the back of his head.

"Ow. Quit," the driver ordered and rubbed his head, swerving the car slightly.

"Well then," said Inez, "I'm willing to do my part and stay quiet."

She'd learned something about Bradley from these young men. Anyone who could outsmart security guards at the mall, prevent his own arrest, have the means to get Kadija out of Afghanistan, could also employ people to help him. If she and Bradley were going to bring Kadija home, she'd better stop being so jumpy.

She watched city streets zoom past and took a deep breath. The driver weaved through traffic doing over 50 mph on Speer Blvd. In no time, they reached Colorado Blvd. and on to Monaco. She could see Interstate 25 beside them. Would their destination be in the Denver Tech Center or onward to Colorado Springs?

When their wheels screeched at the next turn, it forced the driver to slow down on a winding forested driveway that headed uphill. At the top was an eight story building surrounded by a parking lot with fifty or more cars parked in it. They stopped at the front door of the building and, in the dark, Inez could read the sign on the roof, Metro State University in DTC.

Alan Bradley suddenly stood beside the car's door, while each young man got out and saluted him.

"You look surprised, "Dr. Buchanan." Bradley was smiling as he spoke. "Not many people realize that most colleges and universities nowadays have more than one campus." Bradley put his hand inside the car for her to grasp.

"I do feel stupid," Inez responded. Yet she had remembered his mention of the Auraria Campus. Was he deliberately being deceptive? She grabbed his hand for support.

"Well, you're not alone." His smile was gone. "Many people make that same mistake. I confess I relied on your misperception to assure myself you'd be alone."

Inez looked around, hoping to see the green car that the woman with the jacket entered. But no other car appeared. Inez suddenly realized it was meant to be a decoy. And what had happened to Sophie?

As soon as the door of the black car was shut, the young men sped away in the same direction they'd come. Inez felt alone for the first time. Had Trace sensed something about Bradley she hadn't seen? Was that why he wanted him arrested?

"I wonder," said Inez, "if you could do me a big favor? Would you let me use your phone for a minute? I need to make sure my ride knows where to pick me up."

"I've already taken care of that. Those nice young men know they'll be returning for you once I give them a call. Besides, I don't have a phone. The last thing I want is to be tracked by law enforcement."

She was furious. Trace had been right. All she was doing was putting herself and others in danger. Once again she'd arrogantly decided she knew best. She'd made several bad decisions lately and this, she realized, might put the others to shame.

26

Pipes, hammers, pounding. From a garage. Horns honking. Gears yanked into position by someone inside an aging truck, awakened her. Where had she been? She could see nothing, but textureless gray. Her blue cloth was gone. Nothing blue covered her eyes. Her legs were stretched out flat against what? The heels of her bare feet rested on metal perhaps. Why didn't her burka cover her toes? Slowly, as if floating on a cloud, she eased into nothingness.

How long had the nothingness lasted? Jostling against the truck's bed, she began to wonder why the putrid air around her didn't move. Was she, in fact, inside a covered truck. Who was with her? She could feel them all around her. Still she saw nothing. Were her eyes taped shut? Nothingness eased over her again, even as she strained to move her eyelids.

Her right shoulder. In the dark. She could feel her right shoulder pinned down against the metal bed of the truck. By what? Still on her back, her feet uncovered, it was a sweaty hand, she thought, that pressed her shoulder against the metal bed. She heard nothing but breathing, and not her own. Breathing and a motor that sputtered occassionally, before everything faded into nothingness. And then the pain began. Her leg. It burned.

I fear no evil because thou art with me, her mind repeated over and over again, until she heard it. The engine stopped.

"She'll be dead soon. Lost a lot of blood. We should have turned this truck around and made her walk inside." It was a young, raspy male voice speaking in Pashtu.

"I disagree," said another. She couldn't hear what was said next. They mumbled in the distance and she thought she heard her name once. 'Abida.' There it was again. They knew her name. Were they walking away?

There was no movement only the pain in and around her leg. An entire layer of sound had disappeared. She tried to open her mouth and couldn't. Taped shut. Oh, God! Her brain began screaming inside. She twisted her head from side to side against the bottom of the truck until someone pulled her head up by her hair and slammed it against the floor. Again and again her head was savagely thrust against the floor until blessed nothingness consumed her once again.

I ... I hope I can still show them, she said to herself, *that my country 'tis of Thee, sweet land of liberty.*

Male voices rose slowly, then argued loudly around her. They spoke jibberish and some Pashtu. An argument ensued for what seemed like hours. Occassionally, she thought she heard them say the word 'pregnant' and wondered if Malik had told them before he left for Africa. And then the noise stopped. She knew she'd heard the words 'blood,' 'shot,' and 'explosive' many times. But she couldn't lift her head anymore. These men, she thought, they didn't sound like Al Quaeda soldiers and wives she'd lived with. Then nothingness again that pushed her away from the noise. The continuing argument had become part of the nothingness and the ever-present background noise.

Suddenly rough angry hands, came from all directions. They grabbed her skin and ripped the clothes from her body. Those hands pulled at her arms until she was sitting up. She sat on the floor of the truck with men grabbing her breasts and tugging on straps between her legs, while she remembered every last one of her mother's magical incantations. How easily they had worked to make her disappear. All she had to do now was to throw her mind into her past and it could happen again.

A very tiny voice buried deep inside her began to chant. *My ene-mies die for their country. Make my enemies die for their country, not for mine. Help me die for my country. Not theirs.*

Someone from behind ripped the tape off her eyes. She looked through blurred eyes at angry men, about five of them. They sur-rounded her. They were seated on two sides on wooden benches in-side a canvas covered truck. As she looked down, she saw it. She wore a vest covered in wires and sticks of dynamite.

A man beside her, who held her left arm up for a better look at the vest, dropped her arm from his grip. Instead of her hand falling to the floor of the truck, it landed on the man's hip, where a gun handle rested in its holster. How fortuitous she thought for a fraction of a second as she pulled the gun from its leather cradle and fired.

27

Mitchell's phone vibrated atop the nightstand. He rolled to one side, opened one eye, snatched his phone, and rolled back. Unperturbed, he noted this wasn't his apartment. And there she was, the future Mrs. Mitchell. God! He was still at the Brown.

"'Lo," Mitchell said, clearing his throat. The clock on the stand read 7:00 pm.

"You ain't here in forty-five minutes," said a voice with a barmaid's raunchiness, "start countin' your minutes on administrative leave."

Mitchell swallowed spit.

"On your way over, stop by Swedish. Bring your fuckin' report on Freddie Meda. Already heard Schaffer's. I need YOUR take on that explosion. Can't believe you're AWOL. Is this what I get for kicking you up a notch? Come in here after 8:00 pm, and I'll show you what a downhill ride looks like."

The call ended, but in that short time, he had his pants and shirt on, though not zipped or buttoned. He barely kissed Sheila's forehead.

What explosion! What the hell was Jefa, talking about? Was Freddie in a hospital? He spun his radio dial to as many news stations as he could think of while speeding down Broadway. Listening to KOA he thought about calling Inez. She was the best researcher he knew. She'd know about the explosion. But there wasn't time. And there was no sense letting colleagues know how far off the reservation he'd been. He'd wait till he got inside the hospital to call Schaffer.

⅏

Mitchell had already pinned his badge to his breast pocket, not wanting to waste time explaining who he was and his mission to find Freddie.

"Schaffer!" he shouted into his phone.

"Yeah, man."

"What's Freddie's room number?"

"Don't remember."

The answer almost pushed Mitchell against the nearest wall. "So, where the hell are you?" Mitchell asked.

"Home."

That had to be a lie. Confused, Mitchell put his cell back in his pocket. Nothing made sense. The nurse returned. Her eyes never moved from the cards in her hands.

"I swear to you, this room is still assigned to Freddie Meda," she explained. "And there's no record of any change. I even remember a policewoman standing inside this very room with Freddie."

It was dark outside, way too bright inside, and he felt like he'd just stepped into the Bates Motel. "Where's his doctor?" Mitchell asked.

"Signed out for the evening. Mr. Meda was given a sedative that would have kept him asleep the entire night. He's not ambulatory."

"Okay then," Mitchell said, staring first at an empty bed and then back at the nurse, who seemed equally stymied. "Get his doctor in here now. Then find the last nurse, the last nurse's aide, and the last custodian, who was here when Freddie was. Tell them to meet me in this room ASAP. How can I page your security guard?"

She showed him how and left.

Mitchell put his plastic gloves on before picking up the phone, thought better of it, put the phone down, opened the doors to the bathroom and closet instead. Nothing drew his attention. He walked into the hallway and stopped the first nurse he saw.

"Where's the closest exit?"

She thrust her arms in the air and twirled in a circle as she pointed at the sign.

"Wasn't expecting tinkerbell," he muttered, as he tore off his gloves and headed toward the sign.

"Aw, was I too sarcastic? Your fire station crew wrote us up for bogus violations," said the angry nurse. "Aren't you with those people? Didn't you help carry that cot with the dummy on it?"

Mitchell paused at the doorjamb. "Where'd they go?"

"Down those stairs."

Mitchell leapt down one flight and stopped abruptly at the sight of a wall phone. He got a guard on the line and identified himself.

"You in the lobby?" Mitchell asked.

"Sure am."

"See anybody on a gurney, a cot? Anybody look like fire department personnel?"

"What you want is out front. You want me to …"

"Lock the front doors. Don't let anyone in or out. Call Englewood police. Describe that group. They're kidnappers. Tell them that!"

Mitchell dropped the receiver and jumped six steps down. On the next landing, he heard gunshots. When he reached the lobby floor, he dropped to one knee and removed the ankle gun strapped to his thigh, kept for emergencies. With his free hand he pushed a number on his cell phone and with his knee, slowly pried back the door to the lobby. Several frantic people ran through it. Mitchell spoke loud over their epitaphs.

"Mitchell to Chief. 7:45 pm. I'm pinned down by gunfire, Denver police were notified. CBI needs jurisdiction. Send mobile lab to Swedish. I'll need two more agents to search for Freddie. He's been kidnapped or dumped. Hospital personnel can't find him. He could be on a fire truck."

When he heard another gunshot, he stopped talking. An engine started up. Still in a crouched position, he eased forward into an empty lobby. He was in time to see the fire engine drive away.

"And put a tail on the fire truck leaving Swedish now." Mitchell put his phone back into his pocket and took in the unobstructed view through the glass entrance.

On the ground outside lay two bodies. One was a uniformed guard, the other body was covered in a blanket. He dashed through revolving doors to snatch the blanket away. A dead woman in a police uniform stared back at him. She had a missing nameplate and the emblem embroidered on her sleeve said, New York City Metropolitan Museum Association. Mitchell was astonished. The uniform did resemble that of the Denver Police. Two different nurses on Freddie's floor had made a mistake about her being a policewoman. And something about her made her look more African than African-American. Had she been part of the crew of kidnappers? If so, why was she dead?

Mitchell looked at the other body lying face down on the cement. Another guard had rushed toward it. He stood over his dead colleague and took out his cell phone as paramedics swooped in and got to their knees quickly. Which guard had he talked to on the phone? And did it matter now?

An Englewood Police car stopped at the curb and men got out to inspect the scene. Mitchell wanted to ask them about the officer but remembered his instructions to the nurse upstairs. He hurried to the elevator hoping to reach Freddie's room before it got crowded. Sirens approached the hospital as he arrived on Freddie's floor. Three or four white-jacketed personnel moved swiftly through the hallway, all talking at once.

Mitchell pushed past others to stand inside the room himself. "Who here saw Freddie within the last two hours?" he hollered.

"I did," a man yelled back. He wore a white t-shirt under a white lab coat. Everyone else slowly eased out into the hallway.

"Stay on this hall," Mitchell ordered. Then he put his eyes back on the man who had spoken up. "You his doctor?"

"Yes. You the agent who said I had to come back up here?"

"Yes."

"Hmm," said the doctor. "There was a different guy here earlier. Thought very highly of himself."

Mitchell nodded knowingly. Sometimes Schaffer's tilted head seemed to say he was sorry he'd been born rich, but aristocracy was just that. Rich.

"Freddie Meda was brought in earlier today," said the doctor. "Had a mild concussion. He was a scared man and overly dramatic for the benefit of that other agent. Thought he could do with a rest, a reprieve from his interrogation, so I made sure he had a good twelve to fifteen hours sleep before he was locked up."

"You must be new here," Mitchell suggested, getting his notebook from his pocket.

"Not that new."

"Well," Mitchell began, "your confession troubles me because if it turns out you're even indirectly responsible for this fiasco, I'll see you're prosecuted to the fullest extent of the law. I don't know why it takes some people so long to learn that it's not law enforcement you can't trust. It's the people who commit crimes you can't trust."

Mitchell watched the doctor dash from the room quicker than birds poop in flight. In walked Schaffer as the doctor left.

"See you had my back just then," Schaffer said with a weak smile.

"Oh, you heard that? Don't know why people take us for bastards just based on our looks," Mitchell replied.

Schaffer sat in the only chair in the room and asked, "Any leads on Freddie?"

"I bet he's on the fire engine that left here. Is that chair where you interviewed him?" Mitchell asked.

"What do you mean?"

"I mean I missed your report."

Schaffer looked around the room and said. "Well, you weren't here."

"I said you couldn't reach me, you didn't, and I thank you for that."

Schaffer put a faint smile on and continued to sit. Mitchell stood over him.

Schaffer finally spoke again. "I appreciate you calling me so quick and all. Glad to get the head's up. I don't live that far from here."

Mitchell's eyes clung to every movement Schaffer's mouth made. "So what's in it?" Mitchell asked.

"In what?"

"Your report, the report you turned in."

Although there was silence in the room, there was a flurry of activity in the hallway.

Schaffer began again. "The explosion scared Freddie."

Mitchell read outright resistance, in Schaffer's eyes.

"Freddie thought his brother, Morton, killed his mother. She was Dolly David's maid, remember."

Mitchell let that last comment slide, while Schaffer spoke slower than usual.

"Freddie also thought his brother may have been responsible for the explosion of his rooming house. So while you were out, I got a court order to open Morton's juvenile records. Morton may have beheaded a few people as far back as the '80s. I believe it's more likely that Morton Meda killed Dolly David and Joseph Stronsky. I don't think Alan Bradley could have done it. He's a former CEO and founder of Martindale, Inc. I told the heifer we were wasting Bureau time and money looking for a wealthy upstanding member of the community just because his politics pissed some people off."

Mitchell pictured his boss, her spiked bleached hair, popping acid reflux pills, sipping them down with a thermos of diluted tequila, all the while listening to Schaffer's whining. She and her job were Siamese twins and Mitchell could relate to that. Nobody but his boss could keep track of the plethora of details in each and every case that came across her desk. He thought her honesty and no bullshit leadership gave her a right to have some vices.

"You've been quite a busy termite today," Mitchell responded. "Let me ask you this. You want to work under me, get the benefit of my years of experience before you branch out on your own? Tell me now because I'm sure I can fix it, either way."

"Sure I do," Schaffer said, getting to his feet. "I was just …"

"Any report you make goes by me first. That way, we save our boss a great deal of heartburn and other distress. That's clear, right?"

"Right."

Mitchell hadn't finished. "I didn't take this job away from you. You're good. And one day you may surpass my cleverness. But you need to remember that anybody who has the money, power, time, and motive, should never, I don't care how great a pillar of the community they are, be ruled out as a suspect until the last piece of evidence proves somebody else did it. So what I need above all else is EVIDENCE."

"I get that," Schaffer replied.

"Oh and while I'm at it, the word is 'jefa'. Say it incorrectly again and I'll write you up."

An aide walked in and snatched the sheets off the bed. "Heard the latest? The fire truck that left here had an accident at I-25 and Hampden. It turned over. There may be a body under it. It's on the news."

Schaffer reached for the control paddle, dangling from the bed and punched the TV button.

Police say men dressed as firemen jumped off the truck before it drove into a southbound ramp and rolled over. Darkness didn't help. Some onlookers say two men tore off their uniforms as they ran from the scene."

Mitchell snatched the paddle from Schaffer's hand and turned it off. "C'mon. We've got to look for Freddy's body out there."

As they ran to Mitchell's car, Mitchell was still asking questions. "Did you see the woman in the uniform in Freddie's room?"

"Yeah. You requested her, right?" Schaffer answered.

Mitchell stopped in his tracks. Schaffer slowed down and finally stopped.

"Why would I do that?" Mitchell asked. "Denver wasn't looking for Freddie. We weren't either. We were looking for his mom. So who is that dead lady dressed up in a New York City Museum security guard uniform?" Mitchell asked.

Schaffer's face began to crinkle like paper.

"Am I going too fast for you?" Mitchell asked. "Don't tell me. You were so focused on trying to get my job you didn't notice that the black woman was a fake cop? Well, she's dead and we need to know why and who she was working for."

Mitchell pretended not to notice Schaffer's sudden ghost-like stare and continued talking. "I found her body under a hospital blanket outside this place. She was next to a dead hospital security guard. Which door did you come in through?"

"The side door for hospital personnel."

"Then her body and the bullet inside the security guard are our only links to who grabbed Freddie. Get your phone out. Make sure CBI has jurisdiction over both of those bodies."

They walked the rest of the way to Mitchell's car. Schaffer sat in the front passenger seat and punched numbers on his phone locating people he needed to reach in order to find the two dead bodies. Minutes later he was satisfied that CBI had possession of them.

Mitchell then asked, "Did you get a chance to give Dr. Buchanan's phone back to her?"

"Couldn't. Didn't have time after that explosion."

"Sure, you were busy writing a report." Mitchell was never going to let Schaffer forget his mistakes. He'd made too many of them today. But not giving Inez's phone back to her was of little consequence. She probably forgot she had one. If he was lucky, she'd already be in bed for the night. Yet somewhere at the bottom of his sternum he felt a lump of apprehension. There was nothing in this entire world she thought she couldn't do with a little research.

"You got this Morton Meda's address?" Mitchell asked, still apprehensive.

"No."

Mitchell couldn't hide his disappointment in Schaffer. "So what *do* you have on him?"

"He uses aliases wherever he goes. I've only been able to verify one. Saaiq. That name makes him a former resident in the same rooming house that just blew up. He stayed there last year during his mom's birthday. But the name is somewhat common and shows up everywhere. It's on the 'No-fly' list along with hundreds of Omars. He's also been sighted by Interpol in Afghanistan."

28

FALL, 2009 DENVER TECH CENTER

Bradley guided Inez through the revolving doors of Metropolitan State University until they stood inside a circular lobby. A mammoth crystal and brass chandelier hung from three stories above them. The view was more befitting a hotel than a university. But its curved stairs surrounding the edge of a circular lobby floor also suggested an amphitheater.

Inez found the size incredible. Only two things in the lobby suggested a school, two easel style bulletin boards with attached memos. They could easily have been stage props. Inez looked up at him angrily.

Bradley's smile turned into a boisterous laugh. "Okay, you caught me. They're props. You didn't fall for the amphitheater motif. And yet there is a drop curtain, recently hung, for that eventuality." He pointed above the front revolving doors where a black velvet curtain hung. "Students use the lobby for theater practice every morning."

When Martindale's plan for a hotel and conference complex didn't bring in the money we anticipated, we donated the facility to Metro State. Right now there's a chemistry lab in the basement and a psychology class on the top floor. You must have seen the cars parked outside. It may take a few months to get the building up and running as a prestigious school, but ..."

"More like several years," Inez interupted.

"Now don't be so pessimistic," he replied.

"I'm being realistic."

They were both smiling. Inez enjoyed opportunities to brush up on her small talk. So many people nowadays had never learned it from their elders and never therefore, realized it was a skill to be honed.

With one hand on her elbow he led her toward closed doors off the lobby. "The good thing is we have our choice of classrooms to talk in."

He pulled open one side of massive mahogany doors. Inez expected a huge ballroom, but instead saw a wall, maybe 30 feet long, on which hung numerous TV monitors. In the middle of the enclosure sat a console with an assortment of knobs and dials. And along the far wall were drapes which hung below an extremely high ceiling. In front of the drapes, to one side, was a refrigerator. Inez was about to walk over to those drapes to see what was behind them when Bradley spoke.

"It's a fully functional TV station!" he said excitedly. "You can fold it up and truck it out of here, just like those bulletin boards. The beauty is, you only need one person to operate it. But I don't want to bore you with details."

"Looks like you haven't really retired," Inez said. "But will any of this help bring Kadija Campbell home?"

Furrows appeared on Bradley's forehead. He stared at Inez and said nothing.

"I assume then," Inez continued, "that you're still considering my security clearance and how you'll proceed in bringing Kadija out of Afghanistan."

Bradley approached the console. "There's something I want you to see."

He pulled two office chairs on wheels from one corner of the room toward the console and motioned for her to sit beside him.

"I enjoyed our conversation this morning," he said as he tinkered with the knobs and switches. "Oh, I know I wasn't always positive, but ..."

Inez frowned and shook a finger at him. She was already tired of his games.

He looked at her hand gesture and kept talking. "… but I'm afraid I'm about to give you additional reasons to hate my guts."

She chewed on her bottom lip and hoped he wouldn't outright refuse to rescue Kadija. Inez intended to offer him every penny of Dolly's money to retrieve her.

"Our words haunted me all day," Bradley continued, "I'm referring to your thought earlier that I might have driven the Colonel to Fort Collins to meet his granddaughter. Well, I didn't. But I certainly never dreamed he'd try to rape her. My God, the man was in his eighties!" He covered his eyes with one hand as if pretending to be scandalized.

Bradley was acting like a fool.

"Casema Meda," he said, "was fourteen when she started working for the Davids. That's when she got pregnant."

"Was raped, you mean," Inez corrected.

"Yes, that's what I mean," Bradley agreed. "Instead of divorcing him," Bradley went on, "Dolly brought Casema and her baby back to the States. Dolly said she *had* to help cover it up because that's what military wives did in those days. Casema tried to raise Morton on her own but she was too young. Dolly tried to help and failed too. Years later the Colonel contacted the boy, who by then was a grown man. Dolly finally felt betrayed.

"The Colonel got Morton Meda a job at Martindale but the FBI took notice. While conducting his background check they discovered Morton had been to Afghanistan using a string of aliases, most of which I can't even pronounce. Some were the aliases of people the FBI was searching for." Bradley continued to push buttons on the console.

Inez listened politely then said, "I've got so many questions I don't know where to start. But I guess I'll get to the point. How does any of this bring Kadija home?"

Bradley grabbed one of her hands. "Kadija is dead, and …"

Inez snatched her hand back and stood up. "There's no reason to believe that. Stronsky never verified her death. He never even left the U.S. He lied on his documents. No one ever checked them against his travel requisitions for reimbursement."

Bradley's face turned whiter while the muscles at his temples twitched. Inez wondered if he'd known what Stronsky was doing. Stronsky worked for him.

He didn't look at Inez as he spoke. "Stronsky wasn't our only source of validation," Bradley offered. " Kadija was killed inadvertently by friendly fire during our last attempt at a rescue."

Inez stood speechless for a moment. Had he told this to Dolly? Of course he had. Dolly was the love of his life. She took a few steps away from her chair, turning her back to the monitors on the wall.

"You know," Inez said, "I did entertain the thought for a moment that the CIA may have killed Kadija to quiet admonishments about hiring people of color in the first place. For example, suppose she'd been given a husband for this assignment and he was outed somehow as a spy. CIA might want them both dead or rescued."

She turned around and looked at him, his eyes never left the monitors. She'd never voiced this concern before now because there was no one close to her anymore to bounce ideas off. And she had no business asking unstable people like Bradley any question she didn't know the answer to.

"I guess the point I'm continuing to make is that there's no reason to believe Kadija is dead. You're telling me that you believe one unverified story over another. But Dolly talked to Kadija this past January. There's a record of a phone call from Afghanistan to Dolly's house."

Bradley looked ghost-like. "Come. Sit down. Look at the monitors. Here's what's really important. This happened today. Our news crew snatched it off the wire. It's where Morton's stepbrother Freddie lived. Morton is obliterating his past and anybody even remotely related to him. In this case, his brother survived. Morton has already killed his half-sister."

Inez gradually put her eyes on the monitors.

"Aren't you curious about why Morton's doing this?" Bradley continued.

Inez smiled at Bradley, hearing his obsession with Morton in his voice. She'd taught kids that were so stressed, hungry, physically challenged, or generally so obsessed with the condition they found themselves in that they couldn't read, write, or do math. They couldn't listen. Was Bradley likewise so obsessed that he couldn't listen or think rationally about helping Dolly's granddaughter?

"Obviously," she began slowly, "Morton is important to you. And if we have time later, we can talk about him in more detail. I'm more concerned about rescuing Kadija. I know she's alive. I feel it."

Bradley stood up abruptly, his chair falling over behind him. "For God's sake woman! Dolly's phone call had to be a cruel prank played on her by an equally cruel person. Maybe even Morton. Don't you understand that?"

Inez glared at him. Bradley righted his chair and continued to holler as he paced. "In 2001, the U.S. military was on the ground in Afghanistan. They bombed the hell out of Kandahar and later that same year they bombed the hell out of Tora Bora. We … we deployed troops already on the ground in an area in which Kadija was last seen. In a way, we … our friendly fire killed her. We didn't know she was still there."

"I don't need to know government secrets," Inez interrupted, "but as the executor of Dolly's estate, proof of death is absolutely necessary. You've sent me boxes of reports and that's fine. But we need Kadija's body or the woman herself brought back here. Will you put that into motion for me or not? Can I purchase that service from you, or from Martindale, Inc., or another company you're able to recommend?"

Bradley stopped pacing and said, "If I told you about Martindale's attempts to rescue her, which I can't, you'd believe she was dead, too. You think *we* didn't need to have some part of her as proof?"

His mood and facial expression abruptly changed. "I think I will tell you all about it after all. Oh, I'm sorry." He sat down at the console again. "Are you hungry?"

He was unraveling. Inez knew the signs. Harvey Linwood, a student from many years back came to mind. He too didn't know how to stop unraveling.

The explosions on the TV monitors replayed again. The devastated old building again exploded. And for some reason this time, the sound and visuals distracted Inez from Bradley. She hit the replay button to see it all again when she heard a refrigerator door open. She turned away from the monitors. Looking past Bradley she could see a cold feast on all the shelves, including bottles of champagne, wine, and beer.

"What's the occasion?" she asked, knowing her question would feed into whatever he'd planned.

"It's our last supper," Bradley answered. There was no smile on his face and she could see confusion in his eyes.

Inez replied, "You're trying to make me afraid of Morton Meda and ..."

Bradley laughed. "You're talking about the man who killed Dolly and Stronsky," he said, "and who very likely killed his own mother. Those were probably her ashes Martindale mistakenly placed in the vault next to Colonel David's. I'm sure he's aware of you, too. Morton's been through your house at least once, maybe more. That's where he obtained my phone number, isn't it?"

Inez's forehead furrowed, as she watched Bradley pace. Just how much danger was she in?

Suddenly he stopped pacing. "You still think you came here under your own exercise of free will, don't you? But you and I, dear lady, are actually bait inside an elaborate trap which I built. Trace Mitchell still thinks I murdered Dolly and Stronsky doesn't he? Well, somebody had to show him he was wrong. To do that, I had to force Morton out of hiding. He's got a long arm and he won't stop killing until we're dead. His hatred has no bounds, no philosophical end point. No cause is big enough to encompass his hate."

Inez felt her shoulders tense. Bradley didn't sound well. Even his voice was different. "Did you and Stronsky put that first bug in my house?" she asked. "Is that how you know about Trace Mitchell?"

Bradley said nothing at first. He took a deep breath before spitting his words out. "Martindale, Madam, is too damn sophisticated an organization to use 'bugs'. Not even Stronsky could keep up with the technology. I had to threaten him to keep him from using the damn things.

"There was a time when we could put software into any household appliance," Bradley continued. "Few people know what they're buying nowadays anyway. But nobody had to go inside your house to install what we used."

Inez had a general idea of what Bradley was blabbering about but was more concerned about who had placed the bug beside her front door. If the boy with the red shoes had done it that meant he was far more important than she had originally thought. She remembered how quickly he left the Emporium the day she met Sophie, but more important was what Mitchell had said.

"Welcome to the world of high finance 'cause that's who uses this junk. These things self-disintegrate."

What was that boy's connection to high finance?

"What if," Inez said meekly, "I convince Mitchell of your possible innocence? Of course, that's only if you help bring Kadija home."

Bradley sat at the console and leaned back, his eyes growing into saucers. "Why Dr. Buchanan, you're *that* certain of my innocence?" he asked.

"Oh, mercy no! I have no idea who killed Dolly and Stronsky. And now, you're adding Dolly's maid and this Morton guy's mother and sister. I don't mean to sound callous, but I have urgent business too. I'm confident Trace Mitchell will find the murderer and apprehend him, or her, or them. I, on the other hand, made a commitment to Dolly, and if that means dealing with murderers to free Kadija, so be it."

Just then the room lights flickered wildly.

"Morton's here," Bradley said. His eyes seemed to search the bank of fluorescent bulbs in the ceiling. Then he looked down at the console and found several levers, which he switched on.

Inez listened to what seemed like motors running and she knew she'd heard that sound before. But where?

"Don't worry," Bradley said. "My men are just as invisible as his."

"You mean those boys who brought me here?"

Bradley laughed. "The only way to transport a militia of trained men across the country and back is to use camouflage. Each one of them can look nineteen or ninety. They've had acting lessons and makeup instruction as well as SEAL training. You may not have been taken in tonight, but I bet you didn't know they were the security guards you saw at the mall. One of them even hailed you a cab this morning."

"Ingenious," Inez replied. She was genuinely impressed. "I remember the valet. He did look quite young."

Bradley seemed to take pride in Inez's affirmations. His chest expanded and he beamed at her before glancing up at the ceiling again and back at Inez. "By the way," he said, "I see you're carrying Dolly's gun."

Inez tightened her grip on the small purse that hung at her hip. Reflex action made her look up at the ceiling as well. But all she saw were florescent lights which had stopped flickering.

"I wondered what she'd done with it," Bradley said. "I gave her that gun two decades ago. You can still get ammunition for it you know."

"Next time I'll be sure to bring some," Inez responded, through her embarrassment. "How did you know I was carrying it?"

"Ah. Can't tell you all my secrets. I need a drink," Bradley said. "You want anything?"

He'd already opened the refrigerator again.

"No thanks."

"You sure. We'll be here at least until Trace Mitchell arrives."

Inez stood pondering the situation. Gently she said, "All this cloak and dagger stuff hardly makes Morton more important than Kadija Campbell. Spies this country employs put their lives in harm's way so Americans may continue to dream in ways they've become accustomed to. I believe Dolly was very proud of her."

Bradley seemed to move in slow motion as he extracted a bottle of wine from the refrigerator. He was breathing hard, when he turned to face Inez.

"And you think Dolly wasn't proud of me?" he scoffed. "We were both proud of Kadija. Don't you think I want to believe Kadija is alive?

Inez thought she saw a tear begin to roll down his cheek.

"She was MY granddaughter, you stupid ass. Dolly's and Mine! Not Tucker David's!"

Bradley's face had become grotesque and Inez, although disappointed in, and apprehensive of the man who'd shown impeccable manners, knew better than to show him any sign of fear.

"By the time David left Viet Nam," Bradley continued, "he'd contracted everything from gonorhia to syphilis. If I'd thought that animal had put his hands on Dolly or my daughter, I'd have ripped him apart with my bare hands. Eventually, David knew I wasn't someone he could trust to protect him. It took a long time for him to finally believe his own medical reports. That's why he decided to trust Morton."

Bradley's red eyes shimmered. The skin around his mouth shriveled into deeply carved lines. This was no time to commiserate with him over his fatherhood. He suddenly turned his back on Inez, but in one swift arm jerk, threw the bottle of wine against a wall beside her. Shards of glass and splattered red wine flew everywhere, including Inez's clothing and legs.

Staring at Bradley's stooped shoulders, Inez thought she was looking at Harvey Linwood, retained three times in elementary school in Washington, D.C. where she'd completed her student teaching. He'd been a tall kid who one day came to class with a metal wrench, intending to smash the skulls of every sixth grader. No one bullied Harvey Linwood. He was mad that no one in his school let him act like a fifteen year old.

Although Bradley looked at Inez, she knew he didn't see anyone he cared about. His hand still squeezed the neck of what was left of a jagged edged wine bottle. Inez had been in this emotional position before with Harvey, and this time she had no fear at all. Slowly she dragged her chair closer to the console, sat down, and began to turn knobs.

With her back to him, she asked, "Just how does this thing work?"

29

"You're scaring me," Asif shouted into his phone. It was a facetious response to his case manager's pessimism.

"Good! Because that could have been you burned to a crisp in that field. The Embassy won't inquire about it until tomorrow. Far as they're concerned, that body isn't there. It hasn't happened yet. No one's touching his remains tonight."

"But I've got to get to Shamsi. If you're sure that's Jamison's body then there's no one left to fly the Reaper tomorrow. We may never get another opportunity like this."

As Asif talked he rifled through a deck of playing cards, each card carrying a photo of a top Al Queda operative, still alive. He searched the faces of three men just under Bin Laden's.

"Their meeting is still on isn't it?" Asif asked.

"According to latest intel it is."

He stared at each face during every relaxed moment, including times like now, when he was anything but relaxed. He had no business bringing them home to his apartment. Jamison had warned him against it several times. But Asif needed the practice. He needed to keep his mind alert. He wanted to be able to pick each face out of any crowd. It was always Jamison who constantly identified the names of his targets. And maybe he was jealous of that.

"I've got to get there for Jamison's sake."

"Surviver's guilt isn't going to help. Can't go by plane. That's suicide."

"I'll take my car."

"Wish I could tell you that's safer."

"Doesn't matter. They're not going to stop killing American soldiers now that Jamison's dead, are they?"

"You can't drive your own car. They'll spot it. We can get you a better one in a couple of hours."

"Two hours?" Asif repeated. It was a death sentence. He paced his living room floor. "Shamsi's 999 kilometers south of Islamabad. I've got to go now."

"Stay put. That's an order! The shame of it is that the State Department plans to shut the Airfield down in a few weeks. Too much controversy."

Asif sighed. "That *is* a shame." From his fourth floor apartment window, he looked out along the edge of Islamabad's City Park. Morning mist covered the lake and trees. Branches drooped so low only the sound of rippling water could be heard as they swayed. He was too excited to sit down and wait for his handler's next words. He'd need to change clothes. Perspiration soaked the back of his tattersall shirt.

He'd heard rumors they were headed home soon but refused to believe them. "I hate to admit this," Asif blurted, "but I love it here. The food, the people, the scenery, everything ... Are you sure you ...?"

"I remember you once said flying drones was like air sex."

"Ha!" Asif shouted. "You have known me forever."

"For most of your career and I still don't get you. You've done a hell of a job here. But you ought to know by now you can't get deeply invested in this place. Our Company can be a jealous lover."

"You exaggerate my friend, but thank you. I find your occasional pat on the back enjoyable, even your lectures are charming." He chuckled before continuing. "And yet, after all these years, I still don't know your name."

"Only way friendships exist in our profession. However, this situation may end it."

"I've got to go!" Asif shouted. "We'll be ridding ourselves of at least two guys at the very top of the food chain, maybe more. We can't pass this up."

There was a long silence. Asif knew the man on the other end always juggled his own values along side his country's. It was the reason Asif admired him. Not all case managers had standards that the average field agent could comprehend. Asif hadn't been in the field long before observing that some directives, straight from Company headquarters, played into the hands of North America's enemies. Only good handlers kept their agents alive by figuring out cleverer stragtegies.

When the man finally spoke again, Asif swallowed hard.

"You're right. Pack nothing. You won't be returning to Islamabad, but you're not going to Shamsi either. If the Taliban did this, and we're guessing that's who discovered Jamison's identity, then they've already cracked your cover. No one could have anticipated Jamison's murder. And I'm not wasting time guessing who they meant to kill. Your career in this arena is over."

His words, like a blow to the abdomen, made Asif drop into the nearest chair. The chilling silence between them grew longer. For Asif, whatever emotional bond they had, ended on his order, making his stomach churn.

"A Royne cargo plane, bulk-loaded, just arrived from Dubai. It's scheduled to leave Islamabad International in fifty minutes. Wait! I take that back. Icons have changed. It's leaving Benazir Bhutto Airport. Wow, can you beat that? Pakistan renamed their airport that fast. There's room for one loadmaster on that flight. I want you on it and I don't want to hear how sorry you were that you missed it. Keep your Indian passport. Burn the others. Walk straight out the door of your apartment. Catch the first bus. For God's sake don't go to your car or touch the door on it for any reason. When you get to the airport, jump the fence if necessary. Your credit card is still good. I'll have a man looking out for you in case you'll need a uniform. This should be easy. You've done it before. Anyway, Langley thinks you can fly those drones from Virginia."

"What?" Asif felt salt being poured onto his wound.

"There's only one stop. Otherwise, it's a straight shot to Langley. Keep your handgun and cell phone with you at all times. When you get there, turn the phone over to Colonel Jasper Nathan at the Pentagon, in person. Now get going. You've got forty minutes left. Catch that bus and stay safe, amigo."

Asif struck a match and burned the playing cards in an ash tray.

He cursed himself and his case manager the whole way to the airport. How many years would it take him to learn what his mother told him as a boy, that if you put your feelings in the street they'll get trampled? For over twelve years, he'd had the kind of career men killed to acquire: good money, fast cars, beautiful women, opportunities to rid the world of bad guys, and travel perks for preserving American-style democracy throughout the planet. Now it was gone, because the man he'd told of his love for Islamabad decided to take no chances.

The next thirty minutes were exhausting. He attended to everything. If he missed a sound, a smell, an unexplainable image, the mistake could kill him. Ten years ago, he enjoyed the adrenaline rush. But then, he had a partner, another set of eyes to help.

No one stopped him while he walked onto the tarmac toward the only cargo plane he saw. A pilot never loses his strut he told himself. He felt lucky a minute after he was briefed at the duty manager's desk and saw the five-man cargo crew. Someone had taught three of them to play Mah Jong. That meant he could stretch out over their seats to sleep his anguish away. The crew, excluding the pilot and copilot, sat aft on the floor around what his college girlfriend had once called a Lazy Susan.

He hadn't stopped thinking of her since the moment the duty manager told him they were changing their stopover from Kandahar to Kabul. Seated upright, he closed his eyes to shut her out, but sank into a fitful daydream in which he had somehow turned back into the naïve young Sampati Jagjit, Colorado State's Bombay Virgin, that was until Kadija came along. She'd taught him more than a thing or three, some of which he'd forgotten over the years.

She'd heard he'd grown up in the streets of Bombay and convinced him to join CIA the year before they graduated. She'd left Fort Collins so abruptly officials thought she'd been murdered. Years later, after they'd served together in Iraq, he asked his case manager where she'd been assigned. The Company's official statement was that she was presumed dead from friendly fire.

Asif scooted further down across two seats and covered his face with a dirty sheet of bubble wrap found on the floor of the plane. Her death still haunted him on occassion. He'd assumed there'd be time to make peace with her for knocking her out years ago. But for some reason he'd always wondered if his inquiry had prompted her fate? Had they told him she was dead so he'd stop asking questions? Or did he find it impossible to think anyone that vibrant could die?

The pilot and copilot sat in front of the controls. Asif could only catch snatches of their argument over whether to pay the increase in their lease or move from the apartment they shared in Virginia. There was no baracade between their seats and the four passenger seats behind them.

Asif could tell by the way the crew avoided eye contact that someone had probably ratted him out as CIA. Maybe that was a good thing. He'd been told that in much of the Middle East, CIA personnel were considered brutal and militaristic. Maybe he'd be left alone.

Take off was exceptionally smooth and no one asked to see his passport. Was he really going to sleep the entire way to Virginia or was he going to toss and turn with his memories of what could or should have been?

Five years ago, a friend from CSU posted an unnerving question on Facebook. It asked, "If Kadija Campbell was kidnapped, where would her ransom be sent?"

The minute Asif had seen it he discussed the possibility that she was still alive with his case manager. Days later, after first being reprimanded for communicating outside the Company network, his manager's response had been guarded. Kadija's partner, he revealed, had been brutally beaten and left for dead inside the U.S. Embassy in Dar Es Salaam just before Al Qaeda blew it up. So why was her partner's body in Africa while hers was in Afghanistan? His question never got answered. But the answer wouldn't have brought her back from the dead either, if she really was dead.

This wasn't his first sleepless fit over Kadija. Normally he pushed memories of her aside. Suddenly he sat up and looked out the nearest window. Had he dozed off for a time? Slowly, it dawned on him. If he got off the plane and looked for her, he could stop worrying about her fate.

He'd never been to Kabul, but had flown drones over Tora Bora and Kandahar. He knew Kandahar had been bombed relentlessly after 9/11 and that Al-Qaeda left that area. Only the Taliban returned.

"How long are we on the ground?" Asif yelled over the engines to the pilot.

As if uncertain where the voice had come from, the pilot swiveled around to nail his puffy red eyes on Asif. The pilot was not as young as Asif had been when he first began crop dusting in Greeley, Colorado, but almost.

"Cargo shouldn't take mor'n a half hour ta'unload," the pilot said in what could have been a Texas drawl, if he hadn't been so drunk. He hadn't shaved in at least three-days Asif speculated.

"Maybe 'nother half hour 'ta load wha'dey give us. Ya' don't look like no loadmaster. But we shove off in nine'y minutes, or diship's leavin widout cha'."

"Copy that," Asif replied calmly.

Obviously, the co-pilot was the man in charge. Meanwhile, the three men in the back had stopped playing their game to listen and watch. They walked to their seats beside Asif and buckled in.

No one spoke except the co-pilot to the tower. The rest of them sat upright, as if an invisible stewardess stood over them. A man seated next to Asif poked him with his elbow, then pointed in the air at the 2 o'clock position, where a camera was mounted near a storage compartment.

"Safety procedures get filmed," he whispered with what Asif thought was a Russian accent.

He set the seat to upright, remembering that the man had used the term 'filmed,' which was fascinating. And for the first time he realized that everyone on board was as white as snow, another remembered Kadija-ism. Asif smiled as he recalled her voice and the fact that her own skin was as white as snow. As black as his own skin was, he had never seen himself as a man of color, until she'd mentioned it.

"How many people like us," she had asked him, "collect intelligence for CIA?"

Had race always been an important part of their career trajectory? Had he fallen in love with Islamabad because he blended in? Had his handler feared that a man of his color might want to blend in more than the U.S. wanted? Had race played a part in identifying Kadija's body? Spies certainly can never afford to second guess themselves, but he certainly didn't "blend in" on this flight.

He stared at the neck of the drunken blond pilot seated in front of him then glanced down the row of men beside him. There wasn't a tan among them. How does that happen in the Middle East? His first guess was all day Vegas-style gambling.

Just then, the wheels screeched and bounced along the asphalt runway. Was he looking for an excuse to get off the plane? To search for Kadija? Asif decided that in all probability he'd be safer looking for her in Afghanistan than riding to Virginia with this crew. All he'd need was to acquire a few items from the plane first.

30

"Hello, is this Trace Mitchell?" Sophie slid down as far as she could behind the steering wheel so as not to be seen. She pressed her phone tightly against the side of her face.

"Who's this?"

"I know it's midnight, Mr. Mitchell, but I thought Dr. Buchanan would show up by now and ..."

"Who are you?"

"I'm Sophie. Sophie Fortune, Kadija Campbell's friend from high school. Dr. Buchanan told me ..."

"Where is she?"

"She told me to call you if she was ever in trouble and ..."

"Where are you, Sophie?"

She was afraid he'd ask her that. Looking up through the windshield she saw nothing but darkness. "I'm not sure, somewhere in the Denver Tech Center. See, she was to meet Alan Bradley in front of the Library on Auraria's campus near Metro State. But two cars picked her up and I'm sure I followed the right one because I can see the sign that says Metro State University DTC Campus on the only building at the top of this hill. But I didn't want to drive up there in my cab because ..."

"Are you inside your cab now?"

"Yes, sir. See, what I was going to do was climb that hill, stockings and all." She looked down at her legs, wishing they were slimmer though not really seeing them in the dark. "Guess I've always wanted to be an investigator. That's what you are, isn't it? But when I saw men in ski masks, kneeling behind some bushes up there, I hurried back down."

"How long ago was that?" She took her cell phone away from her ear to check the time.

"Oh, maybe five, eight minutes ago."

"Can you keep this phone open, Sophie?"

"Well, sir, my battery's low and Dr. Buchanan doesn't have her phone. Weren't you supposed to give hers back? Hello!"

"I'm still here, Sophie. Listen carefully, make a U turn and get back to an intersection with controlled traffic lights. Situate your car off to the side. Don't block traffic in any direction. Then start honking your horn in two-minute intervals. Can you remember all that?"

With gusto, Sophie answered back, "Yes sir. I'm on my way now sir. This is so dope. What's this gonna do, Mr. Mitchell?"

"Keep those masked bastards away from you I hope. Now don't turn your phone off. If we're lucky, police'll show up soon. Don't let your windows down either, unless it *is* the police. You tell them I'm on the line."

"Did I tell you I'm driving a cab?"

"Yes, Sophie. That's great," Mitchell answered. "Does your cab company know where you are?"

"They sure do. I'm off duty, but I didn't want to be somewhere nobody could find me. You can understand that." She heard nothing for what seemed like minutes. "Mr. Mitchell?"

"Yes, I'm still here, but I need to stop talking for a while. I'm patching this call into another department. Hang on."

"Okay. Okay, I found it! I found a well-lit intersection and now I'm honking my head off. Can you hear my horn? There's hardly any traffic out here though. It's after midnight. Hello? Mr. Mitchell? Mr.

Mitchell? I think my battery just died. Fuck! I mean, oh dear. A car with no headlights just pulled up behind me. NO! They're pushing me. They're pushing me forward. Sir? I can't sit here and wait. I've got to get out of here before they push me into … into oncoming ..."

31

SEPTEMBER 2008 KABUL, AFGHANISTAN

Seated on parched earth and panting hard, Asif searched the immediate area using binoculars he'd stolen from under the pilot's seat. He searched for shelter, but each breath made his chest feel it would split open from the inside. He'd run uphill during the night, having crawled then hidden from airport personnel most of the day.

After landing in Kabul, he'd helped the crew unload, while foraging for items on the plane he'd need to hike through Afghanistan. Once he got his hands on all of it, he hid inside a nearby tool shed, watching as others packed the new cargo onboard. He heard them curse his disappearing act. Asif, meanwhile, tore labels from his clothing, took the battery from his cell phone, and then took a nap.

He was awakened by the noise as the plane took off hours later for Virginia with a sobering pilot, a crew of gamblers, and questionable cargo. They knew they were in no position to report his disappearance until they were airborne.

Twilight eased his paranoia until he opened the door of the shed. There were almost as many people around as there had been during the day. He crawled along piles of luggage on flatbed carts until he reached empty carts that had once carried meals for passenger planes. Because the carts were empty, he had a panoramic view through the slats while tarps on top kept him hidden. The vastness of the Hindu Kush Mountain Range was daunting yet he had to get there and avoid being discovered.

Moving without being seen had been his speciality all of his life. He pulled back the tarps, stood up, and assumed a pilot's attitude of importance as he walked toward a wire fence where a gate had been opened slightly for utility trucks. He kept walking at a normal pace toward the mountains. Only a truck leaving through that gate with its headlights on would notice him. He turned around often as he walked but none came. When the moon went behind a cloud Asif ran as fast as he could.

It took him an almost an hour to run up the side of the nearest hill. When he stopped to rest exhaustion overcame him and he slept where he lay. Three hours had passed according to his wristwatch and the sun was up. He put his binoculars into his shirt and listened for the sound of animals.

"Salaam alaikum," said a voice further up the mountain.

Startled, Asif turned quickly to see a teenaged boy on the mountain above his head holding on to a huge boulder wedged into the dirt. Dressed in a dirty gauze tunic and pants with a vest that had at one time been a deep red with gold colored buttons, he looked like a circus barker who had wandered too far from his movie set.

The boy appeared to be about fourteen or fifteen. He spoke with speed and in Pashtu. Asif could only make out a few words like cargo plane. But as he listened, he slid his hand inside his shirt close enough to his gun to feel the butt in its holster. Suddenly the boy switched to Punjabi.

"You were a stowaway on that plane," he said, pointing beyond Asif. "I watched you sneak into a workers' toolshed. You stayed there until the sun went down, until it was safe to jump the fence. I think you have been trained in the military. You are agile on your feet. I've lingered around the airport for the past three days trying to calculate whether it's humanly possible to stowaway on one of those planes and then you arrive to show me that it is indeed possible. Perhaps you could help me. Tell me how it's done. I have nothing of value to give you in return. Allah has made me his victim as you can see for yourself."

The boy slowly skidded down the mountain toward him, no weapon in his hands. Asif watched him stay two arms lengths away.

"I followed above you on the ridge."

He paused as Asif continued to watch his every movement.

"Kabul," the boy continued, "has an anti-begging commission. No one had heard of such a thing here before now. I'd heard of it but never thought it was anything I'd need to heed. Obviously, I have very bad karma. It is because I have done very bad things. And now police will put me in prison if they think I'll beg again. But I will beg for you, because I am good at it. And I will not get caught. That is something I can do in return. If you want, I will beg for anything you desire, food, money, guns, women, men. I will provide you with anything you need, until I can afford to get back to Islamabad where I am from."

A smile of kinship heedlessly swept over Asif's face.

"I have said something that pleases you? Then perhaps we have a bargain. But first, you want I bring you food? Come, I have friends on the other side of this ridge. You will not need to use that gun you carry. You will see. My name is Quaalude. My friends call me that because I was a very amiable addict for a very long time. That is why I am here in Kabul where I do not belong. I no longer crave drugs and thus have become a much happier but impoverished young man with very few prospects. But all that will change now that you are here. I now have a chance to return home."

Asif watched Quaalude's back from behind as they ascended the mountain. Unable to get a word in, he was at least happy to have found another person from Islamabad. He was used to Islamabadians, their juxtaposition of ideas, their inquisitive youth, their tech savvy students. Nonetheless, his hand never moved from the handle of his gun.

Quaalude's sandals were worn paper thin, his heels calloused, his ankles showing deep scabs. Asif, wearing Doc Martin's as he did wherever he went, didn't feel sorry for the boy who held his shoulders back and his chest straight. He climbed rocks with an air of sophistication that revealed his possible position as the elder son within a prominent Muslim family with money. It also revealed that there was some truth in what he said, that he no longer craved drugs.

As for Asif, he and his three brothers had literally lived off the tin roofs of what was then called Bombay and at a much younger age than this boy in front of him. It was the place that taught him how to size up a tourist and how to survive a cruel, hostile world. All he knew of Hinduism, at the time, was that their mother thought its gods would protect her children when she died. He counted his blessings as he climbed behind the boy, because by the time he was Quaalude's age, all his brothers and both parents were dead. If it hadn't been for the Andersons of Greeley, Colorado, working through their church, he'd be dead, too.

When they reached the top of the ridge, the vastness of the mountain range made his knees weaken. The range seemed never ending in all directions. His stopped and looked below him at three females. One had hair so silver it shimmered in the dawn's light, another with stooped shoulders was seated beside a girl of about ten. The girl sat in a lotus position, with a baby in her lap. On the other side of the woman whose whole body was stooped he noticed a small pit where she was attempting to start a fire with stones.

"They are all my family for now," the teenager announced. "We have only been together this past week. And now approaches a man who is very much like my own grandfather."

A middle-aged man, whose back was so bent his forehead occasionally touched the side of the hill, climbed with a smile on his face. On his back was a large and apparently heavy plastic bag. Quaalude scurried down part way to take hold of the bag and help the man stand taller as he climbed.

"Ah," the man yelled. Looking directly at Asif, while speaking to Quaalude, "I knew you would find more friends. I knew this food would not be wasted. It may look as if I took all the food the airport has, but believe me, I left some behind for others. On the other hand, I did pick and choose. We have only the very best leftovers available."

"Ah, but then we will need to leave here soon," Quaalude said. "Airport personnel are not stupid. They will start looking for the people who daily steal their blankets, pillows, and food. You must not take so much at one time. If you go on this mission again, you must be very careful not to lead them here."

Asif listened carefully to their conversation. The old man used several Arabic words as he spoke and his head was wrapped in ways done by Al Qaeda soldiers. He had a look about him that suggested any and all nationalities.

Both women smiled at the old man and his bag. Only the young girl sat unamused and unengaged, even with the baby in her lap. The baby must have been asleep. Its movements were lethargic compared to other babies Asif had observed. The noise and bustle of people should have attracted the baby's attention by now.

The man's bag was torn open and its contents spread over the bag itself and beyond. Much of it, Asif recognized, came directly from passenger planes, with several meals still unopened and in their own plastic cases. The women made tea from unused teabags and poured the concoctions into clear plastic cocktail cups. Asif thought the food delicious for American fare which he hadn't had in years. The others picked over the meatloaf and mashed potatoes, unsure of what these items were.

Yet another boy, barely in his teens, suddenly appeared. He walked with a long shepherd's hook as short as he was. The boy's quiet approach startled Asif while he ate. He admonished himself for being careless. The younger boy sat beside the girl with the baby. From within the folds of his robe he pulled out a small bottle of milk and began putting drops of it from his fingers into the baby's mouth. Her expression never changed and Asif wondered if it was too little too late, but no one said a word except the silver haired woman, who spoke so others couldn't hear. Gradually, the man, who was still standing, drifted towards the old woman and sat on the ground beside her.

Asif and Quaalude sat apart from the others, Quaalude talking all the time. He began to explain how he came to be in Kabul. He had attempted to buy drugs from a man who sat behind the steering wheel of a truck. As soon as he got inside through the passenger door, the man drove like the wind leaving Pakistan and headed into Afghanistan.

"I pleaded with him to take my money and leave me behind. I feared he intended to sell me. Instead, after many miles, the man stopped the truck, pulled out a hammer, and hit me in the head." Quaalude's hand flew to the back of his head where there must have been a wound. "It was not a good feeling.

"When I awoke I was half naked on the side of a highway somewhere between Kandahar and Kabul. After half a day in the sun without water, a farmer carrying hay in his wagon, took me with him to Kabul where he gave me these clothes he found. And here I am still trying to get back to Islamabad. And you? How did you get that cargo plane to bring you here?"

Quaalude never smiled, but spoke as if speaking to a family member or an older brother. That pleased Asif who hoped he was able to convey a look of sadness caused by the boy's experience.

As the sun rose higher, Asif looked in the distance at the airport and then toward Pakistan. The land was dry and treeless nearer the airport. He had no desire to stay in Afghanistan any longer than he had to and he couldn't return to Islamabad.

Asif was familiar with these mountains, but only on a monitor when he flew drones overhead. Although he hadn't mentioned it to his case manager, he couldn't help wondering why Jamison had been the one kidnapped and left outside headquarters where he was burned alive. The Taliban apparently didn't know that Jamison wasn't the one flying those drones. It was time to put all that aside. He now had a new set of problems. He had to find Kadija or learn why he couldn't. And to do that he would need Quaalude's help.

"If you wish to keep your past a secret," Quaalude said, "I'm not offended. I have no politics at all. None. Knowing the story of your life gives me no advantage. Also I have no wish to learn something that may get me killed by people who may be looking for you."

He seemed to brush imaginary dust off his vest. "Although you can see that I now experience poverty like everyone else here, I am not so poor as to be depressed by my current financial condition. That is because I have experienced life within the high walls of my wealthy family's home.

"Oh, yes, I have disgraced my family many times." He held an index finger up in the air as if he'd learned that gesture from someone who had done that in front of him many times.

"My father," Quaalude continued, "says I must never return home. But I am also determined that my life will once again be blessed. Besides, I am not alone. I have the strength my mother gave me. She was a Senator in the Upper House, before she lost her seat in the last elections.

"So you see, I know I will be taking a chance with my life if I stow away on a plane."

Perhaps, thought Asif, a part of him was willing to die in order to return.

"But I am confident now that I've met you that if you found a way to stow away on a plane, I too, can do it."

Asif was very quiet, thinking about Quaalude's words, wondering whether a young, naive addict with no money to buy drugs could be trusted. They both lay back and watched the sky.

"Your mother is a very intelligent woman, is she not?" Asif asked.

"Ah, finally he speaks. But of course she is."

"Suppose then," Asif continued, "your mother was brought here by the man in the truck and dumped on the side of the road instead of you."

Quaalude sat up and glared at Asif.

"And when your mother awoke, she continued to live in Afghanistan, for several more years. Why would she do that, even though her family, her country, and all she loved was in Pakistan? And because she is so intelligent, she would certainly have devised several ways to come home by now. Yet she stays. Why? Answer that for me."

"I do not understand you. What is it you are trying to tell me? The answer to your question is quite a simple one. Is there some trick to this?"

Asif sat up as well.

"Ah," said Quaalude, looking Asif over more carefully. "It is a woman who brings you here. I thought that might be the reason a man dressed as yourself should come to Kabul."

"So what is this simple answer?" Asif demanded.

"It is myself. My mother would stay here because I am here. It is that simple."

Asif stared into open space for some time, until his eyes fell upon the girl with the listless baby in her lap. "You may be right. It's the only answer that makes sense. But that creates yet another question. Where, in all of Afghanistan, would such a woman as your mother feel safe to care for you? She would not want you to become imbued with hate toward others. And she'd want you safe from ignorance and physical abuse."

"I understand," Quaalude answered. "This answer is not so simple, particularly if my father is not with my mother. Even if I knew this region as well as I know my own, I would be unable to answer that question."

"Are you saying we need to find someone with more knowledge of this region than we have among the two of us?" Asif asked playfully.

"Not necessarily," Quaalude asserted. "A week ago, the old man over there and I traveled through Kabul looking for food in trash containers behind important looking buildings. We reasoned that scraps behind such buildings would be heartier. In our travels we came upon what I thought was an orphanage. A woman came to the back door and said to me that I looked familiar. She thought she knew my mother. She said she was a researcher and that this was a home for abused women and their children. I had never heard of such a thing. She said there were several homes like the one she worked in throughout Afghanistan and soon there would be one in Pakistan. She was very nice and gave us fresh food. She said she had studied in the United States where there were people who donated money to places like the one here because it is very dangerous for Afghan women to live in their own country. It cannot be that dangerous for women in Pakistan, or can it?"

"We must go tomorrow. I must talk to this woman." Asif began breathing quickly. "I won't be here long after all. And here is my promise to you, my wise one. Travel with me while I track down each one of these places for abused women or until I find the woman I seek, and I'll buy you a first class plane ticket to Pakistan. But remember, this may take some time, we could be here for six months to a year, particularly if we travel into other parts of Afghanistan."

Quaalude was ecstatic. He got up from the ground and stood on his head, then turned right side up and jumped up and down. "There is no reason this person you seek isn't nearby," he said. "Allah, of course has known this all along. I could be in Islamabad by the New Year, or maybe not."

"Shhh. I don't want to burden anyone else with my intentions." Asif looked at the middle-aged man, whose eyes were fixed on him, as they had been when he reached the top of the ridge. This man was possibly more than just curious. He had the look of someone who had lived many lives and observed many cultures. Such people were always potentially dangerous, particularly if they stored information they were privy to. How long, he wondered, had that man camped beside the airport?

As a precaution, Asif added, "None of these people can go with us. And certainly not your new grandfather."

The boy plopped down beside Asif. "You are wrong. He is nobody. He has been my only opportunity to change my worthless life. I speak for him. I will feed him. And I will feed you. We will journey together. Wait and see."

"No, Quaalude. I will not wait one minute longer than I need to. There cannot be three of us."

Suddenly, the baby began to cry. It was a loud and healthy cry. The middle-aged man reached over and grabbed the baby under its shoulder with one hand and swung it into the air toward his own lap where it began to cry even louder. The girl's eyes were brighter. The two women smiled and the old man made gurgling sounds with his throat, while he snapped his fingers. The baby became quieter and actively reached out toward the fingers of the man.

"You are right," Quaalude whispered. "That baby needs him." They both continued to watch the others.

Asif lay back down. He'd had a tiring twenty-four hours. Then Quaalude asked, "And what do I call you?"

He thought for a moment. Asif had no desire to use aliases that might later create a traceable path to the Company. "Dilawar," he answered quickly.

"You don't look like a man who would be named Dilawar. But I will call you what you wish with pride because, although you carry a gun and tell nothing about your origin, you are an honorable man. I feel it. Allah speaks to me when I am worthy. And he has told me that I should travel with you. It is my destiny. We should leave here before the others awake. Some will certainly wish to come along."

32

FALL, 2009 DENVER TECH CENTER

At half past midnight a UPS truck turned at the corner of Evergreen Boulevard. Its driver accelerated uphill toward the Metropolitan State University building in the Denver Tech Center, but not before throwing two small items out the window: an empty soda cup and a hamburger wrapper.

At the front door, he stopped the truck, grabbed a small package from the bin beside him, hopped out, and ran to the revolving doors. His bare legs froze in the elevated night air, several degrees colder than downtown Denver. He discovered the doors to the building were locked in place. He jogged in place to keep warm and looked for a night depository drawer. Instead he spied a video camera to the left of the doors.

"Night delivery for," he used his flashlight on the package, "Professor Ulrick," the driver said loudly into the camera lens, "but you don't need to come out to sign anything. I'll leave it right here on the ground at the main door, unless you've got a delivery slot somewhere that I didn't see."

No answer came from the camera itself and he could find no sign of a mounted speaker. He continued to jump from one leg to another for three more minutes. Finally, he did what he said he'd do and left the package on the ground next to the locked doors.

He ran back to his truck, jumped inside, made a U turn, and drove downhill. As he turned the corner at Evergreen Boulevard, the driver picked up speed, travelling due East on Arapahoe Road toward Centennial airport. After traveling a few miles he pulled off the road and stopped. Several police and military vehicles greeted him.

Trace Mitchell banged on the side of the truck to be let inside. Two analysts joined him. Dressed in his brown uniform, Schaffer slid the door back and let them in. With the exception of Mitchell, each man sat on a stool in front of two or more monitors at a time.

"We don't have clear pictures from the satellite yet," Mitchell said, "and no one picked up that package you left out front. Army's blowing up photos you sent back from the camera you're wearing."

"Oh yeah," Schaffer said getting up from one of the stools. He grabbed at the collar of his brown shirt to unpin the very thin nameplate, which hid the camera. "Forgot it was there."

Schaffer climbed back onto a stool and again adjusted a monitor.

"So far we know the lobby is empty," Mitchell continued, "and thanks to that soda cup you threw we discovered two men dressed in camouflage hiding in the front wooded area. The microphone you attached to the front of the building has picked up continuous sounds, perhaps garbled conversation. Analysts think it's coming from a room near the lobby.

"We haven't seen all eight people yet. I'm referring to the eight Sophie claims to have seen, that's four people in two cars. So if two of them are in the wooded area and another two were the ones arrested at Arapahoe and Orchard, where are the other four?"

"I think I got 'em on screen, sir," said one of the analysts. "We've got low clouds otherwise our satellite photos would show contrasts better. The back of the grounds behind the building had human activity about an hour ago. But it's all quiet now."

As the man spoke two other agents came in carrying cable which they hooked up to electric generators.

"You can barely make them out," continued the analyst. "Police are still gathering at the base of the hill. We don't know whether the people in back are aware of that activity or not. We don't have real time data yet. Another fifteen minutes, a few more cable attachments, and we'll have it."

Schaffer busily tried to get a clear image from the building's own security cameras and was having difficulty. What more could he do wrong today he thought. Making an ass of himself was a given. Maybe no one would notice him shivering in short pants.

"And one more thing," Mitchell added, as he put his phone back in his pocket. "Actually, three more things. FBI agents found the phone Bradley used to answer Dr. Buchanan's phone call last night. It was on a man who got off a plane in upstate New York. They think Bradley must have slipped it into the man's pocket. Also, Arapahoe Police just released Sophie Fortune to go home. She was unharmed, but her cab was totalled. And last but not least, Freddie Meda didn't make it. He died a half hour ago of injuries incurred during his kidnapping. We don't know if the same person who took Inez took Freddie, but because it's happening on the same day, it's too coincidental. I'm anxious to get started. I want to be with the first group going in."

"Me too," Schaffer shouted. "Can I hitch a ride?" Before Mitchell could answer, he'd snatched his pile of street clothes from the floor of the truck. "I'll change in your back seat. I'm freezing."

"C'mon," Mitchell beckoned. It had been a long day that was now stretching into morning for both of them.

๑

As they wrapped themselves in body armor from the trunk of Mitchell's car, Schaffer asked, "So you still think Alan Bradley is responsible for taking Dr. Buchanan hostage, thinking it would delay his arrest for murder? It still doesn't sound right to me. His lawyers would give him a better chance of staying out of jail than kidnapping Dr. Buchanan would."

"Even smart people do dumb things."

"What about Sophie's story," Schaffer continued, "that Dr. Buchanan brought a gun but doesn't have bullets for it and that she thinks somebody is watching her. Sounds loopy to me."

Mitchell had his mouth open ready to speak, wondering if he should have left Schaffer back at the truck, when a sheriff walked straight toward them. Mitchell had parked behind police cars from Arapahoe County, the jurisdiction in which the Metro State building was located.

With an Ipad in his hands, the sheriff said, "Take a look at this. We released Sophie Fortune from headquarters about twenty minutes ago. Told her to go home and wait for us to call her with news of this Buchanan woman. Sophie was cooperative. Gave a detailed statement of the incident in the intersection. We arrested the two guys in the other vehicle and sent her home. We fed her statement to you guys in CBI. You've probably seen some of this by now. We even watched her get into a cab to go home."

Mitchell watched video of Sophie standing at the main door of the Metro State building yelling, "I know you're in there. Bring Dr. Buchanan out here. Bring her out now. You hear me? I know you don't want me to come in there after you. Not with my gun you don't."

A cab could be seen behind her, parked at the curb.

"I haven't sent anybody after her yet," said the sheriff. "Wanted to wait for word from you. She could ruin everything."

"I'll get her," Mitchell hollered over his shoulder. He was already running up the hill through the wooded area. "She knows my voice. Tell your men to stay away from the front doors until I give a signal."

Two gunshots and the sound of breaking glass told him he had to move faster. He ran straight through the forest until he stood at the tip of the hill across the driveway. A cab was parked at the curb. Glass from the revolving door was on the ground and from a distance Sophie could be seen standing inside the lobby. Then suddenly, with no warning, there was nothing. A black curtain came down inside the lobby, across the entire glassed-in portion of the entrance, blocking

Mitchell's view inside. Like a curtain onstage in a theater, he could no longer see Sophie.

"Sophie," Mitchell shouted, as he walked toward the broken glass. "Get out of there now."

But there was no reply.

33

Dilawar stood like a statue in front of the glass back door of the women's shelter. The building itself was a cement structure with small windows that imitated several suburban bunker style offices across America. It was out of place in Afghanistan as an office building, but acceptable as a war-time shelter. Quaalude fidgeted beside him, as they waited for the woman in charge.

They watched several young women through the door, each chatted, dusted, washed floors, and fluffed upholstered furniture. They could hear two of the women inside giggle and explain that the beggars standing outside were waiting for Badrah. Not until the woman they waited for walked toward them did Dilawar realize that he and Quaalude were the beggars the women referred to. He had neither shaved nor bathed and his embarrassment made him avoid eye contact while describing the woman he was looking for.

After several minutes of silence with the glass door still between them, the plainly dressed woman with an unmistakable regal bearing finally said, "Abida! That was her name. I think you've described Abida."

Only then did she open the door, asking them to help her down a single marble step to an outside small garden where she could sit. Both Quaalude and Dilawar each took hold of an elbow as they walked with her. They made their way from the back door to a stone bench a few steps away. Both tried to hide a certain amount of joy over finding the one person who could lead them to the woman they sought. As Badrah spoke, Dilawar knew he'd been unusually lucky. She explained that if they had come a few days later, she would have been gone from Afghanistan with no plan to ever return. She had unfortunately suffered a mild stroke a few months earlier. Her arm, she indicated, was now permanently bent. She intended to take advantage of an offer made by a distant relative who had settled in the U.S.

Dilawar couldn't help feeling that he, too, might be closer to going home to than he'd originally anticipated.

"Yes, I knew her quite well," said Badrah, as she spread her skirts over the low bench. A few strands of unruly gray hair fell across her eyes which she attempted to fix with knobby jointed fingers that worked better in unison than individually. Quietly she searched in her pockets until she found hairpins to further fix the damage. All this made Dilawar impatient for her words.

"Abida and I first met in the hospital just outside Khandahar more than ten years ago. I was still a nurse there. She was all alone and had been found beside the main road to Kabul. She'd been there for some time. Motorists thought she was a bundle of trash until someone stopped.

"Such a brave young woman. She gave birth to a premature boy. Also she'd been shot in the leg. And ... there were several rumors at the time, but no way to confirm any of them, because Abida, who had been unconscious when brought to the hospital, said she could remember nothing. She'd been brutalized. The doctor decided not to operate fearing he could damage her ability to ever walk. Then there'd be no question that she'd be condemned to beg on the streets forever with her boy by her side.

Her baby grew to be quite healthy. She stayed in the hospital for many months afterward helping clean and feed other patients."

Dilawar caught Quaalude's eye and smiled at him knowingly, but Badrah frowned. She stared at sand surrounding her own sandaled feet. A much younger woman from inside the shelter brought out one cup of tea and placed it on a stone slab beside the bench. There was no offer of anything to Dilawar or Quaalude. And both understood that as beggars they were of little consequence.

"But I'm not telling you anything that uniquely differentiates her from all the other women inside. Many women have had to bed down in caves with men who have just devoured their entire families, in the hope that they have kept one child alive for one more day."

Badrah sipped her tea and said, "I'd always wondered what happened to her."

"What do you mean?" Dilawar's voice faltered slightly. This woman was revealing his fear and anger at what might have happened to Kadija, and to his own mother, as she too had desperately tried to keep her family alive. Yet he remained observant enough to observe a change in the woman's body language. She was suddenly agitated.

"I didn't see her once she left the hospital. Not for many years. When she and her boy came here I hardly recognized her. She no longer walked with a limp and they looked as if they hadn't eaten in months. Later she told me that during those years she'd found work in three separate homes from three wealthy Afghanis in three different cities: Kandahar, Mazar-e-Sharif, and Kabul. She'd been from one side of Afghanistan to the other. Her adventures kept our ladies in the shelter entertained for over a year. Her stories revealed that her employment always ended in more or less the same way. She was forced to escape with her son when a member of the household wanted her to assume wifely duties. I can tell you it made lots of women here think about their roles as women. They admired her courage, even in the face of the whip."

She took another sip of tea before continuing. Dilawar tried not to bite his tongue but wanted her to hurry the story along, thinking that Abida had very likely edited out the more horrible parts of her survival anyway.

"They stayed here for two years. That was about five years ago. She taught Afghan women skills to support themselves. Abida was always full of ideas, like making and selling jewelry, packaging teas, making bags. She was very clever.

"One day a Warlord came looking for her, a man whose home she had never worked in. He told me he'd heard of her cleverness. He traveled with his own army of mercenaries. Abida peeked at him from behind our drapes, while I told the man she was visiting family members and would return next day. She had seen him before. He was a friend of the master in one of the homes in which she worked. He'd asked her to deliver messages to the man she worked for, but only during moonless nights. Her boy had seen this Warlord before as well."

Dilawar quietly wondered what had really taken place. With an American trained spy like Abida in the mix, she would have discovered exactly what that message contained and determined an appropriate course of action. However, if CIA thought she was dead she hadn't unfortunately found a way to communicate with them.

"Abida," Badrah continued, "was not one to speak about herself often. She disappeared the same day that man came. No, no," she said, rubbing the side of her forehead with her fingers.

She looked up into the sky before looking straight ahead. "I remember now. It was the next day that she disappeared." Badrah placed both her hands in her lap and said, "She asked me the day before, if I knew of a shelter for women in a more remote location. And the next day," she paused again and looked at them both with wide searching eyes, "the next day she and her son were gone."

"Could the War Lord have kidnapped them?" Dilawar asked.

"No. He and his men stayed nearby this shelter for several days afterward, thinking she would come back."

There was something about the way she spoke now that was different from the way she'd spoken earlier. He suspected she was not being completely honest. Was she adding to or subtracting from the truth? And why was she doing that? Dilawar kept his thoughts to himself.

"What answer did you give her?" Dilawar asked. "Is there such a thing as a remote shelter for women?"

Dilawar was actually jogging in place, unable to subdue the energy in his body as he spoke. "Anything could have happened to her in the past five years." He berated himself for not searching for Kadija sooner. He grew more agitated by the minute.

The woman stared up at him. "And who are you anyway, if not someone else, who would make her life miserable? I … I know Abdul here," she said pointing to Quaalude. "Yes, I know his real name. I remember it. You see I first met his mother two years ago. A delightful lady. We met in London at a cultural exchange conference. I was sent by the newly appointed Afghan government. We shared stories and photos of our families and when we returned home we continued to write. I know, for example, she still cries for you, her oldest."

Quaalude sat down in the dirt, obviously distraught.

She looked up at Dilawar. "He was a good boy before he let drugs take over his life," she continued. "See how small a world the Middle East is even with the invasion of infidels."

Quaalude looked away, his face pitiable.

"But you," Badrah said, again looking at Dilawar, "I can't distinguish you from any other invader who finds himself in Kabul. You dress like an American because you think it fashionable. You don't fool anyone. Will it help you get a job or keep you safe? Are you the one who feeds him poison?"

"I no longer am controlled by drugs," Quaalude boasted. "And this man has honorable intentions. I speak for him because I know him well."

Dilawar sat beside Quaalude quietly, recognizing the woman's global awareness. The same young woman who had served Badrh tea returned, this time with a plate of fruit. Once she placed it on the stone slab beside Badrah, she turned to leave, but Badrah's aggressive voice stopped her. "Tell our ladies I'll be with them shortly." The woman nodded and left.

"I don't believe you, Abdul," Badrah continued. "You were here not long ago begging with an older man. You lied about knowing him, too. Don't force the government to arrest you for begging in the streets. Not here." She handed them each a pear from the plate.

The two thanked her for the fruit and they ate.

"I *do* know him," Quaalude pleaded through a full mouth. "His name is Dilawar and he is honorable and good. He means this woman no harm and wants to help her."

Dilawar wanted very much to be more open with Badrah. He knew she was college educated and hardened by years of fighting the good fight. Had Kadija thought of her in the same way? Could Kadija have revealed who she was to such a woman? He noticed her looking at him as he ate the pear.

"She and her son," Badrah finally said, "are very likely dead. I gave her the only map I had of the Hindu Kush mountains. There is a place called the Wakhan Corridor where people are too poor to ask questions, too cold to fight, and where the Taliban don't bother to travel. Even the central Afghan government ignores the place. The mountains are so high the people who live there say birds must cross on foot. I've never been there myself, but foreign tourists who pass through the High Pamir speak of the place and its people lovingly."

"It sounds wonderful," Dilawar said.

"That's funny." The woman seemed more at ease now, as if she'd made a personal resolution of some sort. Perhaps she enjoyed sitting with them in the shade and talking.

"I'm sure I remember Abida saying the very same thing. But I don't believe she had enough clothing or food for such a journey. I gave her what I could and helped her obtain a horse from the husband of a benefactor for this shelter. I wondered if the man who was looking for her might have been the boy's father or grandfather."

"What difference would it make?" Dilawar tried to hide his anger. "The man may have beaten them or tried to kill them."

"But," she answered, "he would be an eternally driven man if she kept his son or grandson away from him. I couldn't understand that about her. As helpful and caring as Abida was, she shared very little about herself. It made me think sometimes that her history was exceptionally horrendous or absolutely fantastic."

Kadija had likely manipulated the woman into thinking that way so that she could obtain help based on the woman's ability to fill in the horrible blanks of an uncertain background story. They both stared at each other, Dilawar wondering if Kadija's ploy had worked.

Quaalude put his hand on Dilawar's shoulder as if to comfort his new friend. But the gaze between Dilawar and Badrah was not yet broken.

"So," Badrah said, finally diverting her gaze, "I gave her my rifle and an ammunition belt I had earlier found near the body of a dead Al Qaeda soldier. You must never tell this. I don't know why I'm telling you this now. Perhaps I believe Abdul when he says you mean her no harm. I believe in very little nowadays."

With a gun, Dilawar thought, she could still be alive. He didn't smile. To do so might disclose his confidence in their covert training.

"Later that man who was looking for her came back and said he was her distant cousin by marriage. I still wouldn't tell him anything about Abida's intentions."

Dilawar noticed her staring across the street. She was about to stand and go inside. Yet there was still much to discuss.

"I'll need to duplicate Abida's journey," Dilawar said. "I'll need the same information you gave her and I may need…"

"You ask for too much."

"There is no one else to ask."

"If the world was a different place, I would pick up my cell phone and call someone in that region to ask if she's there. I've already tried. Every year I've tried. But there are languages there that no one else speaks, political issues that no one else comprehends, and immense poverty. Even if you went, you couldn't be sure you'd find them."

"It's true the world is a dangerous place," said Quaalude. "But if we don't do what we can to help our friends, what good are we?"

Ignoring Quaalude, the woman got up from her stone seat, and taking small steps, hurried to the back door. What had she seen to make her nervous? Dilawar refused to look out onto the street in case there was someone provocative there. She turned to look at them both before entering the shelter. "Meet me here after sunset. I'll have everything I can safely provide. Whatever else you need you must find yourselves."

She spoke angrily, as if she felt forced to help. But Dilawar was too pleased to mention his observations to Quaalude. He had to remind himself that Quaalude was just a boy.

He patted Quaalude on the back, smiling inwardly at his good fortune. As he did so Dilawar caught sight of his nemesis across the street, the man he thought had been an Al Qaeda soldier, and the man they'd left sleeping on top of the ridge hours ago with a sleeping baby in his arms. There was no need to point him out to Quaalude. Dilawar knew enough about human nature to know this would not be their last encounter.

34

SEPTEMBER 2009 DENVER TECH CENTER

Only slightly out of breath from running uphill, Mitchell ran toward the cab he knew would still be at the curb. Empty. Yet in the video, he could have sworn he'd seen the shadow of a driver behind the wheel. Standing in one spot but visually scanning 360 degrees, he saw a man smoking a cigar under a streetlight.

"Your cab?" Mitchell hollered.

"Yeah." A round man waddled toward him, still carrying his lit cigar between his fingers.

"Get in. Go home. Get outta here, before you're arrested," Mitchell said, continuing to walk toward the front door of the building. He heard the man speaking behind him.

"But the sign says …"

"Did you hear me? Go home! You're obstructing justice!"

Just then automatic gunfire could be heard coming from inside the building, then two single shots from a revolver. Both the cab driver and Mitchell had flattened to the ground. Now they each got to their feet.

Mitchell ran up to the driver, grabbing his shirtsleeve and collar. "You're too late," Mitchell said, pulling him away from the cab. "Where are the keys?"

"Here."

Mitchell jerked the man backwards, grabbing the keys from his hand as he did so.

"Go straight down that hill," Mitchell ordered. "Tell the first policemen you see that I'm driving this cab into the building and to have SWAT enter from the back immediately."

The man hollered, "Wait. You can't ..."

"Do it"! Mitchell yelled. "They'll keep you safe down there."

Mitchell had already turned over the ignition, eased his foot on the gas pedal and turned the steering wheel till the cab's two front tires were over the curb. In the rear view mirror he could see the stout man running downhill. With one hand Mitchell took his gun out of its holster, while adrenaline pumped through his body.

"This is Mitchell," he yelled into the microphone on his shoulder. "Send SWAT now!" Then he mashed the gas pedal into the floor.

Blindly, Mitchell drove through revolving glass doors that shattered around the cab. A black theatrical curtain covered the windshield for a second, but he refused to put his foot on the brake until he was all the way inside the lobby. His wheels started up the steps when he realized Sophie was kneeling on his left, behind what may have been a bulletin board. Her gun was drawn, but pointed toward the ceiling.

Mitchell kept his head down and pulled the brake up. He opened the side door and slid out of the driver's seat. The cab with its open side door became their shield. "Where'd that gun come from Sophie? Thought you told police Dr. Buchanan was the only one with a gun."

"You must be Mr. Mitchell then and they didn't asked me if *I* had a gun. I thought they'd go find her quicker if they thought she had one. But she doesn't have ammunition."

"You know you're going to have to surrender that thing over to me don't you?" He paused a moment, then asked, "From which direction did that automatic gun fire come?"

"Up those stairs," Sophie replied. "And I've got a license to carry."

"A license means nothing in a gun fight with law enforcement." Mitchell was preoccupied as he spoke and looked around him. Stairs made a semi circle around the lobby and the cab he'd driven was not quite halfway up those stairs.

"I think I hit one of them," she said. "That's why they haven't rushed down here."

"Yeah?" Mitchell responded. "You're a good shot, are ya'? But you can't use a weapon in a shoot out with police." Mitchell turned away from her and yelled from his crouched position.

"Colorado Bureau of Investigation! You're under arrest. CBI and Arapahoe SWAT have you surrounded. Send Dr. Buchanan out now."

He continued to crouch beside Sophie and listened as a door latch clicked open and slammed shut somewhere further down a hall off the lobby. They could see nothing.

Sophie said, "I thought I heard Dr. Buchanan's voice behind me just before the shooting started, but I could be wrong."

Confused, Mitchell cupped his hand around his ear for amplification. Voices and machinery surrounded them. He could hear the SWAT team arresting men outside the building. Someone was exiting by another door. Voices could also be heard through the forested area in front of the building. And yet, he heard it, the distinct sound of a helicopter's engine and rotary blades overhead. For a moment he panicked. It could have meant anything from a TV news crew to a military style barrage of artillery.

"So why don't you do something?" Sophie shouted. She was a mere foot away from him.

"SHUT UP," Mitchell replied.

Speaking softly into his shoulder microphone he said, "This is Mitchell inside. Somebody take a look on the roof. Sounds like a helicopter. Let me know what you find."

Turning to Sophie again, he said, "Put your gun on the floor and kick it under the cab. When you've done that, I can check out the door where you heard Buchanan's voice."

Neither one of them moved.

"What are you waiting for?" she screamed.

"If you don't put that gun on the floor," Mitchell spit, "you know what I've got to do don't you?" Still crouching, he backed away two steps and pointed his gun straight at her forehead. Her nostrils grew bigger, her shoulders tensed, but she wouldn't move. "Think, Sophie. You've taken enough time away from rescuing Inez as it is. Put it down gently and kick it gently."

She complied.

Without a moment to waste, Mitchell jumped up and leapt toward a carved wooden door then slowly backed away. Sophie was only a few steps behind him. With one foot he suddenly kicked the door all the way in. As he stood at the doorway, he felt Sophie almost push him forward from behind.

"Oh, am I ever glad to see both of you," Inez said, wiping the edges of her mouth with a cloth napkin as she sat at a small card table. "Thought I heard my name, but Bradley here tried to tell me I couldn't possibly have heard it through those thick doors. We convinced each other that we should sit here and wait for whatever comes. Aren't we glad we did?"

Mitchell knew Inez was nervous. She was talking too fast. He just hoped to God she wouldn't *do* anything fast.

She got up slowly from her seat. Alan Bradley, who sat across from her, got up from his chair as well. His expression made Mitchell wonder if he knew what was going on. Inez smiled at him, as she spoke.

"We've been eating very delicious food while we waited for a man named Morton Meda. Did I remember his name correctly?" Inez asked, looking at Bradley.

He did nothing and she continued to talk. "It's hard to believe this Morton person is still coming. It's so late it's past my bedtime. According to Bradley he's coming to kill people, so I'm really not sorry we missed him."

Mitchell and Sophie continued to inch their way into the room as she spoke, Mitchell with his gun straight out in front of him, aimed at Bradley. Mitchell scanned for additional people in the room as he entered. Sophie kept close behind Mitchell's back. It was annoying, but certainly her safest place to be.

Inez gathered up her purse and walked to where Sophie stood behind Mitchell. "Oh my dear, I am so happy to see you. Are you all right?" Inez said.

Sophie was all smiles. "I'm sure glad you're alive, too," she replied.

Mitchell spoke into his microphone. "This is Mitchell again. I'm in the main room off the lobby. Send me three officers. Bring evidence bags. And what about that helicopter I heard earlier?"

There was no reply, but a minute later two men and a woman entered the room, their guns drawn on each person inside with the exception of Mitchell.

"I need one of you to go put the gun that's on the floor in the lobby into an evidence bag," he directed. One policeman holstered his gun and left the room.

Turning his eyes on Inez, Mitchell said, "Now your purse, Dr. Buchanan." He told the policewoman to take the gun out of her purse and hand the purse back to Inez, thinking this would cause Inez the least embarrassment. The policewoman put the gun in an evidence bag and left the room with it.

Mitchell continued to stand at an angle, keeping Bradley in his view at all times. So did the remaining policeman.

"I'm truly sorry I got you into this," Inez said to Sophie.

"Quiet," Mitchell hollered to Inez.

Whispering, Sophie answered, "It's my fault. I told the police you had a gun so they'd move quicker. Then I got scared the police might shoot you because you had one, so I came back here."

Mitchell could not let their distracting words interfere with his duty. "It's your turn Bradley," he shouted to drown out the conversation. "Hold your arms up high."

"I'm not armed," Bradley said.

"Frisk him," Mitchell said to the one policeman. "Then read him his rights and book him. I'd like to take your word for that Bradley but I get paid to be sure."

The officer searched Bradley then handcuffed him, while reciting his rights and shoved him out the door.

Turning to Inez, Mitchell asked, "You all right?"

"I've felt better." She pointed to the monitors, "But whatever you do, don't leave these monitors and amplifiers here overnight without taking a copy of that video that's been playing. Bradley showed it ad nauseum on all these screens and yet I don't think he would have if he'd understood its significance. It'll be important at his trial."

"Yes, we'll save everything in here," Mitchell said with a tired smile. "Isn't it past your bedtime? I don't mean to sound flip. I just know we'll have a lot to talk about in the morning and this is the morning I'm talking about."

"Actually," Inez said, "I made a terrible mistake by not telling you about a robbery that took place in my home the night before." Inez's head was down and she appeared to be concentrating.

"It'll keep. You go along with that officer in the hall," Mitchell urged.

"I was too busy," Inez continued, "reminiscing about how similar it was to a break-in that occurred in Dolly's home."

Inez suddenly lifted her head up and glanced at drapes that hung behind the refrigerator. She walked over to them and yanked them down, then stared into the dark emptiness of a grand ballroom without its chairs and tables.

"What do you see?" Mitchell asked.

"Nothing," she answered. "But I kept thinking there were people in there whispering and listening the whole time I was in here."

Abruptly, she walked to the console of levers and knobs and clicked one on. They heard voices. She clicked a few more and realized the sounds were coming from outside.

"Bradley and his crew must have placed microphones all over this building," Inez said.

Turning around to face Mitchell squarely she said, "You don't still think Bradley killed Dolly do you? Because he didn't. He couldn't have. Bradley and Dolly were lovers all their lives and the young woman Dolly wanted me to find, well she was their love child's daughter."

Mitchell was tired and it sounded like Inez was telling him the details of a soap opera. It took everything his parents ever taught him to keep a civil tongue in his mouth. "And I'll bet you find something important about it by morning," Mitchell exclaimed. "Time you went home to beddy bye."

Sophie took one step closer to Mitchell and shouted in his face. "WHO THE HELL do you think you are? Here's a woman who put her own life in jeopardy to save another, a woman who wants to give you information so you can do your job better. She could have retired and watched TV all day. But no! You see what she's doing, don't you? And you've got the nerve to act as if you're the one that's been through hell and gone. Well let me set you straight about that." Her fists were on her hips.

Inez grabbed one of her arms and pulled her back. "I don't think he meant it that way Sophie."

"The Hell he didn't."

Inez continued to hold Sophie's arm. "We're all a little ..."

Mitchell took a deep breath and rested both his hands on Sophie's shoulders. He said, "You're right Sophie. I misspoke." Just then a police officer passed the doorway and Mitchell called out to him.

"This officer," Mitchell explained to Sophie and Inez, as the man came inside the room, "and another one that I'm sure he'll find outside, will take you and Inez home in separate cars. And Sophie, I don't think you'll need police protection after that officer's shift is over. You've already given your statement to Arapahoe police. I'm sure they'll want to talk to you again before they return your gun to you. And thanks for reminding me what I should never forget about Inez, that I'm damn lucky to have her as a friend. I mean that."

Inez stood where she was and said nothing in response to his orders. Mitchell was only grateful that he could get rid of these women while he sorted this whole thing out.

Sophie followed the officer to the door and turned around. She flung her arms around Inez's shoulders. Inez seemed startled at first, but hugged her back.

Inez smiled. "You helped keep me alive. We'll talk in the morning."

Obviously exhausted, Sophie slowly walked toward the lobby with the police officer in front of her. Inez stood near the broken door to the room she had occupied.

Mitchell, surveying the room, noticed the broken bottle of wine and its splatter against the wall. He suddenly felt bad. Inez had used her wits to stay alive another day and had not been given credit for keeping Bradley where he was.

He glanced sideways and saw Inez still standing at the doorway, staring at the monitors. "I am sorry I was rude and condescending," Mitchell said. "I don't know what ..."

She said, "Oh, I know what you meant. I'm tired, too. Tonight I had to come face to face with the fact that Bradley's in no condition to help bring Kadija home. He blames himself for what may have happened to her. Hopefully, I'll get help from someone on Facebook perhaps who knew Sampati Jagjit."

Mitchell kept shaking his head. "I don't want to hear it right now, because, you know what? As terrific a person as you are, you are not a detective. You have no business carrying a gun. You have not been hired to rescue Kadija Campbell, and you almost got Sophie Fortune killed. I could have killed her in the line of duty in a heartbeat."

She looked at him and said, "I'm sorry I've disappointed you, but ..."

A policeman came running into the room almost pushing into her. "Agent Mitchell?"

"What!"

"They told me to tell you about the helicopter."

Inez stood beside Mitchell and said, "A helicopter! That's how they knew. They must have used it all day long."

The policeman continued. "It landed at Centennial Airport and an arrest was made. Three men in a helicopter were on the roof of this building. Ten minutes later they landed and one of them got away. They still haven't caught him. However, the other two are in custody. So far they haven't said a word."

Inez asked, "Was one of them wearing red sneakers?"

There was total silence between the two men, who stared at each other until Mitchell asked, "So was anyone wearing red sneakers?"

"I don't know sir, but I can find out." The young man put his phone to his ear turned his back on Mitchell and casually walked toward the door. Mitchell tried hard to breath through his diaphragm, knowing it would eventually calm his anger.

Inez said softly, " I don't want to go home until I learn what happened to Freddie and Morton Meda today."

"What do you know about Freddie Meda? Where are you getting your information? I never mentioned Freddie or Morton to you."

"Bradley played video of the explosion at Freddie's place almost nonstop." Inez took hold of Mitchell's arm. "He was trying to pin that explosion on Morton. But I need to hear what happened to them from you. I think my stolen slip of paper with Bradley's cell phone number gave the crook or crooks a way to follow Bradley's every move today. I think I'm right because Bradley's plan to kill Freddie didn't turn out the way he wanted."

Just then the policeman turned to Mitchell again and said, "Arresting officers say the man who ran, the only one they haven't caught yet, was wearing a pair of red Nike's. They're still searching for him at Centennial."

Mitchell turned back to Inez. "Talk to me!"

Schaffer strolled into the room smiling, hands in his pockets. "So, how's it going in here? We've arrested some twenty-five militiamen outside and successfully kept the media from getting into this building. I was even interviewed by a television reporter."

Captivated by Schaffer's imagery, Inez listened to him silently.

"One of those baby-faced militiamen had the nerve to scream over live TV that they were just practicing," Schaffer said. "That it was all a misunderstanding. That these were mock exercises they were doing for the military. State District Attorney thinks it's as good a story as any for the media for the time being."

"Well, I'm awful glad there's nothing left for you to do tonight," Mitchell said with what he hoped was a calm voice to covered up his anger at the half-assed investigator turned TV star.

Inez responded quickly. "That isn't half of Bradley's army. He didn't retire when he left Martindale, Inc. He became the full-time head of his own militia. And I don't think they were the people who rented that helicoptor all day."

All three men looked at one another.

"You've got evidence?" Schaffer asked her. The significance of his question was not lost on Mitchell. Schaffer was being sarcastic, and he hoped Inez didn't notice.

"I know where you can find evidence," Inez answered.

Mitchell took a deep breath. "You sure you won't be too tired if we go to CBI headquarters now?" Mitchell asked in exasperation.

"Just keep some decent coffee warmed up," Inez answered. "I may be safer there than at home. Some of what Bradley said might be right, although he was only trying to cover up his own crime."

Chuckling, Schaffer asked, "And what crime would that be?"

"Why killing Stronsky, of course."

35

JANUARY 2009 WAKHAN CORRIDOR, AFGHANISTAN

Before leaving Kabul, Dilawar bought ski pants and goose down jackets for both of them. Quaalude boasted that he didn't need leather gloves so Dilawar didn't buy them. He was too preoccupied with other matters. But two weeks into their journey north Dilawar realized that Quaalude had no idea how cold the Wakhan Corridor could be.

Both uneasy and surprised that his credit card had worked and that its credit limit had been increased, Dilawar also bought two motorcycles, a 2006 KDX for himself and a newer 2008 Honda CRF dirt bike for Quaalude.

Langley was definitely communicating with him. But what did they want? Walking off the reservation was frowned upon and every agent knew it. Perhaps the Company wanted him to know their generosity was boundless. Dilawar knew better. Generosity always had a price.

He justified his ostentatious purchases as an attempt to let all interested parties know where he was headed. And it wasn't just CIA he wanted to alert. He needed that former Al Qaeda soldier to follow him into the mountains as well. There he could interrogate him without an audience.

Dilawar hated cold even when he lived in Colorado. He wore gloves every day through the Hindu Kush mountains and he taught

Quaalude to pull his undershirts down past the end of his sleeves to cover his hands. But Quaalude enjoyed the sympathetic attention given to him by the women in each village who willingly ~~they~~ gave him pieces of woven wool to cover his hands.

With the help of neighboring Wahki, Khowar, and Kyrgyz villagers they built their own shelter of mud and stone. Inside they kept a fire burning in the middle of the floor, letting smoke out through a hole in the roof.

Dilawar was thankful he'd stolen the Blast Match and binoculars from the plane in Kabul. There was no kindling above timberline. Villagers burned yak turds which gave their shelter a slightly sweet aroma. And although their yurt had a flat roof to naturally dry the feces, Dilawar had not yet disciplined himself in the collection of it, relying on his Match instead.

Villagers were friendly, and offering travelers along the Silk Road what little they had. Dilawar encouraged their generosity by giving them candy, gum, tea, and coffee in return, all of which he'd bought with his credit card in larger towns along the way like Fayzabad, Baharak, and Eshkashem.

Dilawar knew some words in Kyrgyz and Wahki because they were related to Turkic and Iraqi languages he'd studied. Although he'd been able to pass himself off as an international interpreter in Iraq, he had no wish to appear so skilled here. Several villagers however spoke Persian and although Dilawar's Persian was rusty, he listened carefully. He gleaned from idle talk that the past year's snowstorms were unlike any others. Storing their motorcycles inside their yurt helped, but was no guarantee the engines wouldn't freeze.

Months passed before Quaalude moaned, "We know nothing more about this woman than we did before coming here. It's unlikely her horse survived the rocky terrain. And her boy probably couldn't survive the climate. Families here watch half their children die each winter. If I were not your friend I would be dead now, too."

"No," said Dilawar sipping hot yak milk from his clay cup. "You and I haven't the temperment for death," he smiled and marveled that Quaalude had no idea of the strenuous survival courses taught in other parts of the world, or that ordinary people prided themselves on withstanding anything nature mounted against them. He could accept that Kadija was dead, but not that she was killed by something she had been trained to survive. She'd been just that good.

Dilawar sat in one of the clay platform seats they'd molded inside their yurt. Every day he watched Quaalude gain more muscle than he had the day before and was happy with his pupil.

"If I find someone to make you a pair of leather gloves," Dilawar asked, "would you be willing to stay here one more season? She may have wandered across a border like Tajikistan. This place could become our base as we trek north."

Before Quaalude could respond, a faint rubbing sound of wood against stone made them both listen more carefully. Dilawar snatched his gun from its holster and cocked it. Tangled strips of wool which hung from the door to keep the cold out, began to spread apart. Suddenly a woolen oblong object, a little over 100 centimeters long flew inside and landed with a thud on the floor of the yurt.

Dilawar rushed toward it, not thinking about an enemy outside, but a bomb thrown inside. Quaalude crouched behind the flames from the stove and shivered.

A cursory inspection revealed its resemblance to a short mummy, a human form wrapped in strips of cloth. When it absolutely didn't move, Dilawar dropped to his knees and attempted to tear away the cloth. Frantic, Quaalude ran outside, holding on to a few of the strips that hung down from the doorway and providing Dilawar with a freezing view of the outside expanse. Consumed with fear, Quaalude threw up just outside the door.

Moonlight revealed to Dilawar one continuous streak down the hill beside their yurt, a possible path made by the thing in the room. And yet the object had no visible feet. Their closest neighbor's yurt could barely be seen from their own doorway.

"Come help," Dilawar yelled.

Quaalude reentered, determined to help.

"Sorry. I don't know what happened to me," he said, unable to look at Dilawar.

Finally, the head of a barely breathing young boy was visible. It was not the first time they'd been offered a boy on their journey out of Kabul. Night boys, as they were sometimes called, had to eat too, particularly those who had run away from their War Lord owners. Quaalude's face was stricken with sadness, as Dilawar carried what was left of a skinny seven or eight year old closer to the fire. He was breathing, but only faintly and was covered in layers of black linen cloth.

His skin had color. Blood still pumped through his veins and arteries. Even his fingers felt warmer than Quaalude's.

Had a family realized they'd been paying particular attention to the boys and given them one? Wouldn't they have wanted payment in return? This boy was not very brown, reminding Dilawar that neither was Kadija. But his hair was wavy like all the other boys in the area. Dilawar had to admit there was no reason whatsoever to believe him to be Kadija's son. Had this boy come through the cold night alone?

Quaalude frantically searched through packs tied to his battered Kawasaki until he found the first aid kit Dilawar had purchased. As soon as he found the thermometer, he stuck it into the boy's mouth. Though the boy was breathing his eyes were closed and he was otherwise unresponsive.

Kneeling beside him, Dilawar unwrapped linen from around his frail body and wondered if the boy had been prepared for burial. Rolling him to one side revealed what neither of them expected. A mending welt, not quite a week old, stretched from the back of his head above his right ear down across his back.

"A leather whip," Dilawar said coldly. He made certain not to touch the scar to avoid causing pain. Snatching his goose down sleeping bag from the seat of his Yamaha, he worked diligently to unzip it without snagging the feather light fabric. He unrolled the bag over and around the boy's body. The thermometer fell from his mouth.

"Who would do this?" Quaalude asked. He picked up the thermometer. "There are no other tracks in the snow. How could he come down the side of that hill alone? Thankfully, he has no fever."

Quaalude's first question hung in Dilawar's mind. 'Who would do this?' Was the middle-aged man from their camp in Kabul following them at a distance? That's who he thought crashed into their yurt in the first place. If that old man could leave a baby and its mother in the hills near Kabul, could he whip a young boy? But why? And had he known Abida and her son? He was certainly no War Lord, as Badrah had described the man looking for Abida. Dilawar had already convinced himself that the old man was out there somewhere.

"We might have to stay here longer than we'd both originally planned," Dilawar announced. He was prepared for an argument or at least disappointment from Quaalude, even though he planned to send him back to Islamabad when their adventure was over. But Quaalude said nothing.

"I won't feel comfortable until we get this boy," Dilawar continued, "whoever he is, on his feet and back to his family. Look in that first aid kit again and see if there's a tiny glass bottle of crystals. It should say ammonium carbonate somewhere on the label."

"I think you must have been a student of everything during your whole life. You know so much. Is that why you sit quietly sometimes?" Quaalude asked. "You don't want people to know how educated you are? Here it is. I found it."

Quaalude unscrewed the top and smelled the contents, dropping the bottle and its top onto the sleeping bag with a yell.

"Don't waste any," Dilawar shouted. He scooped the crystals back into the bottle and shoved the whole thing, without the lid, under the boy's nose. The boy raised his head slightly and coughed several times. His closed eyes popped open. They were shiny and dark.

"Hello," said Quaalude, first in Pashtu, then in Punjabi. Still stretched out atop the goose down blanket, the boy moved his head to better see the entire room. His eyes fixed on the motorcycles.

"What is your name?" Dilawar asked in Arabic.

The boy looked at him, but said nothing. Dilawar tried Farsi and the boy showed no recognition of that, either. Quaalude then tried French. The boy smiled, but said nothing. None of the languages they knew had assisted them with any of the residents along the Wakhan Corridor.

Softly, Dilawar spoke in the language he was certain Abida would have taught her son. "Do you understand English?"

The boy's eyes locked onto Dilawar for a moment. Then he yawned. His teeth were whiter and his gums pinker than those of other children he'd seen so far. Or was he wishing hard to see these small distinctions.

Aware the boy still watched him, Dilawar poured yak milk into his cup from a pot kept hanging over their fire. Quaalude propped the boy's head up slightly, but he seemed only to wet his lips with the liquid before closing his eyes. As the boy slept, they speculated on his origins until they too fell asleep.

Dilawar's eyes opened, when he felt a pinch on his bare hand. The boy was sitting up speaking a kind of Farsi, thick with a Tajik dialect. Dilawar grabbed Quaalude's arm hoping he'd have a better sense of the language, but Quaalude slept soundly.

The boy pointed first at his tongue, his throat, and then at the doorway. It was a kind of charade in which he jumped up and fell down, made gutteral sounds as if gasping, then shut his eyes very tight. The sounds woke Quaalude.

"I believe he says," Quaalude responded, "that he drank something and passed out."

Someone outside grabbed up the felt hanging at the door. Brutally cold air swept the room. Dilawar was on his feet. Cold sunlight drenched their small yurt, making it difficult to see anything more than a silhouette of a man with a beard against the sun. As he stepped inside, the tip of the man's cane reached Dilawar's arm just as Dilawar was about to move it under the goose down blanket toward his gun.

"Omar!" Quaalude yelled happily. "How did you find us? He was on his feet embracing the old man, although it had been almost a year since they'd seen each other. Quaalude turned to Dilawar and said, "You remember Omar from the hill beside the airport in Kabul."

How silly, Dilawar thought. Some days he'd thought of little else. The mysterious boy had obviously been brought here by the old man Quaalude called Omar. Had Omar slept in the cold all night? What would his explanation be?

"Allah has given me many things to be thankful for," said the old man as he grabbed the little boy around his neck. There was fear in the boy's eyes but he did not scream. "I have found you, my friend, Quaalude, after all these months. You see, I was afraid for you, when you disappeared into the night with this man."

"But there was nothing to fear," Quaalude answered. "He is my friend too. We wanted to leave without disturbing anyone's sleep. I am a man now, able to survive on my own. Come. Sit and drink tea with us this early morning.

"Yes," Dilawar, interjected, "drink with us before continuing your journey into the hills." He was impressed with Quaalude's explanation of their departure from Kabul.

Omar released the bundle of cloth at the door with one hand. His palms were wrapped in tape with the tips of his fingers exposed. He stepped inside, still clutching the little boy. Somehow the old man's back was straighter than Dilawar had remembered.

"My search for you has finally been rewarded! Just weeks ago another remarkable thing happened as well. A family with a dying boy gave him to me, this boy, in exchange for my dead chicken. I see he has recovered thanks to our care for him." Omar smiled and stood on one side of the warm fire. No one else smiled in return.

"I understood from your neighbors," Omar went on, "that two foreigners were looking for a boy. Is that not true?"

"No, it is not true," said Dilawar. "My neighbors must have mistaken my kindness toward their youngsters for a desire to take one."

Quaalude added nothing to that exchange of words, making certain the pot of water was hot. Discreetly, he caught sight of the boy, whose face revealed fear. Finally the boy broke away from Omar's hold on his neck and ran from the yurt, peeing all the way.

Before Omar could respond, Quaalude said, "Sit, my friend. The boy will be fine." When they were seated, Quaalude asked, "Where is the gun you always carried while we camped beside Kabul's airport? Is that how you bought a dead chicken?"

"Yes, I mean no. That is how I bought the camel. Yes, I am riding a camel. It is just outside. I prefer to sleep beside my camel at night. Will you go see what is taking that boy so long?" he asked Dilawar. Dilawar did not move.

Just then the boy crawled back inside and sat silently against the far wall of the warm yurt. Conscientiously, he made certain the strips once again hung as a barrier to the cold. Dilawar never took his eyes off Omar, letting him know who the Alpha dog in the room was.

"I made an exchange," Omar continued, now looking at Quaalude, "with a man who no longer wished to travel but wanted to feel secure within his home. I wished to travel to find peace of mind. I dropped the boy into your yurt last night, unaware of the identity of its occupants, but simply thinking that he'd be given a place to sleep through the night out of the cold. I am used to the cold and chose to sleep beside the warmth of my camel."

"Let me have your cup," Quaalude requested. "I will fill it with tea."

"No. I will have just a pinch of your left over tea leaves and a trickle of hot water."

Dilawar took notice of his caution. The lies he told were fascinating. Was Omar a trafficker in boys? Did he have other business interests as well? Omar removed a shiny stainless steel thermos from among the folds of his pants, another possession of quality belonging to a man who had nothing a year earlier.

"Fortune," Quaalude said, while looking at the stainless steel thermos, "has smiled upon you, my make-believe grandfather."

"Yes, it has. A powerful man, a War Lord, with powerful friends has employed me. Have you not heard of my War Lord's friend, Saaiq Haji?"

Quaalude and Dilawar shook their heads.

"Why would we know him?" Dilawar asked.

"Saaiq is a man much traveled and speaks several languages. He and my employer are about the same age and made jihad together as young men," Omar said.

"And you say this Saaiq is a War Lord?" Dilawar asked.

"I am glad you have taken an interest in my most humble adventures. But no, that is not what I said. Saaiq is not himself a War Lord. Afghanistan is not Saaiq's native country. And I seem to have forgotten your name since last we met."

Quaalude quickly interrupted. "I never told you his name Omar because we left so early the next morning. This is Dilawar from Islamabad."

"Ah, so that is why you two have so much to say to each other." Omar sipped from his thermos, which now contained the pinch of tea, mixed with whatever was inside it already. "My new master, the War Lord, sent me to find Saaiq. They were very good friends until the day Saaiq took one of my employer's women."

Dilawar glared at Omar as he spoke, suspecting their conversation would not end well. Whoever told him about two men looking for a young boy must have told him of their search for a woman as well. Dilawar wondered how quickly he could reach his gun as they talked. Keeping him off guard was key.

"Were you working for this War Lord when you camped near the airport?" Dilawar asked.

"My, but you *have* taken an interest in me."

"Please pardon me," Dilawar replied. "It was not my intent to intrude upon you. I only hoped to make you feel welcome here for the short time you will be staying."

"You see, I was in the right place at the right time." Omar answered. "My War Lord was boarding a plane to return home quickly when I met him. His family, his crops, the government, all needed him. He'd been tracking Saaiq with a small army for more than a year, learning that Saaiq was taking his woman to Jalalabad. I thought she may have left her son with a family in these mountains somewhere, a boy like this one perhaps."

Dilawar knew better than to second-guess a trained operative, but he would not have left a son of his with a village family. He could not imagine Kadija doing so either. He listened to Omar carefully, wondering what, if any, of his story had anything to do with his own mission.

"Do I understand you right?" Dilawar asked when Omar had finished. "You alone are replacing the entire army of an important War Lord in his search for a specific woman? What talent do you have that will make you succeed where others have failed?"

Omar did not look at Dilawar for a long time. Rather he turned to Quaalude and said, "May I trouble you for just two more leaves and maybe a small stem for my magic bottle here." Quaalude was on his feet quickly and this time Omar handed the thermos to him.

"And more hot water?" Quaalude asked.

"Yes, please, if you have any to spare. But I am a beggar at heart. If you say no I will certainly understand and will still hold you in the highest esteem."

His requests of Quaalude made Omar sound sleazy and conniving.

When all was completed, Quaalude again sat on the ground, this time an inch or two closer to Dilawar. They both waited silently for Omar's explanation.

"I'm surprised you have not yet guessed my talent. For although the War Lord and Saaiq were very close friends once, Saaiq and I are much closer. We are as brothers," Omar said. "We have known each other since Russians left these hills. When the Russians left, Saaiq returned home to the Philippines and when American soldiers arrived in Afghanistan, he came back again." Omar took another sip from his thermos and brushed the residue from his lips with the back of his hand.

Was Saaiq real or a fictional character? Was the woman Kadija?

"Your tea is extraordinary," said Omar. "You could not have purchased it here."

"Yes, we did," Quaalude answered. "There is a shop just outside Kabul. You know the one. We went by it several times as we searched for food."

"I would have thought it was European, maybe even American," Omar said slowly. "That place you speak of never had many scraps of food as I remember. And you ... look at you. You are no longer a beggar either, I see."

Dilawar was convinced Omar was saying these things to observe their reaction, as if he too had been trained to isolate discreet body reactions.

"So did Saaiq ever return to the Philippines after his last jihad, the jihad to remove the U.S.?" Dilawar asked politely. "He sounds like a fascinating individual."

Omar smiled before he continued, "I have misgivings concerning my friend, Saaiq. After Bin Laden's training camp was destroyed, Saaiq said he would return home to the United States, not the Philippines." Omar took another sip from his thermos and again brushed residue from his lips with his vest.

"I do not pretend to understand," he went on, "how Saaiq intends to become a wealthy man in the United States, but I do know, because he told me this, that the wife of a former Al Qaeda soldier, is a part of that plan. When that soldier was killed as a traitor, the woman was given to the War Lord I work for."

Dilawar knew very little of Kadija's mission and she knew nothing of his. Yet the things Omar described skirted around the possible. Dilawar knew she would be working with a man named Malik who had been their driver as they escaped Sadam Hussein's military and who was later killed. Now he knew she'd had a child in Afghanistan, a boy.

Dilawar would need as much information as Omar could provide in order to sort his truths from lies. But the man had a silk tongue.

"You were, as you said, in the right place at the right time," Dilawar interjected. "And you are being paid to do what you and your friend Saaiq do normally, that is, to communicate back and forth. How did you keep from laughing in your War Lord's face when he hired you? You must already know where Saaiq and this woman are everyday of every week."

Dilawar laughed in order to make Omar feel at ease. He could only assume Quaalude was doing the same because nothing they'd said was funny. The small boy was the only one not laughing. He had begun to doze against the wall.

Watching him as he slept reminded Dilawar again of Kadija. Why did Omar bring this boy here? Had he thought this was Kadija's boy? Why had Omar been across the street from Badrah's shelter? Omar hadn't followed them there. Dilawar knew they hadn't been followed that day. Omar had taken Quaalude to Badrah's shelter days earlier in search of food. Had the War Lord told Omar about that place? In all of Kabul, had Dilawar stumbled upon the very man who could lead him to Kadija? Dilawar needed answers.

"Of course I know where they are," Omar said finally. "Aren't phones marvelous? They do not always work, but mine works well enough." Omar continued to laugh.

"You are very entertaining, Omar. I see why Quaalude thinks highly of you. Would you care to share our bread and cheese before you go?"

"I feel most entertained as well. You are both quite industrious to have built your own yurt. I still have rabbit left from my last meal yesterday. Its remains would make a fine stew if we add it to your cheese and bread. What is left of my meal of rabbit is tied to my camel."

"Let Quaalude help you bring what you wish inside," Dilawar suggested. "And as our meal simmers over the fire you can tell me the details of your journey here in the Corridor."

When they left Dilawar tried one last time to talk to the boy, but it was no use. There was no language they both understood and the boy was sleepy. Dilawar had convinced himself that this was not Abida's son for no other reason than realizing what he would do in her place. Quickly, he began wrapping the boy back into the same strips of felt he had been wrapped in.

Dilawar needed Quaalude to accompany Omar to his camel not only to get him out of the yurt while he got his gun, but also because he was certain that Quaalude would not permit Omar to bring a weapon inside. Ultimately what he wanted was an opportunity to be alone with Omar.

Shortly both Omar and Quaalude carried four wrapped packages inside.

While continuing to wrap the boy, Dilawar asked Omar, "Where did he come from? Now that you know we don't want a boy, he will need to be returned."

Omar stood speechless for a moment. "Why? He lives far away," he answered. "The nearest yurt to yours is many kilometers away, at least a two day ride. Besides, we couldn't possibly return him now. His family doesn't want him."

Dilawar turned to Quaalude and asked, "Have you ever ridden a camel before?"

"Why yes," Quaalude answered. "And I'm pretty good at it."

Dilawar then turned to Omar. "The boy's family will want him back now that you've made him strong again. The boy will help them survive the winter. Let Quaalude take him back on your camel. He is younger and stronger than you. We have candy he can take with him. That should make his return tolerable. You and I can prepare the stew together. Of course, Quaalude will return much quicker if he rides his motorcycle rather than your camel, but that's up to you. You trust Quaalude with your camel don't you?"

"Yes, I do. But it is better if he takes his motorcycle," Omar sputtered. "I can see that. Then all three of us can be together sooner," Omar said smiling.

Dilawar noticed uneasiness in that smile. Quaalude had taken over the duties of wrapping the boy. Dilawar handed Quaalude his gloves and watched Quaalude's smile broaden deeply. In minutes, the bike was outside and the boy strapped to the back seat. Inside, Dilawar took out his own phone from his pocket, while listening to the purr of Quaalude's motorcycle riding away from the yurt.

36

Schaffer, Mitchell, and Inez, each wearing thick-soled shoes, made broken glass crunch underfoot in the very place where the revolving doors had been. They stood at the curb under moonlight shivering in fall air. A CBI forensics truck was still parked on the sidewalk with its doors opened. Several technicians in white hazmat suits carried suitcases and containers from the building to the truck.

Inez hunched her shoulders and stretched her neck back to gaze at clouds speeding across a bright half moon when a raindrop hit her forehead.

"It's raining, everyone," she said jokingly. "Time to head for cover." Neither man responded and no one moved. She wasn't really in the mood for small talk, but craved interaction with people she felt safe with.

"I wanted Bradley's help so bad," she continued, "I didn't even notice I'd been kidnapped. How's that for senility? And money can't induce him to bring Kadija home. Bradley won't believe his granddaughter might be alive. He's too full of guilt. He's the one who convinced CIA to hire her over Dolly's objections and Colonel David's bad recommendation."

No one spoke until Schaffer said, "You don't have to beat yourself up over it you know."

"What are you suppose to be?" Mitchell asked him. "The feel good police?"

Schaffer looked away. Inez knew exactly how Schaffer felt. Mitchell's question reminded her of her own mistaken intolerances throughout the years when she was too busy to listen to a student. She still stared at the moon, knowing the muscles in Schaffer's face were flexing with anger.

"If we play nice," she reminded them both, "we can go home sooner. And I just felt a few more raindrops."

The roar of yet another truck made them look in that direction. A UPS truck came up the driveway and stopped beside them. An agent wearing a CBI jacket jumped out of the driver's seat, nodded discretely to Schaffer, and walked quickly around it to the back of the building.

"I remember this truck," Inez said, turning to Mitchell. "The first time we met you we were in this truck."

"That was the first time I met Sheila," Mitchell added. "Which reminds me. We're getting married."

"Congratulations! When did that happen?" Inez asked. "And why are we standing beside this UPS truck?"

"Oh, I forgot," Schaffer interjected, "Our beloved boss wanted me to drive the truck back, since we're on our way to headquarters. Police didn't want it parked at Centennial Airport. They're still combing the place for that missing helicopter pilot. Guess I'll be the one who …"

"Nonsense," Mitchell exclaimed. "This is great. We can all fit in here and I can share my news with you both. I won't need my car right away." He opened the sliding side door and helped Inez up. Schaffer climbed into the driver's seat.

"Sheila's at the Brown Palace," Mitchell continued. "She came to Denver just to ask me to marry her. In case anyone's wondering, it *does* pay to play hard to get. That's where I was earlier today. I mean yesterday."

Seated in the passenger seat, Inez beamed at him before shouting, "I'm excited! How long will she be in Denver?"

"Don't know. I don't even know *when* I'm getting married, but I suspect it'll happen before the year's out. Call her when you get a chance will you Inez, and let me know some of these things? But right now," Mitchell stood in the space between the two seats, "I'd rather hear what makes you think Bradley killed Stronsky and not Dolly."

Schaffer chimed in. "Yeah, I'm curious about that too. My money was on Freddie's brother Morton for both killings."

"Really?" Inez said, staring at Schaffer. She took a moment to reflect. "Yes, I can see how you might think that. And that's certainly what Bradley wanted you to think. But I had the benefit of actually meeting Dolly, Stronsky, and Bradley. That can make all the difference in the world." She pretended not to see Mitchell roll his eyes. Instead she pointed a finger at the windshield. "Look, it's really raining now."

"Where I'm from that's called spit," Schaffer said.

"Where's that?" Mitchell asked.

"A little town called Bowbells." He paused as if realizing his audience had no clue to its location. "It's in North Dakota, home of long summer days and short winters like you never experience anywhere else in the States. It was a nice enough place in which to grow up but when my parents died I sold their homestead, moved to Colorado, and never looked back."

They listened to wiper blades rhythmically slice away sheets of water one at a time. Inez smiled at Schaffer's confidence behind the wheel.

"Why did I think you were from New York City?" Mitchell finally said.

"Oh, that's where I went to college. I certainly didn't want anybody to know I'd been a small town boy."

Mitchell sat in a cubicle shaped space on the floor across from the gearshift, stretching his neck to see above the dashboard. He'd designated himself official backseat driver and wondered how long he could stand having Schaffer as his partner.

As the truck moved easily through the wet night, Inez began her explanations.

"When Dolly was young, she was gorgeous," Inez said. "So when Bradley told me they'd been lovers all their lives, I could believe it, even though he was ten years younger. He truly believed she'd committed suicide on Lookout Mountain and was deeply hurt by it. I could also believe that someone as arrogant as Colonel David actually thought, all those years ago, that Dolly was having his baby and not Bradley's. Dolly and Bradley loved their daughter and I even think they tried to make sure the Colonel was never alone with her. Whether they were successful or not isn't pertinent to who killed Dolly, but it may have had its effects over time. What's important is understanding Bradley's mental state."

Mitchell reached inside his jacket for his small notebook and began writing.

"When Bradley finally realized that Colonel David's words and deeds would never align themselves he continued to trust everyone else around him. Bradley believed everything Stronsky told him. Why would his secretary lie to him? Not only was Stronsky a better yes man to Colonel David than Bradley ever was, Stronsky was a better yes man to the Colonel than the Colonel's own son, Morton." Inez stopped talking abruptly and stared out the windshield. "When we get to headquarters, somebody please remind me to check Morton Meda's birth certificate. It just hit me that Dolly was a gofer to the Colonel too early in her marriage. Could she have hoped to avoid scandal by signing Morton's birth certificate as his mother?"

In unison, both men shouted, "WHAT!"

Then there was silence until Schaffer spoke. "I looked for it, but not for very long. I couldn't find it and had other matters to attend to. Maybe that's why Freddie's mother didn't list Morton as one of her children."

"That may be the motive behind all this. Anyway," Inez continued, "when I visited Stronsky, it was the first time Bradley realized his granddaughter might not have died years ago. Bradley believed friendly fire killed Kadija because Stronsky said so. Stronsky was sent oversees to confirm it, but like always, Stronsky never went. And if anyone at Martindale had been reading Stronsky's reports as carefully as I did they would have caught on. What I didn't know until tonight was that Morton Meda could possibly have taken some of those trips to the Middle East on behalf of Stronsky, using Stronsky's vouchers. He could have lived lavishly in the Middle East off Martindale's dime.

"But I digress. There are several ways Bradley could have listened in on my visit with Stronsky, but I believe Bradley bugged his own office before he retired using Martindale technology. He knew Stronsky wanted that office. Workmen were still scraping the 'e' and the 'y' off the door when I visited him."

Mitchell listened attentively, but the rain had gotten louder. "Today was crazy," Mitchell said, "I didn't have time to listen to that conversation you recorded on your phone with him."

"I'm only glad," Inez yelled above the noise, "that you had the time to come get me."

They all laughed far longer than they should have.

"This is what I *think* happened," Inez finally continued, "because it fits all the events. Bradley was so angered by what he heard during my visit with Stronsky that he snapped. He called his militia together. They picked Stronsky up at his office in a chauffeured limousine after I left. His secretary confirms that. I think the theft of my bag was simply to keep me out of harm's way and in the parking garage. Then they must have put him in a freezer inside a hangar at DIA until nightfall. That's when they transferred his body to a private plane and dropped him out over Kansas. Bradley returned to DIA as the sun was coming up. He admitted to me that he slid his phone into the pocket of a stranger boarding a domestic flight and that's probably where he got the greasy old clothes he wore to the Cherry Creek Mall."

Inez paused a moment and visibly shivered. "Glad I wore a jacket," she murmured.

It was getting cold and the rain was unusual only because it kept coming down heavier and heavier. Mitchell got up from the floor and pulled the window behind her half way closed.

"Thank you," she said as he returned to his place on the floor. She looked at their eager faces and wondered if she was sharing too much at once. But she needed someone to talk to about this as well.

After a short while, Inez started talking again. "Bradley was far too trusting for his own good. Dolly, on the other hand, trusted no one, including Bradley, where their granddaughter was concerned. Her jewelry was the only asset that wasn't tied up in Martindale, which is why she sold it to hire investigators to find Kadija. She must have hired people Bradley didn't know. That would make them former MI6 personnel I think, but I can't prove that. I think that's how she knew about the Taliban and the likelihood that the person on the other end of her conversation last January was indeed Kadija.

"Investigators must have told her that Kadija was married. Maybe they took a photograph of them. The CIA may have set her up with a husband for her protection in a Muslim country. Bradley claims he never shared CIA information with Dolly. He was as old guard as the Colonel about government work, never talking about it with anyone. Stronsky described Bradley and Colonel David as being cut from the same cloth. But Bradley continued to work with CIA, and with the sons and daughters of former operatives who later became part of his current militia."

"You're claiming Bradley right now has his own militia aren't you?" Schaffer asked.

"It's not that uncommon. I could call it a gang. The word gang shouldn't be reserved for just rednecks and drug peddlers. It's just a noun.

"And although I find it hard to believe, it may be a step in the right direction, that CIA is finally willing to trust Americans of color in the Middle East with more than military duty. By the way, if you haven't found any reports at Dolly's house from her paid investigators, she may have hidden them at Bradley's place," Inez said. "Dolly lived with Bradley after the Colonel died earlier this year, which is why Bradley never thought to look at the mansion on Albion Street. According to Bradley her maid was sometimes driven to his house and told never to tell anyone."

Mitchell looked up at Inez from the floor of the truck. "Do you know who Freddie Meda is and that he died in a car accident while being kidnapped from his hospital room?"

Inez took a deep breath and listened to the rain for a bit. "Yes, and No."

Her mind was pulled away for a second to marvel at the relationship between step brothers she'd never met. Morton and Freddie had to be nearly a decade apart in age and were treated so differently by their families and society.

"That brings us to the tricky part," she said softly. "I believe two separate groups of people were involved in two separate criminal activities today. There was Bradley's attempt to kill Freddie Meda in order to make it look like Freddie's brother Morton had killed him along with Stronsky and Dolly. And then, as you're telling me now, there was an attempt to kidnap Freddie from the hospital. That was unfortunate because that was meant to keep him safe. Yet, you just told me he was killed."

"Whoa," Schaffer exclaimed. "No offense ma'm but I think you're writing fiction now. There's no evidence that there were two separate groups of people acting today. When the explosion didn't kill Freddie, the same group decided to finish him off."

"Hear me out, first," she said. "Bradley intended to pin several murders on Morton Meda, a man he knew quite well. Bradley's militia planned that explosion at Freddie's apartment building. They focused their cameras on the very place the bomb was set to explode. The camera was already running moments prior to the building's explosion. Bradley's mistake was in showing me that video."

Schaffer hit the steering wheel with his fist. "Damn. I could have been killed along with Freddie had we still been in his rooms."

Inez continued, "The person or gang who stole Bradley's phone number from me the night before also knew the explosion hadn't killed Freddie. They watched from overhead. That group tried to get Freddie out of Bradley's hands. That same person or gang also managed to access the cell phones of the people Bradley talked to that night, namely the members of his own militia. This person or gang knew what Bradley was planning all day long from inside a helicopter that could ping every tower it passed over. You can see the helicopter in one of the videos on Bradley's monitors."

Mitchell and Schaffer were quiet for a moment until Schaffer whistled and Mitchell put his notebook back into his jacket pocket.

Mitchell was very clear, as he spoke. "That's a road too far. And why didn't you tell me someone stole something from your house last night? I can assure you the video covering your front door didn't show anyone entering or leaving."

"That's because whoever stole the number used my back door. It had to be someone who knew the neighborhood well enough to know there's no alley behind my house and that they'd need to climb a neighbor's fence."

"Okay. That was an oversight. I agree," he admitted.

"No, it wasn't an oversight," Inez shot back. "You didn't think I was that important in the scope of things. And I wouldn't have thought I was that important either."

Mitchell sighed, too tired to argue the point with her. "Schaffer?" he shouted over the rain. "Do we know who rented that copter that landed at Centennial Airport?"

"Belongs to a fleet of helicopters just outside Copper Mountain apparently. Wasn't reported stolen because everyone thought they knew who had it."

Have you got any evidence at all about any of this?" Mitchell asked Inez.

"Could have been Morton Meda, like Bradley suspected, or a terrorist cell working here on his behalf or the behalf of a third party involved in the ransom of Kadija Campbell, or maybe all of the above," Inez answered.

Schaffer made a sudden U turn into a 7-11 parking lot. The streets were wet and the truck's tires slid, making a loud screeching sound.

"I'm going to get some coffee, make a pit stop," he said, when the truck finally came to a complete stop. "Anybody else want ..."

Two gunshots cracked through the open window beside Schaffer. He fell sideways in slow motion toward Inez then slid toward the floor behind her seat. The back of his head had separated from the front and laid between Mitchell's feet.

Suddenly horror stricken, Inez heard Mitchell's feet scuffling to avoid stepping on Schaffer's body parts. She couldn't look down. Straight ahead through the open side door was a boy with very black skin wearing dry but filthy gray clothing and he held a gun straight at her forehead. He hopped up into the truck from the bottom step. Despite her rapid heartbeats, she recognized him. An involuntary blink of her eyelids revealed the red shoes on his feet, as he pushed Schaffer's legs off the truck's pedals.

Turning his gun quickly to Mitchell, he stared into his face and slid onto the driver's seat.

"It's suicide," the young man said to Mitchell with a thick African accent. "Don't even think such things. I'm not trained like you. I shoot before I think."

His jacket and hands were covered with splotches of soot and oil. Could he have been under the truck? His eyes switched to Inez again. Those eyes flashed in the light of the store and with stark white teeth revealed a menacing smile.

"You recognize me. But I'm guessing you know nothing about guns. I shall trust in your ignorance because you know what trust is. I heard you speak of it. Reach inside this dead man's jacket and get his gun. Move slowly because that's what old people are supposed to do."

Inez was already out of her seat and kneeling beside Schaffer's blood soaked body. Her eyes collected water while she tried not to hyperventilate. Feeling for a pulse, gave her a chance to be useful without looking at or acknowledging that part of his head which had blown off.

Her ability to concentrate was limited, but she knew the boy's speech patterns came from gangster movies and not American ones. And then there was the gun she had to get from inside Schaffer's holster.

"Hand me the butt. That's right," said the young man. "Now find his cell phone. Ease it out the crack in your side window and let it drop. That's right. Don't get into your seat yet. There is only one reason I don't kill you. I don't have permission. I'd need to have a good excuse to get that permission. So don't give me one. Both of you can stay alive. But I must find out which one of you killed my sister."

Sister? And why was he speaking softly? Making certain no one outside could hear him? He's holding his gun below the windshield. Who was his sister?

He put Schaffer's gun in his left side jacket pocket. Inez wanted to remember. Maybe it would be important later. She tried to stand up.

"You've got to get *his* gun as well," he demanded.

How could she have forgotten it? She dropped to her knees again and reached into Mitchell's jacket, being careful not to look into his face. She had no desire to decipher any message Mitchell might attempt to send her with his eyes. She felt incapable of deciphering anything and was breathing erratically. Was the truck dark or was she losing her peripheral vision? Could she stay conscious? She also wondered from whom this boy needed to get permission. He'd let them know he wasn't working alone. The minute she had Mitchell's gun, he snatched it from her and slid it into his right side pocket.

"Where are your manners?" she said. She couldn't help herself.

"Get his cell," the young man yelled. He briefly looked at it before placing it in his own breast pocket.

"Drag that body to the back, both of you. Lay face down on the floor beside it. C'mon, do it."

When they were about to get onto the floor, Mitchell whispered, "When I get up, press the side door latch and hop out."

With swift bravado, the young man climbed over the driver's seat and headed toward them. "Are you too old Doctor to get down to the floor?" the boy asked.

Using the palm of his free hand he shoved Inez's back, making her fall forward against the sliding door. Her foot slid into the lower foot well, making that fall less damaging.

He raised his arm to hit Inez on the head with the butt of his gun, but his aim was deflected. His gun jettisoned from his fingers. Mitchell slammed his whole body, head first, into the youn man's stomach. Mitchell pushed him to the front of the truck until they were pressed against the windshield. The stranger slid his fingers under Mitchell's shoulder blades and pushed him off. Mitchell stepped back but fell over Schaffer's body and landed on the truck floor.

For a second the young man's eyes scoured the floor searching for his gun. But the truck was still dark. Inez never opened the side door as Mitchell had asked. The man's search was a second too long, because although Mitchell remained seated, he reached for the gun strapped to the back of his thigh and fired straight in front of him. The bullet hit the young man's knee. He cried out and fell.

Inez huddled in the far corner of the UPS truck under a table of monitors. She listened to pounding rain against the unpadded walls of the metal truck and remembered rainy days as a child and the air-raid drills in the halls of her elementary school when they practiced waiting for the atomic bomb to come.

Mitchell had already pulled the boy's jacket off and put handcuffs on him. Inez listened as he talked on his cell phone requesting two ambulances. For the first time in her adult life Inez wished she had a cell phone too but wasn't sure why. Who would she call?

37

FEBRUARY 2009 WAKHAN CORRIDOR, AFGANISTAN

Dilawar was glad he'd sent Quaalude away. Now he could find out whether his skills had become rusty after years of flying drones in Islamabad. Omar smiled at him and Dilawar returned the gesture, hoping to encourage the old man's belief that he'd snared another male into his stable.

"Batteries die frequently," Dilawar said, holding his own phone up to the light of the fire. "It's an old phone that barely works at all when the sun goes down. Your friend Saaiq must be nearby, if you can reach him from here."

"Actually my phone is probably older than yours," Omar said, "but I can still reach Jalalabad from here."

"That can't be right. Jalalabad is over four hundred kilometers away."

Omar smiled. "May I?" he asked, reaching for Dilawar's phone.

"No," Dilawar replied. "You should use your own phone since you're confident it will work."

Reluctantly, Omar reached into his long shearling vest, pulled out a smart phone, punched a single number on it, put it to his ear and waited. "Ah," Omar said loudly, "wrong number," then pushed a button to end the call.

"You see, I'm right," Dilawar said. "Jalalabad is too far from here."

"Saaiq answered my call," Omar replied. "I said wrong number because Saaiq is the kind of person who would get upset if he knew I was just playing. He knew it was me, but that I meant to call another number."

Dilawar said nothing and believed nothing Omar said. What he really wanted was to get to Jalalabad as soon as possible. If the river was high now, it would take a month to cross. He couldn't let himself think about that now.

"Allah has treated me exceptionally well," Omar continued. "Saaiq keeps the woman in a cave and says he'll call me once he has finished with her. Then I can be paid again by my War Lord."

Dilawar's jaws locked hard against each other; he was determined not to show his hatred.

"Where," Dilawar asked, "could a man keep a woman in a city like Jalalabad in a cave and not be discovered? By the way, we should start the stew if we want to eat when Quaalude returns. Where are your pieces of rabbit?"

The old man laughed. "You don't know Jalalabad, do you? Like every other place in Afghanistan, it has more than its share of un-exploded bombs strewn across the area. Abandoned buildings and caves frighten most people away."

As Omar spoke, he carefully picked up a package from the floor covered in butcher paper. Was it the package of leftover rabbit Dilawar thought he'd seen Quaalude carry inside? Dilawar had paid no atten-tion to its shape before but now he could see it had the unmistakable configuration of an Uzi.

With no time to inquire, he leapt into mid-air. Dilawar was across the floor, his hand under the goose down blanket and on the trigger of his own gun. It all happened faster than the old man was able to punch his fingers through a paper wrapping in order to connect to the trigger. In two shots Dilawar had him. The first shot had been diffused by the blanket. The second reached Omar's shoulder, forcing him to drop the Uzi before collapsing where he'd stood.

Dilawar picked up Omar's gun from the floor ripping remnants of wrapping paper from it. He turned his back on the man to place the gun admiringly beside his motorcycle on the far side of the yurt. Meanwhile an occasional glance at the body on the floor told him blood seeping from Omar's shoulder had pooled around his neck. The man's eyes were closed and his breathing labored which was an invitation to Dilawar to search his body.

To say Omar wore several layers of clothing would be an understatement. In the first pocket Dilawar came to he found a small caliber loaded pistol of German origin and a six-inch knife. He stashed them both in his own goose down jacket along with Omar's money and his phone, the phone he'd used to reach Saaiq. Dilawar couldn't help smiling at it, before putting it inside his own pocket and zipping it up.

In another pouch were his thermos, which smelled of ethyl alcohol, loose cubes of sugar, and a British passport belonging to a man named Robert Boydell. Dilawar had never seen the face of that man before, but leaned very close over Omar's face in search of telltale surgical marks denoting plastic surgery. Finding none, he felt assured this was not Omar's passport. Yet it had to be of great importance to Omar, who risked everything by carrying it. Dilawar decided to keep it for a while.

Finding nothing else of importance, he began dressing warmly. When he had finished, he suddenly remembered the camel. He dashed outside wondering what else, if anything, Omar may have left on the camel's saddle. To his amazement, there was no camel. What did it mean? Had there ever been a camel?

Yes. He remembered looking outside when the small boy arrived. The boy could not have made the line of tracks coming down the hill toward their yurt, but a camel could. The boy had been placed over the top of a four-legged animal and brought down the hill.

Still holding his gun, Dilawar made a path in the snow around the perimeter of the yurt until he came to a deep impression made by a large animal. He stared at the tracks from Quaalude's motorcycle and at the hoof marks beside it made by Omar's camel. Quaalude must have thought Omar's life was about to end when he left with the boy. The boy's family would be overjoyed to accept their son back, particularly if they also received a camel.

Dilawar walked back inside and crouched down low beside what he hoped was by now a dead body. But Omar opened his eyes and asked, "Who are you?"

Dilawar, of course, had been wondering the same thing about Omar, particularly since he was carrying another man's passport. But he wasn't curious enough to ask that question just yet. Instead, consumed with getting to Jalalabad and finding Kadija, Dilawar began to stand up again. The old man grabbed his hand with fingers taped together for warmth. No wonder he hadn't been able to fire his gun quickly.

"Don't go …" Omar insisted. He swallowed before speaking, "… without me." He paused to swallow hard. "I must go with you. You will not be sorry. How do you know I told you the truth? And how do you know the man and the woman you seek are the same as the people I described? I know exactly where to find Saaiq. Don't let me die here."

"You will certainly die tied to the back of my motorcycle old man. And anything you decide to tell me could be a lie. I'd have no way of knowing. I gain nothing by taking you with me and I will lose time, maybe an entire month, nursing you back to life."

The man tugged harder on Dilawar's hand, pulling himself up slightly. "We are not who we seem to be. Neither of us. Stop the bleeding so we can talk."

Dilawar stared at the man's skin and his eyes. He had seen all four of the only people of color trained and hired by CIA to spy in this part of the world. In 1996, they'd all been together on the same Jordanian airliner he'd piloted. According to CIA that had been a major management error. They were never supposed to be together in one place again, which was just one of several reasons why Abida and her partner had to be taken off the plane before reaching Khartoum.

Dilawar knew Omar couldn't be a CIA agent. Was that what he was insinuating?

Omar fell back on the floor and closed his eyes. Dilawar finally stood and thought about that day on the plane. Perhaps that was yet another reason why it was so hard to forget Kadija. She would have given him a thousand reasons to stay onboard. He had no choice but to knock her out to get her off the plane quickly. Unfortunately, he'd had to do the same thing with Malik. Yes, that was his name, Malik. He was happy to knock him out. Not only was Malik great with a gun, he was a bully, as well as Kadija's new partner. Malik had hospitalized the regional CIA administrator, his newly appointed cousin, with his bare fists.

Dilawar looked at the man. No, he thought. This wasn't Malik. Malik had been much bigger than this man on the floor. Besides he'd been told by his own handler that Malik's body had been found in Africa. Of course he'd also been told Kadija was dead.

Dilawar continued to stare at the man on the floor. It was one thing to kill in combat or in self-defense and quite another to kill in cold blood. Until now Dilawar would have described himself as the man his mother wanted him to be, a man who behaved righteously according to Dharma.

Dilawar thought of these things as he hurriedly packed, hoping he'd be sitting on his motorcycle waiting for Quaalude soon. Once Quaalude returned, they'd leave for Jalalabad immediately. But what if Omar *had* lied? And who was Robert Boydell anyway? Who was Omar, for that matter?

Dilawar tied his last set of tools and a flashlight onto his motorcycle, then, once again looked at the body on the floor. The man had surely bled to death by now. But Omar's eyes were again staring back at him. He stood very still and listened to the old man's rasping whisper.

"The desert aged me. CIA no longer employs me. I was fired as soon as they flew me home from Khartoum. Me, the one agent whose scores had been higher than anyone else in my department.

But what should Muslims expect? CIA didn't care. I'd only been an experiment. My career ended because of a stupid outburst from my own flesh and blood. That was the excuse the Company used. They said I'd never be able to lead anyone anywhere. It was pure hatred for my cousin that kept me alive and brought me back to Afghanistan." Omar tried to swallow.

This time as Omar spoke, Dilawar slowly walked around the edges of the yurt with his head down. Although listening intently, he gathered straw and stray pieces of felt, trying hard to remember.

"I found friends among Bin Laden's soldiers," the old man whispered.

Dilawar diligently piled the cloth and straw he found under Omar's head, not wishing to think just yet, only listen, as the man spoke.

The man grabbed at Dilawars jacket pulling him down until he was kneeling beside him. "You don't recognize me?"

"I don't."

Omar's eyes grew large again. "I don't believe you," he said, "You're lying. I'm sure CIA told all its Middle Eastern operatives to be on the look out for me. You see I'm the one who informed. I made sure Bin Laden knew about Malik. And I'm proud of it. I am. He dishonored me. But I didn't mean to … to leave the woman alone and helpless. I didn't mean to. As Allah is my witness, I had to help her. In my hatred for Malik I'd forgotten all about her. Such a naïve little thing too. I had to help her." His eyes rolled back into his head.

Dilawar continued to kneel beside the man, still not fully comprehending his identity. But he did understand one thing. If this Omar had betrayed his own cousin, he could certainly do it again to someone he wasn't related to. Whoever he was, he was never to be trusted.

When Dilawar stood, he grabbed his motorcycle helmet and went outside. After filling it with snow, he brought it inside, and dumped it onto Omar's face and shoulder until the man's eyes fluttered. Perhaps if he listened more carefully he could separate the inconsistent from the consistent and by so doing, slowly discover the truth. Was the woman left alone by Malik's death Kadija? It was the only thing Omar said that made any sense. From what little he knew of the man, saying he wanted to help her was a lie.

38

It was cold and the rain had grown more intense. Yet Mitchell took off his own jacket to cover Schaffer's head and shoulders while Inez watched him from under a bolted table that held computer monitors. She listened to the screams and curses from the boy sporting red shoes, a bullet in his knee and handcuffs around his wrists. She watched blankly as Mitchell examined the young man's leg.

Schaffer and Kadija had similar jobs, she mused. Both were young, highly trained, and passionate about protecting the American people. Inez let her intellect exhaust itself with examples of their similarities while gradually she became more and more attentive to the yelling inside the truck.

Another thought came to her. This boy was in this truck and had been in that helicopter all day because he had been busy protecting someone. He was being paid to protect Freddie Meda and he failed. He even failed to protect his own sister.

Over the din of the boy's curses Inez yelled, "How did your sister die?" It had been one of his first accusations.

"Stop it, Inez! I need to caution him," Mitchell said, "before he talks to you or anybody else and you have no right to ask him anything." He was busy trying to stop the boy from bleeding to death. And for the first time that night Inez could feel Mitchell's righteous indignation. His feelings were clear enough for her to understand.

Mitchell was angry not just with people who broke the law but with people who continued to do provocative things. So he was angry with her. And he was angry with his job, which in essence, was to make dangerous things go away.

She stopped analyzing Mitchell as soon as he began to recite the verse that explained how anything the boy said could be used against him in a court of law. She had nothing positive to say to a murderer, a person who thought that only he should have the right to live.

The boy murderer in front of her had become uncharacteristically quiet. He straightened his back slightly to get a better look at Inez over Mitchell's shoulder. She returned his gaze with what she felt was equal venom. His hands held his good knee tightly, as if it helped the pain. When Mitchell finished reciting nothing was said for some time. Inez marveled at how soothing the quiet felt. The rain had stopped.

Finally, the boy replied, "She came two days ago. Never could read well. Picked out the wrong uniform. Always wanted to help me. Militia killed her. She never heard of Bradley before yesterday."

Mitchell interrupted, "Why was she in the same room with Freddie Meda?"

The boy turned his eyes back to Mitchell but said nothing.

"Sorry for your loss," Inez lied. It had been an automatic response, one of politeness. The truck was quiet with the exception of Mitchell tearing the boy's jacket to make a tourniquet.

After a few more seconds, she added, "And you should be sorry for our loss. We're people too, you know."

The boy peered over Mitchell's shoulder again, this time breathing hard. "Not today, Lady."

Without hesitating, Inez asked, "Who did you need to get permission from?"

She wanted the boy to hurry with his response. Paramedics and police would be arriving soon.

"This won't work," Mitchell announced, as if paying no attention to either of them. He threw the boy's jacket on the floor and said, "I need more cloth."

Inez grabbed the jacket and began tearing out the lining.

"How do you contact the person you needed permission from?" she asked again, all the while yanking away the threads of the lining from his jacket.

The boy stared at her and then at the jacket in her hands. "I've never been arrested. That means I'll get out soon, won't I?"

"No," Inez answered quickly. "You killed a CBI agent. They're special. If you've killed anyone else, that'll add more years to your prison sentence. We typically don't execute murderers in Colorado, but there's no guarantee of that."

Mitchell pulled the side door back and jumped out at the sound of cars coming and going inside the parking lot. The rain had indeed stopped, but large puddles of water had formed in the cracked asphalt. Mitchell only looked at the store from the outside but leaned against the truck deeply breathing in cold early morning air.

Meanwhile the boy feebly kicked at his jacket with his good leg, nodding at it with his whole head.

"Didn't want *you* dead," the boy said. "You had to speak to the man." The boy paused to catch his breath. "You call him ... phone him ..." the boy said softly, eyes fluttering. "He's named Saaiq."

"What did he say?" Mitchell asked. "Did he give you a name?" He'd stopped leaning against the truck.

Ignoring Mitchell Inez asked the boy, "Why?" She continued tearing out the last stitch of lining from the jacket then held her arm out the opened door for Mitchell.

The boy did not answer Inez's question, perhaps because Mitchell climbed back into the truck and proceeded to wrap the lining tightly around the boy's leg. The boy's body went limp as Mitchell attended to him.

Inez spied a loose phone near the boy's jacket pocket. There had been other phones and guns placed in the boy's pockets earlier. But Mitchell had already grabbed his own gun and phone out of it. Inez had been keeping track of where the boy put these things. This phone on the floor wasn't Schaffer's. Had Mitchell noticed this one?

"Eye dee," the boy screamed suddenly from flat on his back. "Eye dee. Next month and the month after." He repeated himself just above a whisper. This time Inez thought she understood what he was doing.

She heard ambulance sirens in the distance. Cars in the parking lot began to leave. With outstretched legs and feet she covered the loose phone, then slid them towards her body in an attempt to stand upright on the floor of the truck.

"You okay?" Mitchell asked. "My hands are busy at the moment or I'd give you some help."

"I'm fine," she answered, as she scooped up the phone and squeezed it into her purse.

Inez then stood up and stepped down from the UPS truck. She walked to the curb in front of the store to stay out of the way of paramedics. Mitchell was more than a little busy over the next half hour and so was Inez. Would she ever hand the phone over to Mitchell? First responders had to get the boy breathing again before they could move him.

Inez found herself unable to fight back tears as Schaffer's body was taken away in an ambulance. Or were her tears for Kadija? Several agents put their arms around Mitchell as he hung his head. But Inez didn't feel capable of comforting him. As far as she was concerned, she'd been hired to bring Kadija home regardless of what Mitchell thought. And right now a monumental feeling of failure came over her caused by the sudden loss of someone who wasn't supposed to die so young. The thing that kept nagging at her was the outside chance that Schaffer's death was somehow related to Kadija Campbell. Bradley had said that Morton Meda had aliases he couldn't pronounce. Could 'Saaiq' have been one of them?

Mitchell put Inez into a patrol car at 4 am. A Denver policeman took her home without a word spoken between them. She knew Mitchell was on his way to see whoever was left of Schaffer's family.

A phone rang. Inez awoke wondering about the time. She recognized her own landline ringing but it took a while to orient herself to her living room chair. Her eyes slowly focused on the analog clock on her mantel. 11:00 in the morning. The phone continued to ring.

Reluctantly she got up, not certain why the strap of her purse was wrapped so tightly around her arm. She walked into the kitchen and answered the phone.

"Hi, Dr. Buchanan." Sophie's voice sounded unusually chipper. "Thought I'd let you sleep a while before calling. Have you listened to the news yet?"

"No. What did I miss?" As she listened she looked for her coffee cup.

"Well, Mr. Bradley never arrived at the Denver jail last night. There was a huge car crash and a shoot out between police and his militia. One of the policemen in the patrol car with him disappeared as well. They think he may not have been a policeman after all. The officer behind the wheel has minor injuries. Nobody knows where this guy Bradley is."

"Unbelievable," Inez said.

"Apparently police are concentrating on airports, trains, and buses out of Denver. The policeman out front of my place last night said he'd been reassigned to DIA. There's going to be a press conference shortly on the television. You might want to turn it on."

Inez was quiet. Bradley was now a forever fugitive from justice and what had he done? He'd killed the man who was supposed to have rescued his daughter from death and wouldn't.

"You still there?" Sophie asked.

"Yes. How soon can you get here?"

"Twenty, thirty minutes maybe. Why? You don't think he'd go to your place, do you?"

"No, I don't. Sadly, I don't. Just hurry. We've got things to do." She pushed the button that said 'end' and took a long look at her purse without opening it. Grabbing the phone again, she got a receptionist at Martindale, Inc.

"Hello," Inez said, "I hope you recognize my voice. We've talked before, when Mr. Stronsky was still alive. I'm Dr. Buchanan and I understand I've been assigned to someone in this organization who's taking Alan Bradley's place. I'd like you to find whoever that is and tell that person to come to my house within the next two to three hours. Make sure it's someone with experience in hostage negotiations. Whoever it is needs to start the paper work to transfer funds that I'm the executor of. Did you get all that? A woman's life is at stake. Yes ... I can hold."

She took a deep breath and sat back in her kitchen chair. How long would it take Mitchell to figure out that the young man with the red shoes must have had a phone of his own? She didn't know how long her prison term would be for obstructing justice, but she knew jail was a possibility. If she could bring Kadija home it would all be worth it though. This Saaiq person, whoever he was, *had* to be on the other end of that boy's phone.

39

O mar's eyes were closed but his face grimaced with pain every few seconds.

Kneeling over him, hands wrapped in a blanket, Dilawar pressed against Omar's wound. After an hour, he said, "I think the bleeding has stopped, but you won't survive the journey to Jalalabad."

Dilawar took his pulse. "Yet I need your help to save the life of a woman. Maybe it's the same woman you spoke of. Can you answer more questions?"

Omar's face was still twisted with pain. "Find my thermos," he said. "Brace me up so I can sit against the hearth." He was pale, yet his clothes were drenched in his own dark blood. "I'll be the judge of my chance to survive." His voice was only a whisper.

Dilawar sat him upright and placed his thermos in his hand.

"I arrived in Afghanistan," Omar whispered, "soaked in hate for the cousin who'd ended my career. I joined Al Qaeda without Malik knowing. I met Saaiq and his closest friends, including Omar almost immediately. These were older, wiser, and better skilled men than the rest of the soldiers. They were like brothers. Saaiq and Omar had fought with Bin Laden during the Russian occupation. They planned to grow old together and talked about it constantly." The old man paused for a long time, as if realizing what he'd said.

Finally Dilawar asked, "Your name isn't Omar, is it?"

"Not anymore than your name is Dilawar. Everyone involved with Al Qaeda uses aliases and they use them interchangeably. I have used the names Saaiq, Omar, and Amir, several times."

Dilawar grabbed the man's bloody collar and pulled him to within an inch of his face. Omar let out an agonizing groan to which Dilawar was deaf.

"What did you do with the real Omar, the Omar you've described?" Dilawar growled.

The old man cried with pain, but managed to whisper, "I didn't kill him. Saaiq killed him. I don't know that for sure. I only know they had a terrible fight over several days and weeks. Everyone in camp heard them fight. Omar thought Saaiq intended to take both the woman and his identity. Together they had planned to become as wealthy as the Bin Ladens. Omar believed that this woman stood between him and a fortune in U.S. currency. The thought of it made Omar crazy. He began...he began to distrust people and to forget things he had said not long ago. He ... he no longer wanted anything to do with Saaiq."

"You helped with that didn't you?" Dilawar asked. "You manipulate people well."

They exchanged meaningful looks before Omar took a sip from his thermos and spoke. "One day Omar was drunk and began to speak in Spanish, thinking no one around him in the Middle East would know what he said. I know Spanish, being New York bred, and what he said was he'd kill his whole family before he'd let anyone take money that was rightfully his. I didn't know what he meant and didn't care. I didn't understand how the woman was involved, but he said she was."

Dilawar thought for a moment and said, "You expect me to believe that one old friend killed the other friend when it's you who had your own blood relative killed."

"I knew them both very well," Omar pleaded, "and I'm telling you the truth. At first Omar became obsessed with this woman and then he became obsessed with Saaiq. I don't know if his obsession over her was really about her money. Later Saaiq became obsessed with her. She is the same woman who acted as my cousin's wife, the woman placed in Afghanistan by CIA."

Dilawar's heart stopped.

"I tell you no lie," Omar continued. "I was to be her handler, hers and my cousin's. I knew she grew up in Colorado and had a rich grandmother she rarely saw."

Dilawar sat on the floor, speechless. Who was this Omar other than an extraordinary storyteller? His words were unbelievable. Could Kadija really be alive? But she, like him had no money to speak of, only grants, loans, and gifts. Maybe he was lying or guessing.

Dilawar slowly found his voice and asked, "This Saaiq never lets her out of his sight?"

"Exactly."

"Does he employ guards, personal armies?"

"Of course. Not as many as before. He did have whole armies to protect his interests here and in other countries."

"What interests, what other countries?"

"Guns, drugs, land, property in every civilized nation. When he got older he thought his friend Omar would help him maintain a lavish life style."

Omar and Dilawar stared into each other's eyes and said nothing for a very long time.

"I think I remember you now," Dilawar said. "You wore a silk suit on board our plane from Iraq, which I thought at the time I would never in my lifetime be able to afford. You were on the plane I flew, the case manager for the man and woman headed for Khartoum."

"Omar smiled. "Then you know Malik beat me unconscious after you knocked out the woman. My recuperative powers however are also well known. If you leave me here to die, I will hunt you down until I kill you."

Dilawar closed his eyes for a moment. He pictured Kadija on that plane, young, proud, and anxious to excel in her new career, yet left for dead for over a decade by her government.

"So is there any truth," Dilawar asked, "to what Saaiq says? Can the woman bring him wealth?"

"Listen to me. You must trust me about these things. I'm the only one who can help you," the old man said.

Dilawar laughed and stood up. "That means you don't know the answer to my question and that you probably have no allegiance to any country. Money is the only commodity you work for. Am I right?"

"Listen. Omar claimed to have come from wealthy people but never spent any money. Saaiq never made such claims and yet he spent money throughout his life as easily as he drank water. Money was the source of Omar's hatred toward the United States, the reason for his jihads. He said the U.S. government refused to acknowledge his claim to his family's wealth. At least that's the way he tells the story. The strange thing was that Saaiq heard these stories from his friend Omar as often as he told them to everyone else. In a way, Saaiq became Omar and Omar became Saaiq."

Dilawar paced the floor around the fire. He replayed Omar's words but couldn't quite quell his excitement over finding Kadija in Jalalabad.

"Remember," Omar said, "I know how Saaiq fights. I know how you can get this woman from him. But you must ..." The old man was suddenly silent and looked around the interior of the yurt. "You must let Quaalude decide whether I go with you or not. He can tie me to his back."

Dilawar also heard the crunch of Quaalude's shoes in snow but could tell it was the sound of a young man marching in one place. How long had Quaalude been outside?

"Let Quaalude decide what?" Quaalude asked, as he pulled back the cloth strips in the doorway and walked inside.

The old man straightened his back against the hearth and spoke eagerly. "It was an accident," Omar said. "I got shot in the shoulder. The gun went off by accident and Dilawar thinks I'm going to die. But I know I will live, particularly if you strap me to your back and then to your motorcycle. What do you say to that?"

Quaalude looked at Dilawar with questioning eyes before speaking, then said, "The boy's family swears they never sold him for a dead chicken or anything else. They claim Omar snatched him away on his camel."

"Ha!" Omar scoffed. "Of course they'll never admit to selling him. You've embarrassed his whole family. You understand that don't you?"

Quaalude continued, "They were more delighted to receive their son back than to receive a camel, but ..."

Omar was obviously surprised. "I'll accept your payment for stealing my very best transport animal. Cash, check, or credit card will do. I still have the bill of sale. How dare you give away something that isn't yours."

Dilawar corrected him. "You *did* have the bill of sale."

"I see," Omar said, "I'm not among friends as I originally thought."

Dilawar again corrected him, "Friends don't try to kill friends. His shoulder is no accident."

"Oh, that," Omar said. "Well, I wasn't ..."

"Omar," Quaalude called out.

"And by the way," Dilawar interrupted, " You're right, this isn't the real Omar. I don't remember his name. Maybe I never knew it. I believe he killed the real Omar in the hopes of taking his place, or maybe a man named Saaiq did that instead. I'm only speculating. But that's his excuse for hanging around airports. He hoped he'd see someone he knew or knew something about. That way he could leave Kabul as that person or with that person's money. You know what I forgot to ask you?" he said, turning to the old man. Dilawar pulled out the British passport he'd found in the man's clothing. "Who is this man?"

Omar stretched his neck forward and stared at it until tears ran down his face. He couldn't touch it, not with a bullet in his shoulder and a thermos in his other hand. "A man I once knew," he replied curtly. "We both searched for the same woman together."

Omar's expression was like a balloon leaking air. He began to nod, as if fighting sleep. Gradually, his chin rested on his chest and his eyes closed.

Quaalude walked closer to Omar and knelt beside him. "Omar. I'm going to continue to call you that because I'll never confuse you with my grandfather again. My grandfather is a good man who loves children." Omar's head and jowls drooped more.

"And it's okay with me," Quaalude continued, "if you ride tied to my back. I don't know why you'd want to. It can't be an easy way to die. It took months to get up here. It'll take us months to get down."

Quaalude stood up again, turned to Dilawar and said, "I took the camel because I was certain you were going to kill him. And at the time, I didn't know why, only that you didn't trust him. But because you are like a father to me …"

"Quaalude," Dilawar replied, "stop trying to turn me into the family you yearn for. I don't …

"Hear me out!" he shouted. "Because you are like a father to me, I trusted your reasons. So why didn't you kill him? What in the name of Allah stopped you?"

Surprised by Quaalude's outburst, Dilawar backed away to look at him from a distance. "Killing is not an easy thing to do," Dilawar answered. "It never should be. How many men have you killed?"

"None. But I could kill Omar. You want me to? Where is your gun?"

"What has happened to you?" Dilawar asked. "You left here a re-markable young man and …"

"The boy's family," Quaalude interrupted, "ran to the tent of a missionary who spoke English for them. They went out of their way to do that because they were determined to make me know that this man, Omar, dishonored their older girls. He made them undress in front of him. He did this while the men were away in the mountains with the family's herds. The boy was home because he was sick. And although he was sick, he tried to beat Omar away. Omar took a whip to him. That's how he got that mark and how he got kidnapped. When the boy awoke he was tied to Omar's camel and far from home." Quaalude sat down on one of the levels of the hearth, as if worn out. His eyes filled with tears and Dilawar sat down beside him, realizing there were similarities between what had happened to Quaalude and the boy.

"That boy was ashamed," Quaalude continued, "to tell us what Omar had done to him. We wouldn't have understood anyway. But when he was thrown in here, Omar had wrapped him for burial. The villagers looked for camel tracks in the snow for several days. But Omar had covered his tracks and, of course, he was faster than anyone in the town because they only had yaks. I tried to assure them that the old man was probably dead by now, but the boy assured his family that he knew the way back here to this yurt. Apparently the whole village will meet and decide what to do next, whether to come here to get him or not. They have guns and the missionary has a car. The boy's father let me go. There were others who wanted to take my motorcycle from me in order to return here and shoot him."

They both stared at the man whose eyes were tightly closed and shoulders slumped. His wound was still wet and dark. Dilawar could feel Quaalude's anger with himself for trusting such a man.

"I think," Quaalude speculated, "that Omar wants to come with us because he knows the boy's family will eventually reach this place."

"It's a decent theory," said Dilawar, "But I believe Omar wants to come with us to get a share of the wealth that Saaiq hopes to obtain in Jalalabad. I wish I knew more about how that was suppose to happen. And I wish I knew more about Saaiq."

"Wealthy." Quaalude repeated. "I just watched people living in extreme poverty up close. It wasn't that bad."

"Oh, it's bad," Dilawar answered. "You don't ever want to trade wealth for one day of poverty if you can help it. Poverty is numbing, eternal, hopelessness. It can seep into anything good that happens to you. If you're lucky, poverty is a wound that requires time to heal. I guess you can tell I've lived in poverty for some time. My memories of it will always haunt me."

He took another look at Omar who was still sleeping and said, "I need his knowledge. And since you volunteered to strap him on your back, we'll take him with us. He won't survive the entire journey."

"Now that I know we must leave, I wish I could stay," Quaalude said. "I do want to come back here again one day while I'm still young and strong. It's a mystical place."

"If I wasn't certain I'd need your help," Dilawar said, "I'd encourage you to stay. I've watched yak milk turn you into a muscular giant."

They both laughed. Dilawar remembered that it was no small feat to climb with their motorcycles all the way to the Wakhan Corridor and it would be no easy task to get down. Dilawar's sense of urgency would not permit him to wait for the first thaw. There was no reason to wait for a man to recuperate who should be dead. They would leave immediately.

40

FEBRUARY 2009 HINDU KUSH MOUNTAINS

There was little doubt that Dilawar and Quaalude felt sadness in leaving their yurt beside the snow-clad mountains of the Wakjir Pass. Each hoped to hide their feelings from the other, yet each cherished how the other felt. After Omar had been tied securely to Quaalude's motorcycle they rode off, never once looking back across the meadow again.

Snow fell through scattered clouds, while the sun shone brightly. Hours later they rode slowly and as noiselessly as possible along the outskirts of the small river village of Kashch Goz where the boy that Omar had kidnapped lived. They had no desire to attract attention.

Snow stopped falling around eighty kilometers from where they had started. Skies cleared and wherever the cold air touched their skin it caused pain. Quaalude and Dilawar wore helmets with visors that covered their heads. Omar's head was covered with felt strips, his body shielded from the wind by Quaalude's back. And while Quaalude had no gloves, he wore several windbreaking shirts with sleeves that covered his hands as he clutched the handles of his bike.

Several hours before nightfall, they reached yet another meadow where they let loose their urge for speed. Dilawar's KDX was fast, but not as fast as Quaalude's 2008 Honda CRF dirt bike. They anticipated purchasing gas on the other side of Kashch Goz. Somehow Dilawar's bike managed to find the thrust it needed to pass Quaalude's bike in the dust only to later have Quaalude find additional power to beat him.

Once past the meadow their journey would be a series of downward and upward motorcycle climbs through the roughest of terrain. The thought made Dilawar repeatedly ask himself if he'd made a good decision. Wouldn't they have saved time by waiting out the months for the ground to thaw? Omar was neither as opinionated nor as verbal as he had been when he had pleaded to come along. Dilawar wanted to talk with him about his future confrontation with Saaiq. Omar, on the other hand, seemed to have nailed his mouth shut.

In many ways, motorcycles were as difficult to maneuver as the double humped camel. Ice, snow, mud, and scree could disable any means of transport. As they approached Daliz Pass the earth vibrated, warning of yet another disabling condition ahead. While rounding a turn in the road they spied the avalanche which had not yet entirely come to rest. Ice, rock, and snow continued to fall across what had been a narrowing road of rocks. They sat on their bikes and marveled for some time over the slow moving thrust of ice and earth that took its time coming to rest. As if the enormity of the problem was not enough, it began to rain lightly.

Dilawar immediately got off his bike and reached behind his seat for his boot length hooded poncho, a piece of equipment he'd seen others use several times in Colorado as motorcycle clubs traveled west through Fort Collins during the rainy season. He'd had to get a tailor in Kabul to attach two waterproof tarps together then cut off two opposite diagonal corners to fashion a hood. As the rain began to pour Dilawar wondered if Quaalude wished he'd accepted his offer to have another made for him.

At that moment, a frantic male voice behind them shouted to come back. The mountain was about to collapse again. Dilawar mounted his motorcycle and they both rode back around the bend in the road just in time. A large chunk of the glacier fell with enough noise to echo throughout the meadow behind them.

The warning voice they discovered belonged to a German engineering student, Peter, who spoke Pashtu quite well. After introducing himself and explaining where he was from and what he studied, he professed that his love for this part of Afghanistan was so great he'd come by bicycle every year since turning twenty. This was a land, he declared, that forced him to think outside the box in order to survive and he enjoyed every moment with all of its challenges.

When they asked how he intended to cross over the pass he was almost gleeful. "I will find a place above here that's more stable. Then I'll make a snow pit and do several shear tests, all day, if necessary, before I decide on the best place to cross."

He said he was certain he'd be on the other side with his bicycle by this time tomorrow. As he talked he unfolded a metal shovel and a telescoping pole. Dilawar and Quaalude had more than once spent three weeks to an entire month waiting for snow to melt at several road passes they'd encountered on their way into the Wakhan Corridor. They were impressed with this young man's energy and asked if they could follow him to learn more about avalanches. Perhaps, they suggested, the three of them working together might make shorter work of the whole project.

They all agreed. Even Omar was awake for the handshake. In no time they'd found a path that would take them higher up the mountain. Peter's bicycle folded in half and was used as a back support for the seat behind Dilawar. The knobby tires on their motorcycles and their slowly but ever-developing skills kept their bikes moving up the steep incline.

When they reached the top Quaalude set up camp. He warmed water for a translucent broth and propped Omar up against his bike so he could see and be sheltered from the wind. But Omar slept.

Dilawar felt comfortable leaving the two behind while he followed Peter who said he was judging the direction of the wind and looking for small tell-tale cracks and slabs that might predict instability. Peter listened before commenting out loud on sounds the snow made. He walked with careful steps, Dilawar close behind. Twenty minutes later the rain stopped. They walked for another twenty minutes before the man from Germany stopped and began to dig in the snow, first with his collapsible pole and then with his portable shovel. Using his shovel, he separated a column of snow from a small wall of snow behind it. By continuing to insert his shovel against the uphill side of the wall and pulling it toward him he could determine how loose the layers of snow were. Once he'd done that, he and Dilawar returned to camp without saying a word.

Dilawar took off his poncho and sat by the fire to drink the miserable concoction Quaalude was able to make with the few ingredients they had. He was happy to keep his mind off his mission in Jalalabad. There was too much uncertainty connected with it for Dilawar to feel comfortable. Omar sat attentively while Quaalude and Peter talked about his engineering studies outside Stuttgart. Peter had met a girl last year in Afghanistan, but a girl he was certain would not be in Neshtkwar where he last saw her. Neshtkwar had been his destination when the avalanche blocked the road.

When the sun stood overhead, Peter announced it was time to recheck the bar of snow. Dilawar and Peter returned to the spot where Peter had used his shovel to see how loose the layers of snow were. To Dilawar's amazement, Peter said immediately that they could travel over the top of the mountain and then down to reach the other side of the avalanche that very evening. They determined that the snow pack would even support motorcycles. While Dilawar expressed some skepticism about this declaration, Peter became quite angry with himself for leaving his bicycle on the back of Dilawar's motorcycle. Otherwise he would have left for Neshtkwar at that very moment.

Dilawar reminded him how quickly darkness arrived in the mountains and that patience was a skill worth cultivating. As they walked back to camp, Dilawar deliberately slowed his pace, determined to slow down the entire journey in order to make good rational decisions. There was an irony in the advice he'd given the younger man.

Dilawar pitched their large tent and helped Quaalude get Omar inside. He welcomed Peter to take advantage of the tent, suggesting that a good night's sleep would give him sharper eyes for the next day. Peter accepted the idea but explained that he would depart their group at sunrise.

The next morning Peter was gone. And from flat on his back, Omar shrieked inside the tent. "Help me up. I've got to pee on this mountain. Guess you two have already done that. I haven't."

Both Dilawar and Quaalude went inside and brought him out. Once balanced on his feet, he began to walk on his own. His wound continued to look diseased but he washed it with surrounding snow and the old clotted blood slowly disappeared.

"You're supposed to be dead by now, old man," Dilawar said without remorse or sentimentality.

"As I said before, you will not be sorry you brought me with you. You will see."

"I only hope you've been truthful about the man and woman in Jalalabad," Dilawar replied. "You seem to accrue enemies easily. If you have been truthful about their whereabouts, I will not stand against you."

"I can hope for no more than that," Omar answered.

They decided to stay at least one night in the village of Sarhad-e-Broghil because they were hungry and needed provisions for the continued journey. The food had improved since the first time they'd tried it upon their arrival from Kabul. There also seemed to be more tourists in the area now than before. A man from Italy offered to buy them a drink and, in passing, reported seeing Taliban fighting American soldiers in a town close to Jalalabad. Dilawar took out his map and made a circle around the name of the town. He noticed that Omar's brow furrowed as he looked at the map, too.

The next day, they reached the lower Wakhan where problems continued to engulf them. The rivers were high which meant they had to travel longer distances out of their way in order to find places that were passable. They continued to carry with them the enthusiasm shown by Peter, who had reminded Dilawar that engineered solutions could be found anywhere. He still wasn't certain of his route to Jalalabad thinking that once they reached Eshkashem there would be time to make better decisions. Twice Quaalude commented on something that flew past his arm, and later, his shoulder. It had to be an insect traveling with exceptional speed.

In Eshkashem a host family, well known in the area for treating tourists well, tried to make them forget their purpose. The three female relatives of the one male owner of that small lodge were all talented cooks. The lodge itself was away from the center of town and therefore away from both the European and Russian tourists crossing over from Tajikstan. Many of those tourists were headed toward the Wakhan Corridor, the very place from which they'd come.

The sound and beauty of the rushing Panj River made Quaalude nostalgic for his family's home in Pakistan. But Dilawar could not afford to indulge him. Decisions had to be made. There were too many people in uniform stolling the streets for Dilawar's liking. Eshkashem was after all a border town, and Quaalude was the only one who carried no papers at all.

If they intended to travel to Kabul first they would leave Eshkashem for Fayzabad and its decent road. On the other hand, if they stayed away from asphalt they'd not likely be stopped by military.

Before Dilawar realized it, three weeks had past. When they finished what Dilawar alluded to as their last meal in Eshkashem, Omar leaned closer to him and said, "I sense you want to return to Kabul before taking the highway from there to Jalalabad. It looks safe on a map, the little red lines are fatter. But the map doesn't tell you where the last fights between U.S. Military forces and Taliban occurred nor how the seasons have changed the rivers and mountain passes."

He leaned back against his chair. "Nor does that map tell you where your next near-death experience will happen. I'm sure you didn't notice that Quaalude and I slipped down the side of a mountain of scree near Ork two days before we arrived here. It was as if a hand under the rocks reached out and grabbed the crankshaft of Quaalude's bike, dragging us down the side while we still sat upright upon the bike. Rocks finally peeled us off the seat but we managed to stand and pull the bike out of that mess before you ever turned around. And of course, when you finally did, we'd caught up with you."

Quaalude's face was red with embarrassment and Dilawar stared at him, wondering why his friend hadn't shared that information before now.

Omar meanwhile sipped sweet tea, giving his words time to sink into the ears and minds of his audience. "I wouldn't be surprised, if while you were riding, you'd been preoccupied with some personal debate. Perhaps the debate still rages inside you. Does your passionate desire to help someone mean you're prepared to die for that same someone? You should have had that conversation with your mind before you arrived in Kabul. Where do you stand now in your mission? I ask because all our lives are going to be challenged if we continue this journey."

"To be blunt, Omar," Dilawar said, "I've never considered you an equal member of this threesome. You're beyond cocky if you believe I'd share my inner thoughts with a man who tried to kill me and who has already killed his cousin."

"Then let me share my thoughts with you," Omar said angrily. "A new season is dawning. This is always the time when change occurs worldwide, treaties are made, directions are modified. I believe we must act soon because Saaiq will do the same. He has lived outdoors for many years and is more a creature of nature than a man of industry. We must arrive in Jalalabad as soon as we can in order to tackle Saaiq's plan of action. Yes, the skinny red road on your map is more treacherous but Quaalude has become as strong as you. I have traveled the shorter route before. We could be there in three days, unseen and ready to take the woman if that is what you are after. Is that what you want?"

Dilawar replied, "You know until just now I thought you'd been looking for Saaiq's money, but you've been looking for a very particular woman with a birthmark that CIA would have known about. You've been looking throughout the Wakhan Corridor. And I wonder why, if she's supposed to be safe with Saaiq in Jalalabad. You were looking for her boy, too. Or are you always looking for young boys?" He already knew the answer to that question.

Quaalude silently stared into Omar's face waiting to hear his answer. Dilawar stared at Omar too. But he knew the old man couldn't avenge his verbal assault. He presumed Omar had no preference for one sex over another. The villagers would have wanted him to marry one of the young women he had touched if he had demonstrated traditional sexual preferences.

"Perhaps," Omar suggested, "neither of us should be concerned with the other's motivation."

"Perhaps," Dilawar responded.

Quaalude continued to stare at the old man who again leaned closer to Dilawar.

"I stand by what I've said already," Omar announced. "Here is one more reason for taking the shorter route. Saaiq's location is actually just outside Jalalabad in a house alongside this very road." He placed a burn-scarred index finger on the map just below Asadabad. "You will not be sorry you brought me with you. Once again, it's a promise."

41

Two women sat on either side of Inez at her kitchen table. Both Sophie and Inez watched a woman they'd never met until today, Luella Cavenaugh, red headed and freckled, click the keys of her computer at a frantic pace. She wore a fierce expression and a custom-made menswear suit. Inez still wore what she had on yesterday and Sophie looked perky but out of place in skintight jeans and a sweater two sizes too small.

Luella stopped typing, looked at Inez and said, "There's a Martindale employee in Afghanistan now, but not near Jalalabad. He's in Herat closer to Iran. I'll ask that he be ready in case we need him. By plane it's an hour and ten minutes away. I believe he's there to get a deposition which should be finished by the end of the week."

She began typing again, while Inez looked on and said, "I can't tell you how happy I am you were able to come. I have absolutely no experience or knowledge of what to do in a situation like this. Maybe I should test this phone first and see if what that young man said was true before we go any further."

"I'd highly recommend it," Luella said sarcastically, but never stopped typing.

Inez opened her purse and took out the phone. She was trembling as she held it. What if she made a mistake now and erased important stuff?

Sophie grabbed the phone from her hands and said, "Better let me do this part. You don't use cell phones enough. What was that boy's password?"

"Ten and then eleven."

"Yes, it works."

"Mitchell thought the boy was delirious," Inez said. "He said those words twice. Next month and the month after. He'd lost a lot of blood. Look under Contacts and see if the name Saaiq is there."

"And you spell that how?" Sophie asked.

Inez leaned over to look. "I think it's S-a-a-i-q, but be on the look out for anything similar."

"Here it is," Sophie said. "There's a mobile phone number. I assume we aren't calling it this minute though."

"Right," said Luella. "I'd prefer to get a reply from our man in Herat first. We can't transfer money anyway until we have our hands on our target. Consider that Hostage Negotiations 101."

"Doesn't that phone have a place to put the owner's information?" Inez asked. "I never found out that young man's name. Maybe it doesn't matter, but it would be nice to know what he's called."

"I'm sure I can find it," Sophie answered. "People sometimes put that kind of information in strange places so no one will find it if the phone gets stolen."

"If you can't find it," Luella said, "let me have a go at it. Knowing his name *is* important for several reasons. Somebody at Martindale may have heard of him and that could mean we can find the people in his entire network. I can't believe you've got so little in the way of information about who could be holding Kadija and yet you're willing to go through with all this as if it's going to take place."

Inez wanted to tell Luella, that this probably wasn't going to be the last time she'd fooled someone into thinking she was more intelligent, more important, or more prepared than she was. Twenty minutes passed. Inez began pacing and Sophie still played with the phone.

"Don't upset yourselves," Luella said. "This is going to take time, but I'm sure I'm going to hear back from our man in Herat soon."

Sophie suddenly announced, "This phone is owned by someone named… "

"No! Don't tell me," Inez shouted. "Then I'd have to let Mitchell know what I know and I don't want to give the phone back to him until I talk to whoever this Saaiq person is."

"Actually," Luella said, propping her head in one of her hands, "one of the first things Saaiq will probably ask you is who gave you his number? That will be important to him because it will tell him if he needs to change locations and how fast. If he thinks he needs to run, he may kill his hostage."

Inez looked at both women with frightened eyes and gulped. "Okay. I get it. What's his name?" she asked Sophie.

"Harold Smythe with an 'e' at the end."

"Really?" said Luella in an unimpressed way. "I don't think so. Do you?"

Sophie shoved the phone into Luella's face, "You're welcome to look for yourself."

Luella didn't have to reach far to grab it.

"Maybe," Inez suggested, "he's a British subject or he came from an African country once colonized by the British. How's that for narrowing it down to seven or eight African nations? Or maybe he really was enrolled at East High School and was trying to raise money for their athletic department? Then again, the more I think about it the more unlikely it is. These *are* the kinds of things that need to be investigated on the internet."

"I can find out if he was enrolled at East," Sophie said. She started using her own phone.

"Good." Inez sighed with relief.

"And I can find out whether he's a British subject or not," Luella said, fingering the phone in one hand while also looking at her laptop monitor from time to time. She seemed to be the perfect example of someone who could multitask successfully.

"That's great," Inez replied. "But I've got this scary thought that Mitchell may finally put the pieces together: the phone, Schaffer's murderer, the people in the helicopter, the name Saaiq, and then he'll decide to come here to arrest me for stealing ..."

"... for confiscating an item needed to insure the international safety of an American citizen," Luella interjected.

"Yes, for stealing that phone," Inez continued, "just when we have people on two continents ready to put a deal together for a woman's life."

She remembered Mitchell banging on her door yesterday morning because he was afraid something had happened to her. How embarrassing she thought, that he'd have to come back again, bang on her door, and then arrest the old lady he cared about.

"There's a hot plate upstairs," Inez said. She grabbed a plastic bag, opened the refrigerator, and pulled out a few of food containers placing them into the bag. "Humor me. I know this must seem like some movie you've seen, but I'd like you to get up from your seats and follow me. We're going to do our work from the attic. Neither the police nor CBI will find us up there right away. They'll search the basement before they come looking in the attic. Bring your purse. And if I'm lucky, Mitchell won't remember there is an attic, much less where the door to it is."

"I'm game," Luella said, "if I can plug my devices in up there."

"You sure can," Inez answered.

"What can I do?" Sophie asked as they all climbed the stairs to the second floor.

"When the time comes, you're going to have to be our Miss Congeniality and steer the police every which way but upstairs. And you can't get nervous, even when they get close. We'll be fine even if they do show up. We just need time."

Once they'd climbed the stairs to the second floor, the two women followed Inez into a guest bedroom at the back of the small house. Inside the only closet in that room was a ladder held flat against the ceiling. An innocuous air pump attached to it let Inez use one hand to pull it down. When it was down, she took a key chain from her pocket and pushed the button on it. Her face was all smiles.

"I invested a little money in my own safety after that incident with the Chinese Government. You're the first people to ever see this."

A metal ceiling panel slid away and the women climbed to the attic. A cheery room with slanting walls covered in yellowing flowered wallpaper greeted them. One window looked down onto a sprawling backyard. Sunlight streaming through it covered a long table in the middle of the floor. The only other furniture was a small side table with a hot plate on it, a cot folded upright against one wall, and four folding chairs at each corner.

Although Sophie walked around to see everything, she said, "I know. I know. I should be downstairs. I was just curious to know where I wasn't supposed to bring the police."

"Call me on your phone, if you get lonely or you see them coming," Inez said.

Inez waited until she heard Sophie go down the stairs to the first floor before she pushed the button again on her key chain and the stairs rose up and the metal panel covered the space they had walked through.

"Pull up a chair, Luella." Inez took refrigerator boxes from the plastic bag and stacked them at one end of the table.

Luella opened her laptop and made a peculiar despairing noise. She grabbed a chair and sat down quickly. "Oh, dear. Jeremy Masters, our man in Herat, is supposed to be in Beijing tomorow. He finished the deposition early and plans to leave the city today. He wants to know this minute if he's got to go to Jalalabad." Luella looked up at Inez. "But we don't know yet do we?" Luella answered. "Masters would need to cancel his reservation." She began typing again.

"Where's that phone?" Inez asked.

Luella suddenly stopped typing, reached inside her tote, and pulled out the phone. Inez grabbed it from her.

"Wait," Luella yelled. "Let's find out something, anything about the phone's owner before you call. That may be Saaiq's only assurance that you are who you say you are. Here, let me just finish this check on his citizenship."

Just then Luella's personal cell phone rang. It was Sophie and Luella put her on speaker phone.

"There is no Harold Smythe currently enrolled at East," Sophie said, "and although there were five enrolled over the last eight years, Smith was spelled with an 'i' instead of 'y'."

Inez smiled at the phone. "That was good work. But could he have Americanized his name so he wouldn't stick out?"

"I've got to check further, huh?" asked Sophie.

"You were right," Luella said. "He's originally from Nigeria, twenty-eight years old, and a British citizen now. He's in Colorado, on a student visa."

"Wow! Inez said. "He looked like a high school student. Wonder where and how he got licensed to fly a helicopter. Write his name and nationality on a sticky note for me Luella. I'm going to start now." Inez punched the phone number for Saaiq.

42

No one remembered when the rain started. The sound of it hitting on Dilawar's plastic coated poncho had been so hypnotic that he had no memory of when it became intense. Rain turned the road's stone into clay from its pounding.

A nearby sign, though difficult to read through a mist of water and steam, said 'Asadabad'. The metal pole to which it was attached was bent parallel to the road, giving the appearance that it wouldn't last the whole day.

Finally dismounting, Quaalude and Dilawar stood beside the two motorcycles and cautiously peered down the side of the mountain into the valley below. Their feet slowly sank into wet peat. Dilawar wondered if the sign and the village below had any chance of survival but he didn't speak of it.

Frustrated, tired, and angry Dilawar pushed his bike away from the edge of the road and motioned to Quaalude to do the same. Omar was still seated on it and slowly, with Quaalude's help, dismounted.

Of the three, Dilawar was the driest. His poncho let water roll down like beads. Quaalude stood soaked in his ski jacket, while Omar, wrapped in his long sheepskin vest, wore gauze that held rain next to his skin.

"You want to hear me say it old man?" Dilawar shouted over the roaring sound of running water. "I *am* sorry I brought you along and you're welcome to walk back or just leave us here at any time."

He'd grown tired of pulling their motorcycles out of mud and scree to trudge miles off course to find mechanics to fix what the roads had shaken from their cycles. Just then the sound of stone being chipped by a bullet was clearly audible.

Dilawar pulled out both his binoculars and his gun as he turned his back on Quaalude and Omar. Looking in all directions he saw no one else. What he saw below was devastating. About sixty meters down, rushing water had risen to the top of most flat roofed structures in the valley. Some homes had two stories with people sitting on top waving for help. Dead cows and sheep floated in place on their sides, others bobbed up and down where a harness tethered them. Small groups of people helped each other climb from crumbling homes onto handmade rafts. Other groups foraged up the sides of muddy hills, while some hills had already given away. He suddenly remembered the gunshot. Where had it come from and what did it mean?

What was left of five to seven thousand homes was spread across the valley floor. Torrential rain wasn't good for motorcycles either. Dilawar turned around and saw that Quaalude had moved both bikes under the overhang of the mountain they had just driven across. They were alone and drenched. Omar!

Calling to Quaalude he asked, "Where'd he go?"

"You told him you didn't care if he left. When he heard the shot, he jumped over the side. I don't think he's gone far, he's not doing well. I'm sure you've begun to smell his infected wound. As much as I hate him, I'd hate to see him drown."

"No, I haven't smelled it. He's not tied to *my* back. I've paid little attention to him knowing he couldn't last. I looked everywhere before we left the yurt and couldn't find my bullet so it must still be logded inside him.

I believe what we heard couldn't have been a bullet," Dilawar continued, "but rather was the sound of stones hitting each other. I suspect Omar jumped over the side because he recognizes this place and wants to see the woman before he dies."

He lifted his black poncho over his head as he spoke then stuffed it into his daypack.

"I'm going to follow him," Dilawar said, "not to bring him back necessarily, but to see where he's going. You stay here." He untied a coil of rope from his motorcycle and hung it from a loop at his waist, then handed Quaalude a gun.

"Everybody in that valley down there will want these bikes," Dilawar warned, "both mean people and beautiful ones. And don't forget about the people who walk over this pass. You may need to kill somebody to keep what's ours. There aren't too many places in the world where you can still do that and be considered heroic. On the other hand, that's your decision. Besides, maybe it was a bullet we heard." He smiled at Quaalude, who tried to smile back, but couldn't sustain it.

"And don't forget to release the safety catch. I'll be back soon." Still smiling, Dilawar jumped over the edge.

Hiking up and down moutains had been the most enjoyable part of his CIA training.

Dilawar landed hard, but got up quickly to run across a barely discernible footpath to the next edge, and jump again. He'd last used his climbing skills when a drone flew off course in Pakistan and had to be retrieved from the far side of the Khyber Pass. This time, he landed on rock and lay stunned for a moment before rolling himself close to the edge to see how far down he was. The view made him feel stupid. When he looked up, he was unable to see Quaalude or the motorcycles. The top of the mountain had not been steep, but the rest of the way down would require rope.

Where was Omar? He couldn't be far. He hadn't carried a rope or a hook, or had he? Dilawar sat back from the edge, not wanting to attract attention from anyone below. He took out his binoculars again. Rope had attached Omar to Quaalude and then to the motorcycle itself. Perhaps he took that rope with him. But wasn't he also in pain?

He could hear voices rising out of the valley as people screamed to family and friends for help. Dilawar looked for people along the sides of the mountains. He didn't think he'd find many people as far up as he was, but to his surprise he counted four scattered throughout the valley's walls. Two carried rifles and remained in place for long periods at a time. Had they fired the shot?

Climbing was not the preferred way to escape the flood. More people loaded themselves and their belongings onto cars, trucks, rafts, and boats. Finally, he spotted Omar above him. He must have used his rope to swing to yet another mountain. Dilawar looked horizontally in the same direction as he was traveling. About a mile in front of Omar was a shelter, a home perhaps. Smoke seemed to extend from its chimney and it was camouflaged with bushes. Nothing about the structure itself seemed remarkable. But its placement in the side of the rock made it an incredible engineering feat. There was no movement around it.

He was slow to realize however that Omar could not possibly have seen that house from where they originally dismounted from their motorcycles. Omar knew about this location before today. This was where they would at last find Saaiq.

He stood up and wiped water from his binoculars before looking through them again. He had to find a quicker route to that shelter. Above it he saw unexpected rapid movement. Dilawar had to keep wiping water off the glass lenses to make certain what he saw was no mirage. It was a man dressed entirely in dark gray, a color matching the mountain rock exactly. Was that Saaiq? Had Saaiq seen Omar? Why was he climbing in such a hurry? Instinct told him to scan the mountain again. But there was nothing. No one else was near that shelter.

Where then was the woman he'd known as Sabeen, later to be called Abida, the woman he'd loved in another life as Kadija Campbell? He leaned an elbow against the mountain, watching through the binoculars, cursing the cold, the wetness, and mental exhaustion that engulfed him. She wasn't here. Was she dead after all? The base of his chest burned with the desire to know.

He took the binoculars away from his face and stared up at a gray sky. Rain had turned to drizzle. He stood immobile questioning the sanity of following Omar, a man he knew would be dead soon. A man whose mission he still didn't understand. All along, Dilawar had tried to forget the possibility that CIA had told him the truth, that Kadija had been killed by friendly fire.

Her face had become mentally difficult to recreate, but her infectious curiosity, her zest for action, her love of life, had, over the years become so tangible he had no trouble recalling specific instances.

He looked up again. Returning to the place where he'd left Quaalude and the motorcycles was easy enough. Maybe they'd put their efforts into helping the people below. Once the water receded they could continue to Jalalabad. He'd then charge a ticket for Quaalude's return to Islamabad. Later he would find a military base somewhere in Afghanistan where people would listen to the story he'd create for their benefit. Eventually they'd take him home to the States.

There was less rain than before, but the ground was dangerously saturated. He had to climb now or not at all. If he waited any longer, the stunted trees and rocks around him would cause mudslides as he climbed.

He took one last look at the house on the side of the mountain hoping he'd suddenly see her standing near a door or window. It was not uncommon to leave embers smoldering for a family's return, thus the smoke from the chimney continued. Or maybe those had been fragments of clouds. Nothing appeared out of the ordinary. As his gaze drooped below the house he saw movement around a low plant, maybe from a mongoose or maybe it was the figure of yet another man.

This one wore all black and sat crouched beside a rise in the rocks to watch the catastrophe below. As Dilawar stared he realized this man's head and shoulders were also covered. He wore loose black pants and suddenly leaped to a branch, then swung to a tree that hung perpendicular to the mountain itself. That had been a dangerous move considering the rushing waters below. So this man had not climbed up from the valley floor, if he was so eager to climb down.

Again he jumped, this time to a lower jutting of rock that gave way. Landing feet first on a boulder he was now closer to Dilawar, but far below his position. He seemed to collapse into a crumbled ball, face down onto the ground. There he lay for several minutes before sitting up to rub his leg and breath deeply.

Seeing the figure twist its head to one side, Dilawar stepped back and pressed himself hard against the mountain. He anticipated that person's inclination to look up. Dilawar waited a very long time, six minutes by his own count, then eased forward slightly. In a blink, the face looked up at him from the distance below. Dilawar snapped himself back against the mountain, trying hard to recall what he'd just seen. His heart had already jumped into his throat. Had it been a woman's face? He leaned forward again, this time to boldly see and be seen.

No one was there. It was as if no one had ever been there. He looked through his binoculars and saw no trace, no indentation in the mud, no evidence that a figure in black ever existed.

Suddenly, uncontrollably, he yelled from deep inside his chest and lungs across the entire valley, "NOOOOO!"

His voice reverberated against the wall of mountains before heading back toward him. His echo even scared him. Might he have created a landslide in the twenty audible seconds it took the sound to return? He carefully looked down over a large boulder as the tiny heads of people in the valley looked all around them for the source of the noise. They likely ascribed the sound to someone's personal loss. Had Omar and Quaalude heard it and recognized his voice? It was done now in one moment of insanity, a moment to be Sampati Jagjit, for all it mattered. He shook his head and hoped it wouldn't get him killed right here, right now.

And what exactly had he lost? What had he seen? Had his own desire conjured up the very face of the woman he wanted to find? Was he really that crazy? Had he seen a woman or a skinny man?

He looked through his binoculars. Somehow Omar had trekked half the distance to the shelter. And where was the man in gray? Could he have reached the top of the summit by now? If Omar could be believed, Saaiq was possibly where Omar said he'd be, near a cage holding the woman. If he let himself imagine her existence, perhaps she had escaped and was traveling down the mountain into a flooded valley. Had he seen a woman wearing a burqa? Is that what he saw? It made sense.

His mission suddenly became more urgent. He could head down the mountain to help her. If it was Kadija and she really had survived this long in Afghanistan, she was far more astute a spy than he was. She would either survive that flood or return to the shelter, any shelter she could find.

Obliterating her need to escape on the other hand would be a better use of his skills. Omar and Saaiq had to be eliminated. To avoid being seen by Omar he'd need to follow a lower path across two mountains and do it quickly. And if the man in gray were Saaiq, he'd need to eliminate him next.

Dilawar put his binoculars back in his daypack and suddenly saw his folded black poncho. Putting it on might help him become a decoy for the woman in black. He hoped he was right. There was more energy in his step as he prepared.

૨

Dilawar eased closer to the far side of the shelter and perched himself just above eye level. He could plainly see that the shelter had no foundation. Someone had built it on a natural extension of rock. He swung his rope around a pole that projected out of the mountain, first tugging on it to test if it would hold his weight. He swung into the air and onto the lip of the rock.

He stood in front of a shelter that resembled a mud walled bunkhouse, similar to what he'd seen in western movies. There were horizontal beams of wood that supported the part of the mountain that acted as the roof of a front porch.

Explosives must have been used to blow out the back part of the shelter because he could see that the inside floor of the structure was stone that curved deep down into the mountain itself. Looking around outside he realized this was not a strategic position. And if, in fact, Omar had called Saaiq by phone here, he could not have answered the call from inside the cave. Dilawar backed away slowly to wait for Omar who would soon approach from the far side of what he now knew was a stone façade built to look like the front of a house. On the opposite side where Dilawar positioned himself was a pile of scree.

Five minutes later Omar crawled to the front doorway entrance of the facade. Dilawar barely saw him and assumed he could no longer stand.

Instead of crawling inside Omar rolled over on his back and in English yelled, "Saaiq, where the hell are you?" Omar had little lung power left.

Dilawar stood quietly around the corner of the facade waiting to see if anyone would answer. They both waited while the noise of rushing water and people yelling prevented them from hearing anyone approach.

"Who's there?" Omar finally asked, while still on his back. How could he have heard anything, Dilawar wondered?

He was about to answer Omar when a new voice spoke up. "It's you. I didn't expect you to return. I'm sure Saaiq didn't expect you, either. You've got to leave. I don't know why he didn't kill you the last time he saw you."

"No, no, no. I've got to tell you this before Dilawar gets here. He's on his way. He's coming to save you."

"Who?"

Dilawar could hear Omar being pushed and pulled, probably into a sitting position. Was it a female voice? It was deeper than he remembered Kadija's but that had been so long ago, when they were young and foolish. He couldn't chance being discovered until he knew more about this person.

"I'm responsible for Malik's death," Omar confessed. "I'm the one who betrayed him. I wanted you to hear it from me first. I didn't lie to you. I omitted a lot. My only sorrow is that by being responsible for Malik's death, I jeopardized your life and the life of my nephew. I didn't know Saaiq was so cunning. I tried to find your boy, rather I tried to find a boy, any boy to throw this Dilawar off the track but I ..."

"You've been shot. Some time ago." The whispering voice was very calm.

"Dilawar shot me. You know him."

There was silence.

"No. Don't leave me," Omar pleaded.

Dilawar quickly backed further away as noiselessly as he could, realizing that the whisperer was no longer by Omar's side.

"Where's Saaiq?" Omar cried out. "Where is he?"

The whispering voice returned to Omar's side. "He's been climbing back and forth up to the summit making phone calls, then climbing the summit again in order to answer them. There's a tower up there. Occasionally he can receive calls on top of the roof here. He's left me for weeks at a time, daring me to escape. He's more depressed since Wanted went into hiding in Pakistan. He believes he's not trusted anymore by the Taliban or Al Qaeda. It scares him. His own people may come after him."

"He'll kill you."

"Maybe."

"Has he told you where Bin Laden is?"

The voice was silent. Omar whimpered.

The voice became stronger. "You've come to ask me for forgiveness haven't you? And for all it's worth, I forgive you. In my religion however God is the final arbiter of forgiveness. My place is not to judge."

It was definitely a female voice, deep and seductive.

Omar's voice was more of a whisper. "I tried to bring a boy back here with me to pull at Saaiq's sense of righteousness, but nothing happened the way I planned."

"Be assured," said the female voice, "your nephew, many times removed, is safe. Even I was safe for a while today," she continued. "I escaped from here, but returned because … because I was curious about a voice I heard."

Dilawar came from around the corner of the façade, his gun pointed up and held next to his chest. "It was your Mowgli's voice," he said.

He stood about 300 paces from her. "You remember?"

She was on one knee on the far side of the shelter next to Omar, her eyes moving swiftly over every inch of Dilawar's face.

Omar lifted his head up slightly and said, "This is Dilawar, the pilot who flew us … It's the only name I know him by." His head fell back against the ground. "Saddam Hussein planned to slaughter …" he continued. "The CIA reassigned me … long ago."

Dilawar watched painfully as tears quietly streamed down the woman's face from half closed eyes. Dilawar felt his own face twist in sorrowful happiness but he was also determined not to permit his feelings to interfere with his mission to set her free.

"How long has Saaiq been gone?" Dilawar asked her.

"Not long," said a loud voice above their heads. "I'm expecting a call so I had to make certain the tower hadn't been compromised in this rain storm."

Saaiq was resting on one knee on the part of the mountain that formed the porch roof. He was drenched, while everyone else had partial cover under part of the roof's overhang. Dressed in gray fatigues, he looked as old as Omar, but was obviously more healthy and spry. Dilawar had already seen how quickly he was capable of climbing cliffs and mud encrusted terrain. His face was like a road map with deep wrinkled crevices and raised scars.

It was also a familiar face; he'd seen it on the deck of cards belonging to Jamison. He was Hamid al Magdeed, fourth in command under Bin Laden. He'd been educated in both the UK and the United States.

"And look," Saaiq continued. "We both have guns. Guess you've been sent here to bring your spies home. Well, first things first. Drop your gun, whatever your name is." He quickly stood up, holding his arm out toward the woman and Omar.

"If you don't drop yours," Saaiq said, "one of them will die on the count of three, and I'm not going to tell you which ... One.

"Look at all of you," Saaiq continued. "Who would have thought CIA would become such an equal opportunity employer. I can't imagine them ever hiring Afghanis or Moroccans, but hey, who am I to be critical? Two. You must have those buns of iron, and nerves of steel that they talk about on TV? Three."

Saaiq's one shot through Omar's heart killed him as he lay flat on the ground. Dilawar fired, almost simultaneously in the direction of Saaiq who instantly rolled down the rooftop, flipped over, and jumped off the façade's front porch. Saaiq grabbed at the woman's wrist, but she ably avoided him to leap over Omar's body. Out the corner of his eye, Dilawar saw her do a summersault over the edge of the rock on which the façade was built, crying "Mowgli," as she disappeared.

Dilawar had no intention of leaping over the side after her. The rain had degraded patches of rock and vegetation around them in the short time they'd been there. He'd already found a perfect place to hide where he'd waited for Omar. Besides, he knew, or thought he knew, that she'd try to talk him into leaving Saaiq behind, to find Saaiq another day. That was no option. A man like Saaiq would never accept defeat.

"Don't go anywhere," Saaiq yelled to him. "I've got a deal for you."

"Same deal Omar got?" Dilawar yelled back. He couldn't see Saaiq and Saaiq couldn't see him. But he was certain Kadija was just under the lip of the rock where she had been earlier. He knew she could hear everything from there.

"No, my boy, I've got another deal for you. I ... I plan to go to the U.S. a rich man. I'm tired of war. I plan to live out the last days of my life in the style I've only dreamed of. I'm not here for jihad. I'm here to help me."

"Omar told me," Dilawar answered, "your female hostage is worth tons of money, right?"

"Female hostage. That's funny. Abida would have liked that money too. That make-believe Omar over there, that terrible excuse for a CIA agent, gathered a lot of timely information in his short stay in Afghanistan, but never learned how to use any of it," Saaiq answered.

Dilawar noticed the quality of Saaiq's voice change, as if distracted and distant. Perhaps he was searching Omar's dead body.

"That female hostage as you call her," Saaiq continued, "is supposed to be my step-mother's bastard granddaughter. Can you follow that? That's her relationship to the real Omar. Can you believe how incestuous this whole thing sounds? And how is it that this dead Omar has nothing on his person? Was he your prisoner?"

"Unlike you, I have no need to take prisoners," Dilawar answered.

"And of all times to have cell phone problems," Saaiq answered. "The rainy season started early this year. What was your name again? I didn't catch it. Dilly something wasn't it? Oh, wait a minute. I think I ... Yes. I finally do have a call from the States," Saaiq said.

He could hear Saaiq's knees stretching and stones falling and the phone ringing. Saaiq must have climbed back onto the roof of the porch to receive that call.

"Hello? HELLO?" Saaiq yelled, still in English.

43

D etermined to prevent her voice from faltering, Inez replied, "Please connect me to Saaiq."

"And who, for all the heavens to hear, shall I say, wants him?"

She was taken aback by the sarcasm of whoever answered, but hoped it wouldn't show in her voice. "Dr. Inez Buchanan."

She was not distracted when Luella took out a long cord and plugged it into the phone Inez held to her ear.

"Doctor, is it? Doctor of what?" Saaiq asked. He spoke English with a definite Middle Eastern accent.

"Education."

"Ha! And who said you should call me?"

Luella plugged the other end into her computer, which amplified the voice on the other end.

"I only recently know him as Harold Smythe," Inez answered. "If he has an alias, I don't know it. He gave me his phone and told me to call you. I'm also calling on behalf of the late Dolly David who asked me to do anything to bring her granddaughter home."

There was a long silence. Finally, Inez added, "Did you murder Dolly?"

"If you think that, what makes you think Kadija Campbell is still alive?"

"You still want the money don't you?"

Another long silence followed, until Saaiq began speaking swiftly. "I want all of it deposited into a Swiss account. Can you write down these numbers?"

"Yes. Am I on speaker phone?"

There was another pause in the conversation. "No." Then he recited the numbers. "And I get the money before I release the woman."

"This isn't Hollywood. Our eyes aren't on you. It has to be the other way around."

He chuckled. "Am *I* on speaker phone? And exactly how much money are we talking about?"

"The answer is yes and the figure is $500,000,000.000."

"Why not all of it? And who's listening?"

"You don't know them. They don't know you. And that's the amount because it'll take lots of people and institutions to safely transfer that money and determine if your Kadija Campbell is authentic."

"You sound like you know what you're doing."

"Thank you."

"Yes, but do you? We should be Skyping or something shouldn't we?" Saaiq said. "Our eyes should be on each other."

Inez wondered if that statement indicated the conversation wasn't going well. Was he emphasizing the fact that no one could verify his identity? Luella held one thumb up. Inez said nothing in response. Instead, she began addressing the mechanics of the exchange as she and Luella had mapped them out.

"Kadija must be at the airport in Jalalabad within the next two days. There, a man who will be unable to identify her, will escort her by plane to Greece. She'll be identified through DNA in Martindale branch offices there. The minute we know she's Kadija, the money will be released to the account with the number you gave me."

There was another long silence.

Whispering, Saaiq replied, "I'll call you back."

"NO!" Inez screamed. She held the phone with both hands. "We have protocols to follow too. Our whole situation can drastically change if we hang up now without agreeing on the process."

After a short silence Saaiq whispered, "Right now I'm just outside a cave on the side of a mountain cliff. Explosives are inside the cave with a detonator set to go off in forty minutes. Below me, maybe a whole kilometer down, is a village being wiped away by floodwaters as we speak. I'm sure you don't want to hear my burdens, but maybe you could come rescue us?"

Inez looked at Luella who was busy typing. After what seemed like a minute, she whispered to her, "He's still waiting."

"Be thankful for that," Luella replied. In a few minutes she shook her head and pointed to her screen for Inez to read. Inez recognized it as a map of a mountainous terrain with a blinking message to one side.

"We can't do it in forty minutes," Inez said into the phone. "More like seventy-two hours from a base near what looks like Iceland."

Luella nodded in agreement.

"Who are you kidding?" Saaiq shouted. "Every American military base in Afghanistan has helicopter rescue planes."

"Did you think you were talking to the military?" Inez shouted back. "They'd easily misunderstand this entire transaction."

"You're with Martindale, aren't you?" Saaiq asked.

"The money you seek is with Martindale."

"Martindale *is* the military," he shouted.

Inez looked at Luella for help and when none came, Inez spoke again, "You're thinking of the glory days when Alan Bradley and Colonel Tucker David ran the place. That administration is gone from Martindale and the White House."

There was another silence on his end. She could hear defeat in his voice. "Make it four days from today to report to the airport in Jalalabad. What's your man's name?"

"He'll be holding a sign that says Mission Impossible. And you're going to tell him you're Morton Meda."

"Why? And why would I kill a woman whose money I'm trying to procure?"

Inez was surprised by his words and remained silent.

He spoke again. "And if she *is* dead, how is this transaction possible?"

Luella quickly scribbled a note and handed it to Inez. "And Saaiq," Inez said, "you can't come with her. If you get on the same plane with her, our business ..." Inez could barely bring herself to say the words but Luella, a woman well seasoned in hostage negotiations, looked at her angrily, "... is over," Inez conceded.

"Are you crazy?" he replied.

"And what do you mean," Inez asked, "you're not Morton Meda?"

"Just what I said. I have my pride, too. I'm ..."

A gunshot could be heard over the phone.

"Saaiq?" Inez called. "SAAIQ!"

The connection went dead.

44

Dilawar touched the side of his ear. His fingertips were wet with his own blood. He'd poked his head up too high above the side of the hill of scree thinking Saaiq was very much engaged in his phone conversation. That unanticipated bullet from Saaiq had been too close. It had also stopped drizzling. Slowly Dilawar walked down the hill beside the façade and crouched alongside it.

"Okay, Dilly," Saaiq hollered, "I know you're not dead. About that deal I was ready to offer you. There have been a few changes. I don't need you anymore."

The man's voice lacked the arrogance it had before he answered his phone. Dilawar sat quietly, ready for Saaiq to spring at him.

"Kadija, you listening?" Saaiq hollered. "Yes, I know your real name. You and I are going to America. We get to be wealthy. All we need do is get rid of this Dilly Ware or whatever he's called, so we can get out of here."

There was no answer. After all these years Dilawar could have told him that a spy like Kadija Campbell would never reveal her location willingly. On the other hand, Dilawar knew exactly where Saaiq was. He was seated on the roof, legs dangling over the edge. Dilawar could see just his legs swinging back and forth. However, what he wanted was a straight shot to his heart. If he shot his legs there'd be no way to get him off the mountain and no way for the three of them to help each other.

"Listen," Saaiq continued, "I've just finished talking to a woman on the phone who says we've got to get to the airport in Jalalabad in a few days. You go on ahead. You look for a sign that says Mission Impossible. I'll join you as soon as I take care of this interloper this Dilly person. But you get off this mountain. You hear me?"

Dilawar had heard the part about the explosives. He doubted that Kadija could have heard Saaiq's voice from her location. Shooting his legs had become more appealing.

"Hey, wait," Saaiq said.

Dilawar eased closer to the corner of the façade to take his shot, but Saaiq's legs were gone. He must have been standing on the roof now.

"What's this?" Saaiq asked. "Dilly. You know this guy?"

Dilawar considered it another ploy to get him to show where he was hiding. Quietly he walked up the hill of scree ready to try another shot.

"Does this young man belong to you?" Saaiq asked. "Fifteen, sixteen maybe with a gun and a couple of bullet belts over his shoulders to help him play war games."

Dilawar froze. Quaalude.

"Don't think you know him Kadija. Bet this kid came with Dilly. I'm going to shoot him before he gets closer because he's just one too many ..."

Dilawar did not need to stand up tall to see over the roof. He took one step up the hill of scree, put his eyes above it and shot Saaiq squarely in the back. Instantly, an explosive sound filled the entire valley. Saaiq's back and chest had been torn away enough to see through to the other side.

As Saaiq fell, Dilawar could see the figure of Quaalude off in the distance along the same plane of sight, his gun drawn and smoking. It was miraculous that Dilawar and Quaalude hadn't shot each other. Both were silent for some time and unquestionably shaken by what they'd just done.

Dilawar climbed onto the roof to gaze at what was left of Saaiq.

"Quaalude," Dilawar hollered, "start heading back." The wind carried his words. "We'll come to you."

Quaalude's reply thundered throughout the entire valley. "Okay."

"We've got to help the people down there," screamed a voice from under the stone edge. Kadija climbed over the top and stood for a moment teasingly close to the very edge and looked at Dilawar. "I noticed you had a rope. So did Omar." She continued to talk, as she ran to Omar's dead body to retrieve it.

Dilawar stared down at her from atop the roof. He couldn't help smiling. Her beauty hadn't changed one bit. "It's good to see you, too, he said."

She shook her head as she looked up with tears forming in her eyes, but she kept talking while undoing the knots in the rope around Omar's body. "The quickest, safest way to get out of here is straight up. But this mountain is going to explode soon, which is a good thing because it should dam up the water down there."

"You're still mad at me because I knocked you out to get you off the plane."

"No, I'm not. I love you. You just saved my life. Saaiq had come to the end of his treachery. I believe he intended to commit suicide and take me to paradise with him. But your friend…Quaalude?... needs to move fast. There's enough dynamite inside this cliff to tear down the whole mountain. I've lived inside that cave since January, tethered to that pole. Is that why you're here? Did my grandmother send you? Are they still looking for Bin Laden?"

"No. I didn't know you had a grandmother."

He jumped down from the roof, kissed her cheek quickly, and then stepped back. "I just thought you might still be alive. Guess I love you, too. And yes, they're still looking for Bin Laden."

"You never forgot how much I believe in miracles did you? God has given me so many," she said through her tears.

He snatched the rope from her hands and said, "That young boy's name over there used to be Quaalude. It isn't anymore. He's like a son to me, only he isn't. Let's go get him."

"I have a son. My friend Bedrah has taken him to America with her."

"I know. I could feel it," he said knowingly as he lassoed the pole he'd used to climb onto the rock. "Why did you ask about Bin Laden?" he asked while busily pulling on the rope to test its strength.

Kadija silently wrapped her body tightly around his and kissed his lips. "I know where he is," she whispered. Only Dilawar held on with a sturdy grip to the rope he had just tested. Both of them swung high above the rushing waters below, not knowing when the explosives would ignite.

45

SEPTEMBER 2009 PARK HILL, DENVER

L uella had taken off her stiletto heels. She sat sideways at the table in the attic, legs crossed, hands on her hips. "Other than not being certain what day and time Kadija Campbell will be at the airport," she said confidently, "I don't see a problem. Do you?" She didn't wait for an answer. "Obviously, we can't use our man in Herat. He has other business to attend to. But I think I've got another guy lined up to wait in Jalalabad. And he's even better with a gun."

All the while she spoke, Inez looked out into the room at nothing in particular.

"What's wrong?" Luella asked. "Why didn't you ask him to let you speak to Kadija?"

Inez came out of her personal clouds gradually. "I've never seen or talked to Kadija in person. I had no way to identify Saaiq, either. I thought Saaiq and Morton Meda were the same man. And if I'm not mistaken, I heard a tone of finality in his voice, an exuberant personality that entertained suicide."

She looked at the phone and pushed buttons to read the boy's list of contacts. "There's no Morton Meda here," she said. "We could still be in real danger. Maybe what Bradley said about Morton and his past murders was true after all. And after all, Bradley knew him personally when he worked at Martindale. I think it's time to give Mitchell this phone back."

A creaking floorboard, two floors below, punctuated her sentence. Luella and Inez suddenly sat motionless. Inez grabbed Luella's personal phone and punched in Sophie's number.

"Sophie," Inez whispered into the phone. "Did you make that noise?"

"No," she whispered back. "It's the front door."

"Call Mitchell," Inez said. "Never mind, I'll call him. Oh rats, I still don't have my own phone. I'm sorry Sophie. You tell Mitchell to come quickly because somebody's trying to break in."

Just then they heard glass break over Luella's speaker phone and someone downstairs shout, "You're Inez Buchanan aren't you?"

"No! No," Inez screamed as she frantically pushed the button to force open the stairs that went downstairs. Luella grabbed her phone from the table where Inez had dropped it and called 911.

As Inez reached the stairs to the first floor, a shot was fired and she heard the sound of a body fall to the floor.

"Sophie? Answer me," Inez called.

When she reached the bottom step, she saw a man's figure dressed in jeans and a plaid shirt. His black hair was curly but he never turned around to look at the face of the person calling out. Instead he ran towards the kitchen. Inez assumed he was headed for the back door.

She knelt beside Sophie's body lying in the dining room and held her hand.

"Please Lord, take me," Inez cried. "Luella!" she screamed, "call an ambulance."

The commotion in Inez's backyard: police identifying themselves, gunfire, men with heavy boots, only slightly penetrated her thoughts as she rubbed the hand she held. Then sirens thankfully blared. The ambulance had made good time.

Luella opened the front door and pulled Inez away from Sophie's limp body. Paramedics swooped in and put an oxygen mask on Sophie's face. It was Inez's first sign that Sophie might still be alive. They were very efficient and were quickly headed out the front door with Sophie strapped to a gurney.

"Stay away" said a gruff voice. It had to be Morton Meda's "This will go off. Now.

Inez realized he was speaking somewhere close to the house and to the police. Luella realized it too because as she sat on the dining room floor next to Inez and began praying under her breath.

Morton's voice was deep. "I want to see the stranger my step-mother was willing to sign over her fortune to."

Stepmother? Was he referring to Dolly?

"Inez Buchanan isn't here Morton." It was Mitchell's voice. "I've told you that. That's why blowing yourself up is nonsense."

Inez could hear him plainly. They had to be just outside the back door. Suddenly she heard scuffling and fighting and then the sound of bullets. Bullet fire lasted longer than a minute and then there was silence. Several minutes after that, a policewoman walked into the house, her gun drawn.

"Everybody okay in here?" she asked.

No one could speak.

"You might as well stay where you are," she added. "The intruder's body, what's left of it, is still in the backyard."

A mental image of Dolly's face made her remain seated on the floor with Luella. She had no desire to ever see the man who could do what he had done to Dolly. If Inez were lucky she'd gradually forget what she saw. But she was old enough to know better.

EPILOGUE
SPRING, 2010 PARK HILL, DENVER

Trace Mitchell and Inez sat in upholstered chairs across from each other in her living room, quietly thinking.

"I understand why you continue to be upset," he said after some time had passed, "You still blame yourself. You're not a detective and you don't provide investigative services. You said you told Dolly that. That's when she should have turned around and said, "Thank you very much. Sorry to disturb you," and left. So it's not your fault about Kadija."

Inez stoically stared back at Trace. "Was that supposed to cheer me up?" she asked.

"Maybe I should go." He got up from the chair, still pressing his thighs against it.

She didn't move a muscle and didn't object to his offer to leave. Schaffer's funeral seemed long ago now. She recognized Trace's need to be more careful this time with his new partner. Besides they had new cases to solve. Life went on.

Inez blamed his attitude on the male psyche in general that would never grasp how deep a woman's sorrow could be, or in her case, the sorrow of not bringing Kadija home and her responsibility for Sophie's near death.

She continued to hope and wait for a phone call telling her that Kadija was in Greece or that someone had boarded the plane using her ticket in Jalalabad. But months had passed. Perhaps it was for the best. Someone would have to tell her that her grandfather, if he were ever caught, would be tried for murder.

"I almost forgot," Trace said, as he sat down again. "The DA plans to drop all charges against you related to evidence tampering. He believes that cell phone was given to you and he's convinced he can't prove otherwise."

"Hmmm."

"He's just doing his job, Inez. And I meant to tell you this too. You were right about Morton Meda. A preliminary examination suggested Morton suffered from PTSD, going as far back as the Russian Afghan War. And CBI may look into the death of Colonel David as well."

"What are the odds?" Inez muttered. "And why would CBI care if Dolly finally killed the Colonel." She didn't bother to look at him as she spoke. "In Morton's case, the comaraderie among fighting men partially fulfilled his need for a family. But Freddie was the only person on this side of the Atlantic who wanted him. So naturally Morton wanted to keep him safe. But he couldn't let go of his resentment toward Dolly."

She was silent again and so was Trace.

"Will there ever be a day when minorities in this country will be trusted by the majority and visa versa. Kadija and so many like her are still willing to lay down their life for a country they love.

Trace leaned forward and said, "C'mon Inez. We trust each other don't we? I've never seen you like this before. Kadija Campbell was probably killed years ago, like Bradley said."

"No. Not true. Saaiq asked for a rescue plane for 'us.' He said 'us.' I heard him. And I can't help thinking I heard despair in his voice as well."

"If you weren't depressed, you'd be trying to figure out who this Saaiq really is."

"Does it matter?" Inez replied.

"FBI hit a dead end as well. They know he was part of the same group of soldiers Morton Meda fought with during the 1970s."

"I don't think anybody cares that Bradley is still missing either. I can't help hoping he's decided to take up Dolly's cause and is in Afghanistan trying to find Kadija."

"I care and I'm still looking for him," Trace said. "Come walk me to my car. You need to stop moping." He extended his hand for her to grab.

Outside, the leaves were beginning to unfurl on most trees. Spring was inevitable. A blue car drove up to the curb in front of her house and parked. Three people got out quickly and stood beside the vehicle. Inez had never seen them before. One was a boy of ten or twelve, the man was tall and as dark as night and wore a bindi. The woman was as white as snow with hundreds of minute sandy colored curls.

Inez leaned against the porch railing and stared until her eyes filled with water and she couldn't see them run towards her.

WITHDRAWN
BY
WILLIAMSBURG REGIONAL LIBRARY